*One outrageous family, three lifetime passions!*

# THE ASHTONS: WALKER, FORD & MERCEDES

Three of your favourite authors bring
you three pulse-racing romances
following the scandalous Ashton dynasty

# THE ASHTONS: WALKER, FORD & MERCEDES

SHERI WHITEFEATHER

KRISTI GOLD

EMILIE ROSE

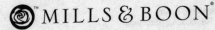

All the characters in this book have no existence outside the imagination of the author, and have no relation whatsoever to anyone bearing the same name or names. They are not even distantly inspired by any individual known or unknown to the author, and all the incidents are pure invention.

THE ASHTONS: WALKER, FORD & MERCEDES
© Harlequin Books S.A. 2010

First published in Great Britain 2010
Harlequin Mills & Boon Limited,
Eton House, 18-24 Paradise Road, Richmond, Surrey TW9 1SR

The publisher acknowledges the copyright holders of the individual works, which have already been published in the UK in single, separate volumes, as follows:

*Betrayed Birthright* © Harlequin Books S.A. 2005
*Mistaken for a Mistress* © Harlequin Books S.A. 2005
*Condition of Marriage* © Harlequin Books S.A. 2005

Special thanks and acknowledgement are given to Sheri WhiteFeather, Kristi Gold and Emilie Rose for their contributions to the DYNASTIES: THE ASHTONS series.

ISBN: 978 0 263 88036 6

64-0510

Printed and bound in Spain
by Litografia Rosés S.A., Barcelona

# BETRAYED BIRTHRIGHT

BY
SHERI WHITEFEATHER

**Sheri WhiteFeather** lives in Southern California and enjoys ethnic dining, attending powwows and visiting art galleries and vintage clothing stores near the beach. When she isn't writing, she often reads until the wee hours of the morning.

Sheri's husband, a member of the Muscogee Creek Nation, inspires many of her stories. They have a son, a daughter and a trio of cats – domestic and wild. She loves to hear from her readers. You may write to her at: PO Box 17146, Anaheim, California 92817, USA. Visit her website at www.SheriWhiteFeather.com.

# THE ASHTONS

Frederick Ashton m Patricia Winston

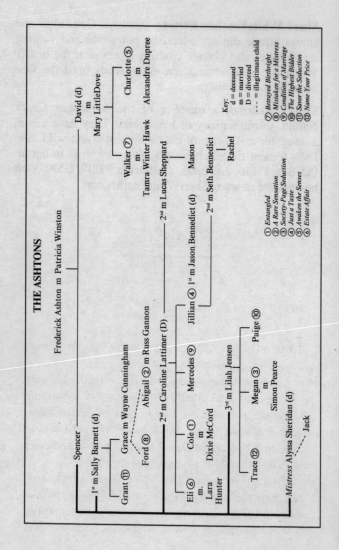

Key:
d = deceased
m = married
D = divorced
--- = illegitimate child

① Entangled
② A Rare Sensation
③ Society-Page Seduction
④ Just a Taste
⑤ Awaken the Senses
⑥ Estate Affair
⑦ Betrayed Birthright
⑧ Mistaken for a Mistress
⑨ Condition of Marriage
⑩ The Highest Bidder
⑪ Savor the Seduction
⑫ Name Your Price

# Prologue

**D**amn David for dying. And damn him for marrying an Indian woman.

Spencer Ashton gazed out the windshield, then blew a frustrated breath. He'd just spent a grueling weekend in Nebraska, taking care of family business. But what choice did he have? Who else would pick up the pieces of David's crumbled life and offer his half-breed kids a better existence?

That squaw wasn't fit to raise David's offspring, and there was no way Spencer would allow her to take them to her freeloading, war-whooping reservation. It was bad enough they'd lived on a farm that had never prospered, a farm Spencer had helped David buy long before he'd married Mary Little Dove.

But in the end, David had been too proud to admit that he and his family were starving.

Spencer flipped the sun visor, squinting into the afternoon light. He was on his way home from the airport, heading to Napa Valley, California, where he owned a thriving winery and a twenty-two-thousand-square-foot mansion. The boy and girl he'd acquired—his dead brother's children—sat next to him in the front seat of his luxury sedan.

He glanced over and saw that three-year-old Charlotte was still behaving like a lost bird. She even chirped every so often, grating on his nerves. He'd tried to put her in the backseat, but she wouldn't leave her big brother's side. Spencer had no use for wounded creatures, but what could he do? She was David's daughter.

The eight-year-old boy, on the other hand, had already garnered Spencer's respect. Walker held his head high. The kid had moxie. Balls. He deserved to be an Ashton.

Too bad he was part Indian.

But Spencer would find a way to get past that. Not that he favored children, Lord knew he had enough of his own. He even had another baby on the way, but Walker was different. He would probably prove to be better than any of Spencer's kids.

Charlotte made another nervous sound, and Spencer gripped the steering wheel.

"She's scared," Walker said.

"Yes, of course. Your parents are gone." Or so they had been told. Their mother was still alive, but that was Spencer's secret. Everyone, except his lawyer, had been fed the same story: Mary Little Dove had died from injuries she'd sustained in an automobile accident, just like David.

Spencer and his attorney had strong-armed her into giving up her kids, but it had been the right thing to do.

Walker was proof. The boy looked dapper in the clothes Spencer had purchased for him. And he hadn't balked about getting his hair cut, either. Spencer wasn't about to take the kids home looking like a couple of ragamuffins.

He turned to study the boy's posture. Although he protected his sister, keeping her close, he still had an air of independence. His mother had called him a warrior. A Sioux at heart. But Spencer sensed otherwise. This kid should have been white.

"I was poor when I was young, too," Spencer said. "But I wanted something better."

Walker glanced up. "My dad talked about you."

"Did he?"

"Yes, sir."

"I would have saved his farm. I didn't know it was in foreclosure, that he was losing it." Spencer knew what people said about him: that he was a bastard, a self-righteous prick. But what the hell did they know? He'd always done right by David, even if his kid brother had been a sentimental fool. "I tried to help your dad succeed."

"And now you're helping me and Charlotte," Walker said.

"That's right, I am. Without me, you and your sister wouldn't have a home."

"I've been praying for Mom and Dad."

Normal prayers, Spencer hoped. None of that heathen crap.

Walker glanced out the window. He had a chiseled profile—handsome, in spite of his brown skin. He seemed to be surveying the land, the wealth of the wine country. Spencer suspected he appreciated what he saw. This kid would be grateful for his uncle's generosity.

"Is my dad going to be buried here?" Walker asked.

"Yes, he is."

"And my mom?"

"No, son. She'll be laid to rest on that Indian reservation. The place where she came from. But it's too far away for you to attend the funeral."

"I've never been there."

And you never will, Spencer thought. He noticed the eight-year-old's voice had turned raw, but he wouldn't dare cry. He was too strong to bawl, to act like a baby. Nope, Walker Ashton wasn't a sniffling coward.

It was hard to believe that mealy-mouthed Sioux had given birth to him. She'd fallen apart at the seams, no backbone whatsoever. But just to ensure she kept up her end of the bargain, Spencer had arranged a thirty-thousand-dollar payment.

A pittance in his bankbook, a fortune in hers.

As for Walker and Charlotte, he supposed they were worth a few bucks. The boy was, anyway. The timid little girl merely came with the deal.

But it was the best deal either of them would ever get. As far as Spencer was concerned, he'd done himself proud.

# One

**W**alker wished his sister had never found out that their mother was still alive. And worse yet, he wished Charlotte hadn't convinced him to look for her.

He sat on the edge of his motel-room bed and blew a weary breath. He was staying in Gordon, Nebraska, but he'd been scouting the South Dakota reservation, traveling from district to district, cursing Pine Ridge, a place that encompassed two million acres and some of the poorest counties in the nation.

He would just as soon forget about that Native American hellhole, let alone claim to part of the Oglala Lakota Sioux Nation. While his sister had romantic notions about Indians, Walker was a realist. A liquored-up Native loitering in one of the paltry little towns had called him a stupid *iyeska* when he'd nearly stumbled over the man's prone form.

*Iyeska.*

It was an insult he couldn't even translate.

Hot and tired, he unbuttoned his shirt and untucked it from his jeans, preparing to take a shower, to wash the grime from his body. He wasn't used to the sweltering heat, to the depressing vastness of the land.

When a knock sounded, Walker came to his feet, anxiety knotting his stomach. He'd left word with postal workers, BIA employees, anyone who seemed educated enough to listen. He'd even spoken with tribal cops, but no one had been particularly helpful. If anything, they'd treated him with indifference. The way he'd treated them, he supposed.

He answered the door and stared at the woman on the other side. He hadn't expected his visitor to be young and beautiful. She stood about five-seven, with shoulder-length black hair and exotic brown eyes.

She wore a simple blouse and a pair of nondescript shorts, but her legs—

When she raised her eyebrows at him, he quit checking her out and remembered that his shirt was unbuttoned, exposing his chest and the sweat dampening his skin.

Uncomfortable, he frowned at her, wondering if she thought he was an *iyeska,* too. Clearly, she was Indian, probably from the reservation.

"Are you Walker Ashton?" she asked.

"Yes." He wanted to wipe his hands on his jeans. He didn't like feeling disorganized and dirty. As the interim CEO of Ashton-Lattimer, an investment banking firm in San Francisco, he relied on cell phones, e-mails, fax transmittals and designer suits.

She tilted her head. "I'm Tamra Winter Hawk. I live with Mary Little Dove Ashton."

His anxiety worsened. Deep down he'd hoped that he wouldn't find his mom. That he could tell Charlotte that he'd done his best but a family reunion wasn't meant to be.

He shifted his stance. "How long have you lived with her?"

"Mary took me in when I was a child."

"I see." His mom had raised someone else's kid while his baby sister had longed for maternal affection? That pissed him off, even if the details weren't clear. "I'd like to speak with her."

"She's at work. And she doesn't know that you're looking for her. She has no idea you're here."

"But you do." Apparently someone had told Tamra about the city-slick stranger who'd been poking around, driving from one poverty-laden county to the next, claiming to be Mary's long-lost son. "So what's the problem? Why are you keeping her from me?"

Tamra didn't respond. With her striking features and regal posture, she reminded Walker of a museum bronze, an untouchable object encased in glass.

"I'd like to see your ID," she finally said.

He squinted into the sun, the hot, fiery ball blazing behind her. "What for?"

"To make sure you're who you say you are."

Who the hell else would he be? A government

agent on the verge of breaking a treaty? Why would he sacrifice his time—his valuable time—to traipse across this godforsaken land if he wasn't Mary's son?

He glared at her. If the police hadn't asked for his ID, then why should she? "I don't need to prove anything to you."

"Then maybe I should leave." Much too elusive, she turned away, her hair spinning in a dark circle.

Walker wanted to let her go, but he knew he couldn't. Charlotte would never forgive him.

Frustrated, he removed his wallet and followed her into the parking lot. "Hold on."

Tamra stopped to face him. For a moment he was struck by how easily she'd managed to stir his blood, to fuel his temper.

Walker didn't let women get under his skin.

Once again she reminded him of a bronze statue. Beautiful, breathtaking, far too aloof. Too bad he'd been taught to behave in museums, he thought. To keep his hands off the glass.

"Will you take it out?" she asked.

Take what out? he wondered, as his brain went numb.

She waited, and he blinked away his confusion. She then asked him to remove his ID from his wallet.

Complying with her request, he handed her his driver's license. She scanned his identification, studying the photo. He knew it was a lousy picture. But those Department of Motor Vehicles cameras weren't meant to be flattering.

"Satisfied?" he asked, his unbuttoned shirt sticking to his skin.

She returned his license. "I'll talk to Mary when she gets home from work."

"Then what?"

"I'll call you and let you know when you can see her."

Right, he thought. Because Mary was queen of the reservation. Or the rez. Or whatever the term for that ghetto plain was.

Aware of his animosity, Tamra sighed. "Your mother has been hurt. I'm only trying to protect her."

No kidding? Well, he'd been hurt, too. He had no idea why Spencer had lied to him years ago, telling him that his mom was dead. And now Spencer was dead, gunned down by an unknown assailant.

Walker's emotions were a flat-out mess.

He motioned to his room, where he'd left the door open. "I'll be here. Do you need the number?"

"No, thanks. I already have it." She paused, her voice turning soft. "Please don't be angry, Walker. At least, not at Mary. She never quit missing you and Charlotte."

His chest constricted, making it tough to breathe.

When he and Charlotte first moved in with Spencer, he used to whisper in the dark, telling her that Mommy and Daddy were angels, watching them from above. But eventually he'd settled into his new life, and he'd quit consoling his sister about the parents they'd lost.

Spencer had become Walker's mentor, the only

person he'd strived to impress. He'd chosen the older man over everyone, including Charlotte, leaving her to fend for herself.

"I'm not angry," he said. But he was, of course. Somewhere in the pit of his stomach, he was mad as hell.

At himself, at Spencer, at Mary.

And at her, too. Tamra Winter Hawk.

The girl his mother had raised.

While the aroma of beef stew wafted through the house, Tamra helped Mary tidy the living room, dusting, vacuuming and fluffing pillows.

Mary turned off the vacuum and looked around. "This place is dingy, isn't it? No matter what we do, it's still an old mobile home."

"It's the same age as me. And I'm not old." Besides, they had cozy furniture, indoor plumbing, heat in the winter and plenty of food in the icebox. To Tamra that was enough.

But she knew how nervous Mary was. She'd been clucking around like a chicken in the rain, preparing for her son but drowning in the fear of seeing him.

"Tell me about him, Tamra. Tell me about Walker."

What could she say that would put the other woman at ease? "He'll be here in about an hour, Mary."

"I know, but I want to know what you thought of him. You never gave me your opinion."

That was true. She hadn't told Mary that he'd triggered her emotions. Or that his intensity reminded her of the past, of the years she'd spent in San Francisco, of the man who'd destroyed her heart.

She glanced at Mary, saw that she waited for a response. "He's stunning." Tall and lean, she thought, with just the right blend of power, of male muscle. "He was dressed casually." And she'd noticed his chest, his stomach, the indentation of his navel. "But he doesn't seem like a casual guy."

Mary frowned. "You could tell he was rich?"

"Yes."

"Fancy watch? Designer labels on his clothes?"

Tamra nodded, troubled by the insecurity in the other woman's eyes. "But you know what?" she said, hoping to soften the blow. "He looks like his dad." She'd seen photographs of David Ashton. She knew all about the farmer Mary had married. "And he resembles you, too."

Walker's mother relaxed a little. "He looked like both of us when he was young." She paused, took an audible breath. "Do you think he'll like stew?"

"Sure." And if he didn't, she doubted he would say otherwise. He would probably go through the motion of being polite. Of course, he hadn't been particularly polite with Tamra. But she'd been harsh with him. She didn't trust his motives, and she suspected he was going to complicate their lives.

Turn their Lakota world on its ear.

Most whitemanized Indians were brash and unyielding. Tamra knew because she'd been one herself. And in some ways she was still struggling with her identity.

"I wonder why he didn't mention Charlotte," Mary said. "Are you sure he didn't say anything about his sister?"

"I'm sure. But you can ask him about her."

"Yes, of course." Nervous once again, Mary smoothed her blouse. She'd chosen a floral-printed top and blue pants, an outfit she'd purchased last summer. She didn't fuss over her clothes and she rarely wore makeup. But this evening she'd put on lipstick. And she'd curled her rain-straight hair.

But even so, she looked older than her fifty-seven years. Her beauty had faded. Tamra had watched it dissipate. Mary had lived a hard life, and the lines in her face bore the brunt of her labor.

The pain of losing her children.

And now Walker was back. A stranger. A man with a distant heart. He hadn't asked about his mom. Nothing that gave Tamra an indication that he cared.

"I'll make the salad," she said, needing to keep busy. The anticipation of entertaining Walker was making her anxious, too.

"I'll bet he's used to steak and lobster." Mary put the vacuum cleaner into the hall closet, then frowned at their cluttered kitchen, at the simplicity of their existence. "Do you think Spencer knows he's here?"

"I have no idea." Tamra knew that Spencer Ashton had taken Walker and Charlotte away from their mother. He was responsible for the constant ache in Mary's chest, for the tears she'd cried.

Tamra washed her hands, running them under the

cold water. She couldn't help being fiercely protective of the woman who'd raised her.

"Is it too hot in here?" Mary asked, stirring the stew. "Should we open another window?"

"It's starting to cool off. It'll be okay."

"Will it?"

"Yes." She hated the shame that had begun to creep into their minds. Tamra and Mary had strived to accept their lifestyle, to be proud of it.

Mary set the table, but when Walker arrived, she was in the bathroom, reapplying her lipstick.

Tamra answered the knock on the screen door, and for a moment she and Walker gazed at each other through the barrier.

He didn't smile. He looked impeccably groomed in a tan shirt and matching trousers. He was cleanly shaven and his short dark hair was combed away from his face, exposing his half-blood features.

Tamra's pulse zigzagged, like invisible footprints racing up her arm.

The last man who'd had that kind of effect on her had given her a child. A baby she'd buried in San Francisco, the city where Walker lived.

"Come in," she said, opening the screen door. It wasn't a fluke that Tamra was connected to San Francisco. That she'd spent her college years there. She'd chosen that region because of Walker and his sister.

"Thanks." He entered the house, then handed her a bouquet of roses. "I was going to bring a bottle of wine, but since they don't sell alcohol on the reservation, I figured you weren't allowed to indulge in it, either." He paused, shrugged a little. "But I've seen plenty of people drinking. I guess everyone doesn't follow the rules."

She merely nodded. The white-owned liquor stores in the border towns catered to Lakota drunks. His mother was far too familiar with that scenario to think of alcohol as a luxury, even an exceptional bottle of wine. Mary's brother had died from alcoholism. "Your mom will appreciate the flowers."

"Where is she?"

"Freshening up. She'll only be a minute."

Or a second, she thought, as Mary appeared in the hallway.

Walker turned around, and Tamra watched mother and son face each other for the first time in twenty-two years.

Tears filled Mary's eyes, but she didn't step forward to hug her boy. He didn't embrace her, either.

Awkward silence stretched between them.

Walker didn't know what to say. Mary didn't look familiar. But he didn't have any old pictures, nothing to refresh his memory.

Was he a coldhearted bastard? Or was it normal that he didn't feel anything? That Mary Little Dove didn't seem like his mother?

When she blinked, the tears that were gathered on her lashes fluttered like raindrops. Should he offer her his handkerchief? Or would that trigger even more tears? Walker didn't want to make her cry.

He moved forward, just a little, stepping closer to her. Why had his memories faded? Why couldn't he see her in his mind? He remembered the farm, but he couldn't recall his mom.

Because it had been easier to forget, he thought. Easier to let her go, to get on with his life.

"My son," Mary said, breaking the silence. "My boy. I never thought I'd see you again. But here you are. So tall. So handsome."

A muscle clenched in his jaw. "We thought you were dead."

"I know." The tears glistening on her lashes fell, dotting her cheeks. "I'm aware of what Spencer told you."

She knew? She'd been part of the lie? Walker wanted to turn away, to shut her out of his life once again, but his feet wouldn't move. He simply stood there, the weight of her words dragging him down.

"Is Charlotte all right?" she asked. "Does she know you came to see me?"

"My sister is fine, and this was her idea."

Mary pressed her hand against her heart. "My baby girl. She was only three years old. How could she possibly remember me?"

Walker didn't respond. But how could he? He didn't remember her, either. And, God help him, he didn't want to. He had no desire to become her son, to be part of Pine Ridge, to embrace his Lakota roots.

Spencer had taught him that being Indian didn't matter. And from what Walker had seen so far, he had to agree.

He glanced at Tamra and saw that she watched him. Could she sense his thoughts? She clutched the roses he'd brought, and the bouquet made her look like a reservation bride, with a summer cotton dress flowing around her ankles.

"These are from Walker." She handed the roses to Mary.

His mother accepted the gift and smiled.

Walker took a deep breath. She looked pretty when she smiled. Softer, like the woman his father had probably fallen in love with. David Ashton had been a sentimental man, that much he knew. That much Spencer had told him.

"Thank you," Mary said to Walker.

He gave her a quick nod. "You're welcome."

"I'll make you a shield." She searched his gaze. "Your dad always wanted you to have one."

His white father wanted him to have a Lakota object? Walker didn't understand, but he tried to pretend that it made sense. He had no idea what he was supposed to do with a shield.

Declare war on another tribe? Hang it on his living room wall? Somehow he didn't see it complementing his contemporary decor. An interior designer had spent months laboring over his hillside condo.

Tamra spoke up. "The meal is ready. We should probably eat now."

"Yeah, sure." Anything to divert his mother's attention, he thought. To make her forget about the shield.

"I'll put these in water." Mary took the flowers

into the kitchen, where a simple table presented casual china, paper napkins and stainless steel flatware.

Walker waited for the women, intending to push in their chairs. But his mom tapped his shoulder and told him to sit, anxious to serve him. When she filled his glass with milk, he wondered if she'd forgotten that he was no longer eight years old.

Finally Mary and Tamra joined him, and they ate a hearty stew, an iceberg lettuce salad and rolls smothered in butter. It was the kind of meal a farmer's wife would prepare, he thought. Middle America. Only this was a South Dakota reservation.

He looked across the table at his mom. At Mary. His mind kept bouncing back and forth. He didn't know what to call her. How to refer to the woman who'd given him life.

"Did Spencer treat you well?" she asked.

He blinked, tried not to frown. "Yes. I was close to my uncle." And probably the only Ashton who could make that claim. No one had forged a bond with Spencer, not the way Walker did. But even so, it had been a hard-earned alliance. Spencer had been a complicated man.

"You're not close to him anymore?"

"Spencer is dead. He was murdered a few months ago. Shot to death in his office. Charlotte found his body."

"Oh, my. Oh." His mom fidgeted with her food. "I'm sorry. I'm so sorry."

When she stopped talking, the walls closed in. The kitchen was already cramped, the table too small for three people. Tamra sat next to him, too close for comfort.

He was still mourning his uncle, still missing him. Yet Spencer's betrayal kept him awake at night.

"Will you tell me about Charlotte?" Mary said.

He nodded, knowing how much this mattered to his sister. "She's engaged to Alexandre Dupree, a winemaker from France. He isn't the kind of man I'd envisioned for her, but they're crazy about each other." Madly in love, he supposed. "My sister was always shy, sort of dreamy. And Alexandre is—" he paused, trying to find a word to describe Charlotte's fiancé "—worldly."

"Like a prince." Mary sighed, already slipping into her daughter's fairy tale.

"I guess, yeah. Women probably think so." Walker knew that Alexandre had given his sister everything she needed, including the strength to investigate their family, to discover that Mary was still alive. "They're in Paris. Charlotte needed to get away after Spencer's funeral. But she made me promise that I'd search for you."

"I'm glad she did." Mary's eyes were watery again. "Do you have a picture of her?"

He shook his head. "I didn't think to bring one. But I'm sure she's going to rush back to meet you. Her and Alexandre."

"I can't wait to see her. And her fiancé, of course." Mary scooted closer to the table. "Is there someone special in your life, son?"

"Me?" Without thinking, he glanced at Tamra.

She turned toward him, and he shifted in his seat, wondering if she had a significant other, if she was sleeping with some big Indian buck.

Then he recalled the blonde in a San Francisco bar who'd tried to pin that phrase on him. A racial slur that had made him feel dirty.

"I'm not involved with anyone," he said. "I'm too busy with my career. Investment banking." More than ready to change the subject, he questioned his mom. "So, what kind of work do you do?"

She smoothed her gray-streaked hair. "I'm a nurse's aid at the PHS."

"PHS?"

"Public Health Service Hospital." She sat up a little straighter, proud of her job. "It's easier for me than some of the other aids. I lived in the white world, so I have a better understanding of the white doctors and nurses who work there."

Tamra interjected. "Most of the doctors are young. Physicians who received government loans for medical school. So they're paying back those loans by performing public health services on the reservation for a few years."

And probably hating every minute of it, he thought.

Tamra continued, "Our society equates wisdom with age, so it's difficult for our elders to accept young doctors. And there's often a language barrier. Far too many cultural differences." She glanced at his mom. "Mary is a valuable asset. The patients trust her. And so do the nurses and doctors."

Unsure of how to respond, he ate another a bite of stew. Mary sounded like a caring woman, yet she'd allowed her children to believe she was dead. He wanted to grill her about the past, to bombard her with accusations, but having Tamra nearby complicated the situation even more.

She'd taken his place. She'd been raised by the lady who'd let him go. And worse yet, he was attracted to Tamra.

A disaster in the making.

When he reached for his drink, he brushed her arm, a touch that made him much too aware.

"Sorry," he said. "I'm left-handed."

"It's okay." She tried to move away from him, to give him more room, but her effort proved useless. There was nowhere to go. They were stuck.

Yet his mother was smiling. "Walker used to do that when he was little, too."

"You mean this?" He lifted his milk, bumping Tamra's elbow, nearly knocking the roll out of her hand.

Everyone laughed. A silly incident. But it felt good. He hadn't laughed in a long time.

A few moments later, silence engulfed him. No one could think of anything to say, so they resumed their meal, making noise with spoons and forks and butter knives.

He glanced at a clock on the wall and imagined it ticking. Like a bomb, he thought. Like the day Spencer had taken legal custody of him and his sister, the day he'd been told that *both* of his parents had died.

Charlotte had been too young to understand, to comprehend the cold, harsh reality of never seeing Mommy and Daddy again. But she'd cried just the same.

Walker stopped eating. His childhood memories were scattered, lost in the darkness of his mind. But not about that day. He remembered it vividly.

"Why did you do it?" he asked Mary, unable to hold back his emotions, to keep faking this reunion. "Why did you give us away?"

# Two

"I'm sorry, Walker." Mary's voice quavered. "I should have explained everything right away. But I thought...I hoped...we could get to know each other first."

He pushed away his plate. "Why?"

"So you wouldn't judge me so harshly. So you wouldn't think I was trying to turn you against Spencer."

"I already told you. My uncle is dead."

"This is his fault," Tamra said. "He forced your mother to give up her children."

"Oh, yeah? With what? A gun?" Unable to sit at the cramped table any longer, he rose from his chair and glared at the young woman Mary had raised.

"Did he force her to take you in, too? To be your mom instead of ours?"

Tamra came to her feet. Suddenly she looked like a female warrior, her mouth set in a determined line, her dark eyes blazing with anger. "That isn't fair."

"You want to talk fair? There's no excuse for what my mom did. None whatsoever." He rounded on Mary. "I prayed for you. I called you an angel." Much too edgy, he blew out a hard breath. "When Spencer rescued us, I was so damn grateful. And so damn scared. Do you have any idea what being an orphan feels like?"

She didn't answer. She just swallowed the lump that seemed to be forming in her throat.

"I know what it feels like," Tamra said.

He spun around, gave her a cold look. "And that's supposed to make me feel better?"

"No. It's just that I understand."

"Yeah, right. You. The perfect Indian."

"Perfect?" She started clearing the table, moving at a frustrated pace. "You have no idea what I've been through. I wasn't raised in a mansion, Walker. My father ran off before I was born, and my mother was all alone, trying to survive on welfare. To find us suitable places to live."

"It's not the same thing." He gestured to Mary, who crossed her arms, hugging herself. "She let me think she was dead. At least your parents were honest."

"Don't point at her." Tamra clanked the dishes. "Don't do that. It's not proper."

"Says who? People on the rez?" As if he gave a

damn about Lakota etiquette. "Maybe someone should have told her that lying to her kids wasn't proper."

"Mary was on the verge of a breakdown when she lost your dad. And Spencer preyed on her emotions. He—"

Walker cut her off. He turned to his mom, needing to hear it from her. "Is that true?"

She nodded, and he realized how frail she looked, sitting alone at the table, listening to him and Tamra argue.

He resumed his seat, his heart pounding horribly in his chest. He wanted to call her a liar, but he knew his uncle had never tolerated gentle-natured women, especially when their wounds were still raw.

Yet he'd loved Spencer. He'd patterned his life after his father's power-hungry brother.

"Tell me," he said. "Tell me what he did."

"He came to see me in the hospital, right after your dad died. I was injured in the accident, nothing life threatening, but I still needed medical care."

"How did he force you to give us up?"

"He threatened me. He said he would get Social Services involved. That he would prove that I was an unfit mother."

"But you weren't." Walker studied the shadows under her eyes, the lines imbedded in her skin. "Were you?"

"Oh, God, no." She reached across the table and brushed his hand. A featherlight touch. The touch of a mother who'd lost her son. "I never abused my babies."

"I have no idea how you treated us." Which made Spencer's threats seem even more plausible, he thought. More frightening. "I can't remember you and Dad. I just can't."

"It's okay." Mary's voice went soft, sad. "It's been a long time."

"Yes, it has." Uncomfortable, he turned in his seat and noticed Tamra stood nearby. She'd fixed a pot of tea, some sort of herbal brew. When she offered him a cup, he looked up at her, and their gazes slammed straight into each other.

Heat. Emotion. The gates of Lakota hell.

He shouldn't be staring at her. Not like this.

Only, he couldn't seem to break eye contact.

And neither could she.

God help him, he thought. Suddenly he feared they were destined to be lovers, like misunderstood characters in a movie who yelled and screamed, then kissed like demons. He wasn't a fortune-teller. He couldn't predict the future. Yet he could feel the passion. The danger that awaited him.

He'd never been involved in a turbulent relationship. His affairs had never bordered on pain, on the kind of emotion that ripped a man apart.

But everything about Pine Ridge tore him in two.

Finally Tamra shifted her gaze, pouring Mary's tea. Afterward she sat next to Walker again, and he could smell the lotion on her skin, a disturbing blend of summer botanicals. A fragrance that made him want her even more.

Soft, airy, far too real.

Mary looked at both of them. "Neither of you deserve this."

"We can handle it." He turned to Tamra, then considered bumping her arm. But he knew no one would laugh this time. His left-handed antics wouldn't ease the tension. Nor would it change what was happening between him and Tamra.

"Yes," she agreed. "We can handle it."

Under the table, her leg was only inches from his, and the near contact made him warm. He didn't understand why she affected him so deeply, why she made him yearn for a forbidden liaison.

Was he trying to punish her? Or was he hell-bent on torturing himself?

"Finish your story," he said to Mary, trying to redirect his focus, to clear his head. "Tell me the rest."

"I was afraid of Spencer. Of his money, his power." She sipped her tea, clutching the cup with both hands. "When I was growing up, Lakota children were being put into foster care. Into white people's homes because their own families were too poor."

"And you thought Spencer could do that to us? That he could convince Social Services to take me and Charlotte?"

"Yes. I'd been away from the reservation for a long time. Married to your dad, being a farmer's wife. But in the end I was just a poor Indian all over again. Except, this time I was mourning my husband and drugged with painkillers from the hospital. I couldn't think clearly."

"But this was the eighties. Wasn't there something your tribe could have done to help you? To stop Spencer from taking us?"

"The Indian Child Welfare Act could have made a difference. But I didn't know about it then. It went into effect after I left the reservation." Her breath hitched, catching in her throat. "My life with your father was over. He was gone and the farm was in foreclosure. There was nowhere to go. Nowhere but here." She glanced at the window, where a small breeze stirred the curtains. "But at the time, all I had to come back to was a rundown shack and an alcoholic brother." She shifted her gaze. "Spencer threatened to use that against me. To drum up phony evidence that I was a drinker, too. That I hurt you and Charlotte. He knew people who would testify, who would lie for him."

Once again, Walker battled his confusion. He wished Mary had fought for her rights. That she'd done whatever she could to keep him and Charlotte. Yet he was glad Spencer had been his uncle.

"I didn't want my children growing up in foster care and thinking that I'd abused them," his mother said. "To me, that was worse than being dead."

Was it? Walker didn't know. He didn't have kids. He didn't have anything in his life but his work, the career Spencer had groomed him for.

"There's more," Mary told him. "Something else your uncle did. It seemed horrible at first. Only it didn't turn out to be a bad thing."

"Really? What was it?"

"Money." She nearly whispered, then raised her

voice a little louder. "His attorney sent me a thirty-thousand-dollar cashier's check after I got back to Pine Ridge. I didn't want to cash it at first."

"But eventually you did?"

"Yes." She reached for his hand. "I did."

Walker wanted to pull away from her. But he allowed her to touch him, feigning indifference, pretending that he could deal with the money.

With the sale of two small children....

The following day Tamra arrived at Walker's motel, per his request. He met her outside, looking like the city boy he was, with his well-tailored clothes and men's-fashion-magazine haircut. He wore the thick dark strands combed straight back and tamed with some sort of styling gel. Short but not conservative, at least not in a boring way.

Walker Ashton's hair had sex appeal.

"Hey," he said.

"Hey, yourself." She noticed that he seemed troubled. She hoped they wouldn't end up in another argument. "What's going on?"

"Nothing. I just want to talk." He reached into his pocket and removed some coins. "How about a soda?"

"Sure." She walked to the vending machine with him and chose an orange drink. He picked grape. From there, they headed back to his room.

She felt a bit odd going into the place where he'd been sleeping. She knew she shouldn't, but being with him in an intimate setting caused her heart to pound unmercifully in her breast.

She looked around his room and noticed the western motif. He'd chosen comfortable accommodations on Highway 20, but he was probably used to five-star hotels. This, she imagined, was foreign to him.

The window air conditioner was on full blast, with color streamers attached, blowing like international flags.

She sat at a pine table, and he leaned against the dresser, a big, sturdy unit that doubled as an entertainment center. She suspected that he'd climbed under the covers last night and watched cable TV.

What else would he do in a cozy Nebraska town?

"How old were you when my mom took you in?" he asked.

"I was five, but my mother was alive then. We both moved in with Mary. My mom and your mom were friends, and we didn't have anywhere else to go. It was winter. We would have frozen to death on our own." She flipped open the top of her soda, memories swirling in her mind. "My mom died two years later. So I was seven when Mary became my guardian."

"How old are you now?"

"Twenty-six."

A frown slashed between his eyebrows. "You're only a year older than my sister."

She nodded. Did that bother him? Did it make him feel even more betrayed? She wanted to ask him if he'd called his sister, if he'd spoken to her in France, but she decided to wait until he finished interviewing her. She could see the unanswered questions in his eyes.

"Is that common on the rez?" he asked. "To just raise someone else's kid?"

"Yes." She tried to relax, but he was making herself-conscious. The way he watched her. His hard-edged posture. "The Lakota have an adoption ceremony called Hunka, the making of relatives. It's conducted by a medicine man or another adult who'd been a Hunka. This ceremony provides a new family for a child who doesn't have a home."

"Did you and Mary do that?"

"No." She lifted her soda, took a sip, placed the can on the table. Walker's gaze followed her every move. She tried to avoid eye contact, but it didn't help. She could feel him looking at her. "In those days Mary wasn't connected to her heritage. She was defying tradition, isolating herself from the community. A Hunka ceremony would have been too Indian. Too Lakota."

"So she just kept you without adopting you?"

"Yes." Tamra tasted her soda again, wishing Walker would quit scrutinizing her. "We could do it now, though. People of any age can become Hunka if both parties agree."

"Don't," he said.

"Don't what? Have a ceremony?" Tired of his male dominance, she lifted her chin, challenging him. "That's not your choice to make."

"I don't want you to be her adopted daughter. I don't want to be related to you." He moved away from the dresser. "And I'm sure you know why."

Did she? She glanced at the bed, at the maroon

and blue quilt, at the plain white pillowcases. Then she looked at him. A bit woozy, she took a steadying breath. "Nothing's going to happen."

"Yes, it is. Sooner or later, we'll end up there."

There.

His bed.

She struggled to maintain her decorum, to seem unaffected. "That's awfully presumptuous of you."

He finished his drink, then grabbed the chair across from her. In one heart-stopping move, he spun it around and straddled it. "I'm not saying that I want it to happen. I'm just saying that it will."

Tamra felt as though she'd just been straddled. Ridden hard and put away…

…wet.

She moistened her lips. "I'm not going to sleep with you."

"Yes, you are." He didn't smile. He didn't flirt. But he shifted in his chair, bumping his fly against it. "We're going to tear off each other's clothes. And we're going to be sorry afterward, wondering what the hell we did."

"I don't have affairs. Not like that."

"Neither do I."

"Then why are we having this stupid conversation?"

"Because I couldn't stop thinking about you last night." He made a tense face. "And it's pissing me off."

She shook her head. He had to be the most difficult man she'd ever met. "Everything pisses you off, Walker."

He squinted at her. "Did you think about me last night?"

Her pulse tripped, stumbled like a clumsy little kid playing hopscotch in the rain. "No."

"Liar."

Yes, she thought. Liar, liar, pants on fire. But she'd be damned if she would admit it. She'd slept with the windows open, letting the breeze stir her hair, her half-naked body. "You're not my type."

"You're not mine, either." He paused, then checked her out, up and down, from head to toe. "But you're hot, sexy as sin. For an Indian," he added, making her scowl.

"I wouldn't go to bed with you if you were the last half-breed on earth."

He smiled at that. "Good. Then it won't happen. We're safe."

She was already safe. She'd been on the Pill since her baby girl died. Since she'd decided that she wasn't getting pregnant again. At least not by a man she wasn't married to.

Walker rocked in his chair, and she tried to think of something to say, something to wipe that cynical smile off his face. She certainly wasn't going to discuss birth control with him. She knew that wasn't the kind of safe he was referring to.

He was talking about their emotions, their feelings. Sex they would regret.

"What did my mother do with the money?" he asked, changing the topic so abruptly, she merely blinked at him.

"What?"

"The thirty grand. How'd she spend it?"

Tamra took a moment to gather her thoughts, to

compose her senses. "Maybe you should ask her about this."

"I'm asking you." He leaned back. "It's easier for me to talk to you. You're—" the cynical smile returned "—not as vulnerable."

He had no idea, she thought. He didn't have a clue. But how could he? She hadn't told him that she'd lost a child. That she understood his mother's pain. "Mary bought the mobile home we're living in. It was used, so it wasn't very expensive."

"So there was money left over?"

"Yes. And she invested that."

"Really?" He seemed surprised. "Were they sound investments?"

"Sound enough. There was enough to help me go to college."

"Damn." He dragged a hand through his sexually appealing hair, messing it up a little. "My mom sent her non-Hunka kid to college. Doesn't that beat all?"

"Beat all what?" Struggling to keep her cool, she blew an exasperated sigh. "I worked hard on my education. I earned a scholarship, too."

"To a tribal college?"

"To San Francisco State University."

He practically gaped at her. "You went to SFSU? You lived in California? Where I live?"

"That's right." She'd spent her entire childhood dreaming of bigger and better things. "And I brought Mary with me."

"Why San Francisco? Why did you choose a university there?"

"Because I knew Spencer had taken you and Charlotte to Northern California. And I wanted Mary to feel like she had a connection to her children, even if she was never going to see them." Tamra finished her soda and cursed her pounding heart. "So we rented a little apartment and tried to make a go of things. I got a part-time job and earned a degree in marketing, and Mary got a full-time job, working at a hospital. Later she became a certified nurse's aid."

He sat on the edge of the bed. "A marketing degree. And you came back to Pine Ridge?"

"Yes, we did."

"Why?"

"Why not? This is our home."

"Fine. Don't tell me the whole story. I don't care anyway."

But he did, she thought. Or he wouldn't be so hurt about Mary letting him go. "Have you called your sister yet? Did you tell Charlotte that you found your mom?"

"Yes." He made a face at the phone, cursing the object as if it were his enemy. "But she's not coming back to the States. Not for a little while. Can you believe it? She thinks I need to spend some time with Mary first. To get to know her."

"Sounds logical to me."

"Because you're a woman. Your kind stick together."

She couldn't help but smile. "I think I'm going to like your sister."

"I'm sure you will." He quit snarling at the phone

and noticed her smile. "Don't patronize me. I'm being serious."

"So am I." But she laughed in spite of herself. "You're just so agitated all the time, Walker. Everything upsets you."

"And you think that's funny?" He grabbed a pillow off the bed and threw it at her.

She caught it and tossed it back at him. Then they both fell silent.

"Want to get a pizza with me?" he asked suddenly.

Was he inviting her on a date? No, she thought, not after his spiel about their warped attraction. He was probably just bored, looking for something to do. "Sure, I guess. But on the rez. Not here. And I have to stop by a friend's house first."

"I noticed the pizza place at Pine Ridge. But I haven't eaten there."

"Don't worry. It won't make you sick."

He shrugged off her sarcasm. "It's a franchise I'm familiar with."

She came to her feet. "I'll drive. And on the way I'll teach you about Lakota protocol." She dug through her purse, snagged her keys. "Indian 101."

"I can hear it now. Don't point, Walker. And don't get drunk on the rez." He followed her out to her truck. "All those winos I saw must have missed your class."

Wiseguy, she thought. "Just listen and learn."

"Yes, ma'am."

He climbed in the passenger seat, and she gunned the engine, wondering what she'd just gotten herself into.

# Three

Walker studied Tamra's profile. He had so many questions about her, about his mother. He was even curious about Lakota protocol. Although he wasn't sure why.

"Who told you I was looking for my mom?" he asked.

"I heard it through the moccasin telegraph. Someone who knew someone who knew someone else." She turned onto the highway. "You're lucky that Mary works at the PHS. That people are familiar with her. It's not easy to locate someone on the rez."

"No, I suppose not." Which was what he had been counting on. "Everything is so spread out."

She continued driving. By Walker's standard, her

pickup was old, an early-eighties model with plenty of mileage. But it seemed reliable enough. At least, he hoped so. He knew there were places in Indian Country where neither cell phones or CB radios worked. But for now they were still in Nebraska.

"Did you forget about my lesson?" he asked.

"No. I'm just deciding where to start."

He examined her profile again, thinking how striking she was. Her prominent cheekbones, the slight imperfection of her nose, the way her hair framed her face. Her eyes fascinated him, too. Whenever she looked at him, heat surged through his veins.

A sexual response, he thought. Lust in the first degree.

"We'll start with respectful eye contact," she said, making him blink, making him realize how closely he was watching her. "In the old way, you're supposed to avoid eye contact with your elders. And children were taught not to stare. When you stare at someone, you're challenging them."

He glanced away. He'd been staring at her from the moment they'd met. Of course, she'd done her fair share of locking gazes with him, too.

"As for pointing," she went on to say, "the Lakota gesture with their lips."

He frowned. "Their lips?"

"Like this?" She moved her mouth in his direction. He tried it and made her laugh.

"You're overdoing it, Walker. You look like Mick Jagger."

He laughed, too. "What other social laws should

I know about?" he asked, deciding he enjoyed her company, her relaxed sense of humor.

"Addressing a family member by a kinship term is part of the old way."

"Like mother, son, daughter? That sort of thing?"

"Yes. But some of the terms are quite specific. Older brother. Younger sister. Male to female. Female to male."

He leaned back in his seat, knowing this would be important to Charlotte. "What's the term for younger sister?"

"From a male to a female? *Tanksi,* I think. Sometimes I get confused. I'm still learning the language."

Walker nodded. He suspected that Mary hadn't raised Tamra in a traditional manner. Not after the things she'd said about his mother avoiding the Hunka and other Lakota ceremonies. "Does my mom speak the language?"

"She's not fluent, but she's working on it. We're both trying to make up for the past. For the years we didn't embrace our culture." She kept her hands on the steering wheel. "But we're still not overly traditional. We just do the best we can, trying to respect others."

Walker tried to picture Tamra in San Francisco, far away from the Lakota. Knowing that she'd chosen SFSU because of him and Charlotte made him feel closer to her. But it made him uncomfortable, too. She'd grown up in his shadow, and now he was struggling to survive in hers.

"Are their different types of Sioux?" he asked,

still trying to absorb his culture. "Or are they all Lakota?"

"There are three branches," she responded. "Lakota, Dakota and Nakota, who are also called the Yankton Sioux."

"So where does Oglala come into it?"

"It's one of the seven Lakota bands. It means 'they scatter their own' or 'dust scatters.'" She sent him a half-cocked smile. "But the Oglala have seven bands of their own, too."

"Okay, now you're confusing me." He shook his head and laughed. "So much for Indian 101. This is turning into an advanced course."

She laughed, too. "It's not as complicated as it sounds."

"If you say so." He glanced out the window and noticed they were on the reservation, heading toward the town of Pine Ridge. He recognized the road.

"What kind of work do you do?" he asked. "What keeps you busy around here?"

"I'm the director of volunteer services for a local nonprofit organization. We supply food and clothing to people on the reservation."

He raised his eyebrows. "An Indian charity?" Was that the extent of her life? Everything Lakota?

"It's important," she countered. "It's meaningful."

"Yes, but being the director of volunteer services doesn't require a marketing degree. Sounds like a waste of your college years to me."

She gave him a quick, sharp look. "I coordinate media events, too."

Small-time stuff, he imagined.

By the time they arrived in downtown Pine Ridge, tension buzzed between them. So much for enjoying her company, he thought. For her easy sense of humor. But he supposed it was his fault. He'd criticized her job.

He considered apologizing, then decided that would be dishonest. Her education wasn't being utilized, not to its full potential. She'd cheated herself by coming back to the reservation, by living on her homeland.

The town of Pine Ridge had one traffic light and four water towers. There was plenty of activity, generated from the Billy Mills Auditorium, tribal offices and the Oglala Department of Public Safety, but Walker noticed that a lot of people were doing nothing, just sitting on a bench, talking away their boredom.

Tamra stopped for gas at Big Bat's, a convenience store, eatery and gathering place for locals. He'd heard it was Lakota owned and operated, unlike some of the businesses on Pine Ridge. He had to admit it was impressive, something he hadn't expected when he'd first arrived. But even so, he hadn't been inclined to hang out there.

The pizza place was in town, too. As well as a taco stand and a market.

"Are you still interested in having pizza with me?" he asked, as they left the gas station. "Or did I blow it?"

"I'll eat with you. But after we go by my friend's house, remember?"

Yeah, he remembered. "Is this a traditional friend? An elder? Should I avoid eye contact?"

"Michele is the same age as me. We went to high school together, and she won't care if you stare at her. She'll probably like it."

A smile twitched his lips. "The way you do?"

"I never said that."

"You didn't have to."

She ignored his last comment, so they drove in silence, past empty fields and into a hodge-podge of unattractive houses.

"So what's the deal with Michele?" he wanted to know. "Why are we visiting her?"

"I'm loaning her some money. Her daughter's birthday is coming up, and she's short right now."

He looked out the window, saw sporadic rows of wire fences, garments hanging on outdated clothes-lines. "Is she on welfare?"

"She's a single mom. And, yes, she receives Aid to Dependent Children." Tamra's truck rattled on the roughly paved road. "Does it matter?"

"I just wondered." He couldn't imagine not having any money for your child's birthday. But he knew his parents had been destitute at the time his dad died. If he looked deep within himself, he could recall the shame it had caused him, the feeling of despair.

For Walker there had been nothing worse than being poor.

Michele's house was a pale-blue structure with a set of worn-out steps leading to the front door. It was, Walker thought, a stark contrast to the diversity of the land. The grassy plains, rolling hills, buttes and mesas. The beauty he'd refused to appreciate.

A little girl, maybe three or four years old, sat on the steps, with a loyal dog, a mutt of some kind, snuggled beside her.

Although a group of older kids played in the yard, he sensed she was the upcoming birthday girl.

"How many kids does Michele have?" he asked Tamra, as she parked her truck in a narrow driveway.

"Just one. The rest are her nieces and nephews."

Walker watched them run through the grass, tagging each other with laughter and adolescent squeals. "Do they all live here?"

She nodded. "Along with their parents. There's a shortage of houses on the reservation. They don't have anywhere else to go."

He thought about his trilevel condo, the sprawling rooms with French doors and leaded-glass windows. The redwood deck and private hot tub. The enormous kitchen he rarely used.

He ran his hand through his hair, smoothing it away from his face, trying to shed the sudden guilt of having money. "That's a lot of people in one house."

"It's a common situation."

"How common?"

"The Tribal Housing Authority is trying to provide homes, but they have a waiting list of at least twelve hundred people. It's been like that for a long time." She turned to look at him. "When I was growing up, before Mary took us in, my mom and I drifted, trying to find a permanent place to stay. In the summer we camped out, but in the winter we had to find some sort of roof over our heads."

He pictured her as a little girl, living like a half-starved gypsy. "Why are these houses so close together and my mom's by itself?"

"Mary lives on her family's land allotment, which is what most families did in the old days. They had log cabins, with gardens and animals." She sighed, her voice fading into the stillness of her truck. "But as time passed, it became increasingly difficult for people to remain on their land allotments. They couldn't afford to improve their homes, to stay in the country with no running water or electricity. And some families lost their land altogether, so they had to move into government projects."

"Like this?"

She nodded. "It's called cluster housing. It was instituted in the 1960s to provide modern conveniences. But the lack of economic infrastructure created reservation ghettos." Tamra reached for her purse. "Cluster housing is only a portion of the problem. There are families who still don't have electricity or running water. People staying in abandoned shacks or old trailers. Or camping out or living in their cars, the way my mom and I did."

He couldn't think of an appropriate response. He'd witnessed the poverty, seen signs of it all over the reservation, but until now he hadn't let it touch him.

They exited the vehicle, and Tamra called out to the older kids. They grinned and waved at her. Walker wondered why they seemed so happy, so lighthearted and free. He could barely breathe.

The little girl on the steps grinned, too. She wore a pink top, denim shorts and a couple of minor scrapes on her knees. Brownish-black hair fell in a single braid, neatly plaited and shining in the July sun. Her feet, dusted with soil from the earth, were devoid of shoes.

When Tamra sat next to her, the child wiggled with familiarity. The dog got excited, too, slapping his tail against the splintered wood. Was the mutt a stray? A hungry soul Michele's abundant family had taken pity on?

Walker moved closer and crouched down. Tamra told him the girl's name was Maya. A bit shy, she banged her knobby knees together, ducked her head and gave him a sweet hello.

He wanted to scoop her up and take her home, spoil her with clothes and toys and fancy ribbons for her hair.

But at this point he wanted to take Tamra home, as well. He envisioned spoiling her, too, making up for her past, for the hardship she'd endured.

As she turned to look at him, he considered kissing her. Just a soft kiss, he thought. Something that wouldn't alarm the child.

The front door flew open, and Walker's heart jackhammered its way to his throat. Romancing Tamra was a crazy notion. They'd already agreed they weren't going to sleep together.

A young, full-figured woman came out of the

house and greeted Tamra. Like most of the people on the rez, she had distinct sound to her voice—a flat tone, an accent Walker was still getting used to.

"Why are you sitting on the stoop?" she asked. "Why didn't you come in?"

"We wanted to visit with Maya first," Tamra told her, rising so they could hug. A second later she introduced Walker.

But the other woman, the infamous Michele, had already taken a keen interest in him. He shook her hand, and she flashed a smile that broadened her moon-shaped face.

"Where did Tamra find you?" She tossed a glance at her friend. "You show up with this yummy *iyeska* and leave me in the dark?"

Yummy *iyeska?*

It was better than being a stupid one, Walker supposed. But since that Lakota word still eluded him, he wasn't sure how to react.

Tamra didn't react, either. "He's Mary's son."

"No shi—" Michele started to cuss, then caught herself. Her little girl was watching the adults like a fledging hawk.

Dark eyes. Rapt attention.

"So you're the boy who was stolen by that mean *wasicu*," Michele said to Walker.

He tried not to frown, to let his emotions show. *Wasicu*. White man, he thought. That was easy enough to translate. "Uncle Spencer raised my sister and me."

Michele stuffed her hands into the pockets of threadbare jeans. "Well, it's good to have you here."

"Thanks." He glanced at the kids playing in the grass, then at Maya, who still sat on the steps with the big mangy dog. "I live in San Francisco. And I'll be going home in a few weeks."

"Too bad." Michele bumped Tamra's shoulder. "*Ennit*, friend?"

Tamra nodded, then made eye contact with Walker. But he knew she wasn't challenging him. It was a look of confusion, of an attraction that was sure to go awry.

Michele guided Walker and Tamra into the house, looping her arms through theirs. Maya popped up and followed them. In no time the other kids came inside, too, joining their parents, who gathered around a TV set with snowy reception.

Two of the older women bounded into the kitchen and began preparing a snack of some kind. Walker hadn't expected them to cook for him. With all the mouths they had to feed, he felt awkward about being fussed over. But he appeared to be an honored guest.

Mary Little Dove's son.

Maya warmed up to him, sitting beside him in a tired old chair. He moved over to accommodate her, and the lopsided cushion sagged under his weight, making him even more aware of his run-down surroundings. The faded brown carpet was worn to the bone, and sleeping mats were stacked in every corner.

He glanced across the crowded room and noticed the exchange of a twenty-dollar bill going from Tamra to Michele. The birthday loan. Walker tipped bellmen at hotels more than that.

He thought about the stocks Spencer had willed to him. Was it blood money? Payment in full? Or was he just lucky that his uncle had given a damn about him?

The Ashton patriarch. The mean *wasicu.*

The snack was a platter of fry bread, a staple among most Indian tribes, accompanied by bowls of *wojapi,* a Lakota pudding made with blueberries, water, sugar and flour.

Following young Maya's lead, Walker dipped a piece of fry bread into the *wojapi* and realized he was surrounded by people who seemed genuinely interested in him. Still seated in the sagging chair, with Maya by his side, he talked and laughed with Tamra's friends.

And for a few surprisingly stress-free hours, he actually enjoyed being in Pine Ridge.

The sun had begun to set, disappearing behind the hills, painting the sky in majestic colors.

For Tamra, this was home. The land, the trees, the tranquility. The impoverished reservation. A place she used to hate. But she would never hate it again. She knew better now.

*Maka Ina,* she thought. Mother Earth.

She glanced at Walker. He sat next to her, watching the horizon. They occupied a rustic porch swing at his mom's house that complained every so often, the wood creaking from age.

He hadn't said much since they'd left Michele's house, but he seemed reflective.

Sticking to their original plan, they'd gotten a pepperoni pizza. But instead of eating it, they'd put it in the fridge, saving it for later, waiting for Mary to come home from work. But for now, their bellies were still full of fry bread and *wojapi*.

"What's an *iyeska*?" Walker asked.

"A half-breed."

"That's it? That's all it means?"

"Yes. Do you want me to translate yummy, too?"

He smiled, just little enough to send her heart into a girlish patter.

When his smile faded, she sensed the hurt inside him, the pain that often came with being a mixed blood. "Michele wasn't trying to insult you."

He gazed into the distance, at the land of his ancestors. Tamra waited for him to respond. Somewhere nearby, birds chirped, preparing for their evening roost.

"I know Michele wasn't putting me down," he said. "But the first day I arrived, a wino called me a stupid *iyeska*. It never occurred me that it meant half-breed. In San Francisco, people think I'm this major Indian. No matter how much I downplay my heritage, they still notice, still comment on it. But here I'm not Indian enough."

"It's the way you carry yourself, Walker."

He shifted on the swing, scraping his lace-up boots on the porch. He wore comfortable-looking khakis and a casual yet trendy shirt. A strand of his hair fell across his forehead, masking one of his eyebrows. "What's that supposed to mean?"

"There's always been dissention between the full

bloods and the mixed bloods on the reservation." A war she understood all too well. "But sometimes *iyeska* refers to someone's attitude, not his or her blood quantum. Full bloods can be *iyeskas,* too. Indians who think white."

Edgy as ever, he frowned at her. "Fine. Then that's what I am."

"You didn't seem like an *iyeska* once you got to know Michele's family. You seemed like a full blood."

"I did?" He smoothed his hair, dragging the loose strand away from his forehead. Then he laughed a little. "I really liked Michele's family, but they weren't totally traditional. I don't know if I could handle that." He released a rough breath. "I'm too set in my *wasicu* ways."

"Maybe so." She grinned at him. "But you're starting to speak Lakota."

He grinned, too. "A few words. My uncle is probably rolling over in his grave."

For a moment she thought his good mood would falter. That his grave-rolling uncle would sour his smile. But he managed to hold on, even if she saw a deeply rooted ache in his eyes.

"What does *ennit* mean?" he asked.

"It's not a Lakota word. It's an interjection a lot of Indians use. *Ennit?* instead of *isn't it?*"

"You don't say it."

"I've never been partial to slang."

"Thank God," he said, and made her laugh.

She looked up at the sky and noticed the sun was

gone. Dusk had fallen, like a velvet curtain draping the hills. Beside her, Walker fell silent. She suspected he was enjoying the scenery, too. The pine-scented air, the summer magic.

He interrupted her thoughts. "I almost kissed you earlier."

Her lungs expanded, her heart went haywire. Fidgeting with the hem on her blouse, she tried to think of something to say. But the words stuck in her throat.

"Did you hear me?"

"Yes." Beneath her plain white bra, her nipples turned hard—hard enough to graze her top, to make bulletlike impressions.

"Would you have kissed me back?"

"No," she lied, crossing her arms, trying to hide her breasts.

"I think you would've," he said.

Tamra forced herself to look at him. A mistake, she realized. An error in judgment. Now her panties were warm, the cotton sticking to her skin. "We're supposed to get past this."

"Past what?" He leaned into her, so close, his face was only inches from hers. "Wanting each other?"

She nodded, and he touched her cheek. A gentle caress. A prelude to a kiss.

She waited. But he didn't do it.

He dropped his hand to his lap and moved back, away from her. "We are." He brushed his own fly, tensed his fingers and made a frustrated fist. "We're past it."

She stole a glance at his zipper, looked away, hoped to God she wasn't blushing. "Then let's talk about something else."

"Fine. But I can't think of anything." He spread his thighs, slouching a little. "Can you?"

"Not really, no." And his posture was making her dizzy, ridiculously light-headed. She could almost imagine sliding between his legs, whispering naughty things in his ear.

He cleared his throat. "How about San Francisco?"

She fussed with her blouse again. "What?"

"We can discuss San Francisco."

"You want to compare notes?" She told herself to relax, to quit behaving like a crush-crazed teenager. "About what? Our alma mater?"

He shook his head. "I went to UC Berkeley."

"Then what?"

"I want to know what happened in San Francisco. Why you didn't stay there." A slight breeze blew, cooling the prairie, stirring the air.

She squinted, saw a speckling of stars, milky dots that had yet to shine.

"Will you tell me?" he asked.

"Yes," she said, drawing the strength to talk about her baby, the infant she'd buried in Walker's hometown.

# Four

Tamra took a deep breath, fighting the pain that came with the past. Walker didn't say anything. He just waited for her to speak.

"I had a baby in San Francisco," she said. "A little girl. But she was stillborn."

"Oh, God. I'm sorry. I had no idea." He reached over to take her hand, to skim his fingers across hers.

She closed her eyes for a moment, grateful for his touch, his compassion. "She's still there. In a cemetery near my old apartment."

"Do you want me to visit her when I go home?" he asked. "To take her some flowers?"

Tamra opened her eyes, felt her heart catch in her throat. She hadn't expected him to make such a kind offer. "That would mean a lot to me. Sometimes I worry that she's lonely, all by herself in a big city. I know that's a crazy way to feel, but I can't help it." She looked up at the sky again. "I should have buried her here. But at the time, I was determined to stay in San Francisco, to prove I could make it."

"But you changed your mind?"

She nodded. "After a while, I realized I was spinning in circles. Mourning my baby and trying to be someone I wasn't." She looked at him, saw him looking back at her. "Mary and I went to San Francisco because we were defying our heritage, because we wanted to be white. But we're not. We're Lakota. And this is our home."

He released her hand, but he did it gently, slowly. "What about your baby's father? How does he fit into all of this?"

"He doesn't, not anymore."

"But he did. He gave you a child."

When her chest turned tight, she blew out the breath she was holding. "He broke up with me when he found out I was pregnant. He wasn't her father. He was a sperm donor."

Walker searched her gaze. "Did you love him?"

"Yes." She shifted in her seat, causing the swing to rock. "His name is Edward Louis. I met him through JT Marketing, the firm I worked for. He's one of their top clients."

"A white guy?"

"Yes. A corporate mogul. The president of a wheel corporation. You know, fancy rims and tires."

"I'm sorry he hurt you." Walker paused, frowned. "Is it Titan Motorsports? Is that the company he represents?"

"No. Why? Does it matter?"

"I have Titan wheels on my Jag. I just wanted to be sure I wasn't supporting the enemy."

She smiled, leaned against his shoulder, decided she liked him. "Your Jaguar is safe."

"Good." He leaned against her, too. "I don't understand how a man could leave a woman who's carrying his child."

"He thought I trapped him. That I got pregnant on purpose. He didn't love me the way I loved him. But I'm not blaming that on his race. It doesn't have anything to do with him being white. Plenty of Indian men walk away, too."

"Like your dad?"

"Exactly."

"I'm still having a hard time with my mom," Walker said. "It bothers me that she didn't fight to keep her children. That she let us go. But on the other hand, I'm grateful that I've lived a privileged life. That I wasn't raised here." He made a face. "I realize how awful that sounds, but I can't help it. It's just so damn poor."

"That was part of Mary's reasoning, I think. Why she didn't fight. Why she let Spencer take you."

"So it was more than him just threatening her?"

Tamra nodded. "It was the hopelessness she felt, the fear of not being able to provide for you and Charlotte. Eighty-five percent of the people on Pine

Ridge are unemployed. There's no industry, technology or commercial advancement to provide jobs."

"She has a job now."

"Twenty-two years after she let you and your sister go. Mary has come a long way since then."

"But Pine Ridge hasn't."

"Maybe not, but we keep trying. Mary knows she was wrong. That she should have fought to keep her kids. We have to believe in ourselves, to teach our young to battle the hopelessness, to rise above it."

"That's a noble concept. But how realistic is it?"

"Come to work with me tomorrow and find out."

He raised his eyebrows. "Is that a dare?"

"You bet it is." She wasn't about to let him leave the reservation on a discouraging note. She wanted him to be proud of his birthright.

"Then what choice do I have?" He gave her a playful nudge. "I'm not the kind of man who backs away from a challenge. Especially from a pretty girl."

She didn't flirt back. At least not in a lighthearted way. She was too emotional to goof around, too serious to make silly jokes. In the waning light, she touched the side of his face, absorbing the texture of his skin.

His chest rose and fell, his breathing rough, a little anxious. "Being nice to me is going to get you into trouble, Tamra."

"Maybe. But you've been nice to me tonight. You offered to visit my baby. To bring her flowers."

"What was her name?" he asked.

"Jade."

"Like the stone?"

"When I was pregnant, Mary bought me a figurine for my birthday. A jade turtle that fit in the palm of my hand. It was my protector."

"Do you still have it?"

She shook her head. "I buried it with my baby. I gave it to her."

He leaned forward. "Jade was lucky to have you."

She tried not to cry, but her eyes betrayed her. They burned with the threat of tears, with the memory of her daughter, with the little kicks and jabs that had glorified her womb. "I wanted her so badly. But toward the end, I knew something was wrong. She wasn't moving inside me anymore."

"I'm so sorry." He touched her face, the way she'd grazed his. And then he brushed his lips across hers. A feathery kiss, a warm embrace.

Desperate for his compassion, she slid her arms around his neck and drew him closer. His tongue touched hers, and she welcomed the sensation, the slow, sensual comfort of his mouth.

He tasted like blueberries, like Lakota pudding. Masculine heat, drenched in sugar. She couldn't seem to get enough. Desperate for more, she deepened the kiss.

And then a car sounded, moving along the road, coming toward the house.

Like kids who'd gotten caught with their pants down, they jerked apart.

"My mother's home." He grabbed the chain on the swing, trying to keep it from rattling, from making too much noise. "I guess we should reheat the pizza."

"Yes, of course." Tamra stood, smoothed her blouse, wondered if Walker's prediction would come true. That they would, indeed, end up in bed.

And be sorry about it afterward.

Walker, Tamra and Mary sat in the living room, the coffee table littered with napkins, sodas and left-over pizza. They'd eaten their meal, and now they battled a round of silence.

Walker wondered what Tamra was thinking, if she was as confused as he was. With each passing hour, he became more and more protective of her. Not that he was happy about it. In some ways, arguing with her was easier. But he wasn't about to pick a fight.

If anything, he should cut his trip short and go home. But he knew he wouldn't. Not until he figured out what to do about Tamra. If he walked away too soon, he would feel like a coward.

"Would you like to spend the night here?" his mother asked, catching him off guard.

He reached for his drink and took a hard, cold swig. Sleep under the same roof as Tamra? Was his mother daft? Couldn't she see what was happening? "I don't think that's a good idea."

"Why not?"

Because I want to have sex with your non-Hunka daughter, he thought. "Because I don't have any-thing with me. All of my stuff is at the motel. My rental car, too."

"Then how about tomorrow night?" Mary gave him a beseeching look. "It's been so many years since I've had my boy with me. I just hate to let you go."

Guilt clawed at his conscience. He hadn't come to Pine Ridge to get hot and bothered over Tamra. He'd arrived in South Dakota to search for his mother. And now that he'd found her, he hadn't given her the time or the consideration she deserved. He hadn't given her a chance.

"Sure," he said. "I can stay tomorrow."

"And the next night after that?" she pressed, her voice much too hopeful.

He nodded, feeling kind of loopy inside. Walker wasn't used to maternal affection. Spencer's wife, Lilah, had all but ignored him, especially when he was young.

Of course, he'd been too enamored of Spencer to worry about getting attention from Lilah. Besides, he'd always seen her as a tragic character, lost in a socialite world, a place with no substance. And from what he'd observed, she wasn't the greatest mother to her own kids. So why would she treat him or his sister with care?

He'd survived without a mom, something he'd gotten used to. And now here he was, sitting next to Mary on her plain blue sofa, with boyish butterflies in his stomach.

The longing in her eyes made him ill at ease. Yet somewhere in the cavern of his lost memories, in the depth of his eight-year-old soul, he appreciated it. He just wished he could return the favor. But as it was, she still seemed like a stranger.

"Walker is coming to work with me tomorrow," Tamra said, drawing his attention. "So he should probably drive his car over in the morning."

"That's a great idea," Mary put in.

Yeah, great. He was being prodded by two decision-making females. He addressed Tamra. "You still have to take me back to the motel tonight."

She chewed her bottom lip. "I know."

Curious, he gauged her reaction. Was she wondering if he would kiss her again? If once they were alone, they would pick up where they'd left off?

Well, they wouldn't, he concluded. He was going to keep his hands to himself, control his urges, even if it killed him. What good would it do to pursue a relationship with her? To get tangled up in an affair? He was the up-and-coming CEO of a company that had been his life's blood, and she was dedicated to her reservation, to a place that would never fit his fast-paced, high-finance lifestyle. One or two heart-felt moments on Pine Ridge wouldn't change him. He would always be an *iyeska*. And he would always be connected to Uncle Spencer—the tough, ruthless man who'd raised him.

"Do you want to see some old family photos?" Mary asked.

Walker glanced up, realizing he'd zoned out, gotten lost in troubled thoughts. "I'm sorry. What?"

"Pictures of you and Charlotte when you were little," she said. "They were the first things I packed. After I was released from the hospital, Spencer told me to grab a few belongings and he would send the rest. But I didn't trust him, so I took mementos I didn't want him to destroy."

His lungs constricted. "Sure. Okay. I'd like to see the pictures."

Mary smiled, her dark eyes turning bright. "I'll get them." She rose from the sofa. "I'll be right back."

After she left the room, he locked gazes with Tamra, who sat across from him in a faded easy chair. The golden hue from a nearby lamp sent shadows across her face, making her look soft, almost ghostly.

A Lakota spirit.

He rubbed his arm, fighting an instant chill. Suddenly he could hear voices in his head, the cry of a woman and a child being gunned down, running from the cavalry, falling to the frozen earth. A play-acted scene from an Indian documentary he'd caught on the History Channel a few months ago.

"What's wrong?" Tamra asked.

"Nothing."

"You're frowning."

He tried to relax his forehead. "It's not intentional."

"Here they are." Mary returned with two large photo albums.

Walker broke eye contact with Tamra, thinking about the baby she'd buried, the child he'd assumed responsibility for. Flowers on a grave.

His mother resumed her seat, handing him the first album. He opened the cover, then nearly lost his breath.

"That's your father and me on our wedding day. It wasn't a fancy ceremony. We went to the justice of the peace."

"You look just like Charlotte, the way she looks now." Stunned, he studied the picture. He hadn't noticed the resemblance until now, hadn't realized how much his sister had taken after Mary. But then, his mother had aged harshly, the years taking their toll.

"Really? Oh, my." She seemed pleased, thrilled that her daughter had grown up in her image. Especially since Charlotte had called Mary earlier, promising that she would return to the States next week. They'd talked easily, almost as if they'd never been apart.

Walker had been a tad envious, wondering how his sister had managed to carry on a conversation like that. Within a few a minutes she'd accomplished more than he had in two full days.

And over the phone, no less.

Mary turned the page. "Here you are. On the day you were born. Look at that sweet little face."

Sweet? He wasn't an authority on newborns, but he wasn't impressed with what he saw. "I look like a prune." A dried plum, he thought, with a cap of dark hair.

When his mom swatted his shoulder, he scrunched up his features, mocking the picture.

And then suddenly he felt sad. He noticed Tamra, sitting alone in her chair, ghostlike once again.

Was she thinking about Jade?

Trying to hide her emotions, she gave him a brave smile. But it was too late. He was already affected by her, already wishing he could hold her, take away her pain.

Too many lost children, he thought. Too much

heartache. Now his mother was watching him with anticipation, waiting for him to look at the next picture.

To remember his youth.

But the only thing that came to mind was the documentary he recalled on TV. The woman and her child stumbling to the ground. A depiction of someone's ancestors.

Bleeding in the snow.

Walker rode shotgun in Tamra's truck, traveling from Rapid City, South Dakota, back to the reservation. They'd spent the morning in Rapid City, where she'd given him a tour of the warehouse that stocked food donations. The Oyate Project, the nonprofit organization she worked for, was a small but stable operation. She claimed there were bigger charities in the area, but she'd been involved in the Oyate Project since its inception.

*Oyate,* Walker had learned, meant "the People" in Lakota. Her people, his people, she'd told him.

He glanced out his window and saw a vast amount of nothingness—grassy fields, dry brush, a horizon that went on forever. Rapid City was about 120 miles from Pine Ridge, a long and seemingly endless drive and they were only halfway through it.

"So this is the route your delivery trucks take?" he asked.

"Yes, but because of the distance, the weather can vary, particularly in the winter. Sometimes a truck leaves Rapid City, where it's sixty degrees and hits the reservation in the middle of a whiteout."

"A blizzard?"

She nodded, and he pictured the land blanketed in snow. "Some of the homes aren't accessible during heavy snows or rain, are they?"

"No, they're not. We try to provide propane fuel and heating stoves. We haul firewood, too. But there are so many people to reach, so many families who need to keep warm."

He thought about the years Tamra and her mother had spent dodging the cold. "Do you have any extended family? Anyone who's still alive?"

"I have some distant cousins on my dad's side, but we don't socialize much. They tend to party, drink too much." She heaved a heavy-hearted sigh. "I've tried to help them get sober, but they shoo me away. They think I'm a do-gooder."

"No one could say that about me," he admitted.

"You've never offered to help anyone?"

"Not firsthand. I send checks to charities, but I've always thought of them as tax write-offs. I don't get emotionally involved."

She slanted him a sideways glance. "You will today."

He tried to snare her gaze, but she'd already turned back to the road. "So where exactly are we going?"

"To meet one of the trucks at a drop-off location. It's my home base, where my office is."

They arrived about forty-five minutes later. The drop-off location was a prefab building equipped with garage-style doors. A group of cars were parked around the structure, where volunteers waited for the delivery truck.

Michele and her daughter, Maya, were among the volunteers, ready to help those less fortunate than themselves. Walker was impressed. Michele was living in an overcrowded home, trying to make ends meet, yet she was willing to drive her beat-up car to other communities on the rez, delivering food to hungry families. He suspected the Oyate Project was paying for her gas, but she was offering her time, her heart, for free.

She greeted him and Tamra with a hug. Maya looked up at them and grinned. Soon another volunteer engaged Tamra in a conversation and she excused herself, leaving Walker with Michele and her sweet little girl.

As casually as possible he removed some cash from his wallet and slipped it into Michele's hand.

She gave him a confused look.

"For Maya's birthday," he said, as the child played in the dirt, drawing pictures with a stick.

Michele thanked him, giving him another hug, putting her mouth close to his ear. "I hope you hook up with my friend. She needs a guy like you."

He stepped back, felt his pulse stray. "I'm not hooking up with anybody."

"You sure about that?"

Was he? "I'm trying to be." He'd been doing his damnedest not to touch Tamra, not to kiss her again.

Michele angled her head. Her long, straight hair was clipped with a big, plastic barrette, and a bright blue T-shirt clung to her plus-size figure. "Maybe you shouldn't fight it."

He shifted his feet. They stood in the heat, with the sun beating down on their backs. "It would never work. I live in California."

"Yeah, but you're here now." She gave him a serious study. "And my friend is getting to you."

So he was supposed to live for the moment? Make a move on Tamra? Have a wham-bam-thank-you-ma'am with a woman who'd been through hell and back? Somehow he doubted that was what Michele had in mind. "You think I'll stay. You think that if I hook up with her, I'll make this place my home."

"Stranger things have happened."

Not that strange, he thought.

Tamra returned and invited him into her office. He entered the building with her, eager to escape. As much as he liked Michele, he didn't need to get sidetracked by her hope-filled notions.

Determined to keep his distance, he refrained from getting too close to Tamra. But once they were in her office with the door closed, he didn't have a choice. Her workspace put them in a confined area: a standard desk, a narrow bookcase, a file cabinet that took up way too much room.

She dug through the top drawer, removed a folder and sorted through it, gathering the papers she needed. Walker took a deep breath, and her fragrance accosted him like a floral-scented bandit. If he moved forward, just a little, just three or four small steps, he could take her in his arms.

Damn the consequences and kiss her.

The phone on her desk rang, jarring him back to reality.

She answered the call, and he cursed Michele for messing with his mind, for encouraging him to be with Tamra. Walker hadn't gotten laid in months. Of course, he knew Michele was talking about more than just sex.

"Are you ready?" Tamra asked.

He simply looked at her. He hadn't even realized that she'd hung up the phone. He'd been too busy feeling sorry for his neglected libido. "Ready for what?"

"To go back outside. Or would you rather wait here?"

"For what?"

"The truck." She made a curious expression. "Are you all right, Walker?"

A bit defensive, he frowned at her. "Why wouldn't I be?"

"How would I know? You're acting weird."

Did she have to be so pretty? So smooth and sultry? She wore jeans and an Oyate Project T-shirt, but it could have been a nightgown, a breezy fabric, an erotic temptation. "Maybe I'm just sick of the reservation."

She crossed her arms. "Then go home."

He didn't want to return to California, not without putting his hands all over her first. "I didn't mean it like that." Anxious, he leaned against the file cabinet. "And I don't want to fight with you."

"Me, neither."

She sighed, and he almost touched her.

Almost.

He decided it was safer waiting outside, even if Michele would probably be dogging his heels, giving him conspiratorial glances.

But luckily that didn't happen. The truck arrived, and the pace picked up. So much so, Walker got absorbed in the activity, helping the driver unload the food.

After the cartons were sorted and stacked, Tamra organized the volunteers and individual cars were packed with bags of perishable items and boxes of dry goods. Walker loaded the back of Tamra's vehicle with groceries from a checklist she'd given him.

Soon they were rolling across the plains again, heading to their first destination. He turned to look at her, knowing she was right. He was getting emotionally involved today. But not only with her charity.

He was getting attached to her, too.

# Five

**W**alker and Tamra had spent the afternoon with families who had no electricity and no running water. People living in abandoned camper shells, in old shacks, in rusted-out trailers. But even so, he'd seen pride in their eyes, determination, kindness, a sense of community.

And now Tamra had taken him to the Wounded Knee Memorial. He wasn't sure why she'd decided to come here, especially today, after driving all over the reservation. They were both road weary and tired.

Walker studied his surroundings. Aside from a Lakota couple selling dream catchers in a shelter of pine boughs, there was no one around. He suspected a few tourists trickled by now and then, or else the enterprising young couple wouldn't have any customers.

A green sign, suffering from vandalism, offered a historical account of the Massacre of Wounded Knee. The word *massacre* had been bolted onto the sign with a sheet of metal, covering something below it.

"What did it say before?" Walker asked Tamra, who stood beside him, her hair glistening in the late-day sun.

"Battle," she told him.

"The Battle of Wounded Knee?"

"That was what the government originally called it."

But it wasn't a battle, Tamra explained, as he gazed at the sign. It was a massacre—a place where more than three hundred Indians, mostly women and children, were killed on December 29, 1890, for supporting the Ghost Dance, a religion that had been outlawed on Lakota reservations.

Fourteen days prior to the massacre, the tribal police murdered Sitting Bull at his home. That prompted Big Foot, another Lakota chief, to lead his band to Pine Ridge, where he hoped to seek shelter with Chief Red Cloud, who was trying to make peace with the army. But Big Foot, an old man ill with pneumonia, and most of his people, were exterminated instead. Those who survived told their story, recounting the chilling details.

"It was the Seventh Cavalry who shot them," Tamra said. "Custer's old unit. The government sent them, along with other troops, to arrest the Ghost Dancers. The morning after Big Foot and his band were captured, a gun went off during a scuffle. And that was it. That was how the massacre started." She paused, her voice impassioned with the past, with a war-torn history. "At first the struggle was fought at close quarters, but most of the Indians had already surrendered their weapons. There were only a hundred warriors. The rest were women, children and old men. When they ran to take cover, the cavalry opened fire with cannons that were positioned above the camp. Later some of the women were found two or three miles away, a sign that they were chased down and killed."

Walker glanced at the craft booth, where dream catchers fluttered, feathers stirring in the breeze. "The Seventh Cavalry got their revenge."

"Yes, they did." Tamra followed his gaze. "The Ghost Dance was supposed to bring back the old way, to encourage spiritual powers to save us. At the time, the government was reducing our land and cutting our promised rations. The Lakota were sick and starving. They needed hope."

"They needed the Ghost Dance," he said.

She nodded, and he thought about the documentary on TV, the reenactment of a woman and child bleeding in the snow. Was that a depiction of Wounded Knee? Of the massacre? He'd only caught a glimpse of it while he was switching channels, but it had affected him just the same.

"Someone found a baby still suckling from its dead mother," she said, her words creating a devastating image in his mind. "And after most of the people had been killed, there were soldiers who called out, claiming that those who weren't wounded should come forth, that they would be safe. But when some of the little boys crept out of their hiding places, they were butchered." She paused, took a breath. "We have an annual event called Future Generations Riders, where the organizers take a group of horseback riders, mostly children, on the same trail as the Wounded Knee victims. Sitting Bull's great-great-great-grandson is one of the leaders. Some of the kids don't know their culture, so it helps them learn, to look to the future. Hope can come from grief. From accepting who you are."

"Spencer told me that being Indian didn't matter," Walker admitted. "That I needed to forget about it if I wanted to succeed."

"I was told the same thing. From my mother, from your mother. But Mary and I have changed. We believe differently now."

"Can we visit the grave site?" he asked, compelled by his heritage, the Lakota blood he'd fought so hard to ignore.

"Yes, of course," she told him, meeting his gaze.

He wondered if she could see into his heart, if she knew what he was thinking. If she did, she didn't say anything. Instead she led him to a road that looped around like a teardrop.

On top of a hill, a rustic archway announced the entrance to the cemetery. A mass grave, hedged by a small slab of concrete, was marked with a stone obelisk, listing the names of the Indians buried there. Native gifts, feathers and tobacco offerings adorned their resting place. Surrounding the memorial were other graves, a bit more modern, scattered in the rough grass.

Walker reached for Tamra's hand and whispered a prayer. She slid her fingers through his, and they stood side by side, a man and a woman who'd forged a bond.

A closeness neither of them could deny.

After they went back to her truck, they sat in silence for a while. Finally he turned to look at her. She moved closer, and they kissed.

Slowly, gently.

And even though the exchange was more emotional than physical, more sweet than sexual, he wished they could make love tonight, hold each other in the same bed. Of course, he knew that wasn't possible. Especially since he'd agreed to stay at his mother's house.

Confused, he ended the kiss, still tasting her on his tongue, still wanting what he shouldn't have.

Tamra lay beside Mary, who snored a bit too loudly. Restless, she glanced at the clock and saw that it was almost one o'clock in the morning. She'd been staring at the ceiling for hours, trying not to toss and turn. But it wasn't the other woman's snoring that kept her awake.

It was Walker.

She'd given him her room, offering him a private place to sleep. But picturing him in her bed was making her skin warm. When she touched her lips, intent on reliving his kiss, she knew she was in trouble.

She couldn't fantasize about Walker, not here, not now, not like this. Guilty, she climbed out of bed, cautious not to wake Mary.

What she needed was a drink of water. A tall glass, full of ice. Something to douse her emotions, to cool her skin.

As she padded down the hall, the floorboards creaked beneath her feet. Once she reached the kitchen, she stalled. Walker stood at the counter, drinking a glass of water, doing exactly what she had come to do.

He hadn't noticed her yet. He faced the tiny window above the sink, gazing out at the night. His chest was bare and a pair of shorts rode low on his hips. His hair, those dark, sexy strands, fell across his forehead in sleepless disarray.

Suddenly he turned and caught sight of her. The glass in his hand nearly slipped. She could almost hear it crashing to the floor.

"I'm sorry," she said. "I didn't mean to startle you."

"It's okay. I was just—"

He roamed his gaze over her, and she became acutely aware of her short summer nightgown, of the soft cotton material.

"Just what?"

"Thirsty," he told her.

"Me, too."

"Then you can have this."

He handed her his water, and she put her mouth on the rim of the glass, sipping the liquid, wishing she were tasting him. The ice crackled, jarring the stillness.

He continued to watch her, taking in every inch of her body. He seemed to like what he saw, the slight cleavage between her breasts, the flare of her hips, the length of her bare legs.

She took another sip of his drink and noticed that his nipples were erect. She wanted to drop her gaze, but she didn't have the nerve to glance at his fly, to be that bold in the middle of the night.

"I couldn't sleep," he said. "Not in your bed."

Tamra returned his glass, giving him the rest of the water. In the process, her hand touched his. "Why not?" she asked, her heart picking up speed.

"Because I kept imagining your scent on everything. The sheets, the pillowcase."

Dizzy, she took a deep breath, dragging oxygen into her lungs. "I don't wear perfume."

"I know. I can tell. You wear lotion. Whenever we get really close, I can smell it on your skin."

"It's just a moisturizer." She knew that was a dumb thing to say, but she didn't know how else to respond. He was looking at her with lust in his eyes, with a hunger so deep, she wanted to crawl all over him.

Right here. In his mother's kitchen.

"It's soft," he said. "Airy. Like the plants and flowers in the greenhouse at my family's estate." He set his glass on the counter and moved forward.

She swallowed, got thirsty again, envisioned his mouth covering hers. She knew he was seducing her, but she didn't care. She liked the erotic expression on his face, the deep, husky tone of his voice.

He took another step toward her, his feet silent on the faded linoleum. "I haven't been with anyone in months."

A vein fluttered at her neck. She could feel it, skittering beneath her skin. "It's been longer than that for me."

"I'm good at controlling my urges," he told her.

She stood perfectly still. He was only inches away, so close they struggled to breathe the same air. "So am I. But I can't seem to do that with you."

"Me, neither." He cursed, just once, before he dragged her into his arms, before he kissed her so hard, her head spun.

When he pinned her against the counter, she nearly wept. His mouth plundered hers, over and over, giving her what she wanted, making the moment last.

Heat. Intensity. A tongue-to-tongue sensation.

She gripped his shoulders; he cupped her bottom and pulled her flush against his body. Then they broke apart and stared at each other.

"We can't do this," he said. "Not here."

She nodded, fighting the pressure between her legs, the desperation he'd incited. "Then where?"

"I don't know." He pulled his hand through his hair. "I can't think clearly."

Neither could she. All she wanted was him. Walker Ashton. A boy she'd heard about since she was a child. A man she barely knew.

"We could go for a drive," he suggested. "In my car."

The SUV he'd rented, she thought. A vehicle with

four-wheel-drive and big backseat. Suddenly she felt like a teenager, a moonstruck girl who should know better. "What if your mom wakes up?"

"We'll leave her a note."

"And say what? That we decided to cruise around the rez in the middle of the night? Or drive to Gordon for a piece of pie?"

He made a face. "Do you have a better idea?"

"At least let me get dressed. Grab something from my room. Mary knows I'd never go out like this."

That made him smile. Apparently, he'd been willing to climb behind the wheel just as he was—half-naked and much too aroused. "My clothes are in your room, too. Will you get me a shirt? A pair of tennis shoes?"

She nodded, but as she turned away, he latched on to her arm. She thought he was going to kiss her again, but he didn't. He frowned instead.

"What's wrong?" she asked.

"I don't have any protection."

"I'm on the Pill."

He was still frowning. "I thought you haven't been with anyone for a while."

"I haven't. But I prefer to be prepared."

He searched her gaze. "Because of the father of your baby?"

She let out the breath she was holding. "Yes."

"I can't make any promises, Tamra. No happily-ever-afters. But I wouldn't do what he did. I wouldn't hurt you like that."

"Thank you." She realized they were whispering,

speaking in hushed tones, talking about something far more intimate than sex.

And this time when she turned away to get their clothes, he didn't stop her.

Walker drove into the night, traveling on a dirt road, thinking this had to be the most strangely erotic moment of his life. Tamra sat beside him with a shopping bag on her lap. He hadn't asked her what was in it. For now he was trying to decide where to park. The reservation was dark, eerie, beautiful. The land went on forever, with trees swaying to the moonlight. In the distance a coyote howled.

"I don't know how far to go," he said.

She turned to look at him. She'd changed into a sundress that sported a row of tiny buttons down the front. On her feet, she wore cowboy boots. He'd never seen a more compelling woman. Her hair was the color of a raven's wing, sleek and shiny and begging to be touched.

"With me?" she asked.

He blinked, wondered what she meant. Then it dawned on him. She was responding to his statement. The SUV hit a slight bump in the road, and he grinned. He knew how far to go with her. "I was talking about how far I should keep driving, where would be a good place to park."

"Oh."

She ducked her head and he suspected she was blushing. He reached over to slide his fingers through her hair, just for a second, just to feel the silkiness against his skin. "I'm going to do everything imaginable to you."

"Oh," she said again, only sexier this time.

Damn if he didn't want to pull over right now, right in the middle of the road. "How about over there?" he gestured to a copse of cottonwoods.

Tamra glanced out the window. "The river is that way. There might be people camped by the water."

"Then we'll go in the other direction." He cut across the terrain, closer to the hills, to a backdrop that took his breath away. He'd never made love in an area so vast, so romantic.

He parked beneath a jagged stretch of moonlight, where stars danced in the sky. "What's in the bag, Tamra?"

She clutched it to her chest. "A blanket. Some extra clothes."

"Extra clothes?" He touched her hair again, toying with a strand that looped across her cheek. "What for?"

"In case the ones we're wearing get torn."

Walker's pulse jumped. Excited, intrigued, far too aroused, he moved closer. "Does that mean we can go crazy?"

She chewed her lip, a girlish habit he'd seen her do before. "You kept warning me that we were going to tear off each other clothes and I—" she paused, leaned toward him "—thought we better be prepared."

He wasn't sure if anything could prepare him for this moment—this middle-of-the-night, heaven-help-him lust. Anxious, he took her in his arms, his hands nearly quaking. She held on to him, too, gripping his shoulders.

And then they kissed, as deeply as they could, tongue to tongue, heart to beating heart.

A second later they went mad. He attacked her dress, sending every last button flying. She did the same thing to his shirt, ripping the denim with feminine force.

When she climbed onto his lap, he thought he might die. He breasts were exposed, only inches from his mouth. She was jammed between him and the steering wheel, but she didn't seem to mind. So much for the blanket, he thought. She'd dropped it, along with their extra clothes, onto the floorboard.

He licked her nipples, switching sides, blowing on each one, making them peak. She pulled his head closer, encouraging him to suckle.

Desperate, he lifted her dress to her thighs, running his hands along the waistband of her panties. She moaned and rubbed against his fly.

He closed his eyes, opened them, smiled at her.

She was watching everything he did, trying to see in the dark. He turned on the dome light, illuminating the vehicle with a soft glow. He didn't care if it drained the battery. He could stay here, just like this, for the rest of his life.

His body was rock hard, thick and solid and eager to penetrate hers. Only, they were still half-dressed, still torturing each other with foreplay.

She looked incredible, with her luscious curves and golden-brown skin. Her neck was long and slender, and her nipples were damp with saliva.

His saliva. His hunger. His insatiable need.

"I could eat you alive," he said.

"Then do it." She rocked forward in his lap, creating friction, giving him a slightly shy, slightly sirenlike smile. "And I'll do it to you, too."

Every ounce of blood rushed straight to his groin. He had no idea how she could be so subtle yet so obvious. Women, he thought, were fascinating creatures.

"This could be a dream." He nuzzled her neck, tongued the shell of her ear and inhaled the fragrance on her skin, the lotion that drove him to distraction. "A wet dream," he added, dragging her into the backseat.

Once again, he hiked up her dress, but this time, he removed her panties, clutching the piece of lace. He wondered if she'd chosen them for him or if she always wore such sexy little underthings.

When he kissed her there—right there—she bucked against his mouth. Wanting more, he pushed her legs open even farther, showing her how naughty he intended to get.

She practically melted against him, dissolving like spun sugar. Then she took off her dress and boots, tossing them aside, offering him every inch of her naked body.

A sacrifice, he thought. A gift.

Within minutes—heart pounding, soul-spinning minutes—Tamra kept her promise, shifting her body so she could pleasure him, too. So they could make love to each other at the same time.

She dislodged his shorts and took him in her

mouth, making his stomach muscles quiver, making his blood swim.

Yet somewhere deep down, he knew this was more than an affair. This was their emotions, a blend of sex and sin, of passion and warmth, of unbridled affection.

A pleasure so deep, he feared he might drown.

He kept tasting her, licking her while she did erotic things to him. And when she climaxed, when she convulsed against his tongue, he fought the urge to come, too.

Knowing he couldn't let her take him all the way, he stopped her before it happened. She sat up and gazed at him, still glassy-eyed from her climax.

Finally she smiled at him, and he realized why. His shorts were halfway down his legs, and he was still wearing his shirt, the fabric she'd torn to smithereens. He grinned and tackled her, pinning her to the seat.

She wrestled with his clothes, and they went crazy all over again. By the time he was completely naked, she dug her nails into his skin, clawing him like a dark-eyed cat, a feline in heat.

He thrust into her, full hilt. She wrapped her legs around him, and they gazed at each other, trapped in a candid moment, in being as close as possible.

She grabbed on to the plastic handhold above her head, bracing herself for a deep, driving rhythm, telling him, without words, what she wanted.

He didn't disappoint. He took her, hard and fast, rough and dangerous.

There was no other way to describe their coupling.

The crush of their mouths, the clank of teeth, the greedy, frantic, carnivorous sensation of pounding straight into her.

The woman stealing his senses.

She made his mind spin, his breath catch, his heart nearly beat its way out of his chest.

Together, they let themselves fall. She clung to him, gasping in his ear, shuddering in his arms. He came, too, spilling into her, warm and wet and drugging.

In the moments that followed, they remained still, afraid to move, to break the connection.

Finally he withdrew, leaving her damp with his seed. Unsure of what else to do, he grabbed his discarded shirt and tucked it between her legs, letting her use it like a towel.

"You're not sorry, are you?" she asked.

"No. Why would I be?"

"Because you said we were going to be sorry afterward."

"I said that before I knew you." He scooted next to her, smoothing her hair away from her face, thinking how beautiful she was.

"I'm not sorry, either."

He smiled, then noticed she looked chilled. He remembered the blanket she'd brought and climbed in the front seat to retrieve it.

"Here." He slipped it over her shoulders, and she invited him to share it with her.

He turned off the dome light, darkening the car, bathing them in the pitch of night. And as they snuggled in the dark, he wondered if they would be sorry later.

When he left the reservation without her.

# Six

Morning came too soon. Tamra heard the clang of pots and pans, the familiar sound of Mary fixing breakfast.

Was Walker awake, too? Was he sitting at the kitchen table, pretending that he hadn't sneaked out of the house last night? Or crept back in several hours later?

She sat up and reached for her robe. She could still feel Walker's touch—his mouth, his hands, the strength of his body, the erotic sensation of flesh against flesh.

Although she kept telling herself it had been lust, a hard-hammering, desperate-for-sex release, she knew better. Because after the sex had ended, they'd remained in each other's arms, not wanting to let go, to break the spell.

And now, God help her, she was nervous about seeing him, anxious about facing the man who was seeping into her pores, the man playing guessing games with her emotions.

They were getting too close too fast, and it scared her. Yet she liked it, too. She envisioned marching into the kitchen or her bedroom or wherever he was and kissing him senseless. But she wouldn't dare, not in front of Mary. Walker's mom had slept through the entire event.

Tamra washed her face and brushed her teeth, but she didn't take a shower or get dressed. She simply tightened her robe and headed down the hall. She wanted Walker to see her this way, to look into her eyes on the morning after, to appreciate her tousled hair, to remember running his hands through it.

She entered the kitchen, but he wasn't at the table. She took a deep breath and decided he would awaken soon. He didn't seem like the type of man who would sleep the day away.

"Oh, my. Look at you." Mary turned away from the stove, from the old-fashioned oatmeal she was stirring. "Did you have a rough night?"

Tamra blinked, forced a smile, fought a wave of guilt. "Rough?"

"Did I keep you up?" The older woman sighed. "I was snoring, wasn't I? I need one of those mouth-piece devices. Or a nasal strip or something."

"It was fine. I hardly noticed." Because she'd been parked on the plains, having carnal relations with Mary's son.

A sin she was sure to repeat.

Dodging eye contact, she poured herself a cup of coffee, grateful it was thick and dark and blasted with caffeine. "Do you need help with breakfast?" she asked, adding sugar to her cup, giving herself another artificial boost.

"Sure. You can fry the eggs. But it's just the two of us. Walker already left this morning."

"Left?" Tamra spun around, nearly burned her hand on the sloshing drink, then set it on the counter. "He went home?"

"No, honey. He drove to Gordon. He said he had some banking matters to take care of."

Her pulse quit pounding. There were no banks on the rez, no financial institutions. "That makes sense."

Mary checked her watch, then went back to the oatmeal. An early riser, she was already dressed for work, wearing a freshly laundered uniform and squeaky nurse-type shoes. Her gray-streaked hair was tucked behind her ears. "Walker seemed preoccupied today."

"He did?" Tamra opened a carton of eggs, took inventory, tried to behave accordingly. "How so?"

"I think he was anxious to see you, hoping you were awake."

"Really?" A teenybopper reaction, a bevy of wings took flight in her belly, making breakfast an impossible task. But she cracked several eggs into a pan, anyway, then realized she'd neglected to turn on the flame. She glanced up and noticed Mary watching her. She'd forgotten the oil, too.

"What's going on with you two?"

"Me and Walker?" Caught red-handed, Tamra faked her response, feigning a casual air. "Nothing. We're just friends."

"Friends, my foot," his mother said. "I think you have your eyes on each other."

Uh-oh. Trying to stay calm, she dumped the mistake she'd made into a bowl, deciding she would fix scrambled instead of fried. And this time, she put a pad of butter in the pan, igniting the stove. "Would it be okay with you if we did?"

"Did what?"

"Had our eyes on each other."

"Of course it would," Mary told her. "But I'd hate to see you do something rash."

Unable to keep pretending, she gazed at the lady who'd raised her, who'd given her everything a child could hope for. "I already slept with him."

"Oh, my goodness." Mary fanned her face. "So soon?" She turned off the oatmeal, ignoring their half-made breakfast. "You need to be careful, honey. And so does he. This is all so new."

"We can handle it."

"Are you sure?"

"No," she admitted, "I'm not. But what choice do we have? We're already involved."

"For how long?"

"It doesn't have to last forever. And he promised he wouldn't hurt me."

The older woman frowned. "Not purposely, no. But what if you fall in love with him? What then?"

It was a question Tamra couldn't answer. A question she feared. Because she knew that when Walker went home, she would have to cope with her loss.

With missing him desperately.

Tamra tried to focus on her job. She sat at the desk in her cluttered office, telling herself to quit thinking about Walker. She had more important issues to deal with: flyers to design, schedules to coordinate, donations to secure for an end-of-the-month powwow.

Obsessing about a man wouldn't accomplish a thing.

A knock sounded on her door and she reached for her coffee, her second cup that day. "Come in," she called out, assuming it was Michele. Her friend had offered to stop by to help with the powwow details. The Oyate Project intended to host a raffle this year, giving away as many prizes as they could wangle.

She glanced up, saw that she was mistaken. It wasn't Michele. Walker crossed the threshold, wearing jeans and a denim shirt, similar to the one she'd torn off his body.

He moved closer, and her heart went haywire.

"Hi," he said.

"Hi." She started stacking folders, trying to compose her senses, trying to look busy, to pretend that she hadn't been thinking about him. "I wasn't expecting you."

He reached for an ancient folding chair in the corner and opened it, positioning it across from her. A pair of mirrored sunglasses shielded his eyes, and his sleeves were rolled to his elbows.

"Do you have a minute?" he asked.

For him, she had all day. All night. All year. "Sure. What's going on?"

"I just got back from the bank."

"Mary told me that's where you went."

"I opened a checking account in Gordon. I figured that would be the most convenient location." He removed his sunglasses and hooked them onto his pocket. "You and Mary will have to go into the branch to fill out some paperwork. Unless you already do your banking there. Then I can add your names online."

She merely blinked at him. "I don't understand."

"What's not to understand? It'll be a joint account. I'll make a deposit every month, and you and Mary can use it for whatever you need."

"You're volunteering to support us?"

"Not completely, not unless you want to quit your jobs. But I don't see that happening. You're both so dedicated to what you do."

"Then why are you doing this?" She sucked in a much-needed breath, wondering how he could sit there—so damn casually—and offer her money. "Is it because you slept with me?"

A sudden flare of anger burst into his eyes, like fire. Like brimstone. Like a man who was used to controlling other people's lives. "What the hell is that supposed to mean? That I'm trying to turn you into my mistress?"

"That's how it seems," she said, refusing to be intimidated by his temper, the all-consuming power that could drain a woman dry. The muscle ticking in his jaw. The hard, ready-to-explode, king-of-the-universe breathing.

He stood and pushed away his chair, nearly shoving it against the file cabinet. "I was just trying to help. To make life easier for my mom." He paused, drilled his gaze into hers. "And for you, too. But I don't keep mistresses. I don't reward my lovers for sleeping with me."

She didn't say anything, so he leaned forward, bracing his hands on her desk. "I can't believe you think so little of me. Don't you get it, Tamra? Don't you see why this matters to me?"

"No, I don't. Mary and I can take care of ourselves."

"I know. But my mom's car looks like it's on its last leg and you're lending money to friends, cash you can barely spare. I don't want to go home and worry about you."

She sighed, wishing she hadn't provoked an argument. Walker was confused, she thought. And he was comparing his life to hers. "You don't have to feel guilty for being rich."

"Easy for you to say, Miss Do-Gooder."

She rolled her eyes, trying to ease the tension, to make him stop scowling. It was the best she could do. Other than fall prey to his machismo and touch him. Kiss him. Tug his stubborn mouth to hers. "Listen to you, Mr. Write-a-Check."

He smiled in spite of himself. Grateful, she flicked

a paper clip at him. He grabbed the worse-for-wear chair and parked his butt down again.

"You should see my office at Ashton-Lattimer," he said. "And my condo. Not to mention the apartment I have on my family's estate in Napa Valley. It's inside the mansion, on the second floor with a spectacular view."

She couldn't even fathom his lifestyle. Edward had been wealthy, but not compared to the Ashtons. "Those are the kinds of things Mary wanted you to have."

"Will you talk to her about the account?" he pressed.

"No, but you can. If you want to help your mom and she's willing to accept your offer, then it's okay with me. But I don't want to be part of it."

"Because you're not comfortable taking money from me?"

"Edward used to give me gifts. He used to buy me trinkets."

"That jerk who hurt you? It's not the same thing."

"When it ended, when he broke up with me, I felt cheap." And for her, it had been the worst feeling in the world. "I don't want to go through that again. Not ever."

"Don't compare me to him. We're nothing alike."

She almost reached across the desk to hold his hand, but she curled her fingers, keeping her distance, recalling the ache that came with being in love. She couldn't bear to fall for Walker, not like that.

"Will you at least accept a check for your charity?" he asked.

She looked into his eyes and saw the sincerity in

them. And then she realized how foolish she was, refusing to hold his hand, to touch him. She knew they were going to sleep together again. Sex was inevitable. "You already wrote one, didn't you?"

"Yep." He removed it from his pocket and handed it to her.

She glanced at the denomination. "That's a generous donation." And sex wasn't love, she told herself. There was nothing wrong with continuing their affair.

"It's tax deductible." He picked up the paper clip she'd tossed at him. Toying with the metal, he altered the shape, bending it back and forth. "Besides, it's for a worthy cause. I know the Oyate Project will put it to good use."

"Thank you." She wrote him a receipt, and when she gave it to him, their eyes met and held.

An intimate look. A deep, heart-thundering stare.

"Will you come home with me, Tamra?"

"Home?"

"To Napa Valley. To the estate."

Panic, instant anxiety, leaped to her throat. His family's mansion? The winery? The place where he grew up? She shifted her gaze, breaking eye contact, dragging air into her lungs. "What for?"

"Because I want to take you and Mary there. It would be the perfect place for my mom to meet Charlotte. And you and I could spend some time together."

"What about the rest of your family? Spencer's wife? Your cousins?" When she and Mary lived in Northern California, they used to scan the society pages for tidbits about the Ashtons, and they'd come across their names quite a few times. "They might not like us staying there."

"Spencer is dead, and he's the only one who would have forbidden it. The others won't interfere."

"That's not the same as welcoming us."

"Fine. Whatever. If I tell them to welcome you, then they will."

His bulldozing did little to ease her mind. "I'm not sure if I can get the time off."

"I'm only asking for a week. Seven measly days. You don't take vacations?"

"Yes, but—"

"But what?"

Tamra fidgeted with the paper clip he'd bent. What could she say? That she was nervous about being thrust into his world? That she didn't belong there?

"I'm sure Mary would be more comfortable if you came with us," he said. "And so would I."

"Would this include a trip to San Francisco?" she asked.

"Definitely. It's only fifty miles from the estate. And it's where I live most of the time, where I work."

"How often do you commute to Napa Valley?"

"On the weekends mostly. But I've been spending more time at the estate since Spencer was killed. I can't help but miss him."

She glanced out the window, felt the cloud of death that floated between them. "I'd like to visit Jade." To kneel at her baby's grave site, to whisper to her little girl.

"We can visit her together. We can take her the flowers I promised." He released a rough breath. "We can do other things, too. Just the two of us. But we'll have to tell my mom what's going on. We can't keep sneaking around."

"I already told her."

"That we're lovers?" He sat back in his chair, frowned a little, pulled his hand through his hair. "How'd she take it?"

"She said we needed to be careful. That this is all so new."

"But it won't be." His gaze sought hers, holding her captive. "Not after we get to know each other better."

"Then I'll go with you. I'll arrange to take some time off." To be with him, to meet his high-society family, to discover who Walker Ashton really was.

Walker sat on the steps of his mother's porch. Tamra was still at work, and Mary was inside, puttering around the kitchen, doing whatever domestic things women did. She'd returned from her job about an hour ago, giving him the opportunity to talk to her, much in the way he'd spoken with Tamra earlier. And just like her non-Hunka daughter, she'd left him with mixed emotions.

Good and bad, he supposed.

"You're not brooding, are you?"

"What? No." He turned to look at Mary, who'd come outside with a glass of lemonade in her hand.

She handed him the drink. "Then you must be deep in thought."

"Maybe. I don't know." He took a sip and noticed that she'd added just the right amount of sugar.

"Are you upset about the checking account?"

"That both you and Tamra turned me down? Yeah, it bugs me. I'm trying to do the right thing, and no one will let me."

She sat beside him. "The thirty thousand Spencer gave me was enough. I don't want to take money from my own son, too."

He squinted at her, trying to shield his eyes from the late-day sun. "I thought Indian families were supposed to help each other. I thought that was the message around here."

"It is. But I'm not poor anymore. I'm not struggling to pay my bills." She smoothed her blouse, a polyester top she'd probably bought at a discount store. "I was ashamed of my house when you first got here, but it was wrong for me to feel that way. It's nicer than what most people have around here."

In Walker's eyes she was still poor. Not destitute, like the out-of-work population on the rez, but a two-bedroom mobile home and a tired old Buick certainly didn't make her rich. "At least you and Tamra agreed to go to California with me. I'm glad about that."

"So am I. I can't wait to see Charlotte."

"She's anxious to see you, too." A rabbit darted by, scurrying into the brush. He watched it disappear, feeling like a kid who'd missed out on his childhood, a boy who'd grown up too fast. "I wish you'd reconsider about the money."

"Goodness gracious. You're just like your father."

"Stubborn?" he asked.

"Pigheaded," she replied.

He snorted like a swine and made her laugh. He knew they were still trying to get used to each other, to have stress-free conversations. "Did my dad have a temper, too?"

"Not as bad as yours."

"Gee, thanks." He bumped her shoulder, and she smiled. He wondered if his father was watching them, if angels existed. Walker couldn't remember his dad, at least not to any degree. But he couldn't remember his mom, either, and she was sitting right next to him.

She sighed, her voice turning soft. "I loved David so much."

Suddenly he didn't know what to say. He'd never been in love. He'd never given his heart to anyone. A bit lost, he stared at the grass, at the coarse, wild groundcover.

"Do you know how I met him?" she asked.

"No. How?"

"I was hitchhiking, and he picked me up. It was my second day on the road, and I wasn't getting very many rides."

"Is that the first time you left the rez?"

She nodded. "I was twenty-three years old, determined to get away from this place and never come back."

"Where were you headed?"

"Omaha. I figured it was big enough to find a job and start my life over."

"Did my dad offer to drive you there?"

"No. He offered to take me as far as Kendall, the town where he lived." Her tone turned wistful. "You should have seen me when I climbed into his truck. Talk about nervous. He was so handsome, so tall and strong, with the greenest eyes imaginable."

Curious, Walker studied her, noticed how girlish she seemed——a woman reminiscing about the man she loved. "I guess you never made it to Omaha, considering Charlotte and I were born in Kendall."

"David offered me a job. He said he was looking for a housekeeper, someone to cook and clean for him and his farmhands. But later I discovered that he just wanted to keep me around."

Walker couldn't help but smile. His old man must have been quite the charmer. "Crafty guy."

"And proud and kind. Everything I could have hoped for. I don't think I'll ever stop missing him."

He glanced away, then frowned, his memories as tangled as the weeds spreading across the plains. "What happened on the day he died?"

"Your father had a heart attack behind the wheel. I was with him, riding in the passenger seat. We were on our way home from the mortgage company, trying to get them to discount the loan, but it was too late. They refused to work with us, to help us save the farm."

"Did you try to take the wheel?"

"Yes, but I couldn't. Everything happened so fast. We hit a tree. Between the heart attack and the accident, David didn't stand a chance."

"Charlotte and I were at a neighbor's house. An elderly woman." He remembered a gray-haired lady, but he couldn't recall his own parents.

Mary blinked back tears. "She was a widow who used to baby-sit now and then. That's where you stayed until Spencer came and got you."

"What did my uncle tell her?"

"That he was going to care for my children until I was well enough to take you to the reservation. She had no reason to question his motives."

As silence stretched between them, he placed his lemonade on the step. The glass had been sweating in his hand, making his palms damp. He wanted to comfort Mary, to abolish her pain, as well as his own. But he didn't know how. He was still struggling to bond with her, to behave like her long-lost son.

"I should get started on dinner." She stood and dusted off of her pants, looking old and tired.

He got to his feet, envisioning her when she was young, like the pictures he'd seen in her photo albums. "How do you say mother in Lakota?"

*"Iná,"* she told him.

*"Iná,"* he repeated.

Her breath hitched, causing a lump to form in his throat. "I'll help you with dinner," he said, even though he was a lousy cook.

She touched his cheek, her hand warm against his skin. They gazed at each other, but they didn't embrace. Before things got too awkward, she led him into the kitchen, where she taught him how to make Indian tacos.

Walker was out of his element, but he did the best he could, trying to please his mother. By the time Tamra arrived on the scene, he was knee-deep in fried dough, lettuce, tomatoes and a pan of ground beef.

Tamra pitched in, and the three of them prepared the evening meal. But soon, he thought, they would be in Napa Valley. On the estate. The mansion where he was raised.

The place Walker called home.

# Seven

The weather in Northern California was perfect, a warm summer day bursting with color. The wine country, with its fertile land and prospering grapes, was surrounded by mountain ranges that rose to the sky.

Tamra sat next to Walker in his car, a silver Jaguar he'd retrieved from a long-term parking lot at the airport. Mary settled in the backseat, but she'd been relatively quiet since they'd arrived in Napa Valley.

Walker stopped at a gate at the entrance of the estate, pressing a keypad with a security code. As they continued, moving closer to their final destination, Tamra drew a shaky breath.

The mansion itself, an enormous cream-colored structure accented with marble, presided from a hill overlooking the vineyards below. A large circular drive boasted an elegant reflecting pool. The water shimmered in the sun, catching the light like magic.

"Oh, my," Mary said, a statement that seemed to convey exactly what Tamra was thinking.

*Oh, my.*

"The humble abode," Walker joked, pulling into the driveway with ease.

He was glad to be home, Tamra thought. To the familiarity of his youth. But his comfort zone only made her more nervous.

To her, the estate seemed like a rich-and-powerful fortress. It had Spencer Ashton written all over it. The dead man still reigned.

"Long live the king," she mumbled.

Walker shot her a quick glance. "What?"

"It looks like a castle," she amended.

He shrugged and killed the engine of his sixty-thousand-dollar car. They climbed out of the Jag, and he gestured to the trunk, where he'd already popped open the lid. "Don't worry about our luggage. Someone will take care of it soon enough."

Someone? The hired help? "You're spoiled," Tamra said.

He frowned at her. "I don't have servants in San Francisco. I prefer my privacy. But things are different here."

She held her tongue, and he opened the door to an expansive foyer. A magnificent library was on the left and a lavish dining room on the right. A double staircase, leading to each wing of the house, made a sweeping impression. Walker escorted her and Mary into a majestic room he called the grand parlor.

Grand indeed: creamy fabrics and ornate antiques, a terrace that presented a breathtaking view of a flourishing garden and the vineyards below.

Tamra didn't want to sit, although Walker offered her and his mother a seat. The furniture, she noticed, was polished to perfection. Tables gleamed and mirrors reflected every carefully decorated angle. There wasn't a thread out of place. Even the tassels on pillows displayed themselves in a don't-touch-us manner.

A woman wearing a black uniform draped with a white apron entered the parlor. She looked about Mary's age, her long dark-brown hair pinned up.

"Mr. Walker," she said, her tone soft and respectful. "It's good to have you home. And with your new family."

"Irena." He greeted her in a detached voice. But even so, he introduced her to Tamra and Mary, letting them know she was the head housekeeper.

If his attitude hurt Irena's feelings, she didn't let it show. Her blue eyes sparkled, especially when she spoke to Mary. Tamra liked her immediately, which made Walker's disposition even more baffling.

Had the housekeeper done something to displease him? Or did he treat all of the employees with mild disdain?

Tamra shifted in her seat. Was it a learned response he'd picked up from Spencer?

"Miss Charlotte and Mr. Alexandre left a message for you," Irena informed him. "Their flight was delayed. They won't be arriving until tomorrow morning."

He frowned. "That's fine. Is Lilah here?"

"Yes, Mr. Walker. She'll be with you shortly."

"Thank you. Will you send in some refreshments?"

"Yes, of course. I'd be glad to." She excused herself and gave Walker's mother a gentle smile on her way out the door.

Mary seemed disappointed about Charlotte's delay, but Irena's kindness had prompted her to relax, helping Tamra relax, too.

Five minutes later, when Lilah Spencer breezed into the parlor, their discomfort returned.

The lady of the manor, a reed-thin redhead, approached Walker with a Hollywood-style kiss, brushing her lips past his cheek. Impeccably dressed, she donned a cream-colored suit that matched the decor. Her makeup was flawless, her skin unnaturally taut.

Botox injections? Tamra wondered.

"I see the Indian people are here," Lilah said.

"Mind your manners," Walker told her, scolding his forty-nine-year-old aunt as if she was a child.

"Was that politically incorrect?" She divided her gaze between Tamra and Mary. "Would you prefer Native American?"

So much for the welcome Walker had promised, Tamra thought. "Indian is fine."

"Well, then. See?" Lilah smoothed her lapel, where a simple gold broach had the audacity to shine, to look as chic as the woman wearing it. "No harm done."

Walker introduced his mother first, and Mary was

gracious enough to extend her hand. Lilah extended hers, too, and Tamra wondered if Spencer's widow was mimicking what she saw, like a Stepford wife who kept switching gears, not quite sure how to treat Mary—the Indian her dead husband had wronged.

Irena arrived with a silver tray bearing iced tea, fresh mint, lemon wedges and sugar. Another maid carried a platter of finger sandwiches and a delicate assortment of fine china.

Lilah made a face at the tea, as though she craved something stronger. The head housekeeper offered the first glass to Mary, who accepted it gratefully. After the drinks were distributed and the sandwiches left in a buffet-style setting, the hired help disappeared.

"Now, then." Lilah sat in a Victorian settee and crossed her legs, her posture as graceful as an aging fashion model. "We need to decide what rooms Mary and Tamra should occupy."

Walker made the decision in two seconds flat. "My mother can take Charlotte's old room, and Tamra can stay in my apartment."

"Your apartment?" Lilah arched her lightly penciled bows.

"That's right," he countered, daring her to challenge him.

She didn't. She backed down easily, but not without a socially acceptable response. "His apartment is in the west wing," she announced to no one in particular. "And it has two bedrooms."

Walker gazed at Tamra from the across the room, and her heart bumped her chest. Fat chance that she would be sleeping in the second bedroom. She and Walker hadn't made love since that night on the plains. They'd decided to wait rather than take liberties at Mary's house. Of course, Walker was going full throttle now, demanding Tamra's attention.

"Will you and your guests be joining us for dinner?" Lilah asked her nephew.

"Yes, we will."

"Then I'll see to the menu." She stood, tall and slim and regal. "If you're weary from your flight, don't hesitate to retire to your room," she said to Mary. "I understand how taxing jet lag can be." She turned to Tamra. "You, too." Then to Walker, "I trust you'll show them to their quarters."

"Absolutely."

"I'll make sure the luggage is taken right up," Lilah concluded. She bade everyone a courtly farewell and left the parlor to tend to her duties.

A queen who was lost without her king.

Walker's apartment was as exceptional as the rest of the mansion, although the decor was quite a bit bolder, with more use of color. It contained a stylish living room, two bedrooms, two bathrooms and a comfortably equipped kitchen. The paintings on the walls exhibited desire, rage, even sadness. They were, Tamra thought, a reflection of Walker's personality.

Their luggage had arrived in no time, and she decided to unpack while Walker sat on the edge of his bed and watched her.

"Is there an another apartment on the other side of us?" she asked.

He nodded. "It belongs to my cousin Trace. He got the balcony."

She looked up, shook her head. "God forbid he should get something you don't have."

Walker rolled his eyes. "Trace irks me."

She reached for a hanger. "Really? How so?"

"He just does. We've always been at odds with each other."

Masculine rivalry? she wondered. Or did it go deeper than that? "Have you ever tried to work things out with him? Talk about your differences?"

He barked out a cynical laugh. "Yeah, right. He's impossible to communicate with."

"What does he do?"

"He manages the Ashton Estate Winery."

"How come you didn't get into that business?"

"Because Spencer wanted me to work with him at Ashton-Lattimer Corporation. The investment banking firm." He removed his shoes and socks and tossed them on the floor. Today he wore a charcoal suit that darkened the color of his eyes.

"Trace is Spencer's son, right?"

"Yep. His only son with Lilah."

"How many daughters do they have?"

"Two. Paige and Megan. Paige still lives here, and Meagan is married now." He took off his jacket. "Can we quit yapping about my family and get cozy?" He roamed his gaze over her, lowered his voice. "I've missed you."

Tamra's skin turned warm, but she refused to give in so easily. "You've missed touching me. That's not the same as missing someone. And I'm not through asking questions."

He made a goofy expression, then pretended to hang himself with his tie. She bit her lip to keep from laughing. "That's not going to charm me into bed," she told him, even though she wanted to tackle him, to kiss him, to let his sexual frustration consume her.

"Then hurry up and finish this interview. I've got a woman to seduce."

"Fair enough." She hung her best dress, black cotton with satin trim, in his closet. "What's the deal with Irena?"

"She's the head housekeeper. I already told you that."

"Why were you so rude to her?"

"I wasn't rude."

"The hell you weren't."

"Okay. Fine. Irena is a traitor. She's been with us since I was a kid and she let her daughter—who also used to work here, I might add—get engaged to the enemy."

"The enemy?" The Ashton Estate was beginning to sound like the setting for a soap opera. Days of Our Disgruntled Lives. "Who on earth are you talking about?"

"Eli Ashton. The SOB who threw a fit about Spencer's will and the Ashton-Lattimer stocks I inherited."

Money, she thought. The root of all evil. Only in

this case, she didn't know if Eli was the evil party or if Walker fit the bill. "How is Eli related to your uncle?"

"He's one of Spencer's kids with Caroline Lattimer, a former wife. The other Ashton family." He walked over to a mini bar in the corner and poured himself a shot of tequila, the first time Tamra had seen him drink. "They have a boutique winery about twenty-five miles from here. But that's not enough for Eli. He'll probably try to steal the Ashton-Lattimer stocks away from me."

"Did Spencer leave Caroline's children anything in the will?"

"Nope."

"And you don't think that's wrong?"

"It's not my place to judge my uncle's decision. Besides, Eli is only making a fuss because his grandfather on his mother's side founded the investment banking business."

"But Spencer ended up with it?"

"Caroline's father left it to him. Of course that was before Spencer divorced her. Then again, it doesn't really matter because their marriage was never legal. Spencer had a wife in Nebraska a long time ago, but he never divorced her."

Tamra could only stare. Her head was twirling like a top. "And what was her name?"

"Sally. He has grown kids with her, too. Oh, and there's a little boy Spencer fathered two years ago."

"He cheated on Lilah?"

"As far as I know, he cheated on all of his wives.

Lilah was one of his mistresses before he married her. She was his secretary. The old make-out-in-the-office routine."

"And this is the man you admired?"

Walker gave her a disturbed stare. "He treated me better than he treated everyone else. What am supposed to do? Hate him for that?"

"No, but you shouldn't be rude to Irena because her daughter is engaged to Eli."

"We're back to that?"

"That's right, we are. Did you really expect Irena to stop her daughter from falling in love?" She paused, looked at him, felt her heart pick up speed. "Love isn't something a person can control. Not a parent, not a child, not a man or a woman."

He frowned, squinted, left his empty shot glass on the bar. "What if Eli contests the will?"

"Then he contests it. That doesn't have anything to do with Irena. You owe her an apology, Walker."

"Listen to you. The voice of compassion." He sat on the edge of the bed again. "But you're right, I do. I'll apologize to her tonight, sometime before dinner. After all, she can't help it if her daughter fell for a selfish jerk."

Tamra doubted that Eli was the moneygrubber Walker was making him out to be. She suspected there was more to the story, and Irena had supported her daughter's decision for all the right reasons. "Good parents try to make their children happy."

"You're talking about Irena, right?"

She gave him a solemn nod. She certainly wasn't referring to Spencer.

Walker gazed out a second-story window, and she followed his line of sight. She couldn't see the view from her perspective, but she suspected he was gazing at his family's vineyards, the way he'd studied Mary's land allotment while he'd been on the rez.

Was he comparing the Napa Valley wine country to the South Dakota plains?

"My mom wants me to be happy," he said.

"Yes, she does. Mary loves you very much."

"I know. I can feel her affection." He turned away from the window. "But I don't understand it. She barely knows me."

Tamra walked away from the closet, taking a seat next to him on the bed. "Most mothers have a special bond with their children. I never knew my baby at all. But I loved her." She placed her hand on his knee, recalling the day she'd buried Jade. "She'll always be in my heart."

He touched her face, running his knuckles along her jaw. A masculine caress, a man-to-woman need. "I wish it was that easy for me. That I could love Mary the way she loves me."

"You will. Someday you will."

She put her head on his shoulder, and he held her so tight she could hardly breathe. But she didn't care. She wanted to be as close to him as possible.

He released the top button of her blouse, and she

lifted her head, grateful, so incredibly grateful, for his seduction.

As he kissed her neck, as his lips sought her skin, she opened her shirt completely, allowing him access to her bra, to the cleavage between her breasts.

He accepted the offering, putting his mouth all over her, leaving warm, damp marks. Branding her, she thought, taking possession.

They slid onto the bed, lying side by side, caressing, kissing, making each and every sensation count.

Sweet and slow. Dark and sensual.

He removed her bra, then skimmed his hand down her stomach, popping the snap on her jeans, playing with the waistband of her panties. When he moved lower, she caught her breath.

They rolled over the bed, scattering pillows, rumpling the quilt. Wanting more, they took turns undressing each other. And by the time she got to his trousers, he was hard and thick and desperate to straddle her. But she worked his zipper slowly, teasing him, making him wait.

"That's not fair," he said.

"Isn't it?" Tamra found her way into his boxers and skimmed the tip of his arousal, where moisture beaded like an iridescent pearl. She rubbed it onto his skin, and his entire body quaked.

"Not fair at all," he reiterated.

"You're impatient," she whispered in his ear.

"Can't help it." He kissed her, swirling his tongue, making love to her mouth.

She finished undressing him, and his breathing accelerated. Finally, when they were flesh to flesh, he braced himself above her.

But he didn't push her legs apart. He simply gazed at her, taking in every feminine curve. Then he cuffed her wrists with his hands, holding her arms above her head, making her his prisoner.

Tamra could only imagine how she looked, her nipples peaked, her areolae several shades darker than her brown skin.

"You're the most compatible lover I've ever had," he said.

"Have there been a lot?"

"It depends—" he lowered his head and flicked his tongue over one of her breasts "—on what someone considers a lot."

She didn't try to free herself, even though he still held her captive. She liked his game, his decisive maneuvers.

Sexual strategy. Her heart pounded with anticipation.

A strand of hair fell across his eyebrows, making him seem like a rebel. She itched to run her fingers down his spine, to sink her nails into his back.

But he offered her something even better. In the blink of an eye, he rolled over and took her with him, shifting until she was poised above him, with her legs sprawled across his lap.

"Want to go for a ride?" he asked.

Her breath rushed out; her pulse stumbled. She envisioned riding him until the end of time, until the sun disappeared and the moon spun in the sky. "Yes."

"Then do it." He gripped her waist. "Do it to both of us."

She didn't have a choice. She wanted him so badly, her life could have depended on it. More than ready, Tamra lifted her hips and slid down, taking him inside.

His fingers tightened around her waist, moving her up and down, setting the rhythm.

Deep, wet, intoxicating.

She leaned over to kiss him, to suck on his tongue. Desperate sex, she thought. Suddenly Walker tasted like the tequila he'd drunk.

Or was that the flavor of passion? Of the heat between them? The spiraling sensation of liquid fire?

They made love like animals on the verge of an attack. He lunged forward, so they were face-to-face, so she could look directly in his eyes while they practically tore each other apart.

She clawed his chest, raking her nails over every muscle. He ravaged her shoulders, using his teeth, nearly bruising her.

"This is insane," she said.

Beautifully crazy.

He didn't respond. He just encouraged her to keep going, to keep milking his body with hers.

Harder, faster, deeper.

The room twirled in a haze of color. Daylight burned bright. She could almost feel the sun melting over her skin, dripping in sweet, sticky rivulets.

A hot, hip-grinding climax shattered inside her, making her shudder, making the wetness between her legs seem like honey.

And then she realized that Walker had spilled into her, that the dampness had come from him.

Her lover.

The man sweeping her away.

# Eight

Tamra stepped out of the bathroom with a thick, fluffy towel wrapped around her. Everything at the Ashton Estate was luxurious.

Too luxurious, she thought, as she walked over to Walker's dresser to get some fresh undergarments.

He lounged on the bed with a towel wrapped around him, too. After they'd made love, they'd taken a shower together, but she'd remained in the bathroom to apply her makeup and blow-dry her hair.

His hair, she noticed, was still a little damp, combed away from his face and styled with a dollop of gel.

He smiled at her, and she slipped on her bra and panties and put her towel in a nearby hamper. Once she found the courage to return his smile, she looked through her side of the closet. She didn't want him to know how nervous she was about having dinner with his family.

"Do the Ashtons dress for their meals?" she asked.

"Nope." He drew his knees up, nearly flashing her. "We eat naked."

She sighed, almost laughed, wished he wasn't so damn charming. "You know what I mean."

"Lilah always dresses for dinner, but you don't have to worry about that. Just wear whatever feels right."

She scanned her modest selection and decided on a white skirt, a white blouse and a beaded belt she'd bought from a Lakota craftswoman. She added a noticeable array of silver and turquoise jewelry she'd acquired over the years.

"Now you really look Indian," Walker said.

She turned to face him, preparing for a fight. "Is that a problem for you?"

"No. I like it."

She let out the breath she was holding. "Thank you."

"You're welcome." He frowned a little. "I'm not ashamed of your heritage, Tamra. Of my heritage," he added. "I'm comfortable with who we are."

"Are you?" she asked, hating how temporary their affair was, how throwaway it suddenly seemed.

A fire ignited in his eyes. "What's that supposed to mean?"

"You would never relocate to Pine Ridge."

"Is there a reason I'm supposed to?"

Caught in an argument of her own making, she fussed with a wide silver bracelet, tightening it around her wrist, squeezing the edges of the metal. "No, of course not."

He didn't drop the subject. "It's a bit late for me to start my life over, to move in with my mom and pretend that we haven't been separated for twenty-two years. Besides, how would I survive on the rez? I'm the interim CEO of an investment-banking firm."

"Interim? You took over Ashton-Lattimer when Spencer died?"

"I was the executive vice president before he was killed. I'm the logical choice."

"So you think the board is going to vote you in permanently?"

He nodded. "I'm on a leave of absence right now. But as soon as you and Mary return to Pine Ridge, I'm going back to work. I imagine it will happen then."

She gave her bracelet another tight squeeze. "And you're going to accept the position?"

"Of course I am. Why wouldn't I?"

She shrugged off his question, as well as the intensity in his eyes. She had no right to challenge his choices. He'd already warned her that happily-ever-after wasn't in the cards.

Then why did she feel so dejected? So fearful of losing him?

"I'm going to check on your mom," she said.

"Dinner isn't for another hour."

"I know, but I want to see how she's settling in."

Tamra put on her shoes and ventured down the

hall, leaving Walker alone in his apartment. She didn't worry about getting lost since Mary's room was located in the west wing, near the upper foyer. She knocked on the door and received an instant welcome.

The older woman smiled, admiring Tamra's ensemble. "You look pretty."

"Thank you." She noticed Mary was dressed in her ratty bathrobe, with hot curlers in her hair, looking as nervous as Tamra felt. "What are you going to wear?"

"I don't know. This place is so doggone fancy." Walker's mother pursed her lips. "What do you think of my wake dress?"

"I didn't know you brought it."

"I figured I should."

"In case someone died?"

"Goodness, no." Mary looked at her, and they both laughed. "In case I needed a simple black dress."

"I think it's perfect."

Mary breathed a sigh of relief, and Tamra helped her get ready, hoping the Ashton dinner didn't feel like a wake.

An hour later they were seated in the formal dining room. The table was graced with fresh-cut flowers, elegant china and pristine linens.

Walker and Trace, the cousin he'd complained about, had acknowledged each other brusquely, but Trace had greeted Tamra and Mary in a much-warmer tone. Tamra thought he was handsome with his athletic build and stunning green eyes. She also sensed that his passions ran deep, that there was more to him than Walker was willing to admit.

Paige, the other cousin who lived at the estate, seemed like a peacemaker, quiet and unassuming yet keenly aware of her surroundings. Her almond-shaped eyes darted between the two men. Was she hoping they would quit giving each other the cold shoulder? Come to their senses and behave like family?

Lilah, on the other hand, pretended not to notice. She dined on the first course, a silver fork in her hand and a row of pearls looped around her neck.

Tamra wished someone would say something. That a conversation would flow. She glanced at Paige, who gave her a comforting smile. Blond highlights dazzled her light-brown hair, framing her face in soft layers. She was, Tamra thought, a breath of fresh air in an otherwise tense situation.

Lilah finally broke the silence. "Do you like your room?" she asked Mary.

"Oh, yes. It's lovely," Walker's mother responded.

"It's been redecorated since Charlotte was a child." Lilah took a bite of her watercress salad, chewed, swallowed, then continued speaking. "I had no idea that you were alive. Spencer told everyone, including me, that you'd died with your husband."

Mary looked at her son, then returned her gaze to Lilah. "I appreciate you taking care of my children."

"Well, yes, of course." The redhead almost fumbled with her fork, proving that she hadn't been happy about Spencer bringing home two half-breed kids. "Charlotte was so shy. I never knew what she was thinking. Now Walker—" she paused to nod her head at him "—he's a bit more predictable."

"Stubborn?" Mary asked.

"Precisely." Lilah sighed. "At least with me. He behaved wonderfully for Spencer."

"Hey." The man in question shifted in his seat, then winked at Mary, teasing her with his "stubborn" charm. "That's not fair. You two can't gang up on me."

His mother smiled at him. "I think we just did."

When Lilah agreed, everyone at the table relaxed. A moment later Irena entered the dining room, informing Lilah that there was an important phone call for her.

Lilah thanked the head housekeeper and excused herself. But when she returned after a short absence, she gripped the back of her chair.

"It was Stephen Cassidy," she announced.

Walker looked up. "Spencer's attorney? Is there news about the will?"

She shook her head. "Stephen heard some rumors about the murder investigation."

Spencer's murder, Tamra thought, as Lilah's knuckles turned white.

"The police are building a case against Grant." She all but spat the suspect's name. "They're going to put that traitor behind bars."

"Are you sure?" This came from Paige, who blew out an anxious breath. Trace was on edge, as well, waiting to hear what else his mother had to say.

She continued in a tight voice. "Supposedly the authorities uncovered something that could be highly damaging, something that goes beyond circumstantial evidence."

"What is it?" Trace asked. "What did they find out?"

"Stephen wasn't able to secure the details." Lilah resumed her seat and reached for her wine, downing the contents much too quickly. "I just wish this nightmare would end. That I could stop envisioning my husband with a bullet in his heart."

"Who's Grant?" Tamra asked.

"Spencer's son by his first wife," Walker responded.

"The one in Nebraska?"

"Yes, but she's been gone a long time. She died when Grant and his twin sister were about twelve." Walker picked up his knife and stabbed his roll. "Grant doesn't have an alibi for the night Spencer was shot, and he was at my uncle's office earlier that day, arguing with Spencer. If what Stephen heard is true, then it's only a matter of time before the police arrest him." He cut the roll into several jagged pieces. "I hope that bastard goes to hell for what he did to my uncle."

Tamra studied the darkness in her lover's eyes, the pain of losing his mentor.

Dinner had, indeed, turned into a wake.

Even if no one eulogized Spencer, he was there.

The murder victim. The man someone, possibly Grant Ashton, hated enough to kill.

As the morning sun shone in the sky, Walker sat beneath a veranda located behind the house. Lost in thought, he scanned the gardens, the plants and flowers that flourished in the dew-misted air.

Tamra sat next to him at a glass-topped table. Charlotte, Alexandre and Mary were there, too. Walker had watched his mother and his sister embrace. He'd seen Charlotte cry in Mary's arms.

Even Alexandre had hugged Mary with ease. And he'd called her *Maman,* French for *Mother.* It had flowed from his lips naturally, and he was only the prospective son-in-law.

Walker had never seen Mary so happy. She and Charlotte paged through the photo albums Mary had brought, the family pictures that had yet to jar Walker's memories.

Why couldn't he remember his parents?

"Look how handsome Daddy was," Charlotte said. She leaned toward Mary, studying David's image.

"And look how beautiful you are." Mary touched her daughter's cheek, clearly awed by the young woman she'd become.

Walker had to admit that his sister was beautiful, with her long streaming hair and petite yet willowy figure. She wore a flowing summer dress, as bright as the garden that surrounded them.

"Charlotte runs Ashton Estate Botanicals," Walker said, gesturing in the distance. "The greenhouse is that way." More flowers, he thought. More plants.

"I plan to set up an independent nursery," his sister added. "But for now, I'll remain at Ashton Botanicals, training someone to take over for me."

"An independent nursery?" Mary asked. "Away from the estate?"

Charlotte nodded. "I haven't decided if I'll establish it in Napa Valley or in France. But either way, it will be my own company."

"That's wonderful. Your father had a green thumb. He could make anything grow."

Yes, Walker thought, their dad had been a farmer. A man who'd lived off the land. Sometimes he wondered why he himself hadn't been born to Spencer and Lilah instead of David and Mary.

A moment later the thought shamed him, making him feel like the worst kind of bastard. He moved his chair closer to the table. "May I have that?" He motioned to a photograph of David, Mary, Charlotte and him. The last picture of all of them together, taken on New Year's Day in 1983. The year their lives had changed forever.

Mary glanced up and snared his gaze. "Of course you can." She removed the faded snapshot and handed it to him.

"Thank you." He pressed it to his chest, just a smidgen away from his heart. "I won't lose it. I'm going to scan it into my computer so I can make a copy."

His mother smiled. "I trust you."

Charlotte and Alexandre smiled at him, too. Self-conscious, Walker cleared his throat. Tamra put her hand on his knee, and he turned to look at her, wishing he could kiss her, hold her, let her absorb his tangled emotions.

"Oh, Mama," Charlotte said, breaking the silence. "It's so wonderful to have you here. To be with you.

When I was a little girl, I would dream of you. Imagine a day like today." She paused, and her voice hitched. "Somewhere deep down, I never believed that you were dead."

Alexandre touched his fiancée's shoulder. *"Ma petite,"* he whispered, lending his support.

The women turned teary-eyed, and Walker wished he could love as deeply as his sister, that he could be more like her. But he wasn't a dreamer. He'd never questioned the tale Spencer had told him. He'd trusted his uncle.

"Will you give me a tour of the greenhouse?" Mary asked her daughter.

"Yes. And you must stay with Alexandre and me, at our new home." Charlotte turned to Walker. "Would that be all right with you?"

"Sure," he said, knowing he couldn't interfere with the precious time his mom and his sister had. "Tamra and I will go to San Francisco while Mom stays with you. Then we can all get together before they go back to Pine Ridge."

"That sounds perfect." Charlotte reached for Mary's hand. "Alexandre and I are going to visit your home, too. As soon as we can arrange a trip."

"Maybe you can come for the powwow at the end of the month," the older woman said.

"A Sioux gathering?" Charlotte beamed. "I've always wanted to be close to my heritage. To know more about it."

"Then I'll teach you." Mary squeezed her hand. "Your father always told me that I should be proud of my culture. That I should encourage you and your brother to be proud. But I kept losing sight of that."

"Is that why he wanted me to have a shield?" Walker asked.

His mother nodded. "A shield reflects a warrior's medicine, everything in his life. Protection in combat, success in the hunt, being a good lover, finding the right mate. Even visions and dreams are represented."

He wished he had visions and dreams. Something beyond Ashton-Lattimer. "That's a nice sentiment."

"It's more than sentiment. It projects who you are." Mary scooted closer to him. "I can make you a shield, the way I'd originally intended to. Or I can teach you how to make one. You can put your own symbols on it. Animals, colors, anything you want."

Would a shield bind him to the Oglala Lakota Sioux Nation? Or would it be a forgery? He'd told Tamra that he was comfortable with his heritage, but was that a lie? Would he stop being Lakota when he returned to Ashton-Lattimer? When he started behaving like a corporate *wasicu* again? Or a brash, citified *iyeska?*

"Walker?" his mother pressed.

"What?"

"Do you want me to make it? Or would like to create it yourself?"

"You can do it." He glanced at the picture of his family. "But will you put something on it that represents us?" He lifted the photograph. "You, Dad, Charlotte and me?" He released a ragged breath. "And Tamra, too?"

Tamra looked up at him, and he wondered if he should have kept quiet instead of mentioning her name. Although she smiled, she seemed surprised, maybe even a little shy, about what he'd said.

Mary glanced at his lover, then back at him. "She's good for you. You're good for each other."

"I think so, too," Charlotte said.

"Oui," Alexandre offered his opinion, as well. "I agree."

Okay, great. Now that everyone had just embarrassed the hell out of him, Walker didn't know how to respond. His relationship with Tamra wasn't meant to last. He wanted her to be represented on his shield because he was going to lose her.

And lose a piece of himself after she was gone.

Several hours later Walker sat at the oak desk in his extra bedroom. He scanned the picture on his computer, created a "family photos" file and printed it. Next he saved it on a disc and packed it for the San Francisco trip.

He was used to switching computers. He had a PC at both home locations, as well as a laptop he carried for airports, hotel rooms and places in between.

Tamra knocked on the open door, and he turned to look at her.

"I noticed some ice cream in your freezer," she said. "Is it okay if I dig into it?"

"Sure." He roamed his gaze over her and saw that she'd changed into a pair of sweats, preparing to relax in his apartment. "Will you get me a bowl, too?"

"Okay. I'll be right back."

He watched her leave, then put the original picture in an envelope and left it on his desk with a self-sticking note, reminding himself to return it to his mother.

Tamra came back, balancing two glass bowls. She'd scooped a mound of Neapolitan into each, with spoons readily available. She handed him one of the frozen treats and sat on the edge of the bed. He remained in the swivel chair.

She started eating the vanilla ice cream first, and he wondered if it was her favorite flavor. He continued to analyze every bite she took. Finally she finished the vanilla and started in on the strawberry. He changed his mind, deciding she liked chocolate the best since she was saving it for last.

Walker had mixed all three flavors up in his bowl, stirring the concoction like pudding.

"Your sister is amazing," she said. "Sweet, bright, beautiful. I really like her."

"She appeared to like you, too."

"Alexandre is amazing, as well."

"Really? You think so?"

"Oh, yes. He's gorgeous. So—" she stalled when Walker raised his eyebrows at her "—attentive to Charlotte."

Envy nipped at his heels, but he let it go. He knew Alexandre was one of those guys women noticed. All those fancy French words. Even his mom had swooned a little. "He loves my sister."

"I can tell." She toyed with her spoon. "It was

weird...what Mary, Charlotte and Alexandre said about us."

"Yeah, weird." He shifted his gaze. "They think we're good for each other."

When silence pulled like taffy between them, he stirred his dessert again. He hated these magnified moments. He wasn't good at easing the tension.

But she got past it quick enough.

"Does anyone ever stay in this room?" she asked.

"No. I never invite guests here."

"Then why do you have an extra bed?"

"I don't know. To fill up space, I guess."

She took her first bite of the chocolate ice cream. "What about your bedroom?"

He nearly cursed beneath his breath. Silence had been safer than the conversation she'd hatched. "No one stays there, either."

"I am," she said.

"Yes, but you're—" he paused, afraid he would say something too revealing "—different."

"Different?" she parroted.

Crafty girl, he thought. Prodding him to spill his guts. "I already told you that you're the most compatible lover I've ever had. I wanted to take advantage of that."

She sucked on her spoon, and he wondered if she was trying to seduce him. If she was, her ploy was working. He couldn't keep his eyes off her mouth.

He dropped his gaze and noticed her nipples through her T-shirt. "Are you cold, Tamra?"

She almost smiled. "I'm eating ice cream."

"Want to christen the bed?"

She gave him an innocent look, then shook her head and laughed. "You're easy, Walker."

So she had been playing a game.

He left the desk, came closer, took away her bowl and nudged her down. "You drive me crazy." He unzipped his jeans and slipped her hand inside. "More than crazy."

She closed her fingers around him, and they kissed, deep and wet and slow. She tasted like chocolate, and the flavor, the sweetness, aroused him even more.

They dragged off each other's clothes, tossing articles onto the floor, leaving cotton and denim in their wake.

She lowered her head, then used her mouth between his legs. He tugged his hands through her hair and felt his blood soar. Oh, yeah, he thought. She drove him crazy.

She paused, looked up at him and made his world spin.

Mind-blowing foreplay. Sexual surrender. He wanted it all. And he wanted it with her.

He lifted her up and kissed her, tongue to tongue, flesh to flesh. He needed to get her out of his system, to drink her in, to drain her of every last drop.

Desperate, he guzzled her like the wine he'd been reared on, getting drunk, forcing the intoxication through his veins.

But he wanted to make her drunk, too, so he went down on her, giving her the oral pleasure she'd given him.

She arched, rubbed against him and fisted the quilt.

He kept doing it, teasing her, urging her to completion.

When she stopped shuddering, he rose above her. And with one powerful thrust, he entered her. She gasped, and he went deeper, submerging himself in wetness, in warmth, in everything he craved.

Sunlight spilled into the room, making summer hues dance across the bed. They clasped hands, their fingers locking.

A bond. A connection. A feral need.

Walker wasn't about to let go.

And neither was she. She wrapped her legs around him, holding him hostage, keeping him unbearably close.

Every cell in his body screamed for a release, but he wanted to make it last. To keep making love to her. Yet he couldn't.

Heaven help him. He couldn't.

Her lotion rose like a mist, filling his nostrils. The scent of seduction. Of heat, he thought. Of a life-altering orgasm.

He looked into her eyes, then let himself fall.

Hard and fast.

As hard and fast as a man could endure.

# Nine

**W**alker's condominium in San Francisco was in the same upscale district as Edward's. Yet Tamra hadn't realized it before now. But why would she? She'd only seen Walker's driver's license once, on the first day they'd met, and she hadn't paid attention to his address, to the zip code that would have revealed the location.

"What's wrong?" he asked, as they stood on his deck, overlooking a view of the city.

"Nothing. Your home is beautiful."

"Come on, Tamra. I can tell something is bothering you. You're acting strange."

She took a deep breath, then shifted to look at him. They'd arrived about ten minutes ago and he'd given her the grand tour: spacious rooms, ultramodern furniture, a hot tub. Luxurious, bachelor-style living, she thought. "Edward lives about six blocks from here."

"Jade's father? The sperm donor?" Walker frowned, his dark eyes turning even darker. "Are you going to be thinking about him the whole time you're here with me?"

"Of course not. It's just a coincidence. It doesn't mean anything."

"The hell it doesn't." He turned away and scowled at the city. "Edward still upsets you. He still matters."

"Losing my baby still matters. And this was a shock, that's all. I hadn't expected you to live near him." She moved closer, trying to shed her anxiety, to control the situation, to lighten her lover's mood. "His place isn't as nice as yours. It's not as high up. His view sucks."

Walker managed a smile. "Are you trying to stroke my ego?"

"Did it work?"

"A little, yeah." His smile turned a bit too sexy. "But stroking something else would work even better."

She smacked his shoulder, and they both laughed. She suspected they would be tearing off each other's clothes before the sun went down. A second later she glanced at the gazebo-framed hot tub. "I've never done it in one of those."

"Really?"

"No. Have you?"

"Yes, but I'm not giving you any details. No kiss and tell."

"That's fine." She didn't want to envision other women at his condo, to create their faces, to hear their names. For now she wanted to pretend that Walker Ashton belonged to her. That he would always be her exclusive lover. Hers and hers alone.

When he gazed into her eyes, her heart jumped, playing leapfrog in her chest.

"Maybe Edward doesn't even live around here anymore," Walker said.

"It's only been three years," she responded, her voice quavering.

"A lot can happen in that amount of time." He continued to look in her eyes. "We've only known each other for a few weeks."

Sixteen days, she thought, but who's counting?

He touched her cheek and her knees went weak. In an ordinary world, they would be little more than strangers. But their world was far from ordinary. They'd become lovers almost instantly. And now she was pretending that he belonged to her, that it was okay to make up stories, to fool her mind.

"Do you miss this city?" he asked. "Do you miss it at all?"

She shook her head, recalling the flavor of the place she'd left behind: cable cars, China Town and the Golden Gate Bridge, the roller-coaster landscape and Victorian houses, the early-morning fog.

Too many memories, she thought. The place where Jade rested in a tiny grave.

"Do you miss the reservation?" she asked him.

"I wasn't there long enough." He lowered his hand, skimming the ends of her hair, letting it slip through his fingers.

Already she could feel herself losing him.

Tamra nearly panicked, nearly gasped for the air that refused to fill her lungs. Was she falling in love? Only deeper this time?

Walker wasn't Edward. He wasn't the father of her lost child. But she wished he was. She wished they'd made a baby together.

He watched her, much too closely. "You're upset again."

"I don't mean to be."

"But you are."

"Just hold me." She reached for him, and he put his arms around her.

Eyes closed, she nuzzled his neck. He brought her closer, and she inhaled his scent, the aftershave that lingered on his skin.

Had she fallen in love? After only sixteen days? Was she losing her mind? "I can't think clearly."

"Why not?"

"I don't know." She clung to him yet she knew she should let go. "Maybe it's your fault."

"Don't blame me. You wanted to come to San Francisco."

"To visit Jade." Not to lose her heart. Not to let Walker strip the layers of her soul.

He rocked her in his arms. "Then we'll visit her."

"Not right now," she heard herself say. She needed

time to compose herself, to change the direction of her thoughts. "Let's do something else."

"You could come to the office with me."

She blinked, stepped back. "You're going to work?"

"I'd like to check in, let my assistant know that I'll be in town for a few days. Besides, I want you to see Ashton-Lattimer."

"Then that's where we'll go." And maybe, she thought, just maybe, the corporate environment would bring her back to reality.

And keep her from dwelling on love.

Thirty minutes later, Tamra and Walker arrived in the Financial District. Ashton-Lattimer Corporation was located in an eighteen-story structure on California Street.

Once they were inside, Tamra looked around the lobby and noticed the turn-of-the-century architecture. Walker had told her that the building had been constructed in 1906, after the great fire. He seemed fascinated by the history connected to it.

She tried to keep her emotions in check, but on the elevator ride to the top floor, the walls started closing in. They were the only two people in the confined space. He'd changed into a suit and tie, looking like what he was: a tough, charming CEO. Spencer Ashton's favored nephew. She could almost see the older man's blood flowing through his veins.

Like poison, she thought.

He smiled at her, and a lump caught in her throat. She knew Walker had a tender side. The side he must have hidden from his uncle.

"You okay?" he asked.

She cleared the raspy sound from her voice. "This is an imposing place."

"I suppose it is. Maybe more so since Spencer died here. He was shot in his office. He was working late and—"

The elevator doors opened and he stopped speaking, letting his words fade into the walls. She wondered if he would ever stop mourning his uncle. If he would accept Spencer for the bastard he was.

The fourteenth floor, where the Ashton-Lattimer executives made their corporate marks on the world, presented a modern decor.

Walker introduced her to a few of the secondary bigwigs, men who treated him with the utmost respect. She wondered if there were any women at the top of the food chain.

Finally he showed her his office—a spacious state-of-the-art domain in shades of gray, with silver-framed watercolors, a shiny black desk and floor-to-ceiling windows. Walker was a man rooted to the city.

This wasn't déjà vu. This wasn't Edward all over again. Being with Walker in San Francisco created a whole new stream of emotions.

New fears. New challenges.

Letting Edward go had been her salvation, a part of her growth, of who she was destined to become. But losing Walker—

"Come on," he said, cutting through her thoughts like a machete. "I'll introduce you to my assistant."

He escorted her to a smaller office, but apparently

the woman at the lacquered desk wasn't who he expected to see. "Kerry?" He gave her a curious study. "Where's Linda?"

Kerry came to her feet, and Tamra did her damnedest not to stare. Tall and curvaceous, the stunning blonde wore a lavender suit and chic yet understated jewelry. Her eyes, a color that could only be described as violet, were framed with dark, luxurious lashes.

Talk about beautiful. This girl had it all.

Tamra prayed she wasn't a former bed mate of Walker's. An office liaison. A hot-tub bunny. She couldn't deal with feminine rivalry, not now, not today.

"Linda called in sick," Kerry said. "She caught that awful flu that's been going around, so I'm covering for her."

"Fine. No problem. You're more than qualified." Walker sent the Ashton-Lattimer employee a professional smile, then turned to Tamra and made the introduction.

Kerry, whose last name was Roarke, extended her hand with genuine warmth, and Tamra knew, right then and there, that she'd never slept with Walker. There was nothing between him and the breathtaking blonde, not even a passing interest.

"Kerry used to be Spencer's executive administrative assistant," he said. "After he died, she transferred to Human Resources, but she helps out wherever she's needed."

Now Tamra wondered if Kerry had been involved with Spencer. Given his penchant for infidelity, she

could only imagine how badly he'd probably
wanted her.

But was Kerry the type to sleep with a married man?

While Walker and the blonde talked business,
Tamra sat in a leather chair. Every so often, she stole
a glance at the other woman, still wondering about her.

Finally the meeting ended.

After Walker took Tamra's hand and led her out
of the building, he stopped to kiss her, to brush his
mouth across hers.

As a moderate breeze swirled around them, she
decided that she was ready to visit Jade's grave, to
bring her daughter and the man she loved together.
Because after Tamra was gone, Walker would remain
in San Francisco, keeping Jade from being alone.

Tamra gave Walker directions to the cemetery, but
he stopped at a florist first. She wandered around the
flower shop, her thoughts spinning like a pinwheel.

She didn't want to go home without telling him
that she loved him. Yet she wasn't sure if a confession was in order. What did she hope to accomplish
by admitting the truth? Did she think it would change
the status of their relationship? That he would abandon his corporate lifestyle and move to Pine Ridge
with her?

Fat chance, she thought. Love wasn't a miracle.

But what was the point of keeping quiet? Of suffering in silence? She studied a bouquet of daisies,
feeling like a schoolgirl who couldn't temper her
emotion-laced whims.

*He loves me. He loves me not.*

Walker was Mary's son. He would always be part of Tamra's life. Seeing him from year to year was inevitable. She couldn't ignore the connection they shared.

"What about pink roses?" he asked, his voice sounding behind her.

She turned, looked into his eyes. Mary had warned her in the beginning about getting hurt, about falling in love. But now Walker's mother thought he and Tamra were good together.

"Pink roses?" she parroted.

He nodded. "With baby's breath. And maybe a toy, too. Something fluffy. They have teddy bears. A lamb that's really cute. The florist said they can add a toy to the arrangement."

She wanted to put her arms around him, to hold him close. He seemed like Jade's earthbound angel. Her tall, dark, masculine protector. "That sounds perfect."

"Okay." He smiled. "I'll be right back with the stuffed animals. We'll have to choose which one we want."

Tamra glanced at the daisies again.

*He loves me. He loves me not.*

Walker returned with a pink teddy bear in one hand and a white lamb in the other. He held them up, wiggling each toy, making them come to life. "Which one do you like better?"

"I don't know." The teddy bear had big expressive eyes and the lamb offered a tender smile. "Why don't you decide?"

He made a puzzled face, giving the stuffed animals a serious examination. "Maybe we should get both. The other one might feel bad if we leave it behind."

Tamra wondered how this could be the same man who'd allowed Spencer Ashton to influence him, to guide him, to mold and shape him into the adult he'd become.

She couldn't imagine Spencer buying toys for a baby's grave. Or, heaven forbid, worrying about the emotional welfare of a white lamb or a pink bear.

"Thank you, Walker. This means a lot to me."

His gaze locked on hers. The cozy flower shop, with its festive colors, refrigerated cases and vine-draped displays, made him look even more masculine. Bigger, broader, stronger in the sun-dappled light.

"Jade is going to be happy to see you. To know you're here," he said. Then he paused for a moment, mulling something over in his mind. "When we get back to Napa Valley, we should take my mom to my dad's resting place."

Tamra couldn't quit looking at him. A strand of hair, loosened from the San Francisco breeze, cut across his forehead, slicing over one dark eyebrow. She had the notion to smooth it into place. Just to touch him, she thought. Just to tempt her fingers.

"Charlotte will probably do that," she finally said.

"You're right. She probably will." He cradled the stuffed animals. "I'll go put in our order. Let the saleslady know what we want."

While they waited for the floral arrangement, she inhaled the gardenlike fragrance, the softness in the air. Walker stood with his hands in his pockets, his designer suit and silk tie still in place.

Tamra wore the same clothes she'd had on earlier. She hadn't changed to go to his office, but she hadn't needed to. Her denim dress and tan cowboy boots reflected her style, who she was and who she would always be.

They arrived at the cemetery, silence fluttering between them. He carried the roses, and she led him through grassy slopes, where ancient trees burst with summer foliage. The headstones scattered across the lawn varied, some fancy, others simple. The one that belonged to Jade was white, with an eagle feather etched upon it.

Tamra knelt, dusting away leaves that had fallen.

"Jade Marie Winter Hawk. Beloved daughter." Walker read the baby's marker, then placed the basket on the ground. Nestled among the flowers, the bear and the lamb faced each other, smiling like friends on a preschool playground.

"Marie was my mother's name." She envisioned Jade the way she might look today—a three-year-old with mixed-blood features, a sweet, beautiful, half-Lakota child.

"It's a pretty name. All of it."

"Thank you." Memories clung to her mind like cobwebs, but she didn't want to cry, to let her daughter know she was sad.

"Will you tell me what happened?" Walker asked.

She nodded, then took a deep breath. "Most fetal deaths occur before labor begins, and that's what happened to me. I suspected something was wrong because she'd stopped moving."

"I remember you mentioning that before. I can only imagine how scared you must have been."

"Afraid and alone. Except for Mary. Your mom was there to comfort me." She dusted another leaf from Jade's grave, where the wind had stirred it from a nearby tree. "An ultrasound confirmed my suspicion, and that's when the doctor broke the news to me."

He reached for her hand, slipping his fingers through hers. Grateful for his touch, she continued her story, wanting to share her past with him. "There was no medical reason for immediate delivery, so they gave me the option of inducing labor or waiting for it to happen on its own."

"Did you induce?"

"Yes. Most women in that situation do. It's too traumatic to wait." She searched his gaze and noticed how closely he watched her, how much he seemed to care. "After I delivered, the hospital did an extensive evaluation, an autopsy and some other tests. They discovered that Jade died from a birth defect. But it wasn't caused by something that's likely to recur in another pregnancy. The risk that I'll deliver another stillborn baby is low."

He brought their joined hands to his lips and brushed a kiss across her knuckles. "You'll have more children someday."

"Yes, someday." Tamra decided she was going to tell Walker that she loved him. Tonight…tomorrow morning…she wasn't sure when. But one way or another she was going to summon the courage to say those three little words out loud.

Just so he knew how she felt. Just to hear his response. Just to see the reaction in his eyes.

# Ten

At dusk Walker and Tamra sat on his deck, sharing takeout Chinese food. A mild breeze blew, awakening the aroma of kung pao chicken, sweet-and-sour pork, egg rolls and fried rice.

They used paper plates and plastic utensils, something Walker did often. He rarely fussed in the kitchen, cooking or dirtying dishes.

"I was wrong," Tamra said.

"About what?" He stabbed a piece of the kung pao chicken, a spicy Szechuan dish with just enough kick to ignite his taste buds.

"I thought we'd be tearing off each other's clothes before the sun went down."

He glanced up at the sky and saw a small stream

of light drifting through the clouds. "There's still time." He watched the golden light shift and fade, then sent her a teasing grin. "But we'll have to hurry."

She managed an appreciative laugh, and he was glad to hear the uplifting sound. He'd been worried about her all day, hoping her anxiety would lessen.

He knew that Edward's proximity, the home her ex-lover owned in the area, had triggered her emotions. This town held a lot of sadness for her. A lot of grief. But Walker wanted to change that. He wanted to give her some warm and caring memories.

He figured that a casual dinner was a good start. His redwood deck offered a romantic ambience, with outdoor lanterns and citronella candles. A wind chime near the back door created a melodious tune, and the hot tub was ready and waiting, steam rising from the water. Plants flowered all around it, vines twisting and twining on the gazebo lattice. He liked the jungle effect, as well as the privacy it afforded him.

Tamra ate another small helping of the sweet-and-sour pork, and he watched her add extra chunks of pineapple to her plate. They occupied a rustic wood table that complemented her unpretentious beauty, her blue-jean dress, the slightly scuffed boots she favored.

He shifted his gaze to the hot tub, thinking about the conversation they'd had earlier. "That isn't the spa I made love in."

She looked up from her food. "It isn't?"

"No. It happened somewhere else."

"Thank goodness." She reached for her bottled

water. "Now I don't have to envision you and another woman splashing around in there."

Her envy, or whatever it was, pleased him.

He smiled and stole the biggest piece of pineapple from her plate, stuffing it into his mouth before she could stop him. "My spa is safe."

She shook her head, but he knew she was enjoying his company, the lazy evening he'd created.

Should he admit where the hot tub rendezvous happened? Break his kiss-and-tell policy? Give her details about his past? The infrequent wildness? The few-and-far-between times he'd sown his rich-boy oats?

Oh, what the hell, he thought. "It was at a college party. A drink-until-you-drop sort of thing."

Tamra made a face. "You did it at a party? With other people around?"

Walker frowned, realizing he should have kept his mouth shut. She probably thought he'd participated in an orgy. "It wasn't like that. The party was over. I was in the hot tub with a blonde who lived there. And my friend, Matt, was in one of the bedrooms with her roommate."

She made another face. "Did you switch partners?"

"I wouldn't have done that." He paused, pondering Matt's sexually abundant lifestyle. "Of course, my friend might have."

"He sounds like a great guy."

Walker ignored the sarcasm in her voice. "He is. Honestly. He's a good person. He's just not the kind of guy I'd let any of the women in my family date." He glanced at the fortune cookies they'd yet to break open. "Don't ask me why he ever tried his hand at marriage. I knew he'd end up divorced."

"Is he wealthy? Does he come from an Ashton-type environment?"

"He's rich. But he earned every cent himself. Matt Camberlane didn't have a damn thing when he was growing up. He was probably as badly off as some of the people in Pine Ridge."

She tilted her head. "And you befriended him?"

He shrugged off her surprise. "I was poor once, too, remember? Before Spencer took Charlotte and me in. I understood Matt's shame. As well as his determination to succeed." He scooped up a forkful of rice. "We're still friends."

"Then I'll try not to judge him." Her gaze slammed into his. "But I agree. You should keep him away from the women in your family."

"I'm not worried about it. I'm sure Matt has enough lovers to keep him entertained."

"And you have me."

The air in his lungs whooshed out. The impact of her words, the depth at which they affected him, belied the *entertainment* aspect of their conversation.

"You're not my toy, Tamra. It isn't like that between us."

"I know." She pushed away her plate. "God, how I know."

He noticed her hands were trembling, that she was riddled with anxiety again. He didn't know what to do, how to respond. He feared their relationship was spinning out of control, like a runaway train, a derailment that would leave them bruised. Battered. Wounded.

"There's something I need to tell you." She fidgeted with a bracelet around her wrist. "I wasn't sure when would be the appropriate time, but—"

She stalled, and he scooted his chair back, scraping the wooden deck. He'd been sitting too close to the table, too close to her. Because somewhere in the seed of his soul, in the cavern of his mind, he knew what she was going to say.

"I love you, Walker."

The words came, just as he'd expected. And so did the panic that erupted inside him. "No one has ever been in love with me," he managed. "No one."

"I am."

She searched his gaze, piercing him with her admission, with raw, agonizing honesty. He knew he shouldn't be scared. He was a single, unattached male who had nothing to lose.

Nothing but his heart.

Did he love her, too? Was all the craziness love? The desperate need? The way he longed to protect her? His fear of losing her? Of surviving without her by his side?

Walker picked up his water and took a long, hard swallow. But the ice-cold liquid didn't sober him. He should've figured it out before now. He should've known. "It's happening to me, too. You're not alone in this."

"Oh, God. Really?" She closed the food cartons, keeping herself busy, nearly dropping the leftover egg rolls. Nervous. Excited. "What are we going to do?"

"I don't know." His pulse zigzagged, beating frantically beneath his skin. "Can't we just ignore it? Forget that we talked about?" He sent her an anxious smile. "Maybe just go nuts in the hot tub instead?"

She smiled, too. But it was just as shaky, just as unsteady as his. "Trust a man to look for sex as the answer."

"You can't blame a guy for trying." He couldn't think of anything else to do, so he stood up and gathered the cartons she'd closed. "I'll put these away."

She rose to her feet, as well. "I'll wipe down the table and throw away the trash."

Cleanup duty took a matter of minutes, which left them in the kitchen, staring at each other beneath bright, blinding lights. He wondered if they should have taken the fortunes out of their cookies, used those silly little slips of paper for encouragement.

"We'll figure something out," he said.

"We will?"

"Sure." He ventured closer to her. One, two, three steps and he was close enough to smell the lotion on her skin, the scent that never failed to linger in his mind. "People fall in love all the time."

"People who live over a thousand miles away from each other?"

"So we've got an obstacle to overcome." He smoothed a strand of her hair. "I'm good at solving problems."

She touched his hair, too, running her fingers through it. Within seconds they were locked in each other's arms, kissing and caressing.

And then she took his hand and led him outside. Together they stepped into the shelter of the gazebo, into the maze of plants and low-hanging vines.

Without speaking, without words to clutter their thoughts, they undressed, dropping their clothes onto the deck. He brought her naked body next to his, letting the sensation arouse him even more.

And as they slipped into the water, he decided there was nothing to worry about.

All he had to do was ask her stay, to leave the reservation and move in with him. It was, he decided, the only answer. The only logical choice. And he would talk to her about it. But not yet, he thought.

Not just yet.

Hands questing, they touched. Everywhere. Skin to skin. Water swirled around their bodies, making steam rise to the surface. He could see her through the haze, as dark and exotic as the night. The sun had set, making way for the moon, for a soft, silvery glow.

He lifted her up, placing her on the edge of the tub. She looked like a siren, he thought, an indigenous goddess from the sea, with her legs spread just for him.

He took her hand and encouraged her to touch herself.

Shy. Erotic. Daring.

The woman he was falling in love with.

He tasted her, licking and kissing between her fingers. She watched him, rubbing and purring, making sweet, naughty sounds.

Walker feared he might explode.

She climaxed, and he dragged her into his arms, desperate to fulfill his fantasy.

To claim Tamra Winter Hawk as his own.

Tamra's head was reeling. From the aftermath of sex, she thought, from the hot, bubbling water and cool San Francisco air. But most of all because Walker Ashton admitted he was falling in love with her, too.

He wrapped her in a towel, and she looked up at him through the chlorine-scented moisture dotting her eyelashes.

Her pulse wouldn't quit pounding.

He grabbed another towel and dried himself off with haste, then secured the terry cloth around his waist. "Let's go inside. I have a robe you can borrow."

She followed him into the condo. She liked the idea of wearing something that belonged to him, of letting it envelop her in warmth.

She waited in the living room, and he returned with a navy blue robe that was thick and plush and far too big.

"It's perfect," she said.

For himself, he'd thrown on a pair of jeans. But his chest was still bare, and water dripped from his hair in jewellike rivulets. Already Tamra itched to touch him again.

"Will you have a glass of wine with me?" he asked.

"Are you trying to get me drunk?"

"So I can take advantage of you? You bet." He gave her a devastating wink. "The lady found me out."

Her heart ricocheted, bouncing off the walls of her

chest. "Okay. But just a little. I'm not much of a drinker."

"No problem." He poured a small amount for her and gave himself a generous helping.

She tasted the Pinot Noir, but since she wasn't a connoisseur, she didn't comment on the flavor. "Is this from your family's winery?" she asked instead.

"Absolutely." He turned the bottle, where he'd placed it on an end table, so she could examine the label. "Nothing but the best."

They sat quietly for a while, and she snuggled deeper into the atmosphere.

"I want you to move in with me, Tamra."

Suddenly a strong, cold dose of reality ripped through her veins. "Here?"

"Yes, here. This is where I live. And I want to share my life with you."

Everything inside her went still. He was asking her to be with him, to stay him, yet how could she say yes? How could she live in the city? Pretend to be someone she wasn't?

Tamra clutched his robe. His scent was on it, she realized. The faded fragrance of wood smoke, of male spice.

She closed her eyes, opened them, felt her body go numb. Was she making a mistake? Would she regret this decision for the rest of her life? Would she cry for him on those long, lonely South Dakota nights?

"I can't leave Pine Ridge," she said, the words nearly sticking in her throat. "I'm meant to be there. To try to make a difference. To help our people."

"This isn't about our people." With her rejection blazing in his eyes, he downed his wine, swigging it like beer, his manners falling by the wayside. "This is about us. You and me."

"Why can't you move?" she asked, the glass in her hand vibrating. "Why can't you relocate?"

"Me? Living on the rez? That would never work, and you know it. My background is in investment banking. That's what I do. That's what's in my blood. How am I supposed to walk away from that? I don't belong in Pine Ridge."

"And I don't belong here."

"You have a degree in marketing," he argued. "You'd do well in San Francisco. You'd fit right in. You've lived here before."

She shook her head, tears flooding her eyes. She couldn't leave the land of her ancestors, the place she'd struggled to accept, to become part of. "Pine Ridge is my home."

His voice turned hard. "Then why did you tell me that you loved me?"

"Because I wanted you to know how I felt."

"For all the good it did." He refilled his wine, drinking it just as quickly, just as brutally as before.

She set her glass on the end table, next to the bottle. She would never use alcohol to pacify her pain. She'd seen too many people on the rez fall into that trap. "Slow down, Walker. That won't help."

"Don't tell me what to do." He stood up, looking tall and dark and edgy. "The last thing I need is the woman I love treating me like a child."

She drew her knees to her chest. They loved each other, yet they couldn't stay together.

He crammed his hands in his pockets, shoving his jeans down a little, making them fall lower on his hips. "All I've been thinking about is how awful it was going to be to lose you. But I'm losing you, anyway."

"Me, too. But I didn't expect a miracle," she said, recalling the warning she'd given herself earlier. "Deep down I knew you'd never change your lifestyle for me. That you'd never move to Pine Ridge. "

"And you won't move here. So what damn difference does it make?"

He picked up the Pinot Noir again and frowned at the Ashton label, and for a moment she feared that he would throw the bottle, smash it against the wall. To just to hear it shatter, she thought. Just to release the tension she'd caused. But he held his temper.

And when their eyes met, when he looked straight at her, she knew she would never be the same. No matter how many years passed, no matter how hard she tried to erase him from her mind, he would always be the man she loved.

Walker and Tamra returned to Napa Valley a day early with discomfort humming between them. He'd dropped her at his apartment at the estate, claiming he had some local business to tend to.

From there he drove to his sister's house to talk to his mother. And now here he was, sitting next to Mary on a teakwood bench on Charlotte's flagstone patio. In the garden setting, trees, flowers and potted plants flourished, with rolling hills in the distance.

A fountain in the center of the yard drew his attention, making him frown. It looked like a wishing well, but Walker knew better.

He'd explained the entire situation to his mom, but she hadn't offered to help. She hadn't offered to do a damn thing.

"I want you to convince Tamra to move to San Francisco with me," he said, still frowning at the fountain. A family of finches was bathing in it, splashing and chirping, looking far too happy.

"Oh, honey." She tucked her hair behind her ears, smoothing the gray-streaked strands. "There's no way I can do that."

"Why? Because you think she's right? Because you think I'm the one who should relocate?"

"This isn't about who's willing to move and where they should go. This is about two people who need to learn to compromise, to work through their problems together."

"Easy for you to say."

"No. This isn't easy for me at all. I love you and Tamra. I want both of you to be happy."

"Well, we're not. We're making each other miserable."

Mary sighed. "When you were a little boy and you were sad, you used to put your head on my lap. But you're a grown man now, and I don't know how to make you feel better."

"I wish I was a kid. Life was simpler then."

"Was it?" she asked. "Are you sure about that?"

"No." His life had never been simple, especially after he'd lost his parents. He gazed into her eyes, tempted to lay his head on her lap, to go back in time and start over. He wished he could remember her, that his memories weren't so scattered. He even carried the family photo he'd copied in his wallet, but that hadn't changed him. It hadn't renewed his identity. "I don't even know who I am anymore."

She touched his cheek. "You're the man Tamra loves."

"But it hurts, Mom."

"I know." She traced the angles of his face, memorizing his features, skimming his unshaved jaw. "She's hurting, too."

"And I promised her that wouldn't happen."

"If you search deep enough, you'll find a solution. Look at Charlotte and Alexandre. Look how they've managed to be together." She lowered her hand. "Alexandre has vineyards and a home in France. But he's content to stay in America until Charlotte is ready to move. And even then, they'll still have this house. They'll still have ties in Napa Valley."

"It's not the same thing."

"Yes, it is. But you're just too mixed up to see it. Give yourself some time. Think through it. Make peace with yourself. With everything and everyone around you, if that's what it takes."

It was honest advice. Advice from the heart. But Walker didn't know how to heed it. Although there were other disturbances in his life, they didn't compare to what was happening with Tamra.

Without thinking, he dropped his head to Mary's lap. And this time, when she touched his cheek, he closed his eyes. "I don't want Tamra to leave."

"She doesn't want to lose you, either. But she's as mixed up as you are."

"Then we'll never figure it out."

"Yes, you will," his mother said. "If you love each other enough, you will."

# Eleven

**O**n the day Tamra was scheduled to leave, she awakened at dawn with a fog-shrouded morning light filling the room.

She rolled over and looked at Walker. He was still asleep. He wore a pair of boxer shorts, and his hair was tousled in restless disarray. One arm was flung over his face, and the covers, which he'd kicked away, were bunched below his hips.

She wanted to move closer, to touch him, to hold him, but she kept her distance. Although they were still sharing the same bed in his Ashton Estate apartment, they hadn't made love since that fateful night in San Francisco.

The night she'd lost him.

But she knew it was her fault. She'd rejected Walker's invitation. She'd refused to live with him, to share his life.

And now she was paying the price.

He shifted in his sleep, moving his arm away from his face, exposing hard angles and handsome features.

Tamra pulled her side of the covers against her body, trying to warm the self-induced chill in her bones. She knew she was making a mistake, yet she didn't know how to repair the damage, how to stay with the man she loved.

He stirred again, and when he opened his eyes, her heart nearly stopped.

"Hi," she said, for lack of a better greeting.

"Hi." He didn't smile, but neither did she.

Instead they simply gazed at each other. For the past few days they'd barely talked, barely communicated beyond forced conversations. Yet neither of them had suggested that they should sleep in separate rooms.

It was insane, she knew, to stay in the same bed, but it was their choice. Their own personal punishment. A need they couldn't deny.

He broke eye contact, glancing at the clock. "It's early."

She knew what he meant. Too early to get ready for the airport. "Do you want some coffee? I can make a pot."

"Sure, I guess." He sat up and smoothed his hair.

She noticed that he hadn't shaved in days. That his jaw was peppered with a coarse texture. But not too coarse. Walker didn't have a heavy beard.

"Are you hungry?" she asked.

"Not really. Are you?"

"No. But I'll probably make some toast. I don't like to drink coffee on an empty stomach."

"Me, neither."

"Then I'll fix some toast for you, too."

As she climbed out of bed, she could feel him watching her. The masculine scrutiny made her self-conscious. She wanted to grab a robe to cover her nightgown, but she didn't have one handy. So she left the room with her pulse pounding in her breast.

When she returned from the kitchen with coffee and buttered toast, Walker was still in bed, still wearing his boxers. She set their breakfast on the nightstand, and he thanked her in a quiet voice.

Tamra reached for her cup, then tasted her drink, trying to think of something to say. "It's a gloomy day," she managed.

His voice turned rough. "It fits my mood." He paused, his gaze searching hers. "It's going to feel strange after you're gone."

"For me, too." She let out the breath she was holding. "Why don't you come back to the rez for the powwow next week? Your sister and Alexandre will be there, and—"

"I can't," he interjected. "I can't take any more time off from Ashton-Lattimer, at least not so soon. I'm behind as it is."

"I understand," she told him, her heart sinking to her stomach.

He glanced at the window, at the fog drifting across the glass. "Maybe I shouldn't go to the airport today." He dropped crumbs onto the sheet, but he didn't bother to dust them off. "Charlotte and Alexandre offered to drive you and Mom, and that might be easier. I don't think I can handle a long goodbye."

Her heart remained in her stomach. "It's okay."

"Are you sure?"

"Yes," she said, even though she wanted him to be there, to walk her as far as the airport security would allow, to pretend that he was traveling with her. "It's fine, Walker. You can stay home."

Three hours later Tamra was packed and ready to leave. Or almost ready, she amended. Lilah had insisted that everyone gather in the dining room for a breakfast-style brunch.

So the Ashton family and their departing guests socialized, with eggs, bacon and strawberry crepes on their plates. Mary, Charlotte and Alexandre spoke to Paige and Trace, while Lilah added champagne to her orange juice.

Tamra didn't eat much. The toast and coffee she'd consumed earlier had been more than enough. Walker didn't appear to have an appetite, either. He simply moved the food around on his plate.

Finally, the meal ended, and Alexandre announced that it was time to leave for the airport.

Soft-spoken farewells were exchanged. Lilah did the best she could, trying to ease the tension. After she gave Mary a peck on the cheek, Spencer's widow offered Tamra a check, a donation for the Oyate Project. Tamra thanked the dazzling redhead, realizing Walker must have told his aunt about the Lakota charity.

Walker said goodbye to Mary first. He embraced her, holding her gently in his arms, promising her that he would keep in touch as often as he could, proving how far he and Mary had come. They were, without a doubt, mother and son.

Tears welled up in Tamra's eyes, but she kept them at bay, refusing to cry in front of everyone.

When Walker turned to her, she waited for him to make the first move, to touch her.

And then time stopped. He brushed his mouth across hers, and suddenly they were the only two people on earth.

She melted against him, her knees going girlishly weak.

"I'm sorry," she whispered, apologizing for not making their relationship work, for not finding a way to be together.

"I'm sorry, too," he said.

She put her head on his shoulder, asking the Creator to give her strength, to let him go without dying inside. But her prayer didn't work.

They separated, and he stepped back, leaving her empty inside.

But that didn't change what was happening. Within seconds it was over. They said goodbye, and Tamra walked out the door and climbed into Alexandre's car, sitting next to Mary in the backseat.

Battling the ache in her chest, she glanced out the

window, wondering if Walker had followed them. But he was nowhere to be seen.

He'd disappeared. Just like the morning fog.

A week later Walker sat in a San Francisco bar, waiting for Trace to arrive. He'd asked his cousin to meet him, but Trace hadn't shown up yet.

He checked his watch. He'd been nursing the same beer for twenty minutes. Not that he cared. He'd chosen a rowdy bar with billiard tables and a blaring jukebox because he needed to be around the activity, to blend in with the noise.

Walker had been working a grueling schedule, putting in even longer hours than usual, but once his day finally ended, he couldn't bear to go home to an empty condo.

He glanced up and spotted Trace coming through the door. His cousin seemed irritated, as if he'd been stuck in traffic.

They made eye contact across the wood-grain room, and Trace approached him, the scowl on his face making him look tough, which was exactly what he was.

An angry Ashton.

"You better have a damn good reason for this meeting," he said, taking a moment to glance around. "And besides that, you couldn't have picked a nicer location? This place is a dive."

"Sit down and shut up," Walker told him, wondering if he'd made a mistake. He and Trace hadn't said a civil word to each other in years. "Let me buy you a beer and we'll get this over with."

"Fine. Whatever." Trace pulled up a chair. In the dim light, his green eyes looked catlike. Wary, sharp, distrustful.

A cocktail waitress, a forty-something brunette, came by and took their order. And soon they both had fresh drinks in front of them. The peanuts on the table remained untouched.

"So what's this all about?" Trace asked.

"It's personal."

"I just drove an hour for an answer like that? Personal how? And what's it got to do with me?"

"I'm trying to make peace with myself, and my mom told me that I should make peace with the people around me, too. So I figured I'd start with you."

"Is this a joke?" His cousin glanced around for a hidden camera. "Or something you did just to piss me off?"

Walker cursed beneath his breath. It did sound rather stupid now that he'd said it out loud. "I'm going through a rough time. I didn't know what else to do."

"I'm not good at giving advice. But if you need a sounding board, go ahead." The other man took a swig of his beer, then sat upright in his chair. "I'm game."

No way, Walker thought. He wasn't about to tell Trace how much he missed Tamra. He wasn't about to admit that he couldn't sleep at night. Or that his chest felt like a limestone cavern, a gaping hole where his heart used to be.

"Well," Trace prodded. "Spill your guts."

"So you can watch me suffer? That wasn't what I had in mind."

His cousin made a stoic expression, something he did far too often. Walker never knew what Trace was thinking. He was good at masking his emotions.

"I don't even know why I dislike you," Walker said. "Other than you were a pest when you were a kid."

That almost made Trace smile. Almost. "I'm four years younger than you. What did you expect?"

"Was it Spencer? Was he the problem? Did he make us enemies?"

"Because you were Dad's protégé?" Trace shelled a peanut. "That didn't help."

"It wasn't a fair fight. Spencer treated me better than he treated you."

"Yes, but considering what he did to you, lying about your mom, I think he evened the score. Dad didn't love anyone but himself."

*Love.* The word bounced off Walker's hollow chest. He'd wanted Spencer to love him. So much so, he'd buried his memories, pretending that Mary and David—his own parents—had never existed.

"Dad did something deceitful to me, too," Trace said.

"He did?"

His cousin nodded. "I was never close to him to begin with, but the real animosity started when he bought off my fiancée."

Walker thought about the money Spencer had given Mary. Apparently that was the older man's answer to everything. "He paid the woman you loved? Why? To get her out of your life?"

"A hundred grand."

"He gave my mom a lousy thirty."

Trace blew out an exhausted breath, and they both drank their beers. He wondered if his cousin still loved his fiancée. "Did your lady take the money?"

"Every dime."

Walker frowned. He barely remembered that Trace had been engaged. He'd never given a damn about other people's lives. He'd been too busy kissing Spencer's butt. "Do you think I'm like him?"

"Who? My dad? You modeled yourself after him, didn't you? Hell, you're even taking his place at the office. Filling his shoes."

Suddenly the image of living in Spencer's shadow made Walker ill. He wanted to be his own man, his own person, to find the peace his mother had talked about. But instead, he was the CEO at Ashton-Lattimer, paying himself off, the way Spencer had paid off Trace's fiancée. "I'm sorry about what he did to you."

"It was five years ago. I'm over it now."

Liar, Walker thought. Trace was still hurting. Somewhere in the depth of those catlike eyes, his cousin's pain was brewing, waiting to explode. "Do you think your dad is still messing with our minds? Even from the grave?"

Trace didn't respond, but it didn't matter. Walker already knew the answer. At least for himself. He'd chosen Ashton-Lattimer over Tamra.

And now he wanted to right the wrongs, to make their relationship work, to be with her. But it wasn't as simple as quitting his job. There were other com-promises to make. And he couldn't make them alone.

He needed Tamra to cooperate.

The following day Walker arrived on the rez. He'd stopped by his mom's house, but no one was home. And that's when he'd remembered the powwow. So here he was, overwhelmed by the festivities. Every-where he turned, there was something happening.

Beneath an endless sea of canopies, families gath-ered in lawn chairs, watching regalia-draped dancers spin in colorful circles. In another congested area, craft-booth vendors peddled their wares and food stands created mouthwatering aromas. But that wasn't the last of it. Nestled in tree-clustered corners, storytellers captured the imaginations of wide-eyed children, who sat cross-legged in the grass, listening with rapt attention.

While Walker scanned the grounds, the host Drum sang a traditional song, the music thumping like a heartbeat, drifting through the sun-warmed air.

Feathers, fringe and fry bread, he thought. He had no idea where to look for Tamra. He assumed his mom and his sister were here, too. And Alexandre, of course, making him wonder what the Frenchman thought of the Pine Ridge gathering. No doubt, he and Charlotte were having the time of their lives.

A group of teenagers skirted past Walker, flirting shamelessly with each other. He smiled to himself, then battled a pang of nervousness.

What if Tamra didn't accept his proposition? What

if she didn't think his idea had merit? There would be sacrifices to make, changes to consider, an unconventional future that might leave her wanting more.

He'd rehearsed his upcoming speech last night, going over the details in his mind, but now he wished he had called ahead and warned Tamra that he was coming.

A bit lost, Walker stood in the middle of the pow-wow grounds, turning in every direction, searching for her.

"If it isn't the yummy *iyeska*," a voice said from behind him.

He spun around and found Michele, Tamra's loyal friend, grinning at him. He smiled, too, grateful to see a familiar face. She sported a jingle dress, the fabric covered with cones made from the metal lids of snuff cans. Her accessories included a silver belt, beaded moccasins and matching leggings. In her hair, she wore a lone feather, held in place with a decorative ornament.

"I didn't know you were a competition dancer," he said, noticing the number attached to her regalia.

"And I didn't know you were going to be here." She tilted her head. "I wonder why Tamra didn't say anything."

His nerves kicked in again. "She doesn't know."

Michele's eyes lit up. "You came here to surprise her? Well, thank goodness. That girl has been miserable."

Relief washed over him. Miserable meant that she missed him. Or so he hoped. "Where is she?"

"Walking around, selling raffle tickets." Michele gestured with her lips. "But I just saw your mom at a fry bread stand. She introduced me to your sister and that hunk of burning love she's gonna marry. Boy, is he a charmer."

"Alexandre knows how to impress the ladies."

"I'll say."

He gazed in the direction of the food stands. "Do you think my mom is still there?"

"Probably. The line was pretty long." She shifted the pouch over her arm. "I'm really glad you came back. I hope you stick around this time."

"I plan to. Sort of," he added, his pulse pounding at his throat. "I'll see you around, okay? I'm going to go talk to my mom."

"Sure. Okay," she said, giving him an obscure look. Apparently his "sort of" comment confused her.

But Walker didn't have time to explain. If he didn't find Tamra soon, his anxiety would probably escalate into a full-blown panic attack.

He found Mary, Charlotte and Alexandre easily, realizing he'd probably walked past them a dozen times. His mom was thrilled to see him. She threw her arms around him, and he nuzzled her neck, grateful that she was part of his life. He still didn't remember her. But he'd loved her. He knew that now, as sure as he knew his own name. He could feel the connection they shared, the bond Spencer had tried to break.

She stepped back to study him. "My son. My boy. I can't believe you're here."

*"Iná."* He addressed her in Lakota and made her smile.

"Did you come for Tamra?"

He nodded, wishing his stomach would quit flopping back and forth. "But I can't find her."

"Then I'll help you."

Although Mary was familiar with the powwow grounds, it didn't prove to be an easy task. They strolled the festivities for at least fifteen minutes, weaving in and out of the crowd.

Then finally Mary got his attention. "There she is."

He stopped, frozen in his tracks. Tamra was about twenty feet away, near a craft booth, selling raffle tickets to a group of tourists.

His mom squeezed his arm. "I think you can take it from here."

He nodded, although Tamra hadn't spotted him yet. "I love you," he whispered to his mom, wanting her to know how much she meant to him.

"I love you, too," she whispered back, a smile touching her lips, a maternal glow shimmering in her eyes. Then she left him alone, encouraging him to approach Tamra, to try to change the course of their lives.

Tamra finished her transaction, and he moved closer. She caught sight of him and gasped.

For a suspended moment in time, they stared at each other. Then she came toward him. She wore a pair of faded jeans, a sleeveless blouse tied at her waist and the tan cowboys boots he'd become accustomed to seeing. Behind her, hills rose in the distance, creating a sacred backdrop.

Mother Earth and the lady he loved.

He wanted to latch on to her and never let go, but he steadied his hands instead, cramming them into his pockets.

"You said you weren't coming to the powwow." Her voice all but quavered. "But here you are."

Yes, here he was, so nervous he could barely speak. He cleared his throat. "Can you take a break?"

"Yes, of course." She fidgeted with the roll of tickets in her hand.

He guided her to a vacant spot on the grass, and they sat on the ground, with the summer heat glaring between them. Her hair fell to her shoulders in a glossy black sheen, and her exotic-shaped eyes tilted at the corners. Around her neck, she wore a beaded medicine wheel, a symbol that represented the four directions and the four cardinal Lakota values: integrity, bravery, fortitude and generosity.

Walker thought it suited her beautifully.

"I'm leaving Ashton-Lattimer," he said. "I don't want to fill Spencer's shoes. I don't want to live the rest of my life in his shadow."

Her gaze locked on his. "What are you going to do?"

"Start my own financial consulting firm."

"In San Francisco?"

"Yes, but I intend to find a partner. Someone who can handle the day-to-day operation, who can run the company when I'm not around." He took a chance, moving closer to her. "That way I can commute between here and there. Live in both places."

Her eyelashes fluttered, and he realized she was

blinking back tears. "Both places? Does that mean we can be together?"

"Yes, but it won't be easy. Not at first," he told her, refusing to sugarcoat the situation, to be anything less than honest. "I'll be putting in long hours, getting the new company started. But eventually I'll get my schedule squared away."

"So you can spend more time here? With me?" she asked, her gaze hopeful, her voice soft.

He nodded, thinking how delicate she seemed. But he'd caught her off guard, probably sending her tattered emotions into a tailspin. "I'm not expecting you to quit your job for me. I know how much the Oyate Project means to you, how important it is to the rez. But I was hoping that you'd come to California once in a while. On your days off or whenever you can manage it."

"I'm willing to do whatever it takes," she said, reaching for him. "I can't bear to lose you again."

He took her in his arms, and when she trembled against him, he stroked her hair. He could feel how much she loved him, how lonely she'd been without him by her side. But even so, he wanted her to be sure.

"Our lives won't be as conventional as most couples, Tamra. I'll be gone a lot. Probably a few weeks a month."

She lifted her head. "That doesn't matter to me. Not if we make a commitment to each other, promises we both intend to keep." She sat back, pressed a hand to her heart. "This is the answer to our prayers, Walker. It's the perfect solution. We need to blend our worlds to make this work."

"Does spending more time in San Francisco scare you?" he asked. "The way adapting to reservation life scares me?"

She released a choppy breath. "Yes, but you can teach me to appreciate the city, to see it through your eyes. And I can help you get settled on the rez, to make it seem like home."

A feeling of contentment settled over him. Substance, he thought. Compromise, the beauty of commitment, of making every moment count. "We're going to need a bigger house. My mom's place is too small."

She smiled. "Does that mean we're going to live with Mary?"

He smiled, too. "It seems like the most logical solution. That way, neither of you will be alone when I'm in California."

"A new house is fine, but nothing too fancy. Don't go overboard."

"When I want fancy, I'll go to the estate and hobnob with the Ashtons. Besides, I'm keeping my condo. I'll have plenty of luxury when I need it." He paused, felt his heart bump his chest. "We can do this. We can make it happen."

She looked into his eyes. "I love you, Walker."

"I love you, too." He took her in his arms again, knowing she was accepting him for who he was.

A Pine Ridge Lakota. A San Francisco *iyeska*.

He was both of those things. Both people. But most of all, he was Tamra's partner, the man who couldn't live without her.

* * *

In the wee hours of the morning, Tamra and Walker were still awake. They were in her room, cuddling and talking, too wired to sleep.

Tamra couldn't stop looking at him, touching him, feeling his skin beneath her fingers. For her this was a dream. A real-life fairy tale, something she never expected.

"What kind of wedding do you want?" he asked.

"Wedding?" Her pulse jumped. "You never said anything about us getting married."

He raised his eyebrows. "Did you think I was asking you to live in sin?"

She laughed and pinched his side, making him laugh, too. "That's a hell of a proposal."

He toyed with the ends of her hair. "Glad you think so."

She couldn't help but smile. They were side by side, half-dressed and full of emotion. "Are we going to have a long engagement or is this supposed to happen fast?"

"A long engagement," he decided. "We should do it right. Maybe even have two ceremonies. One here and one on the estate."

"That works for me. If we're going to blend our worlds, we should get married in both places."

"My thoughts exactly." His expression changed, turning a bit troubled.

Concerned, she studied the angles of his face, the hard lines and deep, dark shadows. "What's wrong?"

"I have no idea what's going to happen with the stocks I inherited. They'll probably be held up in probate for a long time, especially if Eli or somebody from that side of the family contests the will."

"Do the stocks matter all that much?"

"Not really. Not anymore. I'd just sell them, anyway." He propped himself up, leaning on one elbow. "I have other investments I can liquidate."

"To get your business started?"

"To help the rez. I'd like to establish a housing fund, maybe work with a local contractor who's willing to get involved."

Her heart all but melted. "To help solve the housing shortage?"

He nodded. "Even if it's just one or two houses a year. Whatever I can manage. Whatever I can do to make a difference."

"No wonder I love you so much." She took a deep breath, searched his gaze, broaching a subject they'd both been avoiding. "How are other things going? Are you sorting out your feelings for Spencer?"

Walker frowned. "I'm trying to come to terms with what he did, with how many people he hurt. But that doesn't mean I condone his murder. I want to know who killed him." He adjusted the blanket, smoothing a ripple in the fabric. "As for my childhood memories, I'm convinced they'll come back."

"I think so, too." Once again she studied him. A pale-blue lamp bathed him in a translucent glow, creating the illusion of twilight, of moonbeams dancing across his skin. "What about children?" she asked suddenly, realizing it was a topic they hadn't discussed. "Do you want kids?"

He reached for her hand. "Anytime you're ready."

She clasped her fingers through his, awed by his beauty, his masculine strength, the passion, the tenderness, the complexity of his personality. "I'd prefer to be married first."

"Then we'll wait." His voice turned quiet. "Would it be all right to alter Jade's headstone? To give her my last name, too?"

Tamra's eyes misted. "Are you asking to be her father?"

"If you don't mind."

She thought about her baby, about the teddy bear, the lamb, the delicate pink roses. "I'd be honored."

He leaned in to kiss her, and she welcomed his embrace, the strength of his touch. She liked being protected by him.

When he slipped his tongue into her mouth, she sighed. He tasted like mint, like the toothpaste he'd used. Fresh and clean and cool.

Their hands were still entwined, connected like a jigsaw puzzle. Pieces that fit. Pieces that belonged together.

Their eyes met, and she knew he was thinking about their future. She was thinking about it, too.

"Forever," she whispered.

"Forever," he repeated, removing what was left of her clothes, running his hands over her body, his fingers seeking, taking possession, claiming every inch of her flesh.

She arched and sighed, and he made love with her, as slowly as they both could endure. Warm and willing, he moved inside her, the rhythm as deep and erotic as a river, as a current flowing through her womb.

She closed her eyes, inhaling his scent, memorizing his pheromones in her mind. As he touched her, she took in every sensation, every wondrous caress.

Spellbound, she floated, her bones and her muscles melting beneath him. Such weightless pleasure, she thought. Reality, fantasy. Everything a woman could want.

She opened her eyes, looked at him, saw him looking back at her.

His body trembled for hers. She could feel his need, his hunger, the power of being loved, of the vow they'd made.

He increased the tempo, going deeper, thrusting on a dream, on sex and sin and everything in between. She clung to his shoulders, wrapping her legs around his waist.

When it happened, when he came, she let him carve a groove right into her soul. She climaxed, too, absorbing the milky warmth that was part of him.

Minutes later they lay in each other's arms, basking in the afterglow. Her hair was still tangled around his fingers, and her hand rested dangerously close to his thigh.

She pressed her lips to his neck and smiled. He was still hard, still partially aroused, even after what they'd done. "I'm going to like being engaged to you."

He returned her smile. "Just think of how desperate we're going to be for each other when I'm not around."

"We'll make up for it every time you come back."
Here, she thought. To the rez. The place that held her
heart. But that wasn't all of it. She'd agreed to be part
of his existence, too. Part of the places that held his
heart. "I can't believe I'm going to be a full-fledged
Ashton. Flying to San Francisco whenever I can. Attending parties on the estate."

He shook his head. "We've created quite a situation for ourselves, haven't we?"

Silent, she nodded. She knew it wasn't a simple
life they'd chosen. But it was their decision, their way
of being together. And she wouldn't trade it for anything. Walker Ashton belonged to her and she belonged to him.

Anxious to kiss him again, she rolled over, strad-
dling his lap. He grinned and pulled her closer.

But before she could cover his mouth with hers,
he tickled her, sending her into a girlish fit, making
her laugh, making her feel happy and free.

Thrilled to be with him.

The man she would always love.

From now until the end of time.

* * * * *

# MISTAKEN FOR A MISTRESS

BY
KRISTI GOLD

**Kristi Gold** has always believed that love has remarkable healing powers and feels very fortunate to be able to weave stories of romance and commitment. Since her first Desire™ in 2000, she's sold over twenty books to Desire™. A classic seat-of-the pants writer, she attributes her ability to write fast to a burning need to see how the book ends.

As a bestselling author, National Readers' Choice winner and Romance Writers of America RITA® Award finalist, she's learned that although accolades are wonderful, the most cherished rewards come from personal stories shared by readers and networking with other authors, both published and aspiring.

You can reach Kristi through her website at www. kristigold.com or through snail-mail at PO Box 9070, Waco, Texas 76714, USA. (Please include an SAE with return postage for a response.)

Many thanks to the San Francisco Area RWA for answering my call for research assistance, particularly Laura, Cynthia, Alice and Nancy. Your help has been invaluable to this story. To all the "Ashtons" authors, it's been a pleasure working with you.

To Marge and Bob Smith for sitting up half the night on a porch in Pigeon Forge, helping me brainstorm the evidence in this story.

# Prologue

*San Francisco, 1991*

Sally Barnett Ashton was dead. One less complication for Spencer Ashton.

In his upscale office at Ashton-Lattimer Corporation, Spencer regarded the private investigator seated across from him, who looked as if he expected him to react with sorrow over the news of his first wife's demise. On the contrary, Spencer experienced only relief that simpering Sally was now completely out of the picture.

Leaning back in his desk chair, Spencer tented his fingers beneath his chin and prepared to ask more questions, not because he wanted to know, but because he needed to know. "And the twins?"

"They're twenty-eight now. Grant is still in Nebraska. He took over the family farm after your in-laws died."

"Former in-laws." Spencer had hated the pompous Barnetts with a passion.

The man looked somewhat put out over the comment. "Until 1975, when Sally died, they were your in-laws since you never officially divorced their daughter."

Spencer's patience was waning. "Pointless details, Rollins. Now get on with it."

"As I was saying, Grant is managing the family farm. He's turned it into a very successful crop-and-cattle venture."

Obviously the boy had inherited Spencer's business acumen, considering he was raised by a passel of country bumpkins. "What about the other one?"

The P.I. looked somewhat disgusted. "Your daughter, Grace, gave birth to two children, Ford and Abigail Ashton, in 1979 and 1981 respectively."

"Ashton?"

Rollins flipped through a folder containing the report. "Yeah. There's no marriage of record. According to the grapevine in your old hometown, she never named any father."

Spencer's anger threatened beneath the surface of his calm facade, and not because his daughter had made a presumed moral misjudgment by giving birth to two bastards. His anger stemmed from having been forced to marry the town prude in order to give his brats a name, and now his own offspring had not been held to the same standards. But he wasn't surprised. Sally had spoiled her from the day she was born. He could still remember Grace's constant wailing as an infant, even if it had been years since he'd taken off and never looked back. "Where is Grace now?"

Rollins streaked a hand over his chin. "That's a good question. She reportedly ran off with some kind of salesman about five years ago when the kids were barely in grade school. I couldn't find a trace of her, but I can keep looking."

"That won't be necessary." As long as she wasn't bugging Spencer, he didn't give a damn where she was. "What about her kids?"

"Your son is now legal guardian of your grandchildren. He's raising them alone."

Spencer found it somewhat ironic that he had other children the same age as his grandchildren. That wouldn't be unusual for a man who'd been coerced into marriage at a ridiculously young age. "Grant's not married?"

"No. Not so far."

Obviously he'd overestimated his oldest son's intelligence. Why would any man want to saddle himself with a couple of kids that weren't even his? Or any kids for that matter? He'd learned early on that child rearing should fall on women's shoulders.

Spencer sat forward and leveled a serious stare on the P.I. "When you returned to Crawley, you were discreet?"

"Of course. I told anyone who asked that I met up with you when we were both teenagers and we lost touch. I have to tell you, though. You're not very popular in town. If I were you, I wouldn't be visiting again anytime soon."

Spencer didn't intend to ever go back to godforsaken Nebraska. "And I suppose you realize that absolute discretion on your part is imperative."

"Are you referring to my knowledge that your second marriage was never valid because you never ended the first?"

True, but his marriage to his current wife was valid, not that he gave a damn about what Lilah thought about anything. She could also be replaced if necessary, and in many ways she already had. Several times. The advantages of having gullible secretaries and power. "I expect you to keep all of it to yourself. If not, you'll never work in this town again."

Rollins finally looked somewhat flustered, which pleased Spencer. "I'm a professional, Mr. Ashton. You can trust me."

Spencer trusted no one but himself. "Good. I will hold you to that."

The P.I. hesitated a moment before speaking again. "I'm no attorney, but aren't you concerned about someone finding out? And if that happens, wouldn't that mean you'd lose this company since it belonged to your second wife's father?"

"Not a concern. Her father signed his shares in this company over to me. Caroline has no claim to it." Spencer bit back a smile. What a pushover old man Lattimer had been, and so had his daughter.

"I guess you have all the bases covered." Rollins pushed his chair back, stood and gestured toward the folder. "The details are in there, copies of birth certificates and death certificates. And a few photos I managed to come across, one in particular of your son. In case you're interested in what he might look like now."

Spencer was curious, but only mildly. "That will be all." After opening his drawer, he pulled out an envelope and handed it to the investigator. "The amount we agreed upon, in cash, plus some extra to ensure your silence."

Rollins gave him a shrewd grin. "Anytime. Enjoy your trip down memory lane."

Without even an offer of a handshake, which suited Spencer fine, the man strode to the private elevator, leaving Spencer with bits and pieces of the products of his past. After the doors closed, he turned the folder around and flipped through it, coming upon the aforementioned photo of his oldest son included with a feature article in the *Crawley Crier*. He'd received some sort of business commendation from the town known for its stupid sentimentality. A boy who appeared to be about thirteen and a girl about two years his junior flanked Grant in the photo. Decent-looking kids, as far as kids went. But with his genes, Spencer certainly wouldn't expect anything less.

Bored with the whole lot of them, he flipped the file closed, just as he had closed this chapter on his life long ago. He wouldn't have to worry that Sally might someday show up on his doorstep. Most likely, neither would his foolhardy son or his reckless daughter, and even if they did, he certainly had no intention of seeing them. As far as he was concerned, his past in Crawley was as dead as the town itself.

Spencer Ashton lived a charmed life, answering to no one, and no doubt he would continue that life for many years to come. In fact, he planned to outlive them all.

# One

*August, Fourteen Years Later*

Spencer Ashton was dead, and Grant Ashton had been charged with his murder.

For most of his life, Ford Ashton had endured being called the "illegitimate" child of a "tramp" in an unforgiving Nebraska town. He'd survived his mother's cruel indifference and eventually her abandonment. But seeing his uncle—the man who'd put his own life on hold to raise him—wearing prison-issue clothes and shackled like an animal, would go down as the worst moment of Ford's twenty-six years on earth.

Standing at the back of the San Francisco courtroom among a crush of curious onlookers, with a heavy heart and sickening anger, Ford listened as the presiding judge announced, "Remanded without bail." Driven by a strong sense of desperation and blind fury, he elbowed his way through the crowd now moving in the opposite direction. Before he could reach his uncle, before he could tell him how much he meant to him, armed guards steered him away. But not before Ford met Grant's gaze and saw resignation in his eyes.

He couldn't allow his uncle to give up. Not now. Not after everything they'd been through together. With hands fisted at his sides, Ford fought the urge to pound something hard with the force of his despair. Pound something until he released all his building frustration and rage over the injustice.

"Mr. Ashton."

Ford spun around toward the unfamiliar voice and confronted an equally unfamiliar man, a slick-looking young guy wearing a dark suit. No doubt, a media vulture. "I'm not answering any damn questions."

The guy pushed his glasses up the bridge of his nose. "I'm not a reporter. I'm a clerk for your uncle's attorney. If you'll follow me, someone would like to see you."

Finally Ford would get to speak with Grant. Finally he could tell him all the things he'd needed to say that had yet to be said. Without hesitation he stepped into the vestibule, glancing to his left at the mass of reporters dogging both the prosecuting and defense attorneys, held at bay by a contingent of security guards. He followed the clerk down a narrow hallway to a secluded room. When the man opened one door, Ford expected to find his uncle waiting for him. Instead, he found Caroline Sheppard—formerly Caroline Ashton—and her second oldest son, Cole, seated at a small conference table.

After the clerk said, "I'll give you some privacy," then left, Caroline rose and crossed the room, her arms held out in welcome. "I'm so sorry, Ford."

He accepted her embrace, hiding his disappointment with a reserved smile. "I'm glad you're here, Caroline."

Cole soon joined them, his hand extended. "Sorry to have

to see you again under such sorry circumstances, Ford. We weren't sure you'd make it on time with such short notice."

Ford shook Cole's hand and said, "I wasn't sure, either. I had a connection in Denver and spent the night in the terminal, then caught the first flight out this morning."

Caroline's expression showed motherly concern, something that had been totally absent in Ford's life due to his lack of a mother. "That means you haven't had any sleep, have you?"

"No, but I wouldn't have slept, anyway, after getting your message."

She gave a one-handed sweep through her short blond hair. "I'm sorry I didn't speak with you personally. I hated that you had to hear about the arrest on your voice mail, but I didn't know how to reach you."

"Don't apologize, Caroline. You had no way of knowing I was out of town on business. I am surprised Grant didn't give you my cell phone number."

Caroline sighed. "Grant didn't want me to call you at all, but I knew you'd want to know. I also knew it could hit the national news soon, and I didn't want you and Abby to learn the facts in that way."

Abby. Damn, Ford didn't look forward to telling his sister. Although his sibling was strong willed—strong, period— she was also pregnant. With twins. "It's been three months since the murder. I thought maybe they'd marked Grant off the list of suspects. What in the hell made them decide to arrest him now?"

"Aside from the argument he had with Spencer the day of the murder," Cole began, "someone's come forward claiming to have seen him enter the building a few minutes before 9 p.m., Spencer's approximate time of death. This witness picked Grant out of a lineup."

God, Ford didn't want to hear this. If only Grant had come

home to Nebraska, none of this would have happened. If only he hadn't been so damned determined to stay in San Francisco to confront his no-good father, then he'd be home right now, helping with the harvest instead of being accused of that father's murder.

One thing Ford did know—his uncle might have been harboring some serious anger, but he would never resort to killing a man, even if justified. "He didn't do it."

"We don't think he did it, either, Ford," Caroline said. "But Spencer has always left victims in his wake, so it doesn't surprise me that continued even after his death."

Spoken like one of Spencer's victims, Ford decided. Caroline had been one of many. "Do we know who this supposed witness is and why they've taken so long to speak up?"

"We don't know any real details," Cole said. "But you'll be able to meet with Grant's attorney on Monday."

That wasn't good enough for Ford. "Why Monday? Why not now?"

"He had another court appearance today, otherwise you could've spoken with him this afternoon. Unfortunately, he'll be out of town this weekend, too."

"His name is Edgar Kent and he has an excellent reputation as a criminal defense attorney," Caroline added. "I hope you don't mind that I took the liberty of hiring him."

"I don't mind. In fact, I owe you." How could he fault this woman for anything? She'd been nothing but kind since he'd met her six months ago in Napa at Abby's wedding. "When can I see Grant?"

Caroline exchanged a brief look with Cole before saying, "According to Mr. Kent, that's not going to be possible."

The urge to knock a hole in the wall revisited Ford. "Why the hell not if they intend to keep him locked up?"

"They're taking him to one of the jails that houses some

of the worst criminals," Cole said. "You'll only be able to communicate through the attorney."

Ford's anger began to build momentum, threatening the tenuous grip he had on his temper. "I can't believe they didn't allow him to post bail."

Caroline shook her head. "They consider him a flight risk because he has no ties to the community. And because he carries the Ashton name, they also believe he might have the connections and enough money to get out of the country."

Grant might have money and the Ashton name, but not once had he ever run from his responsibility. "That's ridiculous. He's never been anywhere aside from Nebraska and now California." Unlike Ford, who'd traveled abroad the year after college graduation, thanks to his uncle, and several times since, thanks to his successful business. "I can't stand the thought of him being treated like some hardened criminal."

Cole rubbed a hand over the back of his neck and lowered his eyes. "According to the state of California, he is."

The state was wrong. Dead wrong. "What happens next?"

"Kent said the case will go before a grand jury," Cole continued. "If they find the evidence is sufficient, then he'll be arraigned again and a trial date will be set. It's my understanding that process could take some time."

Time might be on Ford's side in this instance. "I'm going to clear him. Whatever it takes."

"Grant said you'd try that," Caroline said. "He also said you needed to let the police and the justice system handle it."

"Handle it?" With every ounce of his waning composure, Ford tempered his tone. "As far as they're concerned, they have their man. I'm not going to just lie down and let Grant rot in jail on the off chance they drop the charges. While I'm here, I'm going to do some digging on my own."

Cole sent him a look of understanding. "I figured you

would, and I don't blame you. I also have some information that might help you do that. It involves Spencer's administrative assistant at Ashton-Lattimer, Kerry Roarke. I saw them together in a restaurant several months ago when I was with Dixie. Maybe she knows more than she's letting on, especially since she's the one who claimed she overheard Grant threaten Spencer."

"Grant told me about that, and he also said it was true. That's why I'm not sure she'll be of any help."

Caroline wrapped one arm around her son's waist, as if she needed physical support. "Ford, we all know that Spencer has left a trail of scorned women. I've always thought that one day he would meet up with one who wouldn't tolerate his antics. Maybe Kerry Roarke is that woman."

A trail of scorned women that had included Ford's own grandmother, and Caroline. "Then you're thinking that maybe this Kerry did him in?"

"She has a solid alibi," Cole said. "Something about taking some kind of night class. But she might have hired someone to do it."

Caroline frowned. "But that would take money, and as far as I know she doesn't have any."

"I'll find out." That, and everything else he could about Kerry Roarke. "Any idea where I can locate her?"

"She still works at Ashton-Lattimer, and that's all I know," Caroline said. "Spencer's nephew, Walker, should be able to help. He was running the company until last month. Even though he was very loyal to Spencer, and not overly fond of us, he should be reasonable."

At least that was something Ford could work with. "If you can give me his number, I'll call him after I get checked into a hotel. Any suggestions on where I should stay?"

"You can stay at The Vines with us." Caroline's voice was soothing despite Ford's turmoil.

"Thanks for the offer, but Napa's too far away from San Francisco. If I'm going to check out this Roarke woman, I need to be in the city." He also needed to be close to his uncle, even if he couldn't see him.

"You're going to have to be careful, Ford," Cole said. "If she finds out you're an Ashton, she's probably not going to talk to you, especially if she's involved in some way."

"I'll handle it." And he would. He had no tolerance for women with little regard for decency. Women like his own mother who'd abandoned her kids, just like her own father had abandoned his children. Spencer Ashton might have had a reputation of being a womanizer, but it still took two to have an affair, so that made this Kerry Roarke as guilty as Ford's grandfather, even if it turned out she wasn't guilty of murder. But someone was guilty, and it wasn't Grant.

Caroline wrung her hands over and over, another sign of her distress. "Lucas and Eli send their regards. They're sorry they couldn't come but they had to stay at the winery to prepare for the crush. Jillian and Mercedes also told me to tell you they hope to see you soon, too. They just couldn't bear to be here, but they're keeping you and Grant in their thoughts."

Ford took her hands into his. "It's okay, Caroline. It would've been tough on the girls, having to confront the man accused of killing their father."

Fury flashed in Cole's eyes. "He wasn't much of a father, Ford. Not like Grant was to you. It's tough on all of us because we believe Grant's innocent, not because of Spencer's death."

Ford shook Cole's hand again. "I appreciate your support."

"Not a problem. You're family." Cole gestured toward the

door. "We can drive you to a hotel. The car's out back. Kent told us we needed to leave that way to avoid the press."

Ford definitely wanted to avoid the press, and any pictures in the paper that might identify him. If he was going to approach this Roarke women, he needed to pretend to be someone other than an Ashton.

Once they reached the door, Caroline turned to Ford and gave him a pleading look. "Please be careful, Ford."

Oh, he intended to be careful. Very careful. He also intended to clear his uncle of all charges, no matter what it might take. Even if he had to lie.

Kerry Roarke had learned one very important lesson early in life: always be wary of a man's motives.

She'd never forgotten that lesson, and some people simply didn't understand why she was so reluctant to get involved with any man. Particularly her gal pals with whom she'd spent the regular Friday-evening preweekend celebration in a trendy Nob Hill bar, listening to them drone on and on about their active sex lives and Kerry's lack thereof. As she'd told them time and again, she wasn't interested in "finding a guy," for reasons they could never understand.

They'd departed a few minutes ago to ready for their routine club hopping, leaving Kerry with the usual admonishments to get a life. They'd also left her with two top-grade condoms that they'd slipped into her purse. Condoms or not, Kerry wasn't on the prowl today, or any day for that matter. She had a career in the making and a bitter past hanging over her head.

That's why she chose to remain at the lounge, a relatively safe place to unwind. Sure, she'd been hit on by her share of businessmen who frequented the place after work, but she'd honed the art of put-downs and prudish airs. For the most part, those skills had left her out of the line of fire of most men with lust on their minds, except for one disgustingly persistent boss who was fortunately now out of the picture, God rest his demented soul.

Despite Kerry's guardedness when it came to the opposite sex, one man standing near the bar's entry, a pilsner of beer gripped in his hand, had definitely earned her interest, mainly because he stood out from the regulars. He wore a plain navy sport coat over a white tailored shirt, sans tie, like most of the bar's male patrons in attendance. But his dark jeans spanning long solid legs and his brown leather cowboy boots didn't quite add up to corporate mogul. Considering his tanned skin and sandy blond hair cut into spiky layers, he might pass as a surfer. A really, really stunning surfer. But most surfers she'd known were a little more lean. A little less buff. Buff worked for her, if she was at all interested. Which she wasn't. Not in the least. All right, perhaps a tiny bit interested, but not enough to call him over to join her for a drink.

*You need to take a few risks, Kerry....*

In an attempt to ignore her friend's unsolicited advice, and the handsome stranger, Kerry concentrated on visually tracking a drop of condensation on the glass of club soda. Still, she couldn't seem to stop the occasional need to glance at him in spite of the lack of wisdom. Yet when he pushed off the wall and headed in her direction, she gave him her complete attention.

He definitely wasn't from the city; his gait alone indicated that. In her world, most people were always in a rush, and that applied to walking, talking and working. Not this particular man. He maneuvered his way through the tables slowly, practically sauntering toward the bar. The closer he came, the taller he seemed, his confidence overt with every step he took.

Yanking herself back into reality, Kerry took a quick drink and set the glass back down. She kept her eyes lowered, as if the soggy cocktail napkin happened to be a work of art. She heard the scrape of a stool and raised her gaze to stare ahead at the collection of liquor bottles stacked on the shelves behind the bar. But in her peripheral vision, she could see that he'd taken a seat two stools down. A comfortable distance, and a definite message he wasn't seeking her out.

That should relieve her, but instead she was disappointed. Though she shouldn't be. No matter how nice looking he might be, this man was a stranger, and most strangers meant certain danger. Right now, she really needed to finish her drink, grab her purse and go home. She really needed to have some dinner and watch a classic movie with Millie, her eccentric and beloved landlady. She really needed to quit shooting the cute guy covert glances lest he catch her. At least she wasn't panting, not yet, anyway.

"Excuse me."

Kerry froze middrink, the glass gripped firmly in her hand, a very good thing, otherwise she might be wearing the remnants of her soda. She took a quick gulp then leveled her gaze on the man not quite beside her—and immediately met a cliché. Bedroom eyes. Blue, blue bedroom eyes. Eyes as brilliant as Millie's collection of Austrian crystal.

When she realized she was staring, Kerry cleared her throat in an effort to clear away the embarrassment. "Were you addressing me?"

"Yes, ma'am. Do you live here?"

A typical pickup line, aside from the ma'am part. "I'm not really into residing in bars. Too noisy."

He grinned, and Kerry nearly slid off the stool. Did he have to have dimples to match the little cleft in his chin? And did he have to have a dark shading of whiskers to match his eyelashes? Which was kind of odd considering the lightness of his hair. But she doubted his blond highlights came from a bottle. Most likely from the sun. Perhaps he was a surfer disguised as a cowboy. Probably not a first in California.

He folded his hands in front of him. Large, sturdy hands with square, blunt fingers. A man's man hands. "I meant do you live in San Francisco?"

"Yes, I do." For ten years now, many of which hadn't been all that great.

"Good. Then maybe you can help me." Fishing into his jacket's inside pocket, he pulled out a number of brochures and fanned them out in front of him on the bar. "I'm only going to be here for a couple of days, and I can't decide what I'm supposed to do first. Any suggestions?"

Oh, she had a suggestion, all right. He needed to put a bag over his head before she went blind from his sheer beauty. She could be polite without fawning over him. After all, he seemed harmless, in a risky kind of way. "Let me see what you have, there."

After gathering up the brochures, he slid onto the stool beside her, bringing with him a subtle scent of cologne. Nothing overpowering, like most men at the office. A nice clean smell somewhere between fresh cotton and cool water. Nice, very nice. And so was he when he stuck out his hand and said, "Ford Matthews."

She took his hand into hers and noticed the calluses immediately, and the strength of his grip, although it wasn't overpowering. Just firm and solid and patently masculine, as she'd expected. After he'd called her ma'am, she'd also expected a little more country in his speech but he had no real discernable accent. In fact, he sounded fairly articulate. "I'm Kerry Roarke," she said right after he released her hand.

"Nice to meet you, Kerry."

"Ford's an interesting name." But not exactly foreign to her.

"For some reason, I think I've heard it recently, although I can't remember where."

"A lot of people own one." He grinned again and streaked a hand over his chin. "I could see you in a red Mustang convertible."

"Not hardly."

"Not even when you were sixteen?"

At sixteen she'd had nothing but the clothes on her back and a huge chip on her shoulder. "I've never owned a sports car."

"Actually, neither have I. I'm more into trucks. That's the going thing where I'm from."

Kerry toyed with the disintegrating napkin beneath her glass to avoid his unbelievable eyes. "Where are you from, Ford?"

"A small town in the Midwest."

"The Midwest covers a lot of territory. What state?"

He hesitated a moment, then said, "Kansas."

That slight hesitation bothered her a bit, but then maybe he was ashamed of his roots. That she could relate to. "What do you do for a living?"

"I'm a farmer. I own a few acres cultivated in corn. A few horses and cows."

Another of Kerry's expectations met, and very refreshing. She didn't like pretentious, wealthy men in the least. "Farming must be a tough business." And the reason for his sun-burnished skin and sun-bleached hair.

"It can be tough. Long hours, but I like working the land with my own hands."

And he owned hands that looked quite skilled, probably at everything. "It sounds intriguing."

"Not really. In fact, it's pretty boring if you're not in the business. But it's a good way to make a living if things are going well."

"And you're your own boss."

"Yep, I am."

*Yep.* Another indication of his down-home heritage. "That must be nice, being your own boss. I hope to be that someday. I'm guessing you're not in town on business then."

"Nope. Just pleasure."

In Kerry's experience, when a man said "pleasure," he usually followed it with a suggestive look. Not this enigma named Ford. He seemed refreshingly real. But what he seemed and what he was could very well be two different things. She'd given up gullible when she'd learned the true definition of "the mean streets."

"What do you do for a living?" He sounded sincere, another rarity for Kerry.

"Right now I'm working in an investment banking firm. I was an executive administrative assistant, but I've recently been demoted to human resources, due to circumstances beyond my control."

"Did you cross the boss?"

"Actually, he died."

"What happened to him?"

"He was murdered."

If Ford was at all shocked, he didn't show it. "Did they catch the guy who did it?"

Warning bells rang out in Kerry's head. Loud ones. "Who said it was a guy?"

He shrugged. "I guess I just assumed it would be."

"You're not lying to me about being a farmer, are you?" She sent him a questioning look to match her query.

A flash of confusion crossed his face. "No, why would you think that?"

"Because for the past three months, I've been hounded by the press. And I wouldn't be surprised to learn that you're a reporter looking for information. If you are, I have nothing to say."

"I promise I'm not a reporter. Not even close." When he slid off the stool, Kerry assumed he was leaving. Instead, he pulled his wallet from his back pocket, thumbed through it then said, "Damn."

She rested her elbow on the bar and propped her chin on her hand. "Forget your credentials?"

"As a matter of fact, yeah, I did. My driver's license. I don't think the guy checking me in at the airport gave it back to me."

"That's convenient."

"Not if I want to get back home."

"I meant that's convenient, not having anything to prove who you are."

He sat back down and released a rough sigh. "I went to college and I have a business degree. I nearly flunked English twice, couldn't write a decent essay to save my life and never even considered writing for a newspaper. Nowadays, I spend a lot of my time walking through manure and talking to heifers." He grinned. "The four-legged kind, so don't think I'm making some kind of sexist comment."

His smile could wither the most stoic woman, even Kerry, and that was more than obvious when she gave him one in return. "You did clean your boots before you came in here?"

"I have on new boots, bought special for the trip. I had to drive all the way into Kansas City to get them. My hometown only has a post office and a drugstore, which also serves as the grocery store. One stoplight, and that's only been there for about five years."

He seemed genuine, but she still had questions. "You don't have three kids and a wife back home, do you?"

"No way. Slim pickin's in small towns these days."

Slim pickin's in big cities, too, Kerry thought. She studied him again and didn't see anything that would indicate he was lying. She would just have to trust her instincts on this one,

and her instincts told her he was sincere, aside from being simply sensational in the looks department. Besides, she didn't
intend to do anything but have a brief conversation before she
headed home.

"Okay. I guess you've convinced me you're not some
media hound." She gestured toward the stack of brochures.
"Now hand over the tourist stuff and I'll tell you where you
need to go." And she would definitely tell him exactly where
he could go if she found out he had been lying to her.

After he slid the brochures in her direction, she began to
eliminate them one by one. "Boring." She came to the next.
"Great, if you like crowded buses." She tossed aside another.
"Too much money." She kept going until she'd exhausted all
possibilities then handed them back to him. "None of this is
worth your while."

"Then what do you suggest?"

"Several places off the beaten path, a few of the better
tourist attractions not to be missed. The night tour of Alca-
traz is pretty interesting."

His expression went suddenly serious. "Prisons don't interest me at all."

More warning bells sounded. "You haven't been in one,
have you?"

Finally his smile returned, a guarded one. "No. But I did
have a distant cousin who did time for cattle rustling."

"People really still do that?"

"Yeah. When they're desperate."

Kerry knew all about desperation. But she didn't know
what prompted her to ask, "Have you had dinner?" Maybe
her attraction to him. Maybe her co-workers voices encouraging her to take a chance now and again. This might
be considered a colossal chance, but one she felt the need
to take.

"Nope, haven't had anything since peanuts on the airplane. Do you have any suggestions?"

"Plenty. What do you like to eat?"

"Steak."

She wrinkled her nose. Beef was by no means her favorite fare. "Since you're in town, maybe you should try something different. Something exotic."

"I can do exotic. I'm not exactly opposed to taking a few risks."

Kerry had given up risks a while back, but for some reason, this man with the sparkling blue eyes, buff body and stunning mouth had her wanting to take a few risks. Small risks, she reminded herself. Having dinner in the daylight in a crowded restaurant would meet that criteria, as long as she left him with only a handshake.

Sliding from the stool, Kerry leaned down, grabbed her purse and smoothed a hand down her skirt. "Okay, Farmer Ford, I'm going to take you to one of my favorite places for a great meal, and I'm going to give you instructions on where you should go while you're in town. As long as you're buying."

He rose from the stool and stood before her, six feet of solid, electrifying male. "That's an offer I'm not going to refuse."

That was the only offer Kerry Roarke intended to make tonight.

# Two

**F**ord had a plan—a chance meeting, some casual conversation, earning her trust and finding out what she knew about the murder. Except, he hadn't exactly planned on Kerry Roarke's appeal.

He would like to hog-tie Walker Ashton for not sufficiently warning him. He'd only provided the name of the bar where the office staff hung out on Fridays and a general description of Kerry—blond hair, light-colored eyes, about five-seven. He hadn't bothered to mention those eyes were a color Ford had only heard about until now—violet. He also hadn't mentioned that her hair fell to the middle of her back and that her body was anything but nondescript, even if she was hiding some serious curves beneath a conservative black jacket and skirt. And damn if she didn't have a dimple. Not dimples like his and Abby's. A Shirley Temple dimple, right in the left corner of her incredible mouth. Thanks to his sister, he'd endured hours of classic movies featuring the precocious kid, otherwise he wouldn't even know what a Shirley Temple dimple was.

All that aside, he had to admit Kerry Roarke was fairly nice to be around. Maybe too nice. He had to remember that she'd been his grandfather's premortem flavor-of-the-moment, and she could hold important information about the murder. She might even be responsible, as Cole and Caroline had suggested.

At the moment, she was holding him captive with her mouth as they dined in the high-class eatery situated in an up-scale hotel not far from his own hotel. She'd wanted to take him someplace more casual, a popular Italian grill full of people, until he'd convinced her he didn't mind paying more for some quiet. Although he'd had to tip big to get seated because of his jeans, the restaurant wasn't all that crowded and the noise wasn't at all intrusive, allowing them to hold a decent conversation. An easy conversation about nothing in particular. He'd answered her questions when she'd asked, and so far he hadn't slipped up and blown his cover. Yet.

Following a slight break in their almost nonstop dialogue, Kerry dabbed at her mouth with a napkin before regarding the remnants of his so-called dinner. "You didn't eat very much."

"I'm not as hungry as I thought." Nor did he have a fondness for French cuisine or fowl.

"You didn't like the duck." She sounded disappointed, and for some reason that bothered Ford.

He took another bite to appease her. "It's just a little rich for my taste."

Tossing her napkin aside, she sat back and folded her arms beneath her breasts. "Well, I admire you for trying the escargot, even though I warned you. Guess you learned your lesson, huh?"

Little did she know, he'd figured that out at a bistro in Paris. A little garlic and a lot of butter didn't mask what they were—

snails. A lesson he'd learned a while back. But he had a feeling keeping up the farm-boy front might be more tricky than disguising his vast dietary experiences. So might keeping his distance from her because, despite who she was, he couldn't deny she was classically beautiful and damn tempting. But until proven otherwise, she was a member of the enemy camp, a woman who helped put his uncle behind bars. A woman who could know important details. He had to remember that, not only tonight but for the rest of the time he planned to spend in her company, if his plan worked.

After pushing her plate aside, she eyed the black folder holding the check, resting next to Ford's arm. "Do you want to split the bill?"

"No, ma'am. I've got it." Ford took out his wallet and paid the exorbitant total with cash, including another substantial tip. At this rate he was going to have to find an ATM, since he didn't dare bring out a credit card with his real name. "Are you ready to go now?"

"Sure."

When he rounded the table and pulled her chair back, she stared at him like he'd grown two heads. "This is rather strange."

"What's strange?"

She accepted the hand he offered and stood. "You're a gentleman, and that's a rare breed these days."

If she knew he'd been lying to her—about his name, the missing driver's license, his real reasons for being in town and being with her—she wouldn't find him gentlemanly at all. And that was something Ford had a hard time dealing with. His uncle had taught him that lying was one of the most dishonorable things a man could do, especially to a woman. He wasn't in the habit of lying to women. Normally, he let them know upfront he wasn't looking for a serious relationship. If that wasn't okay with them, then he'd let them go without any argument. A lonely life at times, but he wasn't ready to settle down, and he wasn't sure he would ever be. Not if he ran the risk that he'd fall for some woman who'd get tired of living in the middle of nowhere, then take off the way his mother had.

At least that wouldn't be a problem with this particular woman, he thought as they headed out of the hotel. As soon as he got what he needed from Kerry Roarke, he would walk away.

"Do you want to walk awhile?" Kerry asked after they moved through the sliding doors and onto the sidewalk.

He paused to face her, coming in contact with those killer eyes. "You're the guide. Lead on."

"We're only going a block or so," she said as they headed up the street.

Kerry walked fast but Ford managed to keep up with her. He suspected she did everything in a rush, from talk to eat, but then, considering what he'd seen of the city that day, it seemed everyone was in a hurry. After about a block or so, she crossed the sloped street, led him into a nicely landscaped, well-lit park and showed him to a bench across from a fountain, their backs to a row of buildings, an impressive cathedral looming large in the distance. The sun had set completely, leaving the sky a hazy shade of oranges and blues. Ford settled beside her, careful to keep a decent space between them. Otherwise he might forget his goal, especially when she crossed her legs and her skirt rode up higher on her thigh. He fought the urge to stare. He fought even harder the temptation to touch.

She sat back and sighed. "I love this place in the evening, especially all the people. Take that woman across the way, walking her dog."

Reluctantly he turned his attention from Kerry's legs to an elderly lady wearing an odd, flower-bedecked hat and gloves, her prissy four-legged hairball sporting a diamond-studded collar. "That's pretty interesting." And not so unlike some of the snooty women in Crawley, at least as far as the hat and attitude went.

"I guess San Francisco might seem strange to someone who lives on a farm," Kerry said. "All of the chaos and eccentrics."

"Yeah. I'm not used to seeing so many people milling around." Somewhat of a lie since he'd seen his share of big cities in the process of hawking his patented livestock feed to various companies. But he wasn't going to tell her any of that, especially since she'd told him several times at dinner how she appreciated spending time with a "common farmer." True, he had the soul of a farmer, but he had a bank account that far exceeded most men who made a living off the land.

He shifted to face her and laid an arm over the back of the bench, fighting the urge to touch that incredible fall of blond hair. "Do you like living here?"

"Sure. It's an exciting place." She turned those violet eyes on him again. "And some might say it's romantic, although I can't speak from personal experience."

Ford's experience had been limited lately too. Three months had passed since he'd visited a "special" female friend in Lincoln. A month ago, she'd moved to Chicago, and Ford had moved into celibacy, but not by choice. "Sounds like the perfect place to live if you're into that sort of thing."

She lifted one shoulder in a shrug. "Like every other big city, it has its downside."

Ford noted the weariness in her tone, as if she'd personally experienced that downside. A good lead-in. "I imagine it does, especially if you can't go to work without worrying about your boss being murdered."

"Honestly, he wasn't necessarily a nice man. Charming on the surface, but he tended to use that, and money, to get what he wanted. That's why I'm not surprised someone got tired of it and took matters into their own hands."

But was that someone her? Ford couldn't imagine that any woman with such an angelic face and pleasant disposition could actually be involved in a murder. Yet she'd basically echoed exactly what Caroline had said about Spencer. Someone had grown tired of his treachery and had done something about it. "Do they know who did it?"

"They've arrested his son." She crossed her arms beneath her breasts and stared straight head. "Can we talk about something else?"

"No problem." As far as Ford was concerned, they had plenty of time to get into that. "What do you want to talk about?"

"We could discuss what we originally intended to discuss, your tour of the city. I need to know your starting point, so where are you staying?"

Ford hooked a thumb over his shoulder. "We passed it back there. The Royalbrook Hotel."

She looked surprised. "That's a ritzy place for someone on a tight budget."

"Well, I don't get out all that much, so I decided to go for broke and stay at the best. I even have a suite with a couple of couches and one of those minibars. Damnedest thing I've ever seen." More lies. Ford had stayed in many hotel suites with minibars. And Cole had directed him to the hotel because of the proximity to the financial district, and the Ashton-Lattimer offices. Money wasn't an issue.

Kerry toyed with the hem of her skirt, drawing Ford's immediate attention. "I guess a suite might come in handy, in case you meet an interesting woman you'd like to entertain."

"I've already met one." And that was the absolute truth.

Even in the limited light, he could see a blush on her cheeks, making her all the more pretty. "I don't know how interesting I am, but I do know the city like the back of my hand. The good, the not so good, and the ugly." She lowered her gaze to her lap. "Since tomorrow's Saturday, maybe I could be your personal tour guide."

The plan was now in place, and better still, it was her idea. "I could go for that in a heartbeat. If you're not going to upset some boyfriend."

"I don't have a boyfriend, so that's not a problem."

A good thing, Ford decided. But his attraction to her wasn't good at all. It was hazardous. He would just have to keep his urges in check and a firm grip on his control and goal. "What time do you want to meet up?"

"How about 9 a.m.? I'll pick you up in front of the hotel."

"In a car?"

She smiled. "I don't think I want to carry you on my back up and down the streets of San Francisco."

Ford laughed, all the while thinking he'd like to carry her to bed. Another hazardous thought. "Okay, 9 a.m. in front of the hotel."

She secured her purse strap over her shoulder. "Great. Now that that's settled, I should be going home."

"Where is home?"

She pointed in the direction opposite the hotel. "That way."

"Where's your car?"

"I'm on foot. The parking downtown is ridiculous, and public transportation's readily available and cheap. But I can walk home from here."

They stood at the same time, coming into close enough contact to make Ford more than uncomfortable. "I can walk you home."

"That's not necessary. It's not that far, and the area is fairly safe."

"That may be, but where I come from, men escort women to their doorstep."

She straightened the lapels on his jacket. "But I'm not a defenseless woman, Ford Matthews. In fact, I'm a lot tougher than I seem."

Maybe even tough enough to have had her boss killed. She might be that tough, but right now Ford was having a huge moment of weakness, especially when she wet her lips. "Guess I'm going to have to behave myself so I don't give you a reason to slug me."

"I wouldn't necessarily slug you if you misbehaved a little."

"Oh, yeah?"

She moved closer until very little space separated them. "Nothing too naughty, of course."

Ford was having some fairly "naughty" thoughts at the moment. In fact, they could be deemed as downright dirty. Right now he really wanted to kiss her, but he realized the lack of good judgment in that. Obviously, Kerry didn't, because before Ford could brace himself, she wrapped one slender hand around his neck and brought his mouth to hers.

He'd never refused a kiss from a beautiful woman before, and he sure as hell had no desire to do that right now. Not when her sinful lips contrasted with her angelic face. Not when he could no longer resist wrapping his arms around her and pulling her against him. Not even when the kiss took on a definite wildness, growing deeper and deeper with every passing moment.

Kerry pulled away first and touched her fingertips to her lips, her blush a deeper shade of pink. "I'm sorry. I guess I got a little carried away."

If she only knew what was stirring below his belt, she'd

realize she wasn't alone. "I'm not sorry at all." Another truth among the lies, but he had to keep a tight rein on reality, and that meant not getting totally caught in her web.

She released a small, self-conscious laugh. "Just so you know, I don't normally behave that way. I've never kissed anyone I've just met. I've never wanted to."

Ford couldn't say the same thing, another fact he decided to keep to himself in a long line of many. "We'll just chalk it up to the moonlight."

She studied the darkening hazy sky. "I don't see any moon."

He took a moment to admire her, and found himself wishing things were different. Wishing they had met under different circumstances, and that she was all she appeared to be—a gorgeous woman, fresh and unassuming. And incapable of being a mistress or a murderer. "Maybe it's not out yet."

She settled her gaze on his. "Maybe it will be out tomorrow night."

Knowing she planned to spend that much time with him pleased Ford, but not for the reasons it should. "I'll see you tomorrow."

"Nine o'clock sharp," she said as she began backing away.

He slipped his hands in the pockets of his jeans. "Are you sure you don't want me to escort you home?"

She paused on the walkway, the fountain behind her providing a nice backdrop for her beauty. "I really don't think that's a good idea."

"Why's that?"

"Because I might ask you to come in, and something tells me that might be dangerous."

With that, she walked away, leaving Ford frozen where he stood as he watched the sway of her hips. No doubt danger lurked around every curve, especially hers. If he had walked her home and she had asked him in, he wasn't sure what he might have done. Probably nothing that would be considered sensible.

When she was no longer in sight, Ford left the park for the hotel. He had a lot to think about tonight, and a few things to do, namely call home. After that, he'd take a shower and go to bed in order to be well rested for his excursion with Kerry Roarke. And he suspected that prospect could very well keep him up all night.

Kerry closed the front door behind her and fell back against it. If luck prevailed, Millie might already be in bed. Otherwise, she could be in for questions she didn't want to answer.

"What have you been doing, young lady?"

So much for luck. Kerry strolled into the cluttered living room to find Millicent Lantry Morrow Vandiver seated in the red brocade wingback chair midmanicure, a turquoise turban wrapped around her hair to complement the matching caftan. She looked much younger than her seventy-eight years, thanks to a few facelifts that left her eyes a bit sunken, but her skin virtually wrinkle free. She was elegantly unconventional, a woman with a heart of gold who'd survived three husbands and had a penchant for picking up strays. Kerry was no exception to that, except that she'd remained with Millie much longer than most.

Tossing her purse aside, Kerry collapsed onto the weathered gold sofa that had seen its share of visitors, from out-of-work actors to persistent suitors to strung-out kids, according to its owner. She reached down and slipped off her heels, her feet greatly in need of a good soak. When she glanced up and noticed Millie was still awaiting an answer, she said, as nonchalantly as possible, "I've been out to dinner with a friend."

Millie resumed filing her nails. "You've been out kissing someone."

Momentarily stunned and speechless, Kerry gaped a good thirty seconds before she asked, "Why would you think that?'

She waved the fingernail file around like a maestro conducting an orchestra. "My dear, you have that look about you. You're veritably glowing. And your lipstick is smeared."

Kerry automatically swiped the back of her hand over her mouth. "How do you know I didn't mess it up during dinner?"'

Millie set the file aside and folded her hands primly in her lap. "My angel, I have been married many times, and in love at least four times as many. I know when a woman has been keeping company with a young man."

Millie's intuition was as amazing as her youthful attitude, something Kerry had learned a long time ago. "Okay, I might have gotten a good-night kiss." In reality, she had delivered that kiss.

"Who is this young man?"

Kerry curled her legs beneath her. "Don't laugh, but he's a Midwest farmer in town on vacation. I met him tonight."

Millie looked both surprised and concerned. "You kissed a complete stranger?"

Kerry felt the beginnings of a blush. "It was only a simple kiss." Yet there had been nothing simple about it. She still felt the effects, remembered the sensations, wanted more of the same.

Pushing up from the chair, Millie crossed the room with measured steps. Kerry had noticed her frailty more and more each day, and that made her heart ache.

Millie settled in beside her on the sofa and took Kerry's hands into hers. "Kerry Ann, when you came to live with me, you were a scared child, full of anger and suspicion, and rightfully so. Since that time, you've blossomed into a more secure woman. Yet I'm concerned that you are still very vulnerable."

"What are you saying?" As if Kerry didn't know.

"I want you to open yourself to possibilities where men are concerned, but I also want you to be careful. I would hate to see you fall in love too quickly or trust too much."

"I just met him, for heaven's sake. I'm not in love with him." But she had to admit, she was very drawn to him. Almost to extremes. "Besides, he'll be leaving in a couple of days."

"Precisely, but one can make grave errors in judgment in two days' time."

Kerry pulled her hands from Millie's grasp and lowered her gaze to the miniature Buddha sitting in the middle of the coffee table. "It's not that big a deal, Millie. I'm only going to show him around tomorrow."

"Perhaps you would like me to chaperone to ensure your safety."

Wouldn't that be lovely? "That's not necessary, Millie. We'll be out in public. I'm just going to take him to a few places around town."

"He could very well try to take you a few places—none having to do with tourism."

Kerry glanced up to meet Millie's somber expression. "You haven't even met him yet."

"True, so do bring him by for afternoon tea. Unless you are otherwise occupied, or fear that I might steal him away."

Kerry smiled in response to Millie's sudden mischievous grin. "Actually, that could be a problem with your charm and his incredible looks."

"Then he is handsome?"

Oh, yes. "You could say that."

"I will have to judge for myself, and suppose I will have to trust your judgment, as well." She pushed off the sofa and faced Kerry. "Now I'm going upstairs since it's getting late."

"I'll be up in a minute to brush your hair." Something

Kerry had done for the past ten years for her mentor, such a small gesture in light of everything Millie had done for her.

Millie waved her hand in a dismissive gesture. "That won't be necessary, darling. You must get your rest tonight and prepare for your day tomorrow. I want you to be totally cognizant of your actions."

After Millie headed away to make the slow journey up the stairs, Kerry remained on the sofa and pondered Millie's words. Maybe she was being foolish. Maybe she was taking too big a chance. But in her heart of hearts she truly believed she could trust Ford Matthews.

Ford sensed Kerry was beginning to trust him, and although that's exactly what he'd planned, he was also beginning to feel like a jerk. But he still had to remember what he hoped to accomplish. Losing control wasn't a part of the scheme, although that's exactly what he had almost done when she'd kissed him.

Tomorrow he would take it easy with her. He'd spend the time necessary to get her to talk to him about the murder. Beyond that, he couldn't allow anything else to happen between them.

But hell, he wanted to kiss her again. He wanted to do a lot more than that.

Right now he needed to call home. Grabbing the tableside phone, Ford pounded out the number and waited, hoping his brother-in-law answered and not his sister. Chances were, Abby had spent a good part of her day fuming since he'd spoken to her husband before he'd left the hotel instead of her.

"Speak."

Damn, for once he'd lucked out. "Hey, Russ. How's it going?"

"If you mean how's your sister, I'm going to let her answer that."

"Wait a minute, I need to talk to you before—"

"Ford Ashton, you are in so much trouble you're going to need a backhoe to dig out of it."

And she would be driving the backhoe, heading straight for him. "Good evening to you, too, sis."

"Why haven't you called before now? I've been sitting here, waiting to hear why you suddenly decided to take a trip to California."

Obviously, the story hadn't made the local news out of North Platte, and cable TV was a nonentity in Crawley. Maybe this time that was a blessing. At least he could break it to her gently. "They had Grant's bail hearing today."

She drew in a harsh breath. "Bail hearing? They've arrested him?"

"Yeah, and the worst part is, they're going to keep him in jail until the trial. They're afraid he's going to skip out."

"Oh, God. Did you talk to him?"

"No. He's not allowed any visitors."

"This is insane! Uncle Grant couldn't have done this."

He hated hearing Abby so upset, especially because of the pregnancy. He knew enough to know that carrying twins was risky enough without emotional stress. "Calm down, Abby. I'm going to clear him of the charges if it's the last thing I do."

"How are you going to do that?"

He explained Kerry's affiliation with Spencer before launching into his plan to garner information from her. When he was finished, Abby asked, "Is she pretty?"

Pretty wasn't the half of it. "Yeah, she is."

"Oh, wonderful. I hope you keep your little brain from taking over your big brain."

"Not funny, Abby. This is serious business. I'm seeing her to get information, not to seduce her. Besides, so far she seems fairly nice." Very nice, unpretentious, and that's what bugged Ford the most. Maybe everyone had been wrong about her.

"You know something, Ford? Maybe you *should* seduce her, if that's the only way you can get information."

"You don't mean that, Abby."

"Normally I wouldn't even consider such a thing. But if this woman is responsible for the murder, or if she's protecting the real killer, then I say you pull out all the stops and do what you have to do. This is Grant's life we're talking about here. Literally. He could receive the maximum penalty for something he didn't do."

He could be executed, what Abby had failed to say, but Ford got her meaning, loud and clear. He couldn't stomach the thought of Grant suffering that fate. He couldn't stand the thought of him spending his life in jail, either.

"I agree, Abby. I intend to do whatever I can to clear him. But Grant also stressed to us the importance of honesty and respect. I'm lying to this woman, and if she's not responsible for any of it, then I'm in the wrong, and I'm going to have to live with that."

"Ford, you've always been fairly cavalier with relationships with women. Don't let this one turn your head around until you can't see straight."

At times he believed Kerry Roarke was already clouding his judgment, and he'd only known her for about five hours. Which made spending all day with her dicey. But he had no choice. "I'll do what I have to do, Abby. And if this all turns out to be a dead end, I'm not going to give up. I'll stay here until I find out who really did this and see Grant walk out of that hell-hole."

"I wish I could be there with you."

Ford hated the hint of tears in Abby's voice. Abby rarely cried, but he could understand why she would feel the need.

"You've got to think about the babies and your health, Abby. This is already stressful enough for you."

"Yes, but I'll handle it. Besides, I have Russ."

Thank God she did have Russ, and although Ford was happy she'd found a life partner, at times he envied them both. "Speaking of Russ, tell him thanks again for keeping the place in order."

"I will. Between him and Buck, everything will get done."

Thank God for Buck Collier, too. The foreman had been around for as long as Ford could remember. In many ways, he'd also served as a surrogate father. At least the men in his and Abby's lives had been great role models. "I'm going to let you go now. Try to get some rest."

"You, too, Ford. And be careful. I don't want to see you get hurt."

Hurt? Where had that come from? Ford Ashton didn't get hurt. He never allowed himself that emotion, not since the day his mother had walked out the door and never returned. He vowed he never would. "I'll be fine, Abby. And if I can find some way to get word to Grant, I'll send him your love."

"You do that. And in the meantime, call every now and then, will you?"

"I'll stay in touch when I have the chance." But tomorrow that might be impossible. Tomorrow he planned to be occupied by Kerry Roarke.

After hanging up from his sister, Ford stripped out of all of his clothes and lay across the bed, a glass half-full of mini-bar whiskey resting on his bare chest. He didn't like feeling this way, at war with his honor and, worse, battling his libido. Kerry had definitely stirred up big trouble, maybe more than he could handle. Right now he had to get a grip on some serious strength. Otherwise, their little sightseeing trip and his fact-finding expedition might get thrown over for a totally different kind of journey. One that involved a good-looking lady who could kiss way too well, and a hot-blooded man who hadn't kept company with a woman of her caliber in quite some time, if ever. A deadly combination. He'd just have to keep his head on straight.

# Three

The minute Ford walked out of the Royalbrook Hotel's revolving doors, his head started spinning. Parked in the circular drive beneath the portico sat a little red Mustang convertible with the top down. And behind the wheel of that hot little car was an equally hot blonde, her hair secured high atop her head, sunglasses concealing her eyes. But Ford remembered every detail of those eyes without having to see them this morning.

He approached the car, gave it a long glance and whistled. "Nice wheels. Mind if I come along for the ride?"

She patted the passenger seat. "Sure. Hop in. I'm in the mood for a little adventure."

Ford shouldn't be in the mood for adventure, but unfortunately, he couldn't deny that he'd looked forward to today. After seeing her dressed in a blue, sleeveless, striped top that tied at the neck and showed a lot of bare arms and back, he also couldn't deny that a strong sense of awareness had begun to surface. The solid matching skirt that came to her thighs only made matters worse, and threatened to make him forget his goal.

This whole day trip was about information, not about his attraction to Kerry Roarke. This outing served only as a means to an end, a way to obtain information that could prove his uncle innocent. That was all it was, all it should be, and nothing more.

On that thought, Ford rounded the car and climbed into the passenger side. He powered the seat back to accommodate his legs and studied her for a moment. "You told me you never owned a Mustang."

She shrugged. "I don't own it. I rented it. It's all ours until tomorrow."

Ford didn't want to consider what tomorrow might bring. He was more interested in the here and now. And her. "What's on the agenda?"

She checked her mirrors, then steered down the drive. "Just a few sights I'd like to show you in the city."

As far as he was concerned, the best sight was sitting beside him—a portrait of prime woman. "Okay. You're the tour guide."

As they began their journey, Ford learned two very important things in a brief time—San Francisco streets qualified as an amusement ride, although he didn't exactly find them amusing. And Kerry Roarke enjoyed driving fast. She skipped the infamous Lombard Street and opted to take him down a less traveled but equally crooked road—laughing all the way. She traveled through Chinatown past the open-air markets and eventually drove down California Street and into the financial district. Ford noted an immediate change in her when they passed by a historic-looking high-rise.

"That's Ashton-Lattimer," she said with a wave of her hand and a frown on her face. "My workplace."

Ford sent a cursory glance in the building's direction—the place where Spencer had been murdered. Maybe that was the reason for her sudden mood change. "Looks like it's been around for a while."

"It has, since right after the big quake."

"How long have you been there?"

"Entirely too long."

"I'm guessing you don't like your job."

They stopped for a light, her grip tight on the wheel. "Not particularly."

"You liked what you did before your boss was killed?"

"The job was fine. But as I told you last night, I can't say the same for my boss."

Ford wondered if she'd been jilted by his grandfather or just disgusted. "That must be tough, working for someone you don't like."

"I managed. And now for the best part of the tour."

Deciding to drop the subject for now, Ford sat back while Kerry took him on a scenic drive around a road that spanned the coastline. Again she resumed tour guide status, pointing out various sights in the city. But all Ford could see were the slight strands of hair raining down from her ponytail, the movement of her lips as she talked, the line of her arm and outline of breasts. Several times he had to force his gaze away from her and back on the sights.

After they'd completed the scenic drive, Kerry took him to Fisherman's Wharf where they strolled past shops concentrated in an area that was twice the size of downtown Crawley. Several times he laid a palm on the small of her back, as if they were any other couple out for a routine Saturday excursion. And several times he'd been tempted to kiss her. He definitely had to hand it to his grandfather—the lying bastard had good taste in assistants. And maybe this particular one had suffered through enough of his disregard for women that she'd taken matters into her own hands. But Kerry Roarke a murderer? He was still having one helluva time believing that, more than before.

Following an hour of acting like serious tourists, Kerry ushered Ford back into the car for a trip to Golden Gate Park. He soon found himself seated in a rowboat on an emerald-green lake, picnic basket onboard, oars in hand, facing a woman who looked every bit the celestial being. The noon sky had become overcast, causing Kerry to discard the sunglasses. Now Ford had a first-rate view of her violet eyes, and he couldn't think of anything more fatal to his control. Except when she crossed her legs and the skirt crept higher. Not to mention the view of her cleavage and breasts that he suspected were unencumbered beneath the top. If it cooled off any more, he'd probably know for sure. If he didn't cool off, he might try to find out with his hands.

Unaware of Ford's questionable thoughts, Kerry gestured to an impressive waterfall and propped the basket on her lap, preventing him from staring at her thighs. "Row over there and we can have some lunch."

Ford complied, skirting a paddleboat navigated by a teenage boy who seemed more interested in making out with his girlfriend than steering.

"Maybe someone should tell them to find a backseat," Kerry said as she spread a blue-checked tablecloth on the deck between them.

He returned her smile, although he had to force it around a vision of finding himself in the backseat of a Mustang—with her. "Yeah. Must be nice, being so young that you don't give a damn what anyone thinks."

After they pulled alongside a rock border separating the falls from the lake, Kerry pulled out two bright-pink plastic plates and handed him one. "I can't say that I've ever been quite that carefree."

"You've never necked on a paddleboat?"

"No. Have you?"

"Nope. Not too many of those in Nebraska."

"Nebraska? I thought you lived in Kansas."

Oh, hell. "I went to college in Nebraska. I was a little more daring at that age, more inclined to take risks."

Fortunately for Ford, Kerry seemed satisfied with that answer. "I'm originally from Seattle," she said as she went back to unloading the basket.

"How did you end up in San Francisco?"

"Blind luck, actually. When I decided to leave home, I got out a map, closed my eyes and pointed. San Francisco was the largest city closest to my finger."

Although she sounded amused, Ford saw a flash of pain cross her expression before she lowered her gaze. "Didn't your folks have something to say about that?"

"My mother died when I was fourteen. My dad died before I was born, in a logging accident."

"I'm sorry to hear that. Who raised you after she died?"

"My stepfather was my legal guardian, but I can't say he was all that active in my raising. He had a lot of money but very little compassion, so I got out from under his thumb as soon as I was old enough to survive on my own. He was always taking but rarely giving back. I've found that to be true with most wealthy men."

An accurate description of Spencer Ashton. But Ford wanted to tell her that not all men with means bore that label. "That must be tough, settling in a strange city, alone."

"It wasn't so tough after I met Millie."

"Millie?"

"Millicent Vandiver, my landlady. She's a former actress and very dramatic, but she has a heart of gold. She took me in and I've been with her ever since. She's the one who packed our lunch."

"You'll have to thank her for me."

"Maybe you can meet her and thank her yourself. She's quite a character." Kerry popped open one plastic container and held it out to him. "Hope you like chicken salad."

Ford reached inside the container and took two skinny finger sandwiches. "Look's fine."

Kerry took one for herself then resealed the lid. "Be glad she didn't make her usual goose liver pate." She wrinkled her nose. "I never have acquired a taste for that."

Neither had Ford. "Did she pack anything to drink?" His mouth was dry, but not from thirst. He'd had a hard time keeping his eyes off Kerry's breasts every time she leaned over to take something from the basket.

"Let's see." Again she bent forward, causing Ford to shift on the bench as she withdrew a carafe. She twisted the lid open and sniffed it. "Mimosas. Although I'm betting there's a lot more champagne than orange juice."

"It's kind of early to be indulging in alcohol." Especially if he wanted to keep his wits about him.

She poured the liquid into a blue plastic cup and handed it to him. "A big guy like you can handle one little drink."

Ford was having one hell of a time handling being so close to her. "Okay, but just one." Being close to her made him drunk enough.

They ate in silence for a time before Kerry asked, "What about your parents?"

A sorry subject he didn't really want to broach. "Both dead." As far as he was concerned, they were.

"I'm sorry we have that in common. It's tough, isn't it?"

"I did okay. My grandparents raised me." A lie since his grandmother died four years before he was born. But he didn't want to mention his uncle for fear he might slip up again.

She offered him some grapes. "Dessert?"

"No, thanks. I'm full." Another lie. Skimpy sandwiches just didn't cut it, but he could grab something later at the hotel. At the moment he envisioned grabbing Kerry at the hotel. He sat back and studied the skies, hoping to clear those images from his head. "Looks like rain."

"I know that's how it looks, but it rarely rains in August."

Right after she said it, a few drops fell from the sky. "Must be one of those rare times," Ford said.

She laughed. "I guess so."

Ford picked up one oar, prepared to head back to the rental dock, when Kerry laid a palm on his hand. "Let's stay for a while. It won't last long." She turned her face toward the graying skies the same as he had. "Besides, I love rain."

He couldn't deny that he appreciated the way she looked right then, drops of water forming on her face and tracking a path down her slender throat. He visually followed one of those drops as it disappeared beneath the knit top. As far as urges went, he had a strong one. He wanted to follow that drop's path with his mouth, trace the line with his tongue—and keep going.

Then the deluge came, hard pelting rain, yet Kerry didn't seem to care at all, unlike most of the other boaters who had long ago headed back in. Without warning, she moved beside him on the narrow bench, their thighs and arms touching. She turned her face to his, and Ford realized he was quickly approaching a point of no return, and facing plenty of regret if he gave in. He had no choice in the matter when she reached down and pulled the tablecloth out of the basket, then draped it around them like a cocoon.

She looked up at him and said, "This gives us a little protection from the elements."

Ford needed more than a flimsy tablecloth to protect him from doing something stupid. Here he was, soaked to the skin with an incredible woman, their faces only inches apart. So he did the only thing he could think to do at the moment—kiss her soundly.

He wrapped his arms around her, and she laid one hand on his thigh, her other hand sliding through the hair at his nape. The rain continued to fall, and so did Ford's conviction to avoid this very thing. He couldn't explain why he couldn't seem to get enough of her. Couldn't explain why he slid his palm up the curve of her hip. Couldn't explain why he kept going beneath her shirt to touch her waist. Her flesh was warm in contrast with the chill of the sudden wind. She was so soft against his callused hand, her tongue smooth as it moved in sync with his. A mix of instinct and need caused him to move his hand higher over her rib cage. And then she flinched.

Reality thrust Ford back into coherency and he broke the kiss. Kerry stared at him for a moment, her eyes as hazy as his brain. She touched her fingertips to her mouth, as if she didn't quite believe what they'd done. "Maybe we should go now," she said, her voice little more than a whisper.

"That's a good idea." His voice sounded gruff and slightly angry. He *was* angry—at himself.

She clutched the wrap tightly around her and glanced away, but not before he saw wariness in her eyes. If he didn't slow down, he was going to blow his plans to hell and back. Worse, he might even forget what he needed from her, and that sure as hell wasn't taking her to bed and forgetting all about Grant's predicament. "I'm sorry, Kerry. I didn't mean to—"

"Don't apologize, Ford. We're both to blame. But I just want you to know that I'm not prone to this kind of behavior."

Although he should be suspicious—especially if she had been Spencer's mistress—he sensed she was being sincere. But his instincts about women hadn't always been on target, and he couldn't afford to let down his guard. "I guess we both just got a little carried away again."

"That we did." She tossed aside the tablecloth. "Now shall I row, or would you prefer to do it?"

He only wanted to do one thing right now—kiss her again. And again. He grabbed up the oars, thinking he should pound some sense into his head. "I'll do it. Might help work off some steam."

She smiled a self-conscious smile, revealing the dimple that threatened to shred the last of Ford's sanity. "I suppose the tour is now officially over."

Ford pushed off the rocks with the oar. "I thought we might have dinner later."

"We'll have to change first since I'm wet."

He sent a long glance down her body. "I kind of like you wet."

The comment hung over them for a long span of silence until she finally said, "Then you should like me a whole lot right now."

Problem was, Ford did like her. A lot. He couldn't let that sway him. He couldn't want more from her than a few answers. But damned if he didn't.

By the time Kerry pulled up Millie's driveway, she wanted to scream. How could she have been such an idiot? And what had possessed her to toss away common sense to the point that she'd allowed Ford Matthews, a man she knew so little about, to kiss her until she'd almost completely forgotten herself? And in a rowboat, no less. At least she was thankful he'd stopped before things had gotten totally out of hand. Of course, when he'd come so close to her scar, she'd automatically tensed. An ugly reminder of her past, one she wasn't ready for him to see, or feel, just yet. But she still felt the effects of his kiss, of his touch. She also recognized he was the first man she'd trusted enough to welcome the intimacy since that one horrible experience ten years before. Unwise, probably. Unwelcome, no. In fact, she wanted more of what they'd shared today. She wanted to feel that alive again.

After putting the car in park, Kerry turned to find Ford staring at the Victorian house, surprise in his expression. "That's a pretty impressive place. Part of the tour?"

"Actually, this is where I live."

His surprise melted into shock. "You're kidding."

"No. I've been here with Millie for ten years. Her father built it after fire destroyed the original."

He skimmed a hand over his jaw. "Is it as nice inside as it outside?"

"Would you like to come in and see? I'm sure Millie would love to meet you as soon as she returns from her investment club meeting."

He glanced down at his rain-soaked jeans. "I'm not exactly presentable right now."

Millie wouldn't mind, that much Kerry knew. But she thought it might be best if they parted company for the time being since they would be alone for another hour or so. Otherwise, she might be tempted to invite Ford into her bedroom. And the way she was feeling right now, a little lightheaded and totally enamored, that wouldn't be a good idea. "Tell you what. You go back to the hotel and change, and we'll meet back up for dinner."

"Okay. Just point me in the right direction."

"You can take the car. I'll write down how to get back to the hotel, and basically you just follow that route to get back here."

"Only one problem. I'm not authorized to drive your rental, and I don't have my license back yet."

"I trust you. Just don't run over any pedestrians along the way. Besides, it's not far at all. Just a few blocks."

"Are you sure?"

"Unless you can't drive anything other than a truck."

He released a low, deep laugh. "I can hold my own in a car."

Kerry just wished he was holding her. But tonight... Well, tonight she planned to have him hold her, and possibly more. She would play it by ear and see how things progressed between them. "Fine. Be back here at 7:00 p.m. You can meet my landlady then."

"Sounds good."

He looked good. No. He looked great, even drenched. Better than any man had a right to look, Kerry decided. She anticipated looking her fill later. "See you then."

Before she left the car, she leaned over and kissed his cheek. Yet when she pulled away, their gazes held for a long moment. That intangible chemistry came back to roost, and once more their lips came together in a fiery joining. They kissed for a long time, stopping only now and then to draw a breath. Kissed as if their very survival depended on it.

After a time, Ford cupped her jaw in his large palm, slid his hand down her throat. As ridiculous as it seemed, Kerry wanted him to keep going. She wanted him to touch her breasts, to know what that would be like to have that experience with a man that she wanted more than anything. A pleading sound escaped from her mouth and she guided his palm down to her breast, showing him what she needed. At the moment, she didn't really care what he might think of her, as long as he touched her. And he did, thoroughly, rubbing his thumb back and forth on her nipple until it formed a tight knot.

She shifted against the surge of heat between her thighs, wishing the console were gone and she could be closer to him.

Wishing for once that she'd been braver and invited him int
the house. Wishing he would touch her beneath her shirt.

Ford broke the kiss and rested his lips against her ear as h
continued to fondle her through the fabric. "We shouldn't b
doing this."

Funny, Kerry was thinking exactly the opposite. "I know.

He kept his hand in motion despite his protest. "You'r
driving me crazy, Kerry."

"I could say the same thing about you."

All too soon, he took his hand away and collapsed bac
against the seat. "I've decided I'm not much better than tha
kid on the paddleboat."

Kerry tugged the band from her ponytail and finger
combed her hair. "Oh, I'm willing to wager you're much bet
ter than that kid. Experience is bound to count for something.
She felt like a vamp, uninhibited and ready to take a few mor
chances.

Ford finally looked at her and groaned. "You are trying t
kill me, aren't you?"

She frowned. "I don't know what you mean."

He reached over and sifted a lock through his fingertip
"You took your hair down. You look sexy as hell. And that
making things really *hard* on me."

She didn't dare look lower to confirm that fact. "Thank you

"Wear it down tonight."

"I will. Any other requests?"

"Yeah. Be sure to wear a turtleneck and pants. Otherwis
I'm not going to responsible for my actions."

She laughed. "I'm probably going to nix the turtleneck, b
I will be wearing some sort of a sweater. And you need to brin
a jacket because the nights in San Francisco can be rather cool

He leaned over the console, kissed her cheek, then whi
pered, "I'll keep you warm."

Kerry shivered at the thought, pleasantly so. "I'm looking forward to it."

After jotting down directions to the hotel on the back of the rental agreement, she grabbed the picnic basket from the backseat, opened the door and stepped outside while Ford did the same. They met in front of the hood, and before she could head toward the house, he pulled her back into his arms and she immediately dropped the basket onto the drive without a second thought. He kissed her again. This time their bodies completely melded together. She could feel every inch of him, from thighs to chest and everything in between. Definitely everything. Five more minutes and she *would* invite him into her bedroom, and quite possibly her bed.

The sound of a honking horn startled Kerry and sent her backward, away from Ford. She looked to her right to see Millie's ancient roadster waiting at the curb.

"That's Millie," Kerry said. "You'll have to back out before she can get up the drive."

"Not a problem." He gave her a crooked grin. "I probably need to get in the car anyway, before I totally lose my respectability."

This time Kerry did look. She just couldn't help herself. "I see." And she did.

"Yeah. I guess you do. But that's your fault."

She raised her gaze to his face. "Not all my fault, but I'm willing to take responsibility."

He took her hand, turned it over and kissed her palm. "I'm willing to compromise on the responsibility if you are."

"Oh, yes. I'm all about compromise." Right now she was all about being a mass of mercurial need.

After following Ford back to the driver's side, she leaned in and gave him another quick kiss before he closed the door. "I'll see you later. Call me if you get lost."

Lost was exactly how Kerry felt at the moment. Lost to a gorgeous Kansas farm boy. Lost to her own feminine urges for the very first time.

Now she had to decide exactly how far she would go to satisfy them.

# Four

Ford had no trouble finding his way back to Kerry. In fact, he'd spent the better part of an hour pacing with anticipation, and chastising himself for losing control again. Now he was sitting in the drive behind a gaudy ancient blue roadster, putting himself through the paces of a mental pep talk.

Tonight he would have dinner with her. He would slowly work his way into a conversation about Spencer's murder. He would keep his hands to himself.

That last directive was bugging the hell out of him because he wasn't sure he could follow through. Kerry Roarke was doing things to him no woman had done in a long time. He'd barely known her for twenty-four hours and already he was thinking things he should not be thinking. Considering things he should not be considering. He would just have to keep reminding himself of his mission, and remember that his uncle was wasting away in jail with a murder charge hanging over his head. And Ford could be the only person to save him from that fate—if Kerry cooperated.

He left the car and walked up the three steps, stopping to survey the grounds before knocking, as much out of procrastination as interest. The paint on the home's facade had begun to peel, and the flower beds had fallen into disarray. He also noticed that the porch's support seemed to be leaning and needed to be bolstered. Other than those few things, the estate still looked refined and shouted money.

After another brief hesitation, he rang the bell and jingled the keys in his pocket. He was still on edge, even more so when a severe-looking elderly woman opened the door. *Flamboyant* immediately came to Ford's mind, from her overly made-up face and jet-black hair to her flowing red-and-purple calf-length dress.

She eyed him curiously for a long moment before saying, "You must be Kerry's young man." She sounded polite but she didn't seem that pleased to see him.

"Yes, ma'am. Ford Matthews. And you must be Mrs. Vandiver." He stuck out his hand, which she took briefly for a delicate shake.

"You may call me Millie." She swept a hand in an almost theatrical gesture, her smile painted on as if also part of the act. "Right this way."

Ford stepped inside the foyer and followed behind her into a musty formal living room. She turned to him and said, "You may sit there," indicating an ancient gold sofa. While Ford settled onto the couch, Millie took a stiff-looking red chair across from him. The fabric was a near-match to the dress and her lips, contrasting with her pale skin. He couldn't quit peg her age, but from the looks of the myriad service awards lining the walls, many dating back decades, he'd guess she was somewhere around seventy.

Scooting to the edge of the chair, she studied him again. "Kerry tells me you're a farmer."

"Yes, I am."

"Do you make a decent living?"

If she only knew. "Yeah, I do all right."

She sat back, crossed one bony leg over the other and clasped her hands together in her lap. "Exactly what are your intentions, Ford?"

"I'm not sure I understand the question." He did understand he was about to get the third degree.

"What do you plan to do this evening with my charge?"

Her tone held a note of suspicion, like she'd channeled his questionable thoughts. "We're going out for dinner."

"And after that?"

"I'm not sure. We haven't discussed it."

She leaned forward and leveled her rheumy blue eyes on him. "May I speak frankly to you, Ford?"

Although she'd posed it as a question, Ford recognized he had no choice but to hear her out. Draping an arm over the back of the sofa, he tried to appear relaxed when he was anything but. "Sure."

"Kerry Ann is a very special young woman. She might appear tough on the exterior, but that is only a front. Inside she is very vulnerable. Wounded, if you will."

Wounded? Ford's curiosity increased. "How do you mean?"

"It's not my place to say, but you must take my word for it. If she trusts you, she'll tell you. And if she does, then you should feel honored. Trust doesn't come easily for her, with good reason."

A good dose of guilt settled over Ford. "I understand."

"No, you don't. Not yet. But if you are lucky, you will. And one more thing."

"Shoot."

"I have protected her for many years, and I plan to continue to do so for as long as I am living. I will do anything, *anything*, to make certain she is not harmed. I suggest you keep that in mind. You certainly don't want to cross me." *And if you do, you won't live to tell about it,* her expression seemed to say.

One helluva scary woman, Ford decided. And it suddenly dawned on him that maybe this frail-looking lady could be a killer. Maybe she'd been the one to take out his grandfather in order to protect Kerry. A possibility, even if it was remote. Or maybe he just didn't want to believe that Kerry Roarke had been involved in Spencer's death. Only time would tell, if they ever got out of there so he could find out. "Do you think maybe Kerry's ready?"

She glanced at the clock set in the middle of a white marble mantel. "You are several minutes early." Again she nailed him with another severe glare. "I've always admired promptness, but then perhaps you are more eager than you should be."

Damn. Ford hadn't gotten this much cross examination since Grant had caught him playing with matches in the barn when he was ten years old. "I promise you I'll treat Kerry well."

"I am going to hold you to that promise, young man. That you can count on." Gripping the chair's arms, she pushed herself up slowly. "I shall go and see if she has completed her preparations."

"I'm here, Millie."

At the sound of Kerry's feather-soft voice coming from behind him, Ford realized he wasn't at all ready. He immediately came to his feet, turned and almost dropped where he stood when he caught sight of her standing in the entry wearing second-skin, low-riding jeans and a V-neck burgundy sweater than didn't quite meet her waistband, providing a glimpse of bare flesh at her belly. Falling to his knees would be a damned bad idea in front of the matriarch of the mansion.

Kerry slipped her purse strap over her slender shoulder. "Are you ready to roll, Ford?"

Oh, yeah, almost spilled out of his mouth before he had the presence of mind to stop it. "Sure. If you are."

"I am." After crossing the room, she planted a kiss on Millie's cheek. "Don't wait up, okay?"

Millie sent her a sour look. "I don't intend to do any such thing. You're a grown woman, Kerry Ann. I trust you." She stared at Ford, hard. "I trust you will take good care of her, young man?"

Ford had the sudden urge to salute. "Yes, ma'am. You can count on it."

"And I'm counting on you to do that very thing. Now, both of you, run along. Have a nice time."

But not too nice a time, Ford thought as he followed Kerry out the front door. Millie might not have said it, but her tone indicated she was thinking it. Sound advice all the way around.

Ford tossed Kerry the car key. "You drive around this maze of a city."

Kerry tossed him a sexy smile. "I plan to."

Five minutes in her presence and she was already driving him crazy. He bordered on crossing over into complete madness when they settled into the car and her perfume hit him full force. She smelled like a hint of flowers mixed with fruit, something he might normally consider an odd combination, but not on her. He imagined she tasted as good, too. All over.

Twitching in his seat, he snapped his seat belt closed while Kerry lowered the roof on the car now that the threat of rain had subsided. The sun was on the verge of setting while Ford was on the verge of kissing her. He decided that was the last thing he needed to do and promised himself to refrain for now.

At least this time, Kerry didn't make a move to kiss him,

either. Instead, she started the car, put it in gear and backed out of the steep drive like a pro. "I hope Millie didn't give you a hard time," she said as she turned onto the street.

"Not too bad. I'm not sure she likes me."

"Millie likes everyone. She's just cautious."

"I kind of figured that out."

She sent him a glance as they stopped at a light. "What did she say to you exactly?"

"Just that I needed to be careful with you."

"She's very protective of me."

"I gathered that right away. Hopefully I put her mind at ease."

She rolled through the light and turned sharply onto a major street. "Don't worry about Millie. The important thing is that I know you're not going to hurt me."

God, he didn't want to hurt her, but he realized he could. Especially if this whole theory about her being Spencer's mistress was in error. "So where are you taking me tonight?"

"To one of my favorite restaurants in one of my favorite places. It's in an area known as The Haight."

Hippie haven, that's how Ford had termed Kerry's old stomping grounds. In many ways that was still true, she realized. But the place had transformed from a flower-child hangout to a trendy hotspot with shops and restaurants, although it still retained a lot of its sixties roots. Kerry knew the back alleys and communal existence very well. She'd spent a lot of days in those places upon her arrival in San Francisco. She'd learned quite a bit about hard living during that time in her life, some of which she still carried with her—on her body and in her soul.

She wanted to tell Ford about that part of her past, minus the really horrible part, but she experienced the burden of being labeled "homeless" and not knowing how people would react to that. Whenever she'd chosen to be honest with her co-workers, some had been accepting and sympathetic, others had been judgmental and treated her as damaged goods. Some saw her as an as easy mark, and that had included Spencer Ashton.

She decided not to contaminate the conversation right now. Dinner had gone so well that she wanted to keep the mood light. Ford had been very pleased that she'd taken him to a place where he could dine on a burger and fries. She had been pleased to have pleased him. But now that dinner was over, she had to decide what would happen next. If she went according to plan, a drive to another special place would be first on the agenda. What happened after that would be up to Ford.

Ford insisted on paying the bill again and that bothered her somewhat. She wasn't broke even though finances were tight. Real estate courses had drained most of her savings but she planned to eventually get ahead as soon as she'd completed the program in two weeks. Then she could quit her current job after she obtained her license and signed on as an agent, concentrating on her dream—finding families permanent homes, something she hadn't really had, aside from her home with Millie. But it still hadn't been the same, because it wasn't hers. One day, she would have a home of her own, and maybe even someone to share it with.

She glanced at Ford and wished that he could be the man of her dreams. Unfortunately, that wasn't reality. Soon he would be leaving, but she refused to think about that now. She planned to make the best of their time together and hopefully restore herself into the land of the living under his guidance. If he happened to be willing. She would just have to convince him that's what she wanted. No strings attached, just memories to make.

Kerry and Ford left the restaurant and strolled up the sidewalk toward the pay-by-the-hour parking lot. Along the way she pointed out the surfer shop with several colorful boards on display in the window. "This might interest you," she said, followed by a laugh.

He frowned. "Why would you think that? I've never even tried surfing. Not many beaches near where I live."

She paused and faced him. "Because when I first saw you in the bar, I thought you looked like a surfer with that blond hair and tanned body. Or is that just a farmer's tan you have?"

His grin gave the streetlight some serious competition. "Are you asking me if I'm tanned all over?"

"Yes, I guess that's what I'm asking."

"Do you want to see?"

Frankly, she did. "It's a little cool to be taking off your shirt." But not cool enough to rid Kerry of some serious heat prompted by that thought.

"You're right, but if you decide you want proof, all you have to do is ask."

She just might ask before the night was over. "Okay, I will. Now let's get back to the car. I have another place I want to show you."

"Okay. You're the boss."

Taking Kerry by surprise, Ford leaned over and kissed her cheek. A simple gesture, but one that touched her in complex ways. "What was that for?"

"For being such a great tour guide. I owe you a lot."

"This whole experience with you has been a pleasure." More pleasure than she'd expected. Hopefully more pleasure to come. "But it's not over yet, unless you're tired and want to go to bed." She regretted the comment that came out sounding like suggestive innuendo. "I meant to sleep."

Ford's provocative smile came into play slowly. "I don't want to sleep. In fact, I'm not tired at all."

"Good." She hooked her arm into the bend of his arm. "Then let's get on with the second phase of the evening."

By the time they made the block, they had their arms wrapped securely around each other's waists, as if they were any other couple out on a date. Kerry felt completely comfortable with this man, totally relaxed, a huge step in the right direction. She couldn't say the same for Ford when he tensed as they came upon a lanky teenage boy with tattered clothes, listless eyes and his hand out.

"Could you spare a few bucks?" the teen said, his voice tentative and almost apologetic.

Suddenly thrust back in time, Kerry did the only thing she could do. She released her hold on Ford's arm and dug through her purse for a ten-dollar bill and a card. She held both up before handing them over. "I'll give you this as long as you promise me no drugs. What's your name?"

"Joe." The boy's gaze faltered. "No drugs. I just want something to eat."

"I understand, Joe." Kerry handed over the money and the card. "You'll find the address for a shelter where you can get a bath and clean clothes. Tell Rosie I sent you. She might even be able to find you a job. How old are you?"

"Seventeen."

Kerry wondered if he was lying about his age because he didn't look a day over fifteen, if that. "Good luck, Joe. And get some help. The streets are no place to be, even for a guy."

Finally he smiled. A small one, but a smile all the same. "Thanks. I'll try."

Ford had stood by silently during the exchange. He remained quiet all the way back to the car and during the drive across the Golden Gate Bridge and up into the hills that comprised the Marin Headlands. Kerry accepted that silence for now, yet knowing the time would come when she would have to offer an explanation, because she knew he would eventually ask.

After she parked in the pull-off spot that offered a spectacular view of the city, Kerry left the car and Ford followed her lead. She opened the trunk and retrieved two blankets, a thick one to cover the ground, the other to shelter them against the chilly night air. Kerry was definitely chilled, but only in part from the weather. Ford's continued coolness toward her made her nervous and fearful that once he knew the details of her past, their evening together could come to an abrupt halt. She didn't want it to end, not yet.

Ford had turned his back on her to stare at the amazing panorama—the outline of the bridge, the water shimmering beneath the three-quarter moon and the city lights twinkling in the distance. Or maybe he was simply avoiding her.

No longer able to stand his silence, she moved to a spot not far away from him on the edge leading to the cliffs. With one hand, she spread the thicker blanket over the grass as best she could and kept the other clutched against her chest. "The view's breathtaking, isn't it?" she said as she studied his strong profile and his lips that formed a tight line.

"Yeah, it is." He still had yet to look at her.

Kerry lowered herself onto the blanketed ground, hoping upon hope he would join her. "It's a lot more comfortable down here."

He turned toward her, his thumbs hooked in the pockets of his black leather jacket. Even in the muted light, he was an imposing, beautiful presence silhouetted against the night sky.

Kerry released the breath she'd been holding when he took his place beside her, yet not quite as close as she would have liked. He rested his forearms on his bent knees, his hands laced together. She sensed he wanted to speak, and he confirmed that by saying, "You handled that kid well. I'm not sure

I would've given him money, though. Especially if he might spend it on drugs."

"He needed some kind of a break, probably even more than the money. I just hope he finds a safe place to land, at least for the night."

Ford sent her a brief glance before he turned his attention back to the scenery. "How did you know about the homeless shelter?"

Exactly what she'd been expecting, and dreading. "I've volunteered there before." Only a partial truth. Once upon a terrible time, she'd temporarily resided there.

"I don't understand why a kid would want to live on the streets."

Kerry reached down and pulled the other blanket over her as if it might provide some protection from his possible reaction. "I'm sure he doesn't want to live this way. He's probably a runaway."

"Running away isn't the answer."

Sometimes it was the only answer. "Try telling that to a teenager who honestly believes he or she doesn't have a choice."

Finally he looked at her straight-on. "I have a hard time believing that things would be so bad at home that someone feels escaping is the only option."

"Believe me, it can be that bad. So bad that you don't think there is another way. You feel so trapped you can't see beyond getting out."

When she saw unease in his expression, Kerry realized she had revealed too much. He confirmed that by saying, "You sound like you know all about it."

Now was the time to tell him the truth and accept his response, whatever that response might be. "I do know because I ran away. And for one solid year, I was homeless."

She saw momentary shock in his expression and possibly sympathy. "How old were you?"

"Sixteen."

"So young and on your own?"

"Yeah. I came to a point where I thought I had no choice but to leave. My stepfather was cruel and verbally abusive. My mother never seemed to notice it when she was alive, or maybe she didn't want to see it. Then one day I stood up to him and he backhanded me across the face. I honestly thought he might try to kill me. Later that night, I packed a bag, stole a hundred dollars from his wallet and caught a bus for San Francisco."

"And he never came looking for you?"

Kerry released a mirthless laugh. "I doubt it. Many times he told me he ought to kick me out. I was worthless and a burden. Funny thing, I was a straight-A student, never in trouble, but I couldn't seem to do anything to please him. I stopped trying."

"I'm sorry," he said, and he sounded that way, as well.

"It's not your fault. Besides, I met Millie a year later, and she was the best thing that ever happened to me."

"How exactly did you meet her?"

That circumstance was getting into territory Kerry wasn't sure she was ready to cover. She decided to settle on a condensed version. "One night I got into a fight and ended up in the hospital with a few scrapes and bruises. A nurse in the E.R. knew Millie liked to help runaways, so she called her. Millie took me in that night, and I ended up staying. She home-schooled me because we didn't want the hassle of having to explain guardianship, and then I eventually got my G.E.D. I also went to community college and majored in business. Unfortunately, I only received an associate's degree so my job options were limited. That's why I've been attending real estate school in the evenings."

He studied her for a time before saying, "I admire you, Kerry. I don't know how you survived on your own at that age."

"That experience made me much tougher," she said. "Survival is the name of the game, and living alone on the streets taught me that." It had also taught her caution, and a definite lack of trust, especially in men. Spencer Ashton had only cemented that mistrust. But Ford Matthews was different, that's what her instincts were telling her. She felt as if she could sincerely trust both them and him.

"At least you did get a decent job," Ford said after a time.

Some job. "Unfortunately, working for an indecent lecher."

"Lecher?"

"That sums up Spencer Ashton in a nutshell."

"What did he do to you?" He looked and sounded angry.

Kerry plucked at a blade of grass and shredded it. "Aside from pawing me, he used to stage these little lunches under the guise of business meetings. Some were even out of the city. When I wouldn't *cooperate,* he buried me in work and refused to give me a raise. I honestly think he believed I would finally give in."

"There are laws against sexual harassment. Why didn't you report him or at least quit?"

"First of all, I needed the money. Second, Spencer Ashton had a lot of power and connections. Even after his death he's still revered as a city leader." She sighed. "And God forgive me for saying this, I understand why someone would want him dead. But I think they might have arrested the wrong person."

Ford leveled a hard stare on her. "Why do you think that?"

"I just do." She couldn't imagine a man as polite as Grant Ashton would be a killer. For months he'd tried to get in to see his father, his anger never directed at her when she'd refused to allow him access, per Spencer's instructions. But Spencer had been known for his charm, so she could be wrong about his son. After all, he was an Ashton, and that name alone made her cringe.

Ford draped his arm around her shoulder and pulled her close to his side. "After hearing about this bastard, I agree with you. I don't think anyone would have blamed anyone for getting even."

Kerry reveled in his warmth, in his compassion. "Oh, I did get even in my own way." Ways she was too embarrassed to tell him. Nothing major enough to risk ending up in the unemployment line, but a few childish things to give her some measure of satisfaction. Proof positive that you could take the girl off the streets, but you couldn't take the street out of the girl.

Ford surveyed her face from forehead to chin, his expression sympathetic, not cynical. "I'm sorry for what you've had to endure, with both your situation at home and with your boss."

"Again, it's not your fault." She reached up and formed her palm to his shadowed jaw. "I've learned to tolerate what life throws me, Ford. I've had to. But I've also learned not to dwell on the past. You just have to move on, otherwise you find yourself too afraid to go forward." And that hit home right then more than any other time in her life. Tonight she refused to be afraid. She only wanted to experience true freedom from fear, and she knew that Ford Matthews could be the man to help her over that fear.

On that thought, she brushed a kiss over his cheek, then one along his jaw, making her way to the corner of his mouth and stopping there. A subtle suggestion, but it worked. He inclined his head and kissed her, carefully at first, until care gave way to carnal.

After pulling the quilt from her shoulders and tossing it aside, Kerry took Ford with her back onto the remaining blanket without disrupting the kiss. She kept her arms tightly around him while his hands roved down her sides. She wanted so much more, enough to break the kiss and tug the sweater over her head. While he watched, with one hand she reached up to unfasten the bra's front closure, with the other she guided his palm to her breast. He touched her with innate gentleness, working her nipple between his fingertips for a time before replacing his hand with his mouth.

Kerry tuned in to every sensation, every light flick of his tongue across her nipple, every gentle pull of his lips as she stared up at the misty sky, her hands buried in his thick hair. The infamous San Francisco fog had begun to appear above them in swirls, giving the moon a muted, dreamlike glow. Everything about this night had taken on a surreal quality, but the overwhelming need she now experienced was extremely real.

Ford lifted his head from her breast and stared at her a long moment. "You are so damn beautiful."

Kerry truly felt beautiful when she noted the approval in his eyes, but that soon turned to concern when he traced a fingertip along the scar spanning from her rib cage to beneath her left breast. "What happened here?"

She'd tried to defend herself and lost. Lost what little had remained of her sense of security, and her innocence. "I'd rather not talk about that now." Doing so would only resurrect more bitter memories. Tonight she only wanted to make more memories. Good ones.

After shoving the leather jacket from Ford's broad shoulders, Kerry worked it off his arms and tossed it aside. Then she pulled the tails of his shirt from his jeans, released the buttons and opened it wide to smooth her hands over his chest.

Although he looked somewhat troubled, she also saw a definite fire in his blue eyes. "Kerry, if we don't stop now, I might not be able to stop."

"I don't want you to stop." She locked into his gaze. "I

don't need any promises. I only need you to touch me again. Everywhere."

As if his last shred of control had snapped, Ford pulled her to face him, molding his hands to her scalp, holding her in place to accept the provocative play of his tongue against hers. After rolling her onto her back, he moved partially atop her and she could feel his erection pressing against her pelvis. Could feel his heart pounding against her breast where their bodies met without any barriers between them.

Kerry wanted all the barriers gone. She wanted to know how it would feel to have him totally naked against her, inside her. She wanted to know all of him and in turn, learn how it felt to truly make love with a man without reservation or coercion.

He broke the kiss and once more rolled her to face him, settling her head against his shoulder, his warm breath breezing over her ear as he let go a mild oath in a harsh whisper. She celebrated her sudden sense of power. Rejoiced in the fact that she could take him so close to the edge. Only, she was following right behind him.

As Ford claimed her mouth in another tantalizing kiss, he parted her legs with his leg and rubbed against the apex of her thighs. The friction the denim created was both delicious and frustrating. She *needed* him to touch her without any clothing constraints. Emboldened by her own newly discovered empowerment, she took his hand from the bow of her hip and placed it on her abdomen where her low-riding jeans began below her navel. She hoped he would take the hint, take the initiative to make her wish come true. She feared she wouldn't get that wish when he pulled his leg from between hers. But when she felt the tug on the jeans' button, then the slide of her zipper, her optimism rose and so did her heart rate.

He kept one hand tangled in her hair and slid his other palm beneath the backside of her jeans, kneading her bottom through her panties. For Kerry, it wasn't quite enough so she pushed against him, letting him know exactly where she needed his attention though he probably did know. In order to be assured, she reached between them and tugged on his fly, only to have Ford catch her wrist before she had it undone.

Confused, she looked at him straight-on and saw indecision warring in his eyes, and something else she couldn't quite identify. "What's wrong?" she asked, her voice as shaky as her body.

Everything, Ford thought. As badly as he wanted to finish this, he didn't dare. As badly as he wanted to lose himself deep inside her, he couldn't do it. Not without losing what was left of his honor.

After tossing the discarded blanket over Kerry to cover her, he sat up, draped his forearms on his bent knees and lowered his eyes to the blanket beneath him.

Kerry's hand coming to rest on his shoulder was almost his undoing. "If you're worried about safety, I've taken care of that."

Ford glanced over his shoulder to see her holding a condom that he assumed had been in her pocket. She'd had all the bases covered, and protection hadn't even crossed his mind. That's how far gone he'd been. He didn't know how he had let things get so out of control. Easy. His head had been screwed up the moment he'd laid eyes on her. God help him, he had totally lost his mind, and had damn near lost his principles. Disregarded everything his uncle had taught him about respecting women. Behaved no better than his bastard of a grandfather.

"I'm not like him," he muttered without thought.

"Like who?"

"Spencer Ashton."

"I know you're not like him."

But he would be if he continued on this course. Right now he had something he had to ask her, before he revealed the truth. But he wasn't quite ready to face her, so he kept his back turned. "I need to know something, Kerry."

"If you want to know if I've been with a man, yes. But only one. And not by choice."

*Not by choice.* "You were…?" He couldn't even force himself to say the ugly word.

"Raped. For a long time I had a hard time saying it, too. But with the help of counselors and support groups and Millie, and even helping others, I've come a long way. It's something you don't ever forget, but you move on and get stronger as the years go by. At least I have. "

Ford's concerns increased and he had to ask, even if he feared the answer. "Was it Spencer Ashton?"

"No. It happened a long time ago, the night I went to live with Millie."

While she was still fending for herself on the streets, he realized. At the age of sixteen. He was only slightly relieved that his own flesh and blood hadn't physically assaulted her even though he'd terrorized her in many ways. He honestly wished he knew who had attacked her because right now he wouldn't think twice about killing him with his bare hands. He'd almost done that very thing to the jerk who'd tried to assault Abby years ago. Still, he'd known for years how much that event had affected Abby, even if she had rammed her knee into a strategic area before it had been too late, saving herself from Kerry's fate.

Ford shifted around to face Kerry again, thankful to find that she was completely dressed, her legs crossed before her, her hands fisted on her thighs. "I wish you would have told me sooner."

She hugged her arms to her breasts. "Would that have

made a difference? I mean, you stopped anyway." She inclined her head and stared at him. "Why did you stop?"

Now for the most difficult question of all, the entire reason why he'd met her in the first place. "I have to know something, Kerry. Did you have anything to do with Spencer Ashton's murder?"

Her eyes went wide. "Why would you even think that?"

"Because you said they've arrested the wrong man. That you found a way to get even with him. And considering what you've been through, I couldn't blame you if you did."

She let go a humorless laugh. "I got *even* as in I put salt in his coffee and scheduled his least favorite clients back-to-back. And for your information, I was at my real estate classes in the Bay area the night he was killed. I didn't even know about it until I came in the next morning." Awareness mixed with anger reflected from her face. "That's why you stopped, because you think I'm a murderer?"

He'd stopped because she had no idea who he was, but before he could spit it out, she uncrossed her legs and came to her knees, leaving very little space between them. "Let me tell you something, Ford. I watched a man die once, and he wasn't considered a good man. In fact, he was a drug dealer. Someone shot him only a few feet away from where I was hanging out. I'll never forget it. And even though I knew he destroyed lives, I also knew that no one had the right to take his life. Believe me, I could never kill anyone, even if I did hate them with a passion."

The sincerity in her expression confirmed what Ford had probably known all along—she hadn't been involved in any way in Spencer's death. She hadn't been his mistress, either. "I do believe you. And I'm sorry I doubted you."

She laid a palm on his arm. "Then can we stop talking and go back to where we were a few moments before?"

After he said what he needed to say, she would probably prefer he go back to Nebraska. "I sure as hell wish we could, but we can't."

She dropped her hand and released her frustration on a sigh. "Why not?"

"Because you don't know me. You don't know—"

She pressed a fingertip to his lips. "I know all that I need to know. I know you're a good man. I know that you've accepted what I've told you about my past without judgment. I also know that I trust you enough to make love with you. It's taken me a long time to be willing to take that step, and I want to do that with you."

She might as well have delivered a two-fisted punch to his gut. "You shouldn't trust me, Kerry, because I've been lying to you."

Her whole frame went rigid. "You're married."

"No, I'm not married. But I'm from Nebraska, not Kansas." The time had come for Ford to lay it on the line. He was more than willing to accept the consequences and her fury. He deserved that much and more. "I'm Spencer Ashton's grandson."

# Five

The exhilaration Kerry had experienced only a few short moments ago disappeared like the moonlight now obscured by the fog. She clutched the blanket to her chest as if it provided security as well as cover. "I don't understand," she said, although she feared she did.

"My name is Ford Ashton, not Ford Matthews. Grant is my uncle. He raised me. I came to California to try and find out anything I can to clear him."

The bitter truth came with a stinging bite of betrayal. "Are you telling me that our meeting—"

"Wasn't an accident. I thought you might have information."

"You thought I murdered him." Her voice held an edge of disbelief, exactly what she was feeling at the moment. Disbelief and so many more emotions crowding in on her all at once.

He lowered his gaze once more. "I was told you might be involved because you were Spencer's mistress."

"Whoever told you that was dead wrong. I hated the man."

"I know that now."

She released a caustic laugh. "This is so rich. You seduced me for the sake of information. I think I would've preferred to be held at knife point."

Finally he looked at her, remorse in his eyes. Probably just another lie, Kerry decided. "I never intended for this to happen," he said. "You have to believe that, even if you don't believe anything else."

"Believe you? Why should I believe anything you say when everything you've told me has been a lie?"

"Not everything. I do want you, more than I've wanted any woman I can think of. And I care about you, that's why this is so damn difficult. I didn't plan on that, either."

Kerry came to her feet and turned her back to Ford, refastened her bra then pulled the sweater over her head. She then grabbed up the discarded blanket with shaking hands without looking at him. She didn't want to see his eyes that she'd thought had been honest. See his hands that had touched her so thoroughly and gently.

All lies. What a fool she'd been to trust him. What a stupid, stupid fool.

He moved in front of her, the remaining blanket bunched in his strong arms. "I want to talk about this some more. I want to try to explain."

No explanation would be good enough, as far as Kerry was concerned. "I have a good mind to make you walk back into the city. But I'm more benevolent than that, although I'm not sure why."

He streaked a hand over the back of his neck. "I'm sorry. I don't know what else to say."

She wanted him to say this was all a bad dream. That what they had shared was as pure and true as it had seemed. "I don't care to hear anything else you have to say. I'm going to take you back to the hotel, and then I'm going to put you and this whole experience out of my mind." Probably not an easy feat because no matter how much he'd betrayed her, she would never forget him, or the feelings for him that had begun to creep into her heart and soul. Feelings for the man she'd thought him to be.

Without another word, Kerry turned away from Ford, headed back to the Mustang and tossed the blanket into the backseat while he did the same from the passenger side. Once they were in the car, she took off in a rush, not bothering to put up the top on the convertible, leaving behind what she'd thought would be good memories in the dust.

As they drove, the wind bit into her cheeks and numbed her face but unfortunately did nothing to numb the ache in her heart. She tuned the radio to a jazz station and turned the volume high, trying to drown out all the questions running through her mind, without success. Ford didn't speak at all, didn't even look at her, and she tried not to look at him although at times her eyes betrayed her. When they stopped at the booth on the bridge, he reached across her to hand the attendant the toll, his arm brushing slightly across her breast. She didn't want to react to that, didn't want to remember, but she did.

They continued on in silence as they entered the city and made their way up the hill, first to his hotel where she would leave him behind and then go home, where she might have a good cry. Once she reached the portico in front of the Royal-brook, she stopped the car alongside the curb but didn't bother to put it in Park. "Good night," she told him, followed by, "and good luck," muttering the words with little enthusiasm.

A few moments ticked off and still he didn't leave. She could feel his gaze on her and sensed he wanted to speak. She doubted he had anything to say that she wanted to hear.

"I'm sorry, Kerry."

Territory they'd already covered, and Kerry still had a hard time believing it. "Fine. You're sorry. Great."

"I hate what I've done to you. I hate myself for feeling like I had to do it. I was so damn desperate to get Grant cleared that I would've done anything to see that happen. That's my only excuse."

Admittedly, she knew all about desperation, but that didn't excuse him in her mind. "Desperate enough to lie to someone you didn't even know, and to assume the worst about her?"

"I'm not proud of it." He reached over and set the gear into Park. "But that much is the truth. Desperation drives people to do things they wouldn't normally do."

She shifted to face him and draped one arm over the steering wheel. "All you had to do was tell me the truth. I would have answered your questions."

"Would you if you'd known I'm an Ashton?"

Probably not, Kerry decided. "I guess we'll never know, will we?"

He rubbed a hand over his jaw. "I just want you to know that I've never done anything like this before."

And she had never done with any man what she had done with him. "What, pretend you're someone you're not? Or pretend you want someone in order to get what you need?"

"You're an incredible woman, Kerry. When I said I wanted you, it wasn't a lie." He reached over and brushed a strand of hair away from her face. "I still do, and that's the honest-to-God truth."

With that, he left the car and strode into the hotel. Kerry watched him until she could no longer see him, then with heavy limbs and an even heavier heart, she drove away. Drove home in a mental haze, thankful the streets weren't all that crowded due to the lateness of the hour.

By the time she walked through the front door, all she wanted was a hot bath and her bed. What she got was Millie sitting regally in her favorite chair, looking expectant. "Did you have a good time, dearest?"

What a joke. "I thought I told you not to wait up." She hadn't meant to sound so cross but she couldn't seem to control her emotions.

"What's happened, Kerry Ann?" Millie kept her tone even, but it didn't mask the concern in her eyes.

Kerry collapsed onto the sofa and tossed her purse aside. "Nothing happened, other than he lied to me."

"Lied about what?"

She didn't really have the energy to rehash the evening, but she knew Millie wouldn't let up until she came clean. "As it turns out, Ford Matthews is really Ford Ashton, the grandson of my deceased boss and the nephew of the man arrested for the murder. He was wooing me in order to find out if I knew anything about Spencer Ashton's death in order to clear his uncle."

"Why would he think you would know anything?"

"Someone told him I was Spencer's mistress, if you can imagine that. The man was a bastard and an egomaniac who saw every one of his assistants as an easy target. I had absolutely no use for him. But I didn't have him murdered, although a few times I did consider knocking him over the head with a paperweight when he tried to grab my butt."

Millie frowned. "Why didn't you tell me this sooner? I know many of the Ashton-Lattimer board members. I could have stopped the man's harassment."

Kerry doubted that, in light of Spencer's standing with the company, governing board or no governing board. "I needed to handle it myself, Millie. I can't keep relying on you to rescue me."

"And this Ford believed you had Spencer killed?"

"He thought it was a possibility, but now he knows he was wrong. At least, I think he does. I'm not sure what to believe anymore."

With narrowed eyes, Millie studied Kerry's face. "Did he do anything inappropriate to you?"

Nothing she hadn't wanted. "Actually, I practically threw myself at him because I thought I could trust him. He stopped before things went too far. He said he couldn't lie to me any longer and then he told me who he is. End of story."

Millie tented her hands beneath her chin. "I must admit my opinion of him has risen."

That almost shocked the life out of Kerry. "You're defending him?"

"You said he's trying to clear his uncle?"

"Yes. The man who raised him."

"And he would do anything to do that, I take it."

"Yes, and that included lying to me even before he had all the facts."

"But when the opportunity presented itself to have his way with you, he stopped."

Kerry's gaze drifted away from Millie's steady gaze. "Yes."

"My dear, it takes a very strong man to pass up such an opportunity since the majority of the male species is ruled by baser urges. It also takes a man with a strong sense of honor."

Kerry had to admit the truth in Millie's assertions even if she wanted to deny them. "I realize that, but he had other opportunities to tell me earlier."

"I assume this is true, but he was on a mission to protect someone he loves. I can understand that. I would do anything to protect you, my angel."

How well Kerry knew that. She also knew Millie meant serious business when she joined her on the sofa. "Kerry Ann sense that you have feelings for this man, despite what he's done to you. Did he express any true remorse?"

"He tried. He said he was sorry he hurt me. He said he cared about me." That he wanted her. That she was an incredible woman. "He also said he had only one excuse for his behavior, desperation."

"And he saw you as his only hope to help his uncle. Perhaps you are still his only hope."

Kerry's mouth dropped open before she snapped it shut. "What are you saying?"

"I'm saying perhaps you should put your anger aside and help him. The good you do for another will come back to you tenfold in blessings."

"I don't know what I could do to help him. I told the police everything I know about the circumstances leading to the murder."

"I'm not referring to the murder. Your young man could use a friend, a 'leaning shoulder,' so to speak. You can offer your support and friendship if you cannot offer anything else. One never knows what might result from an act of kindness, and the true power of forgiveness."

Kerry mulled that over for a few moments while Millie continued to scrutinize her. Could she go back to Ford Ashton and forgive him? Could she simply be there for him as a friend, knowing that in a secret place in her soul, she wanted more? And would she be trading her heart in exchange?

She was a scrapper. She'd survived the streets. She's survived Spencer. She could take on Ford Ashton without losing herself totally to a man who had nothing to offer. Or could she?

"Okay, Millie, I'll think about what you've said. And tomorrow I'll decide if I can be his friend. But only his friend."

Millie's eyes held a world of wisdom. "Yes, my angel, you can be his friend. You might even be his savior."

* * *

Ford had spent most of Sunday dragging around from lack
of sleep, scraping his mind for what to do next and missing a
woman he had no business missing.

After returning a call from Caroline, who'd informed him he
had an appointment with the attorney in the morning, he'd taken
a shower and decided to settle in for the evening on the sofa, not
bothering to put on any clothes. He considered watching baseball, but that didn't seem all that interesting. The selection of
movies on pay-per-view didn't, either. He sure as hell didn't dare
tune in to the adult offerings, considering what had transpired
with Kerry last night. Their confrontation had effectively shut
off his libido, but that had been only temporary. In fact, unanswered need had kept him up most of the night. So had self-
hatred over what he'd done to her, especially now that he knew
the horror of her past. But he still wanted her, more than he could
express. Truth was, he couldn't have her. Not now. Not ever.

When a series of knocks sounded at the door, Ford pushed
off the sofa and grabbed his jeans from the nearby chair,
hopping on one foot to shrug them on while calling, "Just a
minute."

He didn't have a clue who would be visiting him so late in
the evening, but he hoped it wasn't any of the Ashton clan.
He was shirtless, unshaven, sleep-deprived and sexually keyed
up. Not a good combination to greet his newly discovered
family members.

Ford opened the door to discover the subject of his day-
dreams standing on the other side of threshold, her hair
curling slightly over her breasts encased in a form-fitting
off-the-shoulder green top, her long legs exposed by a matching skirt that hit her mid thigh. He was so damned shocked
to see her that he almost closed the door then opened it again
just to make sure his imagination hadn't distorted his vision.

She hugged her arms to her middle. "May I come in?"

Like she really had to ask. "Sure." Ford stepped aside, and she breezed by him. She smelled great, his first thought. She looked even better, his second.

After he closed the door behind him, Ford turned to see her standing in the middle of the sitting area, her purse clutched to her chest. He couldn't quite read her expression, or even guess why she was there. Probably to give him a good tongue lashing, and not the preferred kind.

"Nice suite," she said after surveying the room. "A good view of the city."

The best view was standing right in front of him. "Why are you here, Kerry?"

"I've been thinking about what you said last night," she began. "And I've decided to help you."

Ford hadn't expected that for a minute. But then, she hadn't met his expectations on several levels. She wasn't mistress material. She wasn't a murderer. She was kind and unselfish and forgiving, everything a man could ask for in a woman. Yet he knew that anything beyond a continuing friendship with her would never happen now, and he deserved that. He didn't deserve her compassion, but here she was offering it in spite of his lies.

"Let's sit down," she said, and took the lone chair, leaving the sofa as Ford's only option.

He dropped down onto the cushions, fighting the urge to climb across the coffee table now separating them and kiss her. "How are you going to help me?"

"I've decided I'm going to be your friend, because you're probably going to need one until you get this thing with your uncle settled, one way or the other."

He needed her in ways he hadn't imagined, and it didn't have only to do with sex. "What made you change your mind?"

She moved slightly and looked away. "Because I know what it's like to be up against insurmountable odds and not have anyone to rely on."

In other words, odds were he probably wouldn't find the evidence needed to clear Grant. Nor would he ever be able to hold her again. To kiss her again, although God knew he wanted that. "I appreciate your offer."

She turned her gaze on him. "You sound disappointed."

He was disappointed, but not in the way that she thought. "No, I'm grateful. I'm just beat." But not tired enough to consider taking up where they left off last night.

Kerry quickly came to her feet. "Then I'll let you go to bed."

Going to bed didn't interest him, unless she went with him. "I probably couldn't sleep anyway. Please sit back down."

"I have to be at work in the morning."

He stood. "It's still early." He sounded almost desperate to keep her there. Maybe he was. "You don't have to stay that long."

"Okay. For a while." She dropped her purse at her feet and reclaimed her seat in the chair as Ford collapsed back on the couch.

She studied him a long moment with concern. "Have you had anything decent to eat today?"

Come to think of it, he hadn't, not anything of real substance. Just a few minibar pretzels to go with the shot of whiskey he'd had earlier that afternoon. "Not really."

She leaned forward, grabbed up the room service menu from the coffee table and pored over it. "They have a good selection of beef. I hear the prime rib is good."

"Do you want anything?"

She kept flipping through the menu before wetting her lips, drawing Ford's undivided attention. "I've already had dinner, but I wouldn't mind some dessert. Maybe a chocolate sundae."

What Ford wanted for dessert had nothing to do with ice cream. "Not a problem." Taking a chance, he stood and crossed the room to stand behind the sofa, peering over her shoulder, all too aware that the need to touch her was stronger than his need for food. "Turn back to the entrées."

She looked up at him as if she had no idea what an entrée was. When she didn't respond, Ford leaned down and flipped through the menu, their arms brushing. Even the limited contact did things to Ford that he needed to avoid for the sake of his sanity. He stopped at the all-day dining section and pointed. "I'm going to have the roast beef sandwich."

"Is that enough for you?"

Just having her there would be enough. For now. "Yeah."

"Fine." She slapped the menu closed and handed it to him. "I'd like a slice of cheesecake, strawberry topping. And some coffee."

"Great. I'll call it in."

Ford walked to the desk, tossed down the menu and dialed room service without looking back at her. If he contacted those violet eyes, he wouldn't be able to form a coherent sentence. He couldn't quite explain why she continued to affect him so strongly. Again, he could continue to chalk it up to lust, or admit to himself it went deeper than that. He could handle simple desire. Deeper he couldn't deal with. But he'd have to deal with it or lose his connection with her. He didn't want to face that again, at least until the time came for him to go back home.

After he placed the order, Ford turned to find Kerry had taken a seat on one end of the sofa. Progress, he thought, but decided it best not to act on any of his considerations of what he'd like to do to her. Otherwise he'd be pushing his luck and, in turn, pushing her right out the door. He strode to the sofa and immediately noticed she was sizing him up—and down. And up again. When he sat, leaving only a small space between them, she smiled. He'd give up food for days just to see that smile, that single dimple creasing the corner of her mouth. A really great spot to kiss.

"What?" he asked when she continued to grin.

"I just noticed you do have a tan all over. Or at least on your chest."

"You didn't notice that last night?"

"It was dark last night, and you didn't take your shirt off completely."

Thinking back on the events of last night had big trouble threatening below his belt. He hooked a thumb over his shoulder in the direction of the bedroom. "Maybe I should put one on now."

"Don't do that on my account. You might as well be comfortable."

He wouldn't be at all comfortable in her presence, considering how badly he wanted to touch her again and knowing that wasn't possible. "As long as it doesn't bother you."

"It doesn't. But I am curious about your tan. Maybe you *are* actually a surfer."

"I told you last night I've never surfed." One of the few truths he'd told her. "I sometimes ride the tractor without my shirt. My sister gives me hell about it even though I've told her it's cooler. She claims that wearing a shirt keeps the heat away." And little did Abby know, he'd spent more than a few afternoon breaks lying on the lounge chair poolside at his house, buck naked.

"You know, your sister is right," Kerry said after a thoughtful pause.

"If you ask her, she'll tell you she's always right. Stubborn woman."

"Do you have any other siblings?"

"Just Abby. We're a little less than two years apart."

"I take it you're close."

"Yeah, we've always been close." Bound together by their mother's abandonment and the mystery of their biological fathers. "Lately she's been pretty preoccupied with her new husband. She's also pregnant with twins."

"Twins? Wow. Do they run in your family?"

"My mother was Grant's twin." Grace, the evil twin.

Kerry ran her slender fingertips along the back of the sofa, causing Ford to have an immediate reaction down south. "I didn't have any brothers or sisters. I missed that growing up." Her wistful tone said she'd missed a lot of things and had faced more than her share of heartache.

"I have to admit, even though Abby's a pain in the butt sometimes, I wouldn't trade her."

She slid off her shoes and curled her legs beneath her. "What kind of parent was Grant?"

"He was tough but fair. He kept us in line. He also gave up a lot to raise us. Marriage and kids of his own."

"He was never seriously involved with a woman?"

"Not that we were aware of, although I'm sure he wasn't celibate all those years. Not many women to choose from in Crawley, but he did go out of town every now and then, leaving Buck in charge."

Kerry frowned. "Who's Buck?"

"He's our ranch foreman. Been there as long as I can remember. He started working for my great-grandparents as a teenager. He's as good as gold. Not exactly a pushover, but he let me and Abby get away with more than Grant ever did. Especially Abby. God, he loves her." Ford smiled with remembrance of Abby climbing into Buck's lap for a tall tale, and eventually teaching him to read. "In Buck's eyes, she can do no wrong. In fact, he's the reason she became a veterinarian. He basically taught her everything she knows about treating cattle and horses."

"Is he married?"

"Nope."

"You were brought up by a couple of confirmed bachelors who had to go out of town to find their women."

"That about sums it up."

"Does all of that apply to you? I mean, did you go out of town to find women?"

He wasn't sure he wanted to get into that at the moment. "I'm not celibate, either, if that's what you're asking. But I haven't had many long-term relationships. Most women don't consider living on a farm in the middle of nowhere a great lifestyle."

"I think it sounds intriguing," she said. "What's it like?"

Ford told Kerry about the hard work, hard living but most important, the rewards of owning and cultivating the land. She listened with sincere interest when he revealed he'd developed his own special feed and leased the patents globally, laughed when he told her about his and Abby's antics, and remained silent as he talked about his uncle's commitment to them.

"I'm glad you had Grant," she said after a long bout of silence. "It's hard having to deal with a mother's death."

Ford braced for the last of the revelations. "My mother isn't dead. She left me and Abby when we were in grade school. We haven't heard from her since. All I know is that she ran off with some kind of salesman."

"Is your father dead?"

He tipped his head back against the sofa and studied the ceiling. "I have no idea who he is. As far as I'm concerned, Grant is my dad."

When he felt the gentle touch on his shoulder, Ford turned his head to see compassion reflecting in her eyes. "I'm really sorry, Ford. Sounds like you've had it about as tough as I have."

"Not really," he said, resisting the urge to pull her into his arms. "I've always had a place to come home to."

Taking him by surprise, she scooted closer and took his hand. "That doesn't discount what your mother did to you. It hurts like hell, knowing a parent has such little regard for their child. In your case, children."

He laced his fingers with hers and gave her hand a squeeze. "Yeah, well I guess some people just aren't meant to be parents."

Their eyes met and held for a long moment, suspending Ford between a strong yearning to kiss her and blaring caution buzzing around in his head. Yearning was beginning to win out until another knock sounded at the door, sending Ford off the sofa to answer the summons.

A lanky waiter rolled in a cart containing their limited dinner, and Ford instructed him to put the food on the coffee table. The guy looked at Ford like he was some hayseed, which in many ways he was. But when he tipped him well, the man's attitude changed immediately. He couldn't be more accommodating, groveling all the way out of the room.

After he returned to Kerry, Ford ate his sandwich in record time, realizing he was hungrier than he'd thought. Obviously, she had restored his appetite, in more ways than one. He pushed aside the plate and leaned back, hands laced behind his neck, to watch Kerry nibble at her cheesecake.

"Is your feed business lucrative?" she asked, following another small bite.

He was more interested in watching her mouth than talking, engaging it in something other than everyday conversation. "I do fairly well. It enabled me to build my own house, complete with all the modern conveniences."

She sent him a teasing look. "No water wells and outdoor plumbing?"

"Water well, yes. Outhouse, no. But I do have a pool."

"Wow. That's great, and so is this cheesecake. Want to try it?"

"Sure."

As soon as she had the fork poised at his mouth, the cheese-cake took a dive, rolled down his bare chest and ended up in his lap. "I'm sorry," Kerry said, followed by an uncomfort-able laugh.

"No problem." For Ford, it was somewhat of a problem, especially when he fantasized about her licking her way down his torso to clean up the sticky path.

Instead, Kerry grabbed a napkin, dipped it in a glass of water then worked over the spot. When she reached his groin, he caught her wrist. "I wouldn't do that if I were you."

She looked down, then back up at him, awareness as well as a faint shade of pink on her pretty face. "Oh. Sorry again."

Ford took the napkin from her, picked up the bite of des-sert, rolled it up into the cloth and tossed it onto the table. "No harm done." Not much, although even the ice water hadn't helped his predicament. He was hard as a harrow and couldn't do a damn thing about it.

"Want to try it again?" she asked.

Oh, yeah, he did. He wanted to take up where they'd left off the night before. "If you mean the cheesecake, no."

In spite of the absence of wisdom, he took her hand, laid the fork on the tray, then pulled her against his side.

"Friendship, Ford," she said, but didn't try to move, even when he rubbed his hands down her bare arms.

"I'm just trying to warm you up. You're covered in goose bumps."

"I know, but I'm not cold."

"What are you, Kerry?"

A breathy sigh drifted from her lips. "Crazy for being here. Crazy for wanting you to kiss me again. For wanting you, period."

She didn't have to tell him twice before Ford took full ad-vantage of her sweet lips. He tried to be gentle, keep it light but the rush went straight to his head, causing him to conduct a very thorough, very deep investigation of her mouth.

Without thought, he lifted her up to straddle his lap. Kerry didn't issue a complaint, didn't pull away from him at all. In fact, she responded to the kiss without hesitation, and he welcomed that. Welcomed her hands coming to rest on his chest. Even welcomed his erection as she moved her bottom against his lap even knowing he couldn't do a damn thing about it. Totally on edge, he kept his hands at her waist and fought the temptation to touch her everywhere. Yet temptation won out when she moaned against his mouth and the glide of her hips against his groin grew more insistent.

Keeping his mouth firmly mated with hers, Ford used both hands to push her skirt up her legs, knowing full well that she needed something from him, something he was more than glad to give her. What he'd almost given her last night.

He waited a few moments, allowing her the opportunity to stop him, which she didn't. Instead, she dug her nails into his shoulders, played her tongue against his in a suggestive rhythm, exploring his mouth without reservation, exactly what he planned to do with her body, if she let him.

He lifted her bottom from his lap with one hand and with the other tugged the skirt up around her waist then pushed her panties down to the tops of her knees. Only then did he break the kiss and waited for her permission before he continued. He stroked the back of his knuckles below her navel and slid his free hand beneath the back of her shirt. "I want to touch you, Kerry. I have to touch you."

She locked into his gaze and murmured, "Ford, I need—"

"I know what you need, and I want you to know how it can be with a man who only wants to make you feel good." He traced circles above the golden vee between her legs. "But you only have to tell me no, and I'll stop."

She released a shaky breath, her unfocused eyes locked on his eyes. "This is insane."

He slid his hand lower, but not exactly where he wanted to be. "If you say yes, I'll make you crazy in a damn good way."

She closed her eyes and sighed. "Yes. Make me crazy."

*Yes* was exactly what he'd wanted to hear. *Yes* was all it took to proceed. He turned his palm and cupped her between her thighs then gently slid one fingertip through the damp folds. She bucked when he hit home, but she didn't bolt from his lap. Instead, she tipped her forehead against his to watch him touch her. Ford did the same, totally caught up in the erotic scene—Kerry with a leg on each side of his thighs, completely open to him, his hand in motion between her legs. He made methodical passes over her swollen flesh, intent on giving her a mind-blowing climax like she'd never known. His erection strained painfully against his jeans, and he considered opening his own fly to provide much-needed comfort. But he didn't want to stop until he'd given her what she needed. He also didn't want her believing he had to have more. This was for her benefit. All for her.

When Kerry pushed against his hand, Ford increased the pressure of his strokes and slid one finger inside her. He felt the beginnings of her orgasm, slightly at first then stronger and stronger. A sound caught somewhere between a moan and a whimper slipped out of her mouth. He captured that sound with his mouth, gliding his tongue in sync with the movement of his fingertip while he experienced every wave of her climax. He fantasized about how she would feel when he was buried inside her, almost at his own peril.

Kerry collapsed against him, her cheek now resting against his chest while he rubbed her back as he considered whether he should ask her to come to his bed. That wouldn't be a good idea, he decided. He sure as hell didn't want to rush her and risk she would turn away from him again. He would have to be satisfied knowing that someday soon he might have the opportunity to show her how it could be between a man and a woman when no force was involved.

But he wasn't completely satisfied, his only excuse for holding her face in his palms and saying, "Stay with me tonight, Kerry."

Without responding, she pulled her panties and skirt back into place, scooted off his lap, then turned around on the sofa, her gaze fixed on some unknown point across the room. "I can't, Ford. I know that's selfish on my part, considering what you've done for me tonight, but I'm just not ready yet. In fact, I shouldn't have allowed any of this to happen."

He understood what she was saying, and he didn't blame her. Still, he had to tell her what was on his mind. "Kerry, I know you're still dealing with my deception, but whether or not I told the truth about my identity, I still want to be with you. And I know you want to be with me, too. You proved that just a minute ago."

She sighed. "That wasn't exactly me. I'm usually very cautious."

"You were very hot. And you make me that way." He had half a mind to take her hand and show her. He chose to tell her. "I'm so turned on right now I could make love with you all night. And I know it would be so damn good between us. But I also know that's probably too much to ask of you right now. I'm willing to be patient and let you decide if and when."

Clasping his hand, she pulled it up and held it above her breasts, against her pounding heart. "Ford, there's something you have to know."

His immediate thought was she'd been lying about her relationship with Spencer. "What is it?"

A flash of pain reflected from her eyes. "I've tried to be

intimate with other men, but it's been difficult. You're the first one I've allowed to be that close to me since…" Her voice faltered along with her gaze.

He tipped her chin toward him so she could see how badly he hurt for her. "You may not believe this, but I do understand what you went through. And I hate like hell you had to go through it."

Although Abby hadn't suffered Kerry's fate, Ford had witnessed firsthand what her personal experience had done to his sister in terms of her relationships with men, and that made Kerry's situation all the more troublesome. He wanted to be a man she could trust. He wanted to prove to her he wouldn't hurt her in any way.

Kerry laid her head against his shoulder, their joined hands resting on his thigh, no more words passing between them. Ford enjoyed having her so close, relaxed and seemingly content, even if his own body still burned for her. But he had to take it easy, not be too persistent. And maybe, just maybe, he would have his opportunity to make love with her. Even if that didn't happen, he'd never regret knowing her. He *would* regret having to leave her.

"Did they ever catch the bastard who assaulted you?" he asked after a time.

She sighed. "No. It was dark in the alley, and I couldn't see his face. I couldn't identify him."

He released her hand and wrapped an arm around her shoulder, all he could think to do. He said, "I'm sorry, Kerry," all he could think to say.

"It was a long time ago," she said before raising her head to look at him again, an all-too-apparent ache in her eyes. "I'd be lying if I said I didn't carry a few internal scars from the experience along with the external ones. But when I met you, I decided it was time to take a few risks because I trusted you."

"And then I blew it when I lied to you."

She shrugged. "That's all behind us now. Maybe we should just start over."

Ford could accept that, as long as she was willing to be with him for however many days he had left in this city. "I agree."

"And that means I have to have time to decide how far I want this thing between us to go."

She had to learn to trust him all over again, he realized. "I'll give you all the time you need."

"Speaking of time." She checked her watch. "I really do have to go, otherwise I'll have a hard time getting up in the morning."

"I'm going to have a hard time all night." Ford wanted to take back the comment the minute it jumped out of his mouth. Old habits were damn difficult to break.

Thankfully, Kerry smiled. "I'm sure you'll handle things just fine."

He wanted her to handle "things," but from this point forward, she would have to take the initiative. "I'll manage."

When Kerry left the sofa, Ford came to his feet, hating that she was leaving. He followed her to the door, and once there she turned to face him with a smile. "What do you have planned for tomorrow?"

"I have an appointment with Grant's attorney to see where we stand."

Her smile faded as if she suddenly remembered he was still fighting for his uncle's very survival. Ford had to admit, at times he'd forgotten, too, especially when she'd been in his arms. That served to play up his guilt even more. "I'll stop by after work tomorrow, if that's okay," she said.

That was more than okay with him. "I look forward to it. Maybe we can go someplace to eat that doesn't serve hotel food."

"I'll keep that in mind, and I'll see you then." She walked out the door before he had a chance to kiss her again. Walked out before he could issue another lame apology. Before he tried to invite her once more into his lonely bed.

Ford would keep her in mind all night long, all day tomorrow until she came back to him, and probably long after he left godforsaken California.

# Six

Eventually Ford would be leaving California, a thought that kept playing over and over in Kerry's mind as she tried to work. Adding to her lack of concentration was the remembrance of her lack of inhibition last night, Ford's gentle skill, the absolute pleasure of his touch. Even now she shivered, twitched in the rigid office chair, feeling the effects as if it had happened only a few moments ago, not hours before.

Right now she had to think about her less-than-exciting job, filling in for a vacationing accounting clerk, and on a Monday, no less. Being stuck at a cluttered desk, inputting financial figures, wasn't nearly as exciting as the thought of escaping the doldrums to be with Ford. And that meant to be with him in every way.

Of course, she'd had the prime opportunity the evening before, but she'd squandered that because of a mix of mistrust and fear. At least she was beginning to understand him more, and that included why he'd lied to her. Granted, she didn't care for his dishonesty, but she did comprehend it. His obvious love for his uncle had been more than apparent. He would do anything to protect his family. As Millie had said, there was a lot of honor in that.

She also recognized that after she'd bared her soul, he hadn't pressured her for more intimacy. But that intimacy issue was first and foremost on her mind. She was just beginning to recognize her own needs, a positive step in the right direction. Most men she'd dated in the past had walked away thinking her aloof, unattainable, which she had been. Until now. Until Ford Ashton had come into her life with the promise of showing her the power of her own sexuality, and she couldn't ignore her desire to let him take her wherever he would.

She deserved to be whole again, and she inherently knew Ford could help her on her way. She wasn't looking for him to save her because that would be unrealistic. But she'd arrived at the point where if she didn't have all of him, and soon, she was in danger of going up in a carnal blaze of glory. Some might consider her a fool for even considering such a thing, but Kerry liked to think of it as being a fair exchange. She could offer him her friendship, and he could offer her an experience the likes of which she'd never known. For once, a good experience. No. A *great* experience.

Kerry glanced at the clock on the wall, noting it was only 9 a.m., still three hours away from lunch and eight hours away from Ford. Tonight she planned to take it to the limit by taking Ford up on his offer to stay with him. First she had to get busy, even though she'd rather eat pure horseradish than to return to the dull data entry.

"Would you please take care of this, Kerry?"

Glancing up from the computer, Kerry forced a smile at the

oh-so-cocky Mona Gilbert—or Hormona, as the office girls like to call her—the newly appointed admin to the interim CEO. "Take care of what?"

"This." Mona tossed a pink message note in front of Kerry. "The post office keeps calling. They need you to pick up some mail that I presume didn't get routed to the office after Mr. Ashton's death. I don't have time to deal with it."

Like Kerry had the time. "Fine. I'll get it at lunch."

"See that you do." Mona swayed away, taking with her the stifling scent of overpowering fruity perfume as well as her arrogance. Too bad she hadn't worked for Spencer. They would have gotten along just great. Two peas in the proverbial pod. Bed buddies. Yuck.

Kerry tossed the note aside and sighed, cheek resting on her palm. So much for a relaxing lunch hour. She would grab a sandwich, pick up the mail and then return to her riveting work. Or she could pick up the mail, forget the sandwich and grab Ford.

Kerry suddenly decided that was a great option. In fact, she made another decision, as well. She had two weeks' worth of vacation coming. The company could do without her for a few days. She would finish out the morning, then present the excuse that something dire had come up at home, and spend the time getting to know Ford better. Getting to know all of him, before he was permanently out of her life. And try to help him with his goal to clear Grant. Of course, that meant leaving Millie alone, but Kerry could remedy that with one phone call to Millie's niece. It could also mean getting in too deep, heart first. Worth the risk, as far as Kerry was concerned.

Pumped up on anticipation, she began keying data at a record pace, mentally chanting, "Three more hours until lunch." Three more hours until Ford.

* * *

Ford spent the best part of Monday morning sitting in an upscale office waiting for Grant's attorney. Shortly before noon, Edgar Kent finally rushed into the room.

"Sorry I'm late, Mr. Ashton," he said as he extended his hand to Ford for a quick shake. "Busy morning."

Ford sat back down at the chair across from Kent's desk, tempted to tell him apology not accepted. Instead he asked, "What's going on with my uncle's case?"

Kent scooted his rolling chair beneath the desk and forked a hand though his silver hair. "Right now we're waiting for the grand jury to convene to hear his case."

"When will that be?"

He moved aside some documents to uncover a file and flipped it open. "Probably not until next week, maybe later."

That sure as hell wouldn't do. "And Grant has to waste away in jail until then?"

Kent closed the file and folded his hands on top of it. "If the grand jury finds that the evidence supports holding him over until trial, then he could be in for a long stay in jail. He'll be arraigned again if that happens, and I'll request bail again, but I'm not counting on having that granted."

Ford leaned back and released a rough sigh. "Do you think the evidence will hold out?"

"The witness who says he saw your uncle entering the building the night of Spencer Ashton's death is fairly compelling, especially since he picked him out of a lineup."

"Who is this witness?"

"I only have a name right now, but I'll be interviewing him when the time comes."

Ford leaned forward, his hands gripped tightly on the chair's arms. "Why don't you let me interview him? Because he's damn sure wrong about Grant."

Kent scowled. "The last thing we need is to have you harassing a witness. You need to allow the justice system to work."

Ford let go a cynical laugh. "Justice? What justice? An innocent man's sitting behind bars right now. That's not justice. That's immoral as hell."

Kent tented his fingers beneath his chin. "Mr. Ashton, you have to understand that your uncle doesn't have a good alibi other than he supposedly returned to Napa. No one saw him return. Spencer's assistant heard him threaten Spencer earlier that day. So he had motive, as well. The police know that he leaked the information of your grandfather's bigamy to the press. They also know he attempted to see him several times before they finally did meet."

"They don't know him at all. My uncle wouldn't kill anyone, even if the bastard did deserve to die. If Grant said he went back to Napa, then he did."

"Yet he has no proof he did return."

Ford leveled a hard stare on the man. "Are you saying even you don't believe him?"

Kent shifted under Ford's continued scrutiny. "It's not my job to believe him. It's my job to represent him to the best of my ability."

"And I just put down one helluva retainer for you to do just that." He came to his feet, no longer trusting he could keep his anger in check. "In the meantime, I'm going to keep digging until I find out who did this. And you're going to do whatever it takes to get him out of that hell hole."

With that, Ford turned away but before he could leave, Kent called him back. He turned around to find the attorney holding out a folded piece of yellow legal paper. "This is from your uncle. He asked me to give this to you."

Ford crossed the room, took the paper and slipped it

into the jacket's inside pocket. "Thank you. I'll be in touch."

On the way out, Ford was tempted to read the letter in the elevator but decided to wait. He considered reading it in the cab but the trip to the hotel was practically over before it had begun. But when he entered the hotel room, alone with his anger and frustration, he shucked off his jacket, sat on the sofa and finally unfolded the page. And soon his fury was replaced by a sadness the likes of which Ford had never known.

Ford,

I don't know what's going to happen to me, so I need to tell you a few things. First, keep your nose clean. Don't do anything that's going to get you into trouble, although I know you're probably bent on getting me out of here. Second, take good care of Abby in my absence, like you've always done. I know she has Russ now, but she still needs you, too. I'd hate to think I wouldn't be around to see the babies, but that's a possibility.

And in case you're wondering if I regret having to raise you and your sister, I wouldn't trade that time for anything in the world. Not even for my freedom right now. You two are the best things that ever happened to me, and although I hate like hell what Grace did to you, in a way she did me a favor. And now I'm going to ask a couple of favors from you.

First, don't let what your mother did to you keep you from trying to find the right woman. Second, when you have the time, check on Anna Sheridan. She became a good friend while I was at The Vines. Just tell her I'm going to be okay and she will be, too.

Last, I probably didn't tell you enough while you were growing up, bud, but I'm telling you now. I love you and Abby, more than I love my own life. Just keep remembering that, no matter what happens.

Grant.

Ford tossed the letter aside, laid his head back and closed his eyes. The last time he'd cried, he'd been eight years old and Grant had told him his mother had left. He never let anyone see those tears because he'd cried them at night in his bed. Since that time, he'd been determined to be the consummate tough guy, the one who had no use for emotions. Had no use for feelings in general because it was just much easier to feel numb.

Right then he came as close to crying as he had since that day. Tightening his jaw, he fought the emotions as fervently as he fought to save his uncle. Fought not to feel at all. Regardless, he experienced the keen bite of sorrow mixed with the fury over the unfairness of Grant's situation.

He needed a strong drink, but alcohol would only cloud his head. He needed to think about what to do next. Most of all, he needed someone to talk to. And that someone was Kerry Roarke.

Kerry stood at Ford's hotel door, barely able to contain her excitement. She'd cut out of the office at 11:00 a.m., gone by the house and packed a bag while Millie was out for her Monday bridge game, and then she dropped by the post office. The final stopover had led to the discovery of something she hadn't expected. Something very encouraging. It might not mean anything in the grand scheme of things, but it could very well be the key to clearing Grant Ashton. And she couldn't wait to tell Ford the news.

Yet when Ford answered her summons after two knocks, Kerry's excitement faded into deep concern. He looked totally weary and wasted. His hair was ruffled, as if he'd run his hands through it several times, his eyes reddened, turning them an even brighter shade of blue. He simply stared at her for a moment, and without speaking, Kerry dropped the nylon tote and her purse at her feet and walked into his arms. He held on to her tightly, as if she had become his lifeline. She welcomed that he needed her right then, even if she didn't welcome his obvious despair.

After a time he dropped his arms from around her and stepped back, looking somewhat self-conscious. "You're early."

"I hope that's not a problem."

"Not at all. I've never been so glad to see anyone in my life."

Kerry could say the same for herself. She'd imagined this moment all morning, although she hadn't imagined how great he would look in a white tailored shirt, pushed up at the sleeves, and a pair of form-fitting navy slacks. Nor had she imagined he would look so discouraged. Hopefully she could help ease that with her news.

He pointed to the bag at her feet. "What's in there?"

"A change of clothes in case I need them later." Several changes of clothes, but she decided to save that information until later.

He gestured toward the living area. "Come in and I'll tell you how my sorry morning went."

Kerry picked up her belongings and moved into the room, allowing Ford to close the door. She headed to the sofa while Ford walked to the wet bar in the corner and poured a cup of coffee. Without looking at her, he said, "Do you want a cup?"

"No, thanks. I've had more than my share today." Kerry set her things on the coffee table, dropped onto the sofa and waited until Ford settled beside her before saying, "I take it things didn't go well with the attorney."

He took a drink of coffee, then let go a rough sigh. "You

could say that. He pretty much told me there's not a lot that can be done. The evidence against Grant is strong. He's been identified in a lineup and he had motive. All I can do is wait and hope something breaks in the case, although I don't know what that something could be."

"Maybe I do." Kerry rummaged through her purse and withdrew two pieces of mail and held them up for Ford's inspection.

He set his coffee cup down on the end table. "What is that?"

"Mail for Spencer from his private P.O. box. I'd forgotten all about it until I got the message this morning these needed to be picked up."

"Do the police know about this P.O. box?"

"I'm not sure. As far as I know, Spencer had the only key. I only went there one time because he was too busy. I received strict instructions not to open anything. That's why I've always assumed he rented it so he could receive love letters from his latest girl-of-the-month."

"So are they love letters?"

"Not exactly." She slipped the paper from the longest envelope, unfolded it and handed it to him. "That's a bank statement. Best I can tell, it's a biannual recap of transactions, beginning last January. You'll notice that every month this year until May, he deposited ten thousand dollars, and the funds were withdrawn in the same month."

Ford studied the statement for a moment. "I'm not sure what this proves."

"Maybe nothing without this."

She handed him the letter from the second envelope and allowed him time to read it, which he did out loud. "'If you stop paying me, you will pay one way or another.'" His gaze zipped to hers. "Someone was blackmailing him."

"That's my guess. Question is, who is that someone? And did they murder him?" Kerry showed him the empty envelope. "It has an Oakland postmark dated in May, but no return address. Whoever sent this was in the vicinity at the time of Spencer's death."

Ford slid his hands through his hair. "Yeah, and that means Grant, too. This could implicate him if they believe he was doing the blackmailing."

"Regardless, we have to turn it over to the police."

"I know that, but I want to wait a day or two."

"Why?"

"Because I have something else I need to check out." Ford leaned over and picked up a piece of legal pad paper from the coffee table. "This is a letter from Grant. Read it."

Kerry took the page and read it silently, her eyes soon clouding with a mist of tears that threatened to fall when she comprehended the depth of Grant Ashton's commitment to his nephew. No wonder Ford was so distraught. No wonder he was fiercely determined to clear his uncle. "Do you think he's giving up?"

"Grant's a strong man, physically and mentally. I wouldn't believe he would ever give up. But then, I have no idea what he's going through right now. I'm not sure I want to know, because it would probably kill me."

Kerry laid a comforting hand on his arm. "You can't give up, either, Ford. We'll keep trying as long as it takes to see him out of jail."

"I plan to, and I've been wondering about something else." He pointed to a passage near the end. "I know this is probably a long shot, but do you know anything about this Anna Sheridan?"

More than she'd wanted to know. "As a matter of fact, I do. Her sister, Alyssa, used to be Spencer's assistant." And mistress. "I replaced her because she was pregnant. She died not long after the baby was born and now Anna is raising him. That baby is Spencer's son."

Ford tossed the mail onto the table and leaned forward. "Damn. The man knew no shame when it came to screwing up people's lives. First he leaves my grandmother high and dry to raise his kids alone. Then he jilts Caroline out of the family company and fathers four more kids he practically abandoned. Then he moves on to another woman and fathers three more. God only knows what he's done to them and his current wife, although I don't know anything about her or that branch of the Ashtons."

"Believe me, Ford, you don't want to know Lilah Ashton. I had to deal with her when she visited Spencer at Ashton-Latimer. She's a shark."

Ford sent her a cynical smile. "Good. I hope she made his final years pure hell." He collapsed back against the couch. "I'm still wondering about Grant's connection to Anna. He says he met her at The Vines, but from the looks of the letter, I suspect they were closer that he's letting on. I'm kind of surprised he never mentioned her, but Grant can be fairly secretive about that sort of thing."

The cogs in Kerry's brain started turning. "I met Anna once when she brought the baby into the office and demanded to see Spencer. Spencer was in a meeting at the time, so she left, but she wasn't very happy about it. I'm sure she wasn't too thrilled when the press got wind that the little boy was Spencer's. More than likely they've made her life chaotic. I certainly know how that feels."

Ford's expression told her he truly sympathized. "I'm sure you do, and I'm also sorry you got caught up in all this mess."

Kerry put the letter next to the other mail and curled one leg beneath her. "Honestly, I feel guilty for telling the police about the argument I overheard between Spencer and your uncle. For months I had to turn him away, and he was always so nice to me, even though he was furious with Spencer. But that afternoon…" Her gaze drifted away along with her words. Confession might be good for the soul, but her soul was being ripped to shreds.

"What about that afternoon?"

Kerry looked up and met his gaze. "I felt sorry for Grant so I let him back without telling Spencer. If I hadn't done that, maybe none of this would have happened."

He touched her face and rubbed his thumb over her cheek. "Hey, it's not your fault. You were just trying to help Grant. And you had to tell the truth about the argument. You didn't have a choice."

Kerry appreciated his understanding more than she could express. "Any ideas on what to do next?" She had one in particular but felt it wouldn't be appropriate to present it. Not yet.

"I called Caroline earlier and told her I'd be driving to Napa this evening to see her. I want to find out what she knows about Anna and Grant's relationship."

So much for dinner plans. So much for all her lovemaking plans, at least for the time being. "That sounds like a good idea."

"Even more so now. From what you say, I can't help but wonder if maybe Grant's protecting Anna in some way. Maybe she was involved and he went back to the building to stop her."

"That could be. What time do you have to leave?"

"Caroline told me to be there around 6:30 for drinks and invited me to stay on for dinner. I've already rented a car."

Kerry smiled around her disappointment. "Another Mustang?"

"Actually, an SUV, and I'd like you to come with me, if you're game."

Oh, she was game, for that and much, much more. "Sure." She checked her watch. "It's twelve-thirty now, it takes about an hour and a half to get to Napa, so that leaves four and a half hours before we need to leave."

"Do you have to go back to work?"

Time to unveil the plan, and prepare for possible rejection. "Actually, I don't have to go back today. I don't have to go back until next Monday. I took the time off to spend it with you. As long as you don't object to having a roommate for the remainder of the week."

He looked positively shocked. "You want to stay here?"

"If you have room for me."

"I only have one bedroom, Kerry."

"I realize that."

"Do you want me to sleep on the couch?"

She released a ragged breath. "No, I want you to sleep with me. And not only to sleep."

Ford shifted on the cushions. "Are you sure?"

"Positive."

His expression went suddenly serious. "I'll be leaving eventually."

"I know, and I want to make the most of our time together. We've both been through a lot, past and present, and I don't think there's anything wrong with escaping together, even if only temporarily."

Ford stood and paced the room for a few moments. He seemed to be mulling over her words while Kerry seemed to stop breathing. If he refused, she would handle it. She wouldn't like it, but she'd deal with it.

Finally he stopped and stood before her, his expression no less somber. "One question."

"Okay."

"Do you still have that condom?"

Kerry smiled from relief and anticipation and just plain giddiness. "I can go one better than that." Leaning down, she rifled through the bag, pulled out the box and tossed it into his hands. "I believe in being prepared."

He turned the condom box over then nailed her with a devastating grin, emphasizing his gorgeous dimples. "This should be enough to last us tonight."

Kerry kicked off her shoes and shed her tailored black blazer. The rest she would leave for him to remove. After coming to her bare feet, she circled her arms around him.

"I don't want to wait until tonight."

"You want to make love now?" His voice was hoarse and incredibly deep.

"Yes. I need to see your face in the daylight."

Comprehension showed in his expression. "Anything you want I'll do it. You only have to ask me."

"I can tell you one thing I don't want, Ford."

"What's that?"

"I don't want you to treat me like I'm fragile, because I'm not. As far as I'm concerned, this is the first time for me, and I don't want you to hold anything back, and neither will I." She brushed a kiss across his lips. "I want you to treat me like you would any other woman."

She wasn't like any other woman he'd ever known—Ford's first thought as they stood in the bedroom, tossing away clothes like dried leaves caught in a wind current. His second thought centered on slowing down, the reason why he left her panties and his briefs intact, for now.

Without bothering to turn down the spread, Ford took Kerry down on the bed. He held her face in his palms and kissed her, trying desperately to stay grounded. That seemed almost impossible when she stroked her tongue against his and moved her hips beneath him. After breaking the kiss, he rolled to his side and ran one fingertip along her throat then over the rise of her breast.

The light streaming in from the window allowed him to see all the details as he touched her, and that alone was almost more than he could take. Lowering his head, he flicked his tongue over one nipple, then the other. She slid her hands in his hair as if she might be anchoring herself, as well.

He raised his head to watch her, keeping his gaze centered on hers as he slid his finger slowly down her belly. She trembled and a slight gasp slipped out of her mouth. Ford was on the verge of some serious shaking, too. But he vowed to keep it together for a while longer. He also vowed to pull out all the stops, at her request. He planned to crush out all her bad memories, and replace them with good ones. Beginning now.

Coming to his knees, he told her, "Lift up," and when she complied, he slid her panties down her legs and tossed them away.

Ford didn't know what he'd done in his lifetime to deserve this, seeing Kerry lying there, looking so damn beautiful. He'd viewed his share of nude women, but he'd never been as moved by any of them. Her hair formed a golden halo on the pillow still covered by the burgundy spread. Her face was flushed a slight shade of pink that almost matched the color of her nipples. Her breasts were full, her curves generous, her legs long and made to wrap around his waist when he made love to her. She was a mix of saint and seductress, and he wanted her so badly he almost couldn't think.

His gaze wandered down to the light shading between her thighs and every muscle in his body clenched in an effort to maintain control. Overpowering need had him considering parting her legs and sinking inside her. Common sense took hold and told him to focus only on her. To make sure she was more than ready to take the next step.

Regardless that she'd told him not to hold back, he still felt the need to tell her what he intended to do. On that thought, he snaked out of his briefs, stretched out beside her again and pushed her hair back from her ear to whisper, "I want to kiss you. Everywhere."

She turned her face toward him. "I want you to do that, as long as you let me return the favor."

Since that request hadn't totally sent him over the edge, Ford realized he was a lot stronger than he'd believed. He touched his lips to hers and pulled back to study her face. "I want you to do that, but I'm barely hanging on here."

She gave him a shaky smile. "I understand. Later, then."

Later worked fine for Ford, and no way would she understand how he felt at that moment. He didn't understand it himself. But here and now held the most importance. He worked his lips down her body, placing a light kiss on each of her breasts, another above her navel, before he bent her knees and positioned himself between her legs. Sliding his hands beneath her bottom, he lifted her slightly to meet his mouth.

Kerry drew in a sharp breath when he reached his goal, much the same as she had last night. He kept the pull of his lips light, the stroke of his tongue steady until she moved her hips in a telling rhythm. Only then did he slide one finger inside her, determined to feel the surge of her climax. It hit her fast, hit her strong and in turn served to increase the heaviness and strength of Ford's erection. He couldn't remember when he'd needed someone so badly. Needed to be inside her. Needed to hold her close to his pounding heart.

In a matter of moments, he would be exactly where he wanted to be, as close to Kerry as he could possibly be. And he inherently knew that by doing so, he could be forever lost in her. To her.

# Seven

Trembling, Kerry kept her eyes closed as she tried to recover from the impact of the orgasm. Her mind fought the voyage back to earth, but her body told her she needed more. She was mildly aware of Ford leaving the bed and the sound of tearing paper. She was very aware when he skimmed his taut body up her body. She welcomed his weight. Welcomed his intense kiss. Welcome the feel of every ridge and muscle against her palms as she sent her hands on a journey over his back and bottom.

He slid one hand in her hair and slipped the other between them, nudging her legs apart with his thigh. "Look at me, sweetheart."

Sweetheart. At one time she might have found that archaic, but not with Ford. Such a simple endearment said with a world of emotion. She opened her eyes to his beautiful face illuminated by the light of day and the heat of desire. His eyes were bright and oh, so blue and he kept them fixed on her eyes as he pushed inside her. She felt no pain, no fear, only fullness. Completeness, as well, both at the place where they were now joined and deep in her heart.

He tipped his head against her shoulder, and she felt a slight shudder running through him.

"Ford?" Her voice sounded unsure, exactly how she felt at the moment.

He raised his head and traced her lips with a fingertip. "You feel so incredible."

"So do you." And he did, so very, very good.

He looked concern, and she loved him for that. "Are you sure?"

"Positive."

"I don't want to hurt you."

She could tell by the hard set of his jaw that he was fighting his natural instinct. And Kerry would have none of that. "You won't hurt me." She ran her tongue along the seam of his lips. "So don't hold back."

Those simple words unleashed something inside of Ford that both thrilled and excited Kerry. He moved inside her slowly at first, then harder and wilder. Touched her everywhere, including the place that his mouth had so tenderly manipulated only moments before.

She relished every sensation—the power of his body in motion, the feel of his hair-roughened legs entwined with hers, the strength of his broad back beneath her palms, his whispered words of praise so soft at her ear. The way it should be, she recognized, a mutual joining with a seductive and skillful man. A man who didn't know the meaning of brute force but instead knew how to treat a woman.

Then one sensation overtook all others, the onset of another release bearing down upon her. She lost track of place and time until the steady pulse began to subside. Ford tensed in her arms and muttered an oath that Kerry considered the most sexy thing she'd ever heard leave a man's mouth. His breath rode out on a long hiss, followed by a low groan. He claimed her mouth with a drugging kiss, his hands still in motion over her body, and hers roving over his. They remained that way for a long time, kissing and touching and holding on to each other, as if they couldn't quite get enough of the contact. Kerry wondered if she would ever get enough of him.

Still joined to her body, Ford smiled, both his dimples and eyes shining. "Damn, that was great," he muttered, bringing about Kerry's laugh.

"I have to agree," she said.

"No regrets?"

She palmed his jaw. "None at all. Thank you."

"No. Thank you."

They kissed some more, touched some more until Ford finally rolled onto his side with Kerry still securely in his arms. She kept her head nestled against his chest until she heard his breathing grow steady and deep. That sound, along with the solid beat of his heart, lulled her into sleep. She didn't know how long she'd been out when she awoke to find Ford had flipped onto his belly, his face turned toward her.

Kerry grabbed the opportunity to take in all the little details, beginning with his features now slack in sleep, his brown lashes fanning below his closed lids, the deep bow of his lips and the tiny cleft in his chin. She studied his arm covered in golden hair contrasting with his tanned skin, his large hand spanning the pillow next to his face. She visually scanned his back, broad and bronzed, and kept going right down his spine to his incredible butt. Incredible bronzed butt. He had absolutely no tan line at all. Anywhere.

Somehow, someway, the man maintained an allover tan. Kerry seriously doubted it was product-enhanced, because it looked too natural. She supposed he might drive a tractor in the nude, but that seemed highly unlikely. Yet the vision caused a giggle to bubble up in her throat and threaten to explode into a laugh. Before that occurred, she decided to take a shower and let him sleep a while longer.

Kerry made quick work in the bath, hoping the hotel hair dryer didn't wake Ford. But when she left the room, she discovered he hadn't moved an inch. After checking the clock, she realized she probably should wake him. Otherwise they would be late for their dinner in Napa.

Perched on the edge of the bed in a lush terry robe provided by the hotel, Kerry watched Ford again while she ran a brush through her hair. When she cleared her throat and he still didn't rouse, she patted his bare bottom and said, "Time to get up, Farmer Ford."

His eyes drifted open and he came fully awake with a grin. "You smell good." His voice was grainy and gruff and so patently sexy that Kerry considered shedding the robe and forgetting about everything but him.

"And you sleep very soundly," she said.

He rolled onto his back, totally secure in his nudity, and ran a palm down his torso, from chest to belly. Even though Kerry should be totally satisfied and sexually sated, she felt the familiar stirrings of wet heat between her thighs, sensations she had denied for too long. She certainly couldn't deny them now. If they had more time, she just might suggest they do something about her need, and Ford's, which had grown very obvious right before her eyes.

His grin deepened as he slid his hand lower as if to taunt her. "Something else is coming awake."

Kerry pushed off the bed and stood. "I see that." Boy, did she.

Crooking his finger at her, he said, "Why don't you come over here and give me a good-afternoon kiss."

As tempting as that sounded, she didn't dare. Not if they intended to get on the road soon. "I'm thinking you should probably go shower before we keep Caroline waiting."

He laced his hands behind his neck and bent one leg at the knee. "I'm thinking we should be fashionably late."

She waved the brush at him as her heart rate did double time. "Now, now. That would be rude."

He glanced down and so did Kerry. "Considering my current state, I'm liable to embarrass both of us, unless we do something about it pretty soon."

Kerry considered his words, and although she was sorely tempted, she decided she would find the time to help him out when they had more time. "The quicker we learn about Anna Sheridan, the quicker we can plan what to do next. And the quicker we can get back here and settled in for the night."

Ford stared at the ceiling. "You're right. I can't forget about Grant or why I'm in San Francisco."

Kerry hated that she'd reminded him of that. Hated that his uncle's arrest was the only reason he was there and that after it was resolved he'd be gone again. "I left you a towel, so have fun with your shower."

He turned his blue eyes on her again. "I'd have more fun if you'd join me."

Again, temptation came calling, but logic won out. "We can do that later. Otherwise we will be late."

Following a sigh, Ford climbed out of the bed and thankfully headed to the bath. If he'd taken one step toward her, Kerry's resolve would have weakened and they might never leave the hotel room.

She watched him walk away, all the while admiring his muscled bottom flexing with each step, still intrigued by his allover tan. Before he closed the bathroom door, she said, "Ford, you don't have any tan lines."

He turned, one large hand braced on the jamb. "No, ma'am, I don't."

She crossed her legs against another rush of heat when her gaze drifted down the stream of hair below his navel and didn't stop there. After forcing her gaze back to his face, she asked, "Care to explain?"

He smiled again. "There's something to be said for a pool and a privacy fence after coming in from the field at lunchtime. You just strip down, dive in, then lie around for an hour or so and daydream."

"What do you daydream about?"

"Nothing much, but I guarantee when I go back I'll be having some really nice ones about you."

With that he closed the door and left Kerry alone with another reminder of his imminent departure. She allowed herself a private daydream, one that involved living a simple life surrounded by simple people. Spending lazy days and endless nights with a gorgeous guy who was anything but simple. Never again having to worry about locking doors or dealing with big-city hassles.

And that seemed about as probable to Kerry Roarke as having a future with Ford Ashton.

When they arrived at The Vines, a housekeeper showed Ford and Kerry to the living room where they found Caroline waiting. She rose from a black chair and gave him a brief hug. "I'm glad you're here."

"Caroline, this is Kerry Roarke," he said. "She's been helping me out with details about the murder." Helping him out with a lot more.

If Caroline was at all surprised by Kerry's presence, Ford

couldn't tell from her relaxed smile. "Welcome to The Vines, Kerry."

Kerry took the hand Caroline offered for a polite shake. "Thank you for having me here." She looked around the room with an awed expression. "This is a beautiful place. Millie would love all the antiques."

"Millie is Kerry's landlady," Ford offered.

"Well, let's make ourselves comfortable," Caroline said, indicating a striped couch while she took a nearby chair.

Ford and Kerry sat on the sofa, keeping a decent berth between them. When he noticed Kerry wringing her hands, he fought the urge to take them into his hands to calm her nerves. Not a good idea. The less Caroline knew about their relationship, the better.

Caroline picked up a bottle of white wine from an ice bucket set out on the coffee table separating them and held it up. "Would either of you like a glass? It's one of our best Chardonnays."

Ford waved off the offer. "None for me. No offense, but I'm not much of a wine drinker."

"Would you prefer something else, Ford?" she asked.

Yeah, whiskey straight up from the bottle. "No, thanks. I'm driving."

"I'd love some wine," Kerry said.

She looked like she could use a drink, Ford decided. Or two or three. Maybe he shouldn't have brought her here, and he wasn't really sure why he'd thought that necessary. Easy. He didn't want to be away from her for any length of time.

Caroline poured a glass for Kerry, handed it to her and then took one for herself. She leaned back in the chair, looking every bit the refined lady, not a blond hair out of place or a single wrinkle in her pink suit. Kerry wore the clothes she had on from work, the skirt and blouse he'd gladly removed and would be glad to remove again later. With his jeans, boots and polo, he was definitely underdressed.

Caroline took a sip of her wine, then rested her hand on the arm of the chair. "You mentioned on the phone you had something you needed to ask me, Ford?"

He crossed one leg over the other and tried to loosen up. "Yeah. It's about Anna Sheridan."

"What about her?"

"I need to know what you know about her relationship with Grant."

Caroline frowned. "Why?"

"Because Grant sent a letter to me through Edgar Kent this morning. He mentioned her. In fact, he asked me to come here and tell her he's going to be okay."

Caroline took a small sip of the wine, keeping a firm grip on the glass. "I suppose they're only friends."

Ford wouldn't bet on that, considering Caroline's lack of conviction. "You didn't notice anything other than friendship going on between them?"

She leaned forward and topped off her glass. "To be honest with you, I've been distracted lately. My daughter Mercedes is having a few problems."

"Anything serious?" Ford asked.

"Boyfriend problems. It seems hers has suddenly disappeared. But that's the least of your worries. Are you suggesting that perhaps Anna and Grant were having some sort of tryst?"

Ford ran a hand over his jaw. "I don't know about that, but I find it kind of strange he asked about her. He's usually pretty guarded about that sort of thing."

Caroline raised a finely arched eyebrow. "You mean women?"

"Yeah. And the tone of the letter makes me wonder if he's

protecting her in some way. Maybe she's got something to do with Spencer's murder."

Caroline toyed with the pearls at her throat. "I can't imagine Anna would be involved in anything like that. Granted, she did try to confront Spencer at the estate and encountered Lilah, poor girl, and never got in to see him. That's how she ended up here with little Jack. She had nowhere else to go and frankly, she was afraid someone would hurt the baby after she started getting some threats on his life."

"Threats?" Kerry asked, the first word she'd spoken since they'd gotten past the pleasantries.

"Yes, and that's never been solved, but they've ended now."

As far as Ford was concerned, everything about this situation was growing more bizarre by the minute. "I'm guessing Spencer never claimed Jack."

"Of course not. Why would he bother?"

No reason to bother at all, Ford thought. "I need to talk to Anna. I have to know if she's hiding something."

"She's here, as far as I know," Caroline said. "She's staying at the cottage by the lake."

Ford stood. "You two have a nice visit. Hopefully this won't take too long."

When he felt a hand on his shoulder, Ford turned to see Kerry standing beside him. "Why don't you let me handle this, Ford?"

"Why would you want to do that?"

"I did meet her the time she came into Ashton-Lattimer, so I'm not a total stranger. I'm also a woman. If you charge in there and toss out presumed allegations based on theory, she's not going to talk to you."

Although she didn't say it, Ford knew exactly what Kerry was thinking. He'd nearly screwed up their relationship because of his preconceived notions about her. "Okay. I'll go with you."

"That's not necessary. I can give you a full report later." She turned to Caroline. "Mrs. Sheppard, the wine is wonderful. I would love to have another glass on my return, if that's okay."

"Of course it is, dear." Caroline stood and gestured toward the opening of the room. "Just go left and after you exit the rear of the house, follow the path to the right that leads to the cottage. If you have trouble, I'll have my husband escort you. He should be coming in at any moment for dinner."

"I have a good sense of direction, so I'm sure I'll find it without any problem. And please don't wait dinner on me. This could take a while."

Ford watched Kerry walk out, feeling somewhat powerless even though he trusted her to do whatever she could to aid Grant's cause. He also felt somewhat guilty when he realized he'd been following the movement of her hips in that skirt. Clearing his throat, he sat back down and said, "I think I'll have that drink now. Do you have any bourbon?"

"I certainly do." Caroline rose gracefully and walked to a decanter set atop some kind of a bureau across the room. "Ice?" she asked after she poured a highball glass full of the amber liquid.

"Nope. Straight up."

Caroline crossed the room, handed him the tumbler and this time sat beside him. "Kerry seems like a lovely girl. I'm not surprised Spencer hired her."

Ford took a long draw off the drink and welcomed the liquor burning down his throat. "He hired her, but he didn't have an affair with her."

Caroline looked at him curiously. "Are you absolutely sure?"

"Yeah. She hated him. And I believe her."

"Is that your head talking or your heart?"

"I don't know what you mean." He knew exactly what she'd meant, and he hated being that obvious in his admiration.

She gave him a knowing smile. "I've seen the way you look at her, and the way she looks at you. I sense quite a bit of mutual admiration between the two of you."

Ford stared at what was left of the booze in his glass. "Once I found out she had nothing to do with Spencer's murder, I realized I liked her a lot. Actually, I liked her before I found out. Crazy, huh?"

"No, not crazy at all. I understand completely. I knew I was in love with Lucas not long after we met."

In love? Ford sat back and drained the glass dry. "I didn't say that, Caroline."

"Love truly isn't so horrible, Ford. And you know, California isn't, either. It's really a rather nice place to live. Especially in the Napa area."

He knew where this was leading. Time to rein her in. "I have a farm. And a business. Abby's there. My life is there. In Nebraska, not California." Funny how he'd sounded like he was trying to convince himself as well as Caroline.

She didn't look the least bit ruffled. "Then perhaps you might consider taking a souvenir back with you."

Normally Ford might be angry over the less-than-subtle hints, but he couldn't be mad at Caroline. Playing dumb was his best defense. "Well, I thought about picking up some of those weird spices from Chinatown for Abby."

Caroline stared at him like she could see right through him. Probably because she could. "Ford, I hope that you don't let what your mother did ruin your chances of finding someone special. Not every woman is like her. And I hope you forgive me for trying to sound like your mother."

If only she had been his mother, then maybe his history with successful relationships might not be nonexistent. "I hear what you're saying, Caroline. But I just met Kerry. I have no idea how long I'll be here, and it's probably best to keep things light between us."

After a pat on his arm, she took her hand away and laced it with the other in her lap. "Of course, dear. You know what's best for you. I trust you'll find that special someone some day. Maybe sooner than you think."

Ford already had a special lady. Kerry Roarke was special in many ways. And he hadn't realized until that moment how much she'd begun to affect him. But he didn't care to confess that to Caroline—or even to himself.

Kerry knocked twice and was almost ready to give up when the door swung open to Anna Sheridan. "May I help you?"

A polite enough greeting, but Kerry noted the wariness in her brown eyes. "You probably don't remember me, but we've met before. Kerry Roarke, Spencer Ashton's former assistant."

"I remember you. Why are you here?"

From her distrustful tone, no doubt Anna believed Kerry had replaced her sister in every way. "If I could come in for a minute, I'll explain. It's important."

Anna didn't budge. "Can you at least give me a hint?"

"I have a message to give you from Grant Ashton."

Kerry immediately noticed the change in Anna. Her stern expression brightened and her shoulders seemed to slump, as if hearing Grant's name made her boneless. "You've seen Grant?"

"No, but his nephew, Ford, received a letter from him. I'm here on his behalf. And I promise this won't take long."

Finally Anna moved aside and allowed Kerry to enter a small living area decorated with rough-hewn furnishings and a lot of quilts. "Have a seat and I'll be right back," Anna told her before disappearing down a hallway.

Kerry took a seat on the sofa and nervously thrummed her fingers on the cushions as she prepared a mental laundry list of questions to present to Anna. She had to be kind, considerate and above all, cautious. Otherwise, Anna could very well boot her out before she had answers.

Anna returned shortly thereafter and sat on a small chair catty-corner to the sofa. "I've put the baby to bed early because he didn't have his nap today. He could wake up a few times before he's down for the night."

In other words, make it quick, Kerry. "I understand. First of all, Grant wants you to know he's going to be okay."

She looked away. "But he's not okay. He's still in jail."

"True, he is. But Ford's trying very hard to get him cleared."

"Anyone who came in contact with Spencer Ashton suffered for it." Her acid tone indicated the extent of Anna's hatred.

Discretion was definitely in order, Kerry decided. Otherwise, Anna might stop talking altogether. "I know. I worked for Spencer Ashton. He could be very charming. It's understandable why a woman like your sister would have fallen victim to that charm and suffered for it."

Anna finally brought her attention to Kerry. "But you didn't?"

"No. I'd heard about him through the office grapevine, and I knew immediately he couldn't be trusted. He was a master manipulator."

"How well I know. He definitely manipulated Alyssa." She leaned forward, a world-weary look on her face. "And I hold him responsible for her death. He wanted her to get rid of the baby, and when she wouldn't, he wrote her off completely. He didn't even have the decency to check on her when she called and told him she was in labor. By the time she got to the hospital, she was hemorrhaging. It's a miracle they saved Jack. But they couldn't save her. In a way, I think she gave up."

Although it was bad form to think ill of the dead, Kerry despised Spencer Ashton more now than she ever had. "I'm sorry, Anna. At least Jack has you now."

"I'm all that he has."

Which would give Grant prime motivation to protect her if, in fact, she was somehow involved in the murder. "Anna, I hate to ask this, but I have to know. Do you have any knowledge about what happened the night Spencer was murdered?"

Her shoulders tensed, but she failed to look at Kerry. "I don't know what you mean."

Oh, but she did. Kerry had become well versed at reading people, although Ford had been the exception. But in a way, she'd probably known he was hiding something; she just hadn't wanted to see it. Anna Sheridan was definitely hiding something.

"Did you have anything to do with his murder?"

Surprisingly, Kerry saw no anger in Anna's expression. "I hated him, but I would never risk leaving Jack alone. So the answer to your question is no. I did not kill Spencer Ashton, even though I never shed a tear over his death. And I am positive Grant didn't kill him, either."

"How do you know that for sure?"

"Because he was with me that night, all night, right here."

That was not what Kerry had been expecting. She hesitated for a moment, trying to regroup from the shock. "If that's true, why haven't you come forward?"

Anna's eyes welled with tears. "Because he told me not to. He was afraid for me and for Jack. Afraid for Jack because of some threats we received on his life. And afraid for me because he thought the police might believe we were in on the murder together. I asked him to let me tell them, but he made me promise I wouldn't." A few tears drifted down her cheeks, and she swiped them away with the back of her hand. "But I can't do it anymore. I'll come forward. I'll take a lie detector test if I have to. Anything to get him out of that horrible place."

Kerry considered going to her and giving her a hug, but Anna stiffened her frame and resumed her calm in short order. "So now you know the truth. If you'd like, I'll ask Caroline to stay with Jack and I'll go with you back into San Francisco to talk to the police tonight."

At the moment Kerry wished Ford were there to hear the truth and to advise her on what to do next. All she knew right then was Anna looked as if she might crumble in a mild wind. "One night isn't going to matter, Anna. I'll have Ford call you in the morning and arrange a time for you to come in to the police station. I'm sure he'll want to accompany you."

She pressed the heels of her palms against her eyes. "I can't stand the thought of Grant being in that place even one more hour, much less another night."

Unfortunately, Kerry was in the position to see the reality of the situation where Anna was not. "I seriously doubt they'll release him immediately."

"Why?"

"Because it's going to take time. I suspect they'll want to know why you waited to come forward, and they'll have quite a few questions." They really might believe she was in cahoots with Grant, a fact Kerry didn't feel Anna could handle at the moment.

Leaning over, Kerry pulled a tissue from the holder set out on the end table, stood and handed it to Anna. "Are you going to be okay in the meantime?"

Anna dabbed at her eyes, sniffed, then tucked her auburn hair behind her ears with one shaky hand. "Sure. I'll be fine. As long as I know Grant will finally get out, I'll take whatever might come."

If only Kerry could be so sure Grant would be released, but she wasn't. "I'm going back to the house to talk with Ford. Is there anything else I can get for you?"

"Only Grant's freedom."

Spoken like a woman in love, something that was more than obvious to Kerry, even if Anna Sheridan hadn't admitted it to herself, or to him. And as Kerry traveled back to deliver the news of Grant's alibi, she also recognized she had fallen in love with Grant Ashton's nephew.

During the drive back into the city, Ford tried to be optimistic, but even in light of Anna's revelations, he was too afraid to let himself believe. "It might not be enough," he muttered without taking his attention from the road.

"We'll have to wait and see. I personally think we have enough to get Grant cleared. Or at the very least, get him out of jail for the time being. We just have to keep hoping."

He reached across the console and took her hand. She had become his sanity, keeping him grounded yet providing an escape when he'd needed it most. "Thanks for everything. I owe you."

She lifted his hand and brushed a kiss across his knuckles. "You can pay me back when we get to the hotel."

Ford intended to do just that, with a long, hot session of lovemaking. He looked forward to holding her all night, waking up to her in the morning. Just thinking about that made him want to punch the accelerator and speed all the way back into the city. In deference to safety, he refrained.

After a few moments passed, Kerry pointed to a bend in the road that separated the highway from a gravel drive. "Turn right."

He shot her a look of confusion. "Why?"

"Because I want to see something."

Ford wanted to see her naked, and soon. But he couldn't refuse her anything right now, if ever. "Okay, but this better be good."

"It will be."

When he turned onto the narrow road, Kerry instructed him to pull over to one side. Once he had the vehicle parked, she hurried out of the car and rounded the hood, signaling him to follow. By the time Ford got out, she'd already crossed the street to stand on the other side.

As he approached her, she said, "It's beautiful, isn't it?" without turning around.

He had to admit that the rows of grapevines, turned gold by the light of the three-quarter moon, were pretty impressive, but not as impressive as Kerry.

Moving behind her, Ford wrapped his arms around her waist and pulled her against him. "You're beautiful."

She looked back at him and kissed his cheek before returning her attention to the panorama. "Does it look like this at midnight in Nebraska?"

"Yeah. Minus the vines, of course. Lots of corn, especially right before harvest. Abby and I used to play hide-and-seek in the stalks when we were kids. In fact, we hid from Grant or Buck on more than one occasion."

"That must have been wonderful."

At times Ford hadn't realized how much he'd taken for granted, until he'd seen the world through Kerry's eyes. "I had a good childhood." Even with an absent mother, who'd never been much of a mother at all.

"You know, mine wasn't so bad when my mom was alive. She used to take me on long walks and never told me I couldn't climb trees or swim in the creek. I miss being that carefree. I still miss her."

He was going to miss Kerry when he had to leave. Badly.

"I can't even imagine what it would be like not having Grant around."

"Then don't imagine it. Don't invite that into your life." She turned into his arms to face him. "Do you know what you need?"

"No, what do I need?"

She smoothed a hand over his chest. "A distraction."

He couldn't agree more. "Oh, yeah? What kind of distraction?"

"This kind." Clasping his nape with one hand, she bent his head to meet her lips and kissed him but good. A long, hot kiss that caused Ford's body to jolt to life.

She pulled away and smiled. "Did that help?"

"Some, but I could use a little more distracting."

"And I have the perfect way to do that."

Ford expected her to kiss him again, but instead she caught his hand and led him to the back of the SUV. After dropping his hand, she raised the rear door and climbed inside. Ford definitely enjoyed the view of her butt while she pulled a latch and pushed the rear seat forward.

Turning, she sat down at the edge of the cargo space, her long legs dangling, her skirt riding up her thighs, and patted the space beside her. "Come here and let me get your mind off your troubles."

Just thinking about what she might do had Ford close to losing his mind. Once he settled beside her, she slipped off her heels, tossed them behind her and then nudged him to his back.

"What exactly do you plan to do to distract me?" he asked although he was fairly sure he already knew the answer to that.

"Guess you'll just have to wait and see," she told him as she pulled the tails of his shirt from his jeans.

He sucked in a deep breath as she raised the polo until she had his abdomen exposed. "Now you really have my curiosity up."

Slowly she lowered his fly, keeping her gaze on his face as she traced the outline of his erection through his briefs. "I do believe your curiosity isn't the only thing that's up."

Quite an understatement. "You're definitely right about that."

Lowering her head, Kerry placed soft kisses right below his navel as she grasped his waistband. He gritted his teeth when she worked his slacks down his thighs. This kind of distraction could very well kill him. "Kerry, I…" He couldn't even form a coherent sentence.

After raising her head and nailing him with a sultry look, she reached up and pressed her fingertips against his mouth. "Hush and just let me do this."

"Someone might drive by," he muttered as she pushed his briefs down to join his slacks.

Surprisingly, she laughed while Ford didn't find a damn thing funny about the situation. Hot, but not humorous.

"We're on a rural stretch of road at a quarter past midnight," she said as she ran a slow fingertip down his length. "And if someone does happen to come by, too bad."

Too good, Ford thought when she enveloped him in her warm, sweet mouth. He twisted his hands in her hair to secure himself against the total sexual charge. With every pass of her tongue, every draw of her lips, he grew harder than stone, balanced on the brink of coming completely unwound.

As much as he enjoyed what she was doing, Ford didn't want it to end this way. He wanted to be inside her when he couldn't hold out any longer. He wanted her to take this trip with him.

Pulling her head up, he kissed her hard, kissed her quick, then said, "Do you still have that condom in your purse?"

She grinned. "Yes, sir, I sure do."

"Get it."

When she crawled forward and leaned between the front

seats, Ford couldn't resist lifting her skirt and forming his palm her between her thighs. As he'd predicted, she was hot and damp and ready for some action. And while she rummaged through her purse, he slipped his hand beneath the silk panties and touched her without mercy.

He heard her gasp before she declared, "Found it."

So had Ford, and he knew just what to do with it. Kerry went limp, her arms braced on the back of the passenger seat, her hips moving in sync with his fingers. He lifted her skirt, pressed his open mouth to her bottom and slipped a finger inside her. This time she moaned as he stroked her, inside and out, her breath riding out in an uneven tempo. She trembled as Ford quickened the pace, determined to rock her world the way she had rocked his. He didn't let up until he'd brought her to a climax than made her knees buckle.

She regarded him over her shoulder, her body still limp against the seat. "You are determined to drive me crazy."

"That's the plan."

"Plan or not, now it's my turn again." She scooted back and stretched out beside him, tore open the condom and did the honors herself. Ford realized they didn't have a lot of room but he was damn determined to make this work. While he was considering how he was going to get inside her without knocking himself out in the process, Kerry shoved his pants farther down, slinked out of her panties and then straddled his thighs. She guided him inside her, her hair flowing down in a golden veil around him. For a brief moment, he considered how this would look to anyone who happened by—his legs still partially out of the SUV, his pants down around his ankles and an incredible woman on top of him. Frankly, he didn't give a tinker's damn how it looked, not when Kerry took him on a reckless ride straight into oblivion.

He kept one hand on her breast and the other in motion between her legs as she moved in a slow rhythm up and down his shaft. "Don't hold back," he said in a harsh whisper, relinquishing all his control to her.

He saw understanding dawn in her expression before she resumed a wilder pace. He witnessed a total look of awe as the pleasure took over. He felt the pulse of her orgasm while he was seated deep inside her, and that nearly drove him over the edge completely. But he didn't want it to end now, even though his body was saying something different. Even though every muscle in his gut constricted with the effort to prolong the experience. Unable to fight any longer, he clasped her hips beneath the skirt and lifted his own hips to meet her with one final thrust. He shook from the strength of his own climax and automatically pulled her down against his racing heart.

When the world came back into focus as his breathing steadied and his body calmed, Ford felt the need to say something to Kerry, express his gratitude with words that wouldn't quite form. But what he was beginning to feel for her had only partially to do with appreciation of all that she had done in terms of lovemaking. She'd also disregarded his deception and given him a reason to hope for Grant's release. She'd decided to help him when most women would've probably sent him packing without a second glance. She'd inspired him more than any woman in his past.

Lifting her head, she smiled the sweetest smile and gave him the softest of kisses. "How do you feel now?"

He couldn't begin to tell her without sounding like a fool. "Like I could sprint all the way back into the city." Like he could fall for her completely.

She laughed quietly, a sound he could hear every day for the rest of his life and never tire of it. "I think it's probably best we drive so you don't wear yourself out, because there's plenty more distraction where that came from."

"You have my permission to distract me all night." And most likely she would distract him long after they parted ways.

# Eight

**K**erry had never before experienced going to sleep curled into a masculine body. She'd never known the pleasure of being awakened by a man's callused hands streaming up her body, or the joy of making love in the first light of dawn.

She'd also learned the benefits of showering with a gorgeous guy who had no qualms about engaging in some very devilish water play. Right now she sat on a vanity stool wearing the hotel robe while watching that same gorgeous guy rub a towel along his beautiful body—over his broad chest, across the flat plane of his belly and down his very masculine legs. He grinned as he worked his way back up his groin, totally uninhibited by the fact that she followed his movements.

After coming to her feet, she took the towel from him, wrapped it around his narrow hips and tucked it in below his navel. Holding her face in his palms, he kissed her lightly, then deeply until she considered yanking the towel away and stripping out of her robe.

Instead, she chose to end this little vacation from reality knowing they still had a lot to do today that unfortunately didn't include making love for the remaining hours. Stepping back, she pointed behind her at the door. "I'm going to make some coffee and get the paper. Want me to bring you a cup?"

He caught her hand and pulled her back against him. "I want you naked again. I just plain want you."

She patted his bare chest, battling the urge to slide her hand down to find out exactly how much he wanted her. "You need to call Grant's attorney and Anna and arrange a time for them to meet us at the police station."

He released a rough sigh without releasing her. "Yeah, you're right. But I'm not holding out much hope Grant's alibi is going to hold any real weight."

"We don't have any choice. We have to try."

He studied her with a somber expression. "I know. But I'm worried we'll make matters worse, especially if they believe Grant is the one who blackmailed Spencer and Anna is somehow involved."

Kerry recognized Ford had a point. "I just have to believe that with all the investigative techniques at the police department's disposal, they're going to prove that theory wrong."

He pressed a kiss to her forehead. "You're going to have to believe enough for both of us."

"Don't give up, Ford. Somehow, someway, we will get your uncle out of jail."

Turning her around, he patted her bottom. "I need some coffee, woman."

She shot a stern glance over her shoulder as she headed toward the door. "Woman? Aren't we a regular little macho man this morning."

"Little?"

Kerry turned, hand braced on the door, to find Ford had re

moved the towel. Her gaze tracked downward to discover he was impressively aroused. "Okay. Big macho man."

He favored her with a dimpled grin. "That's better. Are you sure you don't want to come over here and sit on my lap for a while?"

"You are too much, Ford Ashton."

"And I can't get enough of you, Kerry Roarke."

Before she discarded good sense, Kerry walked out the door, chafing her terry-covered arms with her palms in reaction to the succession of heady chills. But beneath the bottom of the robe, she was extremely hot.

After setting the coffeemaker in action, she strode across the room, opened the door and bent to get the paper. The headline calling out from the page froze her solid:

Prosecution's Star Witness in Ashton Murder a Street Kid.

Straightening, she backed into the room and read the article with curiosity and major questions. She cataloged the facts—a homeless teenage street artist sketching passersby, identified only as Eddie, had seen Grant enter Ashton-Lattimer. At nine o'clock at night?

"Something interesting in there?"

Kerry faced Ford and held up the paper in both hands like a sign. "Yes, this."

Ford streaked a hand through his damp hair before taking the paper from her. He read silently for a time before turning his attention back to her. "They're hanging their case on a kid?"

"Obviously so, and I found several things odd about it. First, it says he was drawing when he saw Grant enter the building. It would have been dark by then. Second, street artists draw for money, so it doesn't make much sense for this kid to be down in the financial district when he could have been at the Wharf or The Haight hitting tourists up for a few bucks."

"Those are all good questions."

"Yes, and I intend to get some answers."

Ford rolled the paper in his fists. "How do you plan to do that?"

Kerry tightened the robe's sash and lifted her chin. "Easy. I'm going to find this Eddie and ask him. I know people who will know how to find him, and we will find him even if it takes all week."

"Even if we do find him, and that's a big 'if,' what makes you think he'll talk to you?"

"Because it takes a one-time street kid to know one. I have a few theories on what might have happened."

"Care to share them with me?"

"I will on the drive. First, you and I need to get dressed."

He approached her slowly and palmed her cheek. "You've been a godsend, Kerry. I don't know what I would've done without you these past few days. Thank you for everything."

She didn't know what she would do after he was gone from her life. Survive, the way she always had. But it wasn't going to be easy. Not in the least.

Laying her hand on his palm, she smiled to conceal her sudden sadness. "Don't thank me yet. This could be a dead end." Exactly like their relationship.

"It's a possibility," he said. "And for some reason, I have this gut feeling something good will come out of this with you in charge."

Kerry hoped it would, even the good they'd found together would be over soon if they were successful.

Ford has postponed calling Anna for the time being, at least until they could talk to the kid named Eddie. That proved to be a serious challenge. They'd been to The Haight, to Fisherman's Wharf then to a couple of shelters, with no luck.

Kerry refused to give up and by the time late afternoon had set in, they found themselves back at the Wharf.

Now Ford stood outside a small restaurant, waiting for Kerry to return from speaking with the owner. He leaned back against the red brick wall, arms folded across his chest, and prayed this time she might be successful.

"Eureka!"

Ford pushed off the wall to face Kerry who was coming toward him, a vibrant smile on her face. "You found him?"

She slipped her hand in the crook of his arm. "Her. We've been looking for a boy and she's a girl. I talked to J.D., the owner of the restaurant, and he says she left just a while ago after he gave her something to eat. He also said she's been skirting the press and the police, so she's been trying to lay low, but he thinks she probably headed over to where several homeless kids hang out. I imagine she's been hiding out there, with some help."

"Then she probably won't talk to us."

"She might talk to me, that's why I need to do this alone."

"But—"

"It's better this way, Ford. I know what her life is all about because I've lived it, and she could very well be wary of men. You're going to have to trust me on this."

Ford did trust her. He also realized how much he cared about her. So much it made him hurt. "Just promise me you're going to be careful."

She rose up on her toes and kissed him. "I will. First, I'm going to drop you off at the hotel and you can wait for me there."

"How are you going to find her? They didn't publish any kind of picture."

"J.D. described her to me. And I know where to look."

Ford took a moment to simply hold Kerry against him, probably tighter than he should. In adulthood, he'd learned to rely on himself and he'd liked it that way. Now he'd learned to rely on her for many things, and he'd discovered that hadn't been bad at all. In fact, it had been good. Damn good. Now he hoped she would come through for him once again.

Money definitely talked. Thanks to a kid who needed some quick cash, Kerry managed to locate the place where Eddie often hung out. A place all too familiar to a woman who had been there before.

Kerry spotted her sitting on a side-street curb, a sketch pad propped up against her black corduroy-covered knees, her long brown hair pulled back and secured at her nape, a dirty white baseball cap pulled low on her brow. The black T-shirt etched with Life Sucks was partially hidden by a frayed blue flannel shirt. Exactly how J.D. had described her.

Kerry moved cautiously toward the teen, calculating each step, planning each question. Stopping at a nearby light pole, she leaned a shoulder against it, her hands tucked away in the pockets of her navy blazer covering her jeans. She pretended to be hanging out, the misty evening fog beginning to set in as well as a definite chill.

Eddie seemed oblivious to her presence, her brows drawn down in concentration as she swept charcoal over the blank page, creating a picture of a field of flowers surrounding a child, the sun high in the imaginary sky.

"Wow, you're good," Kerry said.

Only then did the teen look up. "What?"

Kerry gestured toward the canvas. "The picture. You're very talented."

She flipped the page over to a blank one. "For ten bucks, I'll draw you."

"Okay." After dropping down on the curb beside her, Kerry retrieved a ten-dollar bill from her pocket and handed it to Eddie.

After shoving the money in her sneaker, Eddie asked, "You want a real picture or a caricature?"

"A caricature might be fun. Can you draw me sitting in a red Mustang convertible?"

"Yeah, I can do that. My mom owned a Mustang once." She opened a box containing assorted colored chalk and started to work.

"How long have you been living on the streets?" Kerry asked as she watched Eddie outline the car in accurate detail.

She continued to draw without looking up. "Who said I live on the streets?"

"Not too hard to figure out, considering where you are. I used to hang out here, too."

She gave Kerry a quick once-over. "You don't look like it."

Kerry folded the hem of her jacket when the memories assaulted her. "It was a while ago. How long have you been here?"

"About eight months."

"I lived on the streets for a year. I was sixteen. How old are you?"

"Fifteen." Eddie sent her a hopeful look. "But you got out."

"Yes. A woman helped me one night after I ended up in the hospital after an attack. I was lucky."

She shrugged. "It's not so bad. Better than home, that's for sure."

"I thought the same thing at the time. My stepfather kicked me out. At first I enjoyed the freedom, but it came with a price." Namely, the last vestiges of naïveté.

Eddie's strokes were so angry, Kerry thought she might break the red chalk in half. "My mom's boyfriend started messing with me. She just pretended not to see, so I took off."

Kerry's heart broke for her. "Where are you from, Eddie?"

Her hand froze and her gaze zipped from the page to Kerry. "How do you know my name?"

Kerry determined the time was right to tell her the truth, and take her chances. "Because I saw it in the newspaper. I've been looking for you all day."

Her eyes narrowed with suspicion. "Are you a cop or a reporter?"

"No, but I am a friend of the man you picked out in the lineup. I also know there's no way you could have seen him, because he wasn't there."

She lowered her gaze, but not before Kerry glimpsed her guilt. "I saw him."

"You couldn't have. He wasn't even in the city."

Eddie slapped the top back on the box and closed the sketch pad. "I've got to go now."

Kerry touched her arm to detain her. "Eddie, if someone threatened you and told you that you had to identify Grant Ashton, then you have to tell the truth."

She swiped a shaky hand over her cheek, leaving a streak of red in its wake. "Telling the truth gets you nowhere."

"It will in this case. Don't throw away your honor, Eddie. Even if that's all you have, it will see you through during the tough times."

Eddie raised her gaze, her eyes looking frightened and fatigued. "If you're right, and I'm not saying you are, what would they do to me if I change my story?"

Kerry's spirits elevated, knowing she was close to discovering the facts. "I don't know. You might have to spend some time in a juvenile facility."

"Maybe that wouldn't be so bad if I had some food and a bed. As long as they don't try to send me back home."

Some home, Kerry thought. "I'm sure they'll be lenient if you try to make it right before it's too late. Before they put the wrong man in jail. Especially if someone said they'd hurt you if you didn't lie."

Eddie wrapped her arms around her bent knees. "He didn't say he would hurt me. But he did give me money."

"He?"

"Some creepy guy. He came up to me when I was down at the Wharf and told me I could make a hundred bucks if I did what he said. At first I thought he wanted me to…you know."

How well Kerry knew. "Did he tell you his name?"

"No. He showed me a picture of that Grant and told me to go to the police and tell them I saw him going into the building around nine. They wanted to keep me there at the police station after I picked him out of the lineup, but I snuck out because I was afraid they'd call my mom. I've been hiding out ever since, but I figure they're going to find me soon."

"That's why you should go to them first and tell the real story. I'll be right there with you. Can you remember what this guy looked like?"

Eddie presented a sudden smile, easing some of the worry from her face and showcasing her youth. "I can go one better. I can draw him."

Ford stopped midpace when he heard the key slide into the lock and the door open, his heart jamming his throat. He turned to see Kerry enter the room, a bright smile on her face and optimism reflecting from her violet eyes.

Before he could reach her, she rushed him and hugged him hard. Ford pulled away first, only because he had to know what happened. "God, I was starting to worry about you when I couldn't find you."

Kerry's expression showed her confusion, understandably so. "Couldn't find me?"

"I followed behind the trolley until I saw you get off. I couldn't find a place to park and I lost sight of you, so I gave up and came back here."

"You were following me?"

"Yeah. I was worried sick the whole time. If something happened to you, I would never forgive myself. I was imagining all sorts of things."

She sent him a slight smile. "I promise, I'm okay. And you can't even imagine what happened, but it's all good. I found our star witness."

"Did you talk to her?"

"Yes, I did. She's waiting downstairs in the restaurant, consuming a cheeseburger. I have the waiter looking after her, in case she tries to slip out."

"What did she say?"

"You won't even believe it."

"Try me."

Kerry stepped out of his arms and withdrew a rolled-up piece of paper from her jacket pocket. "Do you know who this is?"

Ford studied the black-and-white sketch of a guy with thinning dark hair and beady eyes. "I've never seen him before." He handed the picture back. "Who is he?"

"I don't know, and neither does Eddie. But it seems he paid her to say she saw Grant going into the building the night Spencer was murdered. She sketched this picture of him."

"Then this means—"

"We should have enough evidence to clear your uncle."

Ford could only stare at Kerry for a long moment, speechless and in awe that she had somehow managed to help put all the pertinent pieces together. Had it not been for her, he doubted he would have been able to achieve this success. In fact he *knew* he could never have done this without Kerry Roarke—a woman who was as selfless as she was beautiful.

When he failed to speak, she frowned. "Why do you look so serious? This is great news. You should be shouting from the hotel rooftop."

Ford said the only thing he could think to say. "You are amazing." Amazing in more ways than he could begin to express.

She grinned. "All in a day's work. But if it makes you happy, I'll let you tell me how amazing I am, as soon as we get Eddie down to the police station."

"I plan on showing you later." All night long.

"That sounds extremely intriguing. But first you need to call Anna and see if she can meet us down at the station to give her statement."

As much as he wanted to show her how much he appreciated her right this instant, reality took hold. "I've already talked to her. She should be there in the next half hour. Caroline's driving her in. I'll call Edgar Kent on the way to the station."

"Then we should be on our way. The quicker we get out of here, the less time Grant spends in jail."

Kerry turned away but before she could open the door, Ford took her hand and tugged her back into his arms. He held on tight, never wanting to let her go. He didn't want to consider that their time together was almost over, barring any unforeseen glitches. He didn't want to think about not having her around. Not having her this close again. But he did think about it despite his concerns for Grant's well-being and his responsibility back home in Nebraska.

He gave her a quick kiss, then let her go. "Okay. I'm ready now." Ready to get back to the business of what he'd come here for—obtaining his uncle's freedom. But he wasn't ready to leave her just yet. Not until absolutely necessary.

"Looks like I won't be leaving for a while," Ford said as he pulled away from the police station.

Kerry experienced a solid bout of guilt that she wasn't at all displeased over that fact. "What exactly did the attorney tell you?"

"He said he'd file a motion for dismissal and that it could be Monday before they let him out."

"You'd think with everything they have now, they'd let him out tonight, not five days from now."

"Kent said it's a complicated process. Some crappy process, if you ask me. He also said he believes the D.A. still isn't convinced that Grant isn't behind this whole thing. Hopefully Kent can convince a judge there's enough doubt."

Reaching across the console, she took Ford's hand and rested it on her thigh. "It's going to happen, Ford. I can feel it in my bones."

He shot her a quick glance. "I hope you're right."

"I am. I just know it." She also knew that telling him goodbye would be the most difficult thing she'd done in years, and that time would come all too soon. Maybe even tonight.

Ford let go a long sigh. "That Eddie's a pretty sad case. It killed me to see her beg them not to send her back home."

"I know what you mean. That was tough. But unfortunately, she's only one of many lost kids in this city and throughout the country."

"What's going to happen to her?"

Kerry loved him for the true concern in his question. "The detective said she'd go to a halfway house for now. She promised she wouldn't put Eddie back into the home with the abusive boyfriend without some sort of investigation. However, it seems they can't even locate the mother, so it looks as if Eddie might eventually end up in foster care or a group home."

"How did she take that?"

"She seemed resigned to it all. I want to think that any place is better than the streets, but it's hard not knowing what will happen to her. I do plan to keep in touch with her."

"I have no doubt you will."

A few minutes later Ford turned into the hotel drive and

relinquished the SUV to the valet. Together they walked into the hotel, arms around waists, and didn't let each other go until they'd traveled up the elevator and arrived at the room. Only then did Ford drop his arms from around her to unlock the door. Yet they didn't take two steps inside the room before he had her backed up against the wall, kissing her, touching her, stealing her breath and her sanity in one fell swoop.

He left her lips to breeze his lips along her neck before working his way back to her ear. "We haven't had any dinner yet."

"I know," Kerry said while ruffling her fingers through his hair.

He ran his hands up the sides of her sweatshirt. "Anything in particular that you'd like?"

"Oh, I can think of one thing." She reached between them and ran a slow finger up the prominent ridge beneath his fly.

He caught her hand and held it there, pressing her farther back against the wall. "Do you want it now?"

"Yes."

He dropped his hand and cupped her between her legs. "Right here?"

"Yes."

"Then it's all yours."

He took her hand and led her to the hallway, but before they reached the bedroom, he backed her up against that wall. Off went her jacket, shirt, bra and jeans, leaving her wearing only her panties and panting as if she'd run a three-mile marathon. Ford was still dressed, not for long she hoped, but she stopped thinking altogether when he went to his knees and pulled her underwear down her legs, lifted each foot to remove it completely, then tossed it aside.

He pushed her legs apart with his palms and then kissed his way up the inside of her thighs, stroking his tongue over the territory. Kerry was virtually boneless, especially when he halted his journey to use his mouth on her in some terribly creative ways in a very intimate place. He suckled and nibbled and caressed with his lips and hands. She anchored herself by clutching his head, held on until she neared the edge of release. But before that happened, he kissed his way back up her trembling body, pausing to suckle her breasts. A slight groan of protest slipped out of her mouth before she could stop it.

"Don't worry," he whispered. "I plan to finish you in bed, while I'm inside you. I want to feel you climax."

Kerry wanted that too, but she also wanted to be daring and different. "Why the bed when we have a perfectly good wall?"

"You sure about that?" He sounded and looked concerned.

She traced the cleft in his chin with a fingertip then smoothed the worry from his brows. "Very sure. Unless it's too hard to manage."

His smile came into play slowly. "It's hard all right, but I can definitely manage it." He backed away and pointed to her. "Don't move."

As if she could really move at the moment. Then again, she might wilt onto the floor in a pool of need, a distinct possibility as she watched him walk toward the bedroom, stripping out of his jacket as he went. He came back a few moments later, wearing only a condom. He looked very proud. All of him.

Standing in front of her, Ford draped her arms around his neck, then pulled her legs around his waist and said, "Hang on."

She did, tightly, as he pushed inside her, going deeper than she ever dreamed possible. And when she immediately climaxed with the second thrust, her nails inadvertently dug into his shoulders with the strength of the release.

"Damn," he murmured. "This is almost too good."

Kerry couldn't describe how good she felt as he took her on a trip straight into the realm of a sexual place she'd never been before. She marveled at the strength of his legs as he bent to thrust inside her, his arms holding her and protecting her from the wall. Reveled in the power of his body and the sound of his ragged breathing. His skin grew damp with the effort and his eyes took on a hazy cast as he kept them locked with hers. She knew the moment he couldn't hold on any longer by the tautness in his jaw and the hiss that filtered out of his parted lips. He closed his eyes, tipped his forehead against hers and, with one last thrust, his body shuddered. Kerry continued to cling to Ford, holding him close to her body and her heart.

After lowering her legs, Ford kissed her thoroughly yet gently, then swooped her up and carried her into the bedroom. He set her on her feet and turned down the covers but not the lights before laying her back onto the crisp white sheets. He took a quick trip to the bathroom and when he came back he joined her on the bed and rolled her on top of him.

"I knew there was a wild woman residing somewhere beneath that sophisticated exterior," he said, his hands in motion on her bottom.

"And I knew beneath that innocent-farm-boy act I'd find a really wild man, too."

With a laugh, he flipped her over and hovered above her. "Have I told you how amazing you are?"

She tapped her chin with her fingertip. "I believe you did say that earlier. But it takes an amazing person to know an amazing person."

"I guess we'll both agree we're pretty amazing, at least together."

A wave of melancholy rode over Kerry, unwelcome after such a wonderful time. "I guess you won't be needing my services any longer now that we've solved the mystery."

He stared at her long and hard. "First of all, I don't like you using the word *services* like that's what this is all about. I didn't service you. I made love to you because I wanted to.

Second, I know it's selfish to ask, but I'm going to ask, anyway. I want you to stay with me."

"For how long?"

"Until Grant's out of jail."

Of course. He couldn't promise her more than that, and she'd known that all along. Still, it didn't hurt any less to know that she might be nothing more to him than a diversion, regardless of what he'd said. "Then you're asking me to hang around until Monday?"

"Yeah. But only if you want to."

Kerry wanted to, all right, even though she ran the risk of falling in so deep with him that she'd have to claw her way out. "I'll have to call Millie and tell her. It shouldn't be a problem since her niece planned to stay throughout the weekend."

"And you'll stay with me?"

Foolish or not, Kerry just couldn't pass up the chance. Besides, who knew what might happen in five days? Maybe she could somehow convince him that he couldn't live without her. And she would be certifiably stupid if she really believed that. But she'd be crazy not to try.

"Okay, I'll stay."

# Nine

**K**erry Roarke soon found herself caught up in an erotic world created by Ford Ashton. On Thursday morning they began their day by showering together, interrupted by the untimely arrival of housekeeping. Dressed in matching hotel robes, they allowed the maid to make up the room while they cuddled on the sofa in the living area, discreetly touching each other until they bordered on getting caught in some fairly illicit behavior. After the maid finished, Ford requested a surplus of extra towels, bade her goodbye, hung the privacy sign on the door and then made incredible love to Kerry on the sofa.

After that, they dispensed with clothes altogether, donning the robes again only if necessary, parting only when necessary, rarely more than a touch away. They watched the night set on the city and the sun rise over the bay, concealed by the sheer curtain covering the window while Ford stood behind her and made love to her. For the next few days they ordered in-room movies that they hardly watched and meals they rarely finished, consumed partial bottles of wine using most of the contents on each other's bodies.

Kerry learned it took Ford some recovery time between lovemaking sessions, but she also learned that, in regard to her own body, that wasn't always the case. And Ford had discovered that quickly, taking any opportunity he could to bring her to climax when she'd least expected it, using his hands or his mouth or both. She never viewed herself as being such a strongly sexual being before, but then she'd never let herself be that open and trusting with any man. Ever.

On Saturday evening Kerry convinced Ford to go out for dinner and they dressed for the first time in almost three days. She took him to Chinatown for a quick meal and a stroll among the weekly market set up at Portsmouth Park. But they only lasted a while among the chaos because they couldn't seem to keep their hands off each other. They openly kissed on the cable car during the return trip, and the minute they arrived back in the privacy of the hotel room, off went the clothes again, and they become sexually entangled on the living room floor.

By the time Sunday rolled around, Kerry had explored every inch of Ford's body, as he had hers. She'd willingly experimented with lovemaking in every way imaginable, and quite a few that she hadn't imagined. He'd always treated her with the greatest of care, even when their shared passion turned completely unrestrained.

She now knew the way he looked when he slept—tousled and beautiful and almost innocent—because she'd watched him on more than one occasion. She'd also awakened to him watching her with his sultry blue eyes, and invariably that would lead to more touches, more kisses, more incredible couplings.

During the times when they'd both been exhausted and sated, totally replete, they talked about Ford's fury over his mother's careless disregard; her anger over her stepfather's callousness. Both had decided to come to terms with their pasts and forgive, even if they couldn't forget. They'd also discussed all their likes and dislikes, faults and downfalls, goals and dreams. Yet when Monday morning arrived all too soon, they had yet to discuss one important thing—Ford's impending departure.

Kerry had also failed to tell Ford that she loved him, though she did with all her heart. In her life, she had never known a stronger truth. She had never known a more lovable man. But as they waited on the sofa for the call confirming Grant's release, Kerry didn't feel it was time to broach that subject. Even though she was wrapped securely in his arms, she sensed his tension and an underlying impatience. She understood that; he was ready to get on with his life. Without her.

His fingers idled on her arm as his deep voice drifted over her like a warm blanket when he asked, "What do you plan to do today?"

Nothing nearly as exciting as what they'd done the past few days. "First, I'm going to go home and change, visit with Millie, then go into the office. I'm going to have to work a little harder to catch up on my night courses since I missed a couple of classes last week."

"I'm sorry. I didn't even think about your school."

She whisked a kiss over his clean-shaven jaw, drawing in the scent of his cologne and taking it to memory. "I'm not sorry at all. I'd have to say I've learned quite a bit over the past few days."

He sent her a smile. "Yeah? What did you learn?"

That she'd fallen in love with him so deeply she didn't think she'd ever surface. "Mostly about myself. I had no idea I had that in me."

"And I had no idea that I had that much stamina. Must be the company I've been keeping."

"What do you plan to do when you get back home?"

"It's harvest time, and I have a few appointments with some feed suppliers. Just the same old thing I do every day."

"Plow the fields? Herd the cattle? Sun naked by the pool?"

"Something like that, except when I get naked, I'm going to be thinking of you."

There it was, the truth of the matter. She had been his distraction for days, but beyond that, he would think of her only in a sexual sense. "Have fun," she said without looking at him.

He pulled her face toward him and ran his thumb along her jaw. "I'd prefer to have the real thing instead of the fantasy."

"Guess you're just going to have to settle for the fantasy, huh?" She held her breath and waited, hoped for something, although what, she couldn't quite say. Maybe an invitation to come and visit, as if that would really happen.

He pressed his lips against her forehead. "I'm going miss you a helluva lot. I wish we didn't live so far apart."

Kerry wished that more than he would ever know. "But we do, and that's a problem. But you can e-mail me now and then, let me know how you're doing."

"I can do that now and then but we don't have good Internet access in Crawley. At least, not yet."

"Oh, well. It was just a suggestion."

"I could call you, if that's okay."

"Sure."

"Maybe you could come out to Nebraska for a couple of days in the spring."

Well, at least it was something, although Kerry realized not quite enough. "You know, Ford, I'm thinking it might be better if we just leave everything as it is. We've had a great time together, but having a long-distance relationship doesn't work."

"Have you ever had one?"

She'd never had a real relationship, period. "No, I haven't had one, but I don't think it's logical to assume that distance makes the heart grow fonder."

"Then you're saying after I leave, that's it? No phone calls. No visits."

Kerry was surprised by the anger in his tone. "Don't you agree that would be best?"

Taking his arm from around her, he leaned forward and studied the carpeted floor beneath his boots. "Maybe you're right. But I'm not going to forget you."

"And I'm not going to forget you, either."

Straightening, he pulled her to his side again. "I'm not going to fly out until tomorrow. Will you stay with me one more night?"

"I have a class. Remember?"

"Yeah, I remember. But it doesn't last all night, does it?"

"No, but I need to study."

Kerry needed to resist him, but when he kissed her again so completely, she wanted to forget everything but this moment. He was so tempting. So very, very tempting.

They parted, yet he still kept his arms around her, as it had been during the majority of their time together. "I'm glad we met, Kerry."

*And I love you, Ford.* "I feel the same, too. You're a very special man."

He hesitated a long moment, his heart seemingly calling out from his wonderful blue eyes. "What I'm trying to say is—"

When the phone rang, Ford bolted off the sofa and grabbed the receiver, leaving Kerry feeling incredibly bereft. He spoke in low tones, but when he ended the call with, "I'll be right down," she knew that the inevitable was upon them.

Kerry came to her feet, picked up her purse and bag and slipped both straps over her shoulder. "I guess that's the news you've been waiting for."

He shoved his hands into his pockets. "Yeah. Caroline's downstairs. She's going to give me a ride to the jail. Grant's being released as we speak."

"I'm so glad, Ford. I truly am."

"And none of this would be happening without your help."

Regardless of the fact her heart would surely break when he was gone, she didn't regret a minute of their time together. Didn't regret that she'd taken a chance on him after he'd deceived her, because now, more than ever, she knew his honor as well as she knew the touch of his hand, the sound of his voice, the feel of his body so close to hers. "I'm glad I was able to help. Please give your uncle my regards and tell him I'm very sorry for what he's suffered."

"Why don't you tell him yourself?"

"I really have to go, Ford. I need to get back to work." She needed to have a long cry.

He streaked a hand over the back of his neck. "Okay. I understand. But I'd like to at least talk to you before I go tomorrow."

"Sure. I'll give you my number. We can talk for a while tonight. Right now you better get downstairs. I'm sure Caroline's wondering where you are."

Fighting back a rush of tears, Kerry started for the door, but before she could grab the knob, Ford was there, pulling her around into his arms. He kissed her again, soundly, gently, movingly, until she felt as if she would never be able to react to another man in this way.

He released her and thumbed away a rogue tear that had fallen down her cheek despite her effort to stop it. "I'm going to miss you a lot."

"Me, too," she said, worried that if she said more, she ̇ight actually begin to sob. "I really need to get going."

"So do I. Will you at least walk down with me?"

"Sure."

He took her bag, took her hand and held on tightly to her ̇ven in the elevator. When they exited the car, the lobby was ̇rowded with both businessmen and tourists checking out of ̇e hotel. Kerry spotted Caroline first, standing alongside ̇nna Sheridan who was holding a precious little red-haired ̇oy on her hip. And positioned beside Anna, the very tall, very ̇andsome Grant Ashton.

Ford tightened his grip on Kerry's hand, then muttered, ̇I'll be damned."

"Looks like you have a nice surprise."

He stared at her momentarily, shock in his eyes and some- ̇ing else she couldn't quite name. After taking the bag from ̇is shoulder, she smiled. "Don't just stand there. He's wait- ̇g for you."

"Come with me."

"This is your reunion. I'll be right here." At least for a few ̇ore moments.

Following another squeeze of her hand, Ford let her go, in ̇very sense of the word. Kerry watched as he elbowed his way ̇rough the crowd and immediately embraced his uncle. Al- ̇hough she saw little resemblance between Ford and Grant ̇shton, they both wore jeans and boots. Both emitted a con- ̇dence that was palpable even in the jam-packed lobby. Two ̇en who stood above the crowd in every sense of the word.

The family gathered round then, his family, not hers. She ̇idn't belong in this picture, would never be a part of his ̇orld. That realization sent her toward the revolving doors, ̇ut before she left she took one last look at the beautiful man ̇ith the unruly blond hair, the heartbreaker smile and the hypnotic blue eyes. The man with a heart of gold and hardwork ing, wonderful hands. The man who had totally captivated he from the moment they'd met.

Ford caught her gaze in that instant, and as if her heart pro tested the hasty departure before she'd revealed its secre Kerry raised her hand in a wave and mouthed, "I love you."

Stunned by the spontaneous act, she rushed out the exit an hailed a nearby cab, leaving Ford Ashton behind, not know ing if he'd deciphered her declaration. Even if he had, woul it make a difference? Probably not. But at least she could sa she'd tried. The rest was up to him.

"You okay, bud?"

A long moment passed before Ford found the mental re sources to join back in the conversation. He turned his gaz from the place Kerry had been to Grant. "Yeah. I'm fine."

He wasn't fine. Not in the least. Unless he'd imagined i the woman who'd spent the better part of a week in his arm and his bed had just told him she loved him. And he didn' know what the hell to do now. He was torn between runnin after her to make sure his eyes hadn't deceived him, and re maining with the man who had devoted the better part of hi life to raising him.

"I told Grant that Kerry Roarke was instrumental in gath ering the evidence," Caroline said. "She's such a sweet, swee girl, isn't she, Ford?"

Sweeter than any woman had a right to be. "Yeah. She' one in a million."

"And she wasn't tangled up with Spencer?" Grant asked

"No. She was too good for that." When Ford realized hi screwup, he sent Anna a look of apology. "I'm sorry. I didn mean to insult your sister."

Anna smoothed a hand over the boy's head. "No apolog

ecessary. Alyssa made a huge mistake getting involved with
im. Except, because of it, she had this little one. He'll never
e a mistake."

Both Grant and Anna looked at the baby simultaneously
efore turning their gaze to each other. Ford saw something
at looked like a lot more than just simple friendship. Right
ow he didn't have time to ponder anyone's love life other
an his own.

"Ford, can I see you alone for a minute?" Grant asked.

Looking around the crowded room, Ford wasn't sure where
ey could go to have a private conversation. "Do you want
go back to my room?"

Grant pointed behind him. "Caroline and Anna need to get
ack to The Vines, so this will only take a minute. We can step
tside." He regarded Caroline again. "If you'll excuse us, I
ve a couple of things to discuss with Ford."

Caroline waved a hand in dismissal. "Go ahead and take
ur time. We'll go into the restaurant and have some coffee."

"I'll make it quick," Grant said.

Ford was more than curious about the content of the im-
nding conversation. He presumed Grant would want to
ow how things were going back at the farm, maybe how
bby was doing, too. When they stepped outside, Ford im-
ediately scanned the sidewalk hoping to find Kerry. Obvi-
sly, she'd headed home to get ready for work. He planned
call her tonight, although he wasn't exactly sure what he
ould say to her.

Ford stayed in step with Grant as they strode down the side-
alk in silence, past a steady stream of tourists. After they
ent a block, he indicated the park where he'd sat with Kerry
at first night ten days ago and told Grant, "Let's go over
ere."

They took the same bench in front of the same fountain,

and once they were settled in, Ford decided he'd had enoug
of the suspense. "What's on your mind, Grant?"

Grant leaned forward, hands clasped together between h
parted knees. "How's Abby?"

"She was fine as soon as I called her and told her you'd b
getting out soon."

"And the farm?"

"Russ and Buck have everything under control. We'll se
for ourselves when we get back. By the way, I made your re
ervation last night, so we're set to go tomorrow."

"Cancel it."

"What?"

"I'm not leaving California yet."

"Why the hell not?"

"Because the D.A. strongly suggested I stick around un
they find the murderer. I think he still assumes I had som
thing to do with it."

After all they'd done, Grant was still under suspicion. Th
didn't sit well with Ford at all. "Where are you going to stay'

"At The Vines like I was before. Caroline asked me to, a
I agreed."

Ford strongly suspected that Anna had something to c
with that decision, too. "How long do you intend to stay gone

"Until my name is cleared and I find out exactly who kill
Spencer."

"That could take years, if ever."

"Then I'll be here that long."

Ford wanted to knock some sense into his uncle, but eve
a left hook to the jaw wouldn't cure him of his stubbo
streak. Not that he would ever actually punch Grant. Not
he wanted to live to tell about it. "Okay. Have it your wa
Abby's going to be pissed off if you're not there when t
babies are born."

"Maybe we'll get lucky and I'll be home by then."

A span of silence passed before Ford asked, "Anything else you want to talk about?" He figured at some point in time, Grant might want to discuss his jail experience, although he wasn't one to be that open with his feelings. But then, neither was Ford.

"I just wanted to say thanks. You've done me proud, as always."

"Again, I only had a small hand in it. If Kerry Roarke hadn't helped me, I doubt we'd be sitting here together now."

"You like her," Grant said in a simple statement of fact, not a question.

"Yeah."

"Did you spend a lot of time with her?"

Not nearly enough. "Every day since I've been here."

Without straightening, Grant glanced back at him. "Every night, too?"

Ford started to lie but realized Grant would see right through him, as he always had. "For the most part, yeah. Are you going to lecture me about it?"

"You're a grown man, Ford. I'm not going to tell you how to run your life even if you are in love."

In love? "I didn't say that." He did sound way too defensive.

Finally Grant leaned back against the bench. "You don't have to say it. I saw you looking at her when she left, and I saw what she said to you. It's pretty damn obvious to me how you two feel about each other."

"I admit, I do care about her. A hell of a lot more than she realizes."

"Did you tell her that?"

He'd wanted to that morning, but the timing just hadn't been right. Either that, or he'd been too afraid of his own feelings, a more logical explanation. "No, I didn't tell her."

"Then I suggest you go find her and talk this out. What I said to you in that letter about settling down, I meant it. Don't let the right woman pass you by."

"What exactly are you suggesting I do?"

"Ask her to come back with you."

"She won't do it."

"She might."

"She wouldn't stay."

Grant's jaw tightened, and Ford braced for a verbal assault. "Dammit, Ford, not every woman is your mother. If this Kerry feels the same way about you as you do about her, she might be willing to make your home her home."

"She has a home here, Grant."

"Well just maybe she might believe her home's with you. If not now, eventually. All you can do is try. Otherwise you're going to end up like me, in the prime of your life without a good woman to share in it."

"You're only forty-three, Grant, not ninety. One of these days you're going to find the right woman."

Grant looked cynical. "If you say so."

Ford started to ask Grant if he might have found that woman in Anna Sheridan but thought better of it. Grant could dish it out, but he sometimes couldn't take it. The last thing Ford wanted was to get into a heated discussion about relationships. But he was beginning to see the wisdom in his uncle's words.

As soon as he saw Grant off, he would go back to the hotel room and think about it. He had until tonight to decide whether it would be best to return home never knowing the possibilities, or to shore up some courage and tell Kerry exactly how he felt about her. He would have to weigh the risk of asking her to come back to Nebraska with him and face her rejection. Worse, she might agree and then eventually, leave him, too.

* * *

"I was beginning to wonder if you'd run off with your fellow, my dear."

With only a cursory glance at Millie, Kerry started up the staircase to her room. "I'm here, and I'm running late. I need to get dressed and get back to work."

"Kerry Ann, I need to speak with you about something now."

With one hand braced on the banister, Kerry faced Millie and sighed. "Can it wait? We can have a nice dinner together tonight and catch up."

"I would prefer not to wait. I wouldn't ask if this were not of the utmost importance."

Resigned to the fact her mentor wasn't going to give up, Kerry trudged down the three steps she'd taken and followed Millie into the kitchen. They sat across from each other at the oak dinette in the usual places, Millie's prim hands folded before her, Kerry's white-knuckling the edge of the table.

"Did Sandra leave?" Kerry asked.

"Yes, dear. Early this morning, as soon as we finalized our plans."

"Plans?"

Millie looked disturbed. Very disturbed. "She has asked me to come live with her, and I've agreed."

Kerry swallowed around her shock. "When did you decide to do this?"

"While you were with your young man."

Millie was mistaken. Ford wasn't hers at all. "What about the house?"

"I'm afraid I'll have to sell it."

And Kerry had thought she couldn't be more stunned. Wrong. "But it's been in your family for years. It's your home."

"A home that I have mortgaged to the hilt. My pension will no longer cover the payments, much less the upkeep."

"I can help out more."

Millie reached out and pulled Kerry's hand into hers. "My angel, your salary can't begin to cover my debts. I admit that I have squandered my fortune, but I did so with the best of intentions."

She'd given most of it away, Kerry realized. To foundations, to the needy, to her. "You don't have anything at all left?"

"Only a small amount of savings and the roadster, as well as all the furnishings. And you are welcome to anything here that you wish."

Great. She would have furnishings, but no house. No home. "I couldn't do that, Millie. Besides, I'm sure Sandra would like to have some of your things."

Millie waved her free hand. "Posh. Sandra has her own furnishings. And she will never cherish my things the way you will."

Kerry felt as if Millie had told her she was about to pass on to the great unknown. "You've always told me you've never gotten along that well with your niece. How are you going to live with her?"

"As best I can. I have no choice."

Kerry bit her bottom lip, hard, to stop the threat of tears. "I wish there was something I could do."

Millie squeezed her hand. "My dear, you have done so much already. You have been the best companion. The best daughter a woman could ever hope for. I only wish…" Her gaze drifted away.

"You wish what?"

"I wish that I wasn't forced to put you out in the street." She leveled her sad eyes on Kerry. "Perhaps Ford will be asking you to go with him?"

The hopefulness in Millie's voice only added to Kerry's despair. "I'm afraid that's not going to happen. He's leaving tomorrow. He has a life somewhere else, not with me."

"But you wish that weren't so, don't you?"

This time Kerry looked away. "I'm a realist, Millie. I had a wonderful time with Ford, but I knew all along it couldn't last." And though she owned that knowledge, she still didn't hurt any less.

"You say he isn't leaving until tomorrow?"

"That's right."

"Then perhaps between now and tomorrow he will have a change of heart."

"That's not likely, Millie. Again, we had a nice time together, but it was less than two weeks. You can't make a decision like that in such a short time."

"My second husband and I only knew each other five days and we married on the sixth. Anything is possible."

Kerry wanted to believe as strongly in miracles, the way Millie always had. But she had yet to see anything that qualified, except for the miracle of making love with Ford. Tugging her hand from Millie's grasp, she came to her feet and offered a smile. "You go on believing that, but it's time for me to go back to the real world. And that means going back to work."

"Yes, dear. You do that. In the meantime, I have errands to run and a bridge game tonight, so you might return from your class before I get home. Do you want me to drop you at work?"

"No, thanks. I'll probably walk." Kerry needed to walk off her melancholy. In fact, she probably should run in hopes of escaping thoughts of Ford Ashton. But that would require a lengthy marathon and even then she couldn't guarantee she would forget him. Not today. Not tomorrow. Not ever.

# Ten

**H**ow could he forget her when everywhere he looked she was there? Standing by the window. Lounging on the sofa. Lying in his arms.

Ford paced the hotel room, restless with each hour that passed. He'd picked up the phone twice to call her at work, stared at the receiver, started to dial, then hung up. He didn't know what to say or what to do. He hated the thought of leaving without at least a proper goodbye, another kiss. Maybe even another round of lovemaking. But it wouldn't be fair to ask her to be in his bed if he couldn't offer her more than that.

A sharp rap came at the door, sounding like wood against metal. Ford started not to answer, but the prospect of Kerry standing on the other side sent him across the room in a rush. But he didn't discover Kerry on the threshold. He did find Kerry's landlady leaning both hands on her cane, a look of disapproval on her face made worse by her severe scowl.

"I have a bone to pick with you, young man."

Ford had no doubt she did, considering she looked like she could beat him about the face and head with her walking stick. "Come in, Mrs. Vandiver."

She hobbled past him and before he even had the door closed, she spun on him. "I have a question to ask you, and I want you to think about it before you answer."

Ford slid his hands into his jeans pocket. "Okay. Shoot."

"Do you realize what you'll be losing if you let Kerry Ann go?"

"Yeah, I do."

Ford was taken aback by the ease of the admission, and so was Millie, apparently, when she said, "You do?" in an awed tone.

"She's a special woman," he said. "Probably the best woman I've ever met."

Millie pointed her cane at him like a weapon. "Then why in heaven's name would you take off without her?"

"Because I don't think she'd consider leaving you. And even if she did, I'm not sure she'd be happy in Nebraska. She's told me several times San Francisco's her home."

Millie clucked her tongue. "My dear, Kerry has never really had a home. True, she has shared my house, but it's never been her own in the way most of us know. And now I'm afraid she won't have that any longer."

"You're going to put her out?"

"In a way, yes. And I hate that more than anything I've hated in my lifetime."

The woman was making no sense to Ford. "Then why would you do it?"

"Because I have no recourse but to move in with my niece. For all intents and purposes, I am broke."

She was broke, and Kerry would be homeless again. No one should have to suffer that once in a lifetime, much less twice. Especially not the woman he loved.

*The woman he loved.*

There it was, the cold, hard truth. A truth he was more than willing to accept.

"When are you going to have to move?" he asked, like that really mattered.

"By the end of the month. Kerry can remain until the house sells, but after that she'll have to find a new place to reside." Her thin lips curled up into a smile that revealed what Ford suspected was a fine set of dentures. "I hear Nebraska is a very nice place to live."

Ford had rarely heard anyone say that; at least, not any woman he'd known before. "Are you telling me I should ask her to come live with me?"

"Yes, but only if you love her. Only if you're willing to give all of yourself to her and pledge to make her happy. And only if you promise me you will bring her and your children to visit me often."

Children. He'd never let himself consider having any. But he'd want that with Kerry. Want to see her belly swollen like Abby's. Want to make love to her every night of his life. But would she want that, too?

Ford rubbed a hand over his neck and studied the floor. "I'm not sure she'll agree."

"Have you asked her?"

"No."

"Do you love her?"

He raised his gaze so Millie could see the sincerity in his eyes. "Yes."

"How much?"

More than he realized. More than he loved his freedom from commitment. "Enough to ask her to marry me, as insane as that sounds."

Millie tossed back her head and laughed. "Oh, my dear, that's not insanity. That's the voice of love speaking. And you'll do well to listen to it."

Driven by a sudden sense of purpose, Ford snatched the keys to the rental off the table and pocketed them. "Where is she now?"

"I imagine she's at home, studying. I'm certain she will enjoy your company. Myself, I have a card game that could go well into the night, especially if I happen to find myself on a winning streak for a change."

The woman was a real piece of work. "You bet on bridge?"

Taking Ford by surprise, Millie moved to his side and linked her arm in his. "Truthfully, my friends and I prefer a good game of penny poker. Much more interesting, don't you agree?"

He grinned. "Yeah, I guess so."

"Now you may escort me to my car, and then you will see to my charge."

"Sounds like a plan."

Once they reached the hotel door, Millie faced him again. "I didn't trust you when I first met you because I sensed you were hiding something. And now I know what that something is."

Ford frowned. "What do you think I've been hiding?"

"Your heart. But now that it's in the open, you must give it all to Kerry."

He patted her hand resting in the bend of his arm. "I already have, Millie."

Broken hearts sucked as much as calculating interest rates. Kerry sat in the middle of the bed she'd slept in for the past ten years, a book sprawled in her lap, plagued with the beginnings of a mild headache and a heartache the size of the home she would soon be forced to leave.

She couldn't concentrate on the text before her, even knowing she was behind in her studies. Her goal to obtain her real estate license wasn't as pressing as facing the prospect of never seeing Ford Ashton again, or hearing his voice one last time. He hadn't bothered to call, even though she'd stared at the bedside phone several times for the past two hours, as if she could will it to happen. But she couldn't force him into doing something he didn't want to do, and obviously her little spontaneous declaration had meant nothing to him. Either that, or it had prompted him to catch a plane tonight instead of tomorrow.

When she heard the bedroom door creak open, Kerry didn't bother to look up. No doubt Millie had opted to leave her bridge game early and would now embark on a session of "let's grill Kerry about her love life" for Lord only knew how long. She was simply too tired to deal with it.

"Lose all your pennies?" she asked, pretending to peruse the page.

"Nope. Just my mind."

Kerry's whole body went rigid at the sound of the deep, endearing voice. Her entire heart took a tumble at the same time. Slowly she lifted her eyes to find him standing there, all six-foot-plus of potent male wearing washed-out jeans that showcased his long legs and a starched pale-blue shirt that contrasted with his golden skin and highlighted his luminescent eyes.

When she failed to speak, he asked, "Am I interrupting something?"

Only her ability to take in a decent draft of air. "No. I'm

just trying to catch up on some things." Trying not to launch herself off the bed and into his solid arms.

"Mind if I sit down and talk to you for a minute?"

She would mind if he didn't. "Sure." After tossing the book aside, she patted the space beside her. "Take a load off."

He crossed the room with the same confidence she'd noticed the first time she'd seen him. But his eyes looked much less self-assured as he slid onto the edge of the mattress.

"I'm surprised Millie sent you up here without insisting on serving as a chaperone," she said, keeping her tone light.

"Millie's not here."

"Then how did you get in?"

"With Millie's key."

None of this was making any sense to Kerry. "Excuse me?"

He shifted slightly. "Millie paid me a visit today at the hotel. We had a talk."

So that's why he was here, at Millie's insistence. That made Kerry's heart even heavier. "I'm sure that was interesting."

"You could say that. She told me she was going to move."

Kerry sighed. "I was afraid of that. If you're worried about me, I'll be okay."

"I'm sure you will. Have you thought about where you might go?"

She shrugged. "I can't stay in this area because I can't afford it. I'm sure I'll find an apartment somewhere."

"I know of a place that might interest you."

"Where?"

"It's a house. Three bedrooms, three baths—"

"I can't afford anything like that."

"Yes, you can."

"Trust me, I can't."

His expression remained unreadable. "Just hear me out, okay?"

Kerry wasn't quite comprehending any of this scenario. "Okay. First of all, where exactly is this place?"

"It's kind of in the middle of nowhere, surrounded by a lot of land. The only disadvantage is you have to drive a ways to find a mall. Entertainment's hard to come by, but the people are simple and basically good."

"This doesn't sound like California."

"It isn't in California."

A little glimmer of hope began to shine through Kerry's confusion. "Then where is it?"

"In Nebraska. I know the owner personally, and so do you. Better than any woman has ever known him."

Although things were beginning to make sense, Kerry was still hard-pressed to let herself believe. "Who is he?"

Ford took her hands into his and held them against his heart. "A man who loves you more than he's ever loved anyone or anything in his life."

Tears stung the backs of her eyes. "Ford, I don't understand what you're saying."

"You know exactly what I'm saying, even if I'm not saying it that well. I love you, Kerry, and I want you to come back to Nebraska with me. As my wife."

She felt faint and giddy, but all she could do was stare at him in disbelief. "Are you serious?"

"As serious as I've ever been about anything in my life. But I have to know two things. First, if what I saw you say to me is true—that you love me. And if you'll even consider marrying me, if not now, then whenever you're ready."

She raised his hands to her lips and kissed them. "Yes, I love you. I wanted to tell you that last night, out loud, and I almost did, but then…" She smiled. "You know the rest."

He inched off the bed and pulled her up into his arms.

"Yeah, I know the rest. I've been thinking about it all day. Thinking about you."

"Me, too," she said, followed by a rogue sob. "I can't believe this is happening. And I can't believe I'm seriously considering your offer."

"You are?"

"Unless you're only doing this because you're worried I'm going to end up back on the streets."

He swept a warm kiss across her forehead. "No, I'm worried you'll end up with another man, and I couldn't stand the thought of that happening. In fact, I can't stand the thought of being without you even a day from here on out. So?"

She couldn't help teasing him just a little. "So what?"

"Are you going to marry me?"

"Well, I do have school to consider. I'll be finished by the end of the month, and I've worked so hard to get my license, I don't want to blow it now."

"You can sell land in Nebraska. We have more than our share there. I'll have to go back to the farm and check on things, but I'll be back for you, as long as I know you'll be waiting for me."

Waiting with all the love in her heart. "Promise?"

He studied her face and touched her cheek. "Sweetheart, nothing could keep me away from you, you can count on that."

Kerry knew she could count on that, and him. But now it was time to broach a more serious issue. "There is another consideration. Millie. I know she'll be taken care of, but I hate to think I'll never see her again."

"You'll see her. I promised I'd bring you and our kids back for visits."

Her smile came full force. "Kids, huh?"

He grinned. "Yeah. I never thought I'd have any, but I want that now, as long as it's with you."

"I want that, too." More than she realized until this point. "I think we'll be good at it."

He whisked a kiss over her lips. "I'm sure we will, considering how good we are at the baby-making process."

"You're right about that." She pressed against him. "Maybe we should get in a little practice."

"Not until you tell me yes."

She frowned at him, mock serious. "You're going to refuse to have your way with me until I officially agree to marry you?"

"Yeah, I am."

"Well then, I guess I'll have to marry you."

He picked her up off her feet, swung her around, then set her back down to deliver a kiss so full of emotion and passion, Kerry's head whirled from the effects. Once they parted, he told her, "I have another idea."

"You want to make love on the floor?"

"Not a bad suggestion, but this has to do with Millie."

She released the first button on his shirt. "Millie will have to get her own man."

He caught her hand and stilled it against his chest. "I've been thinking about her situation and I've decided I'll pay off her mortgage so she can live out the rest of her days right here. No one should ever have to leave their home."

Oh, how she loved him in that moment. "She's got a lot of pride and because of that, I'm not sure she'll agree. Plus, she's not getting any younger. She needs someone to stay with her."

"I thought about that, too. I know a lost and lonely teenager who might fit the bill."

Kerry was confused again until the light of comprehension suddenly snapped on. "You mean Eddie?"

"Yeah. Do you think Millie would agree to that?"

"I know she would. And I would find comfort knowing that she'll have someone to replace me."

"You're wrong about that, Kerry. No one could ever replace you. You can take my word on that."

This time Kerry kissed him, putting all of her love into the gesture. "You're a remarkable man. Did you know that, Ford Ashton?"

"We're remarkable together. So when are you going to marry me?"

"As soon as we find a suitable place to do it."

His gaze shot to the bed and without warning, he grabbed the hem of her top and tugged it over her head. "I believe right here will do fine."

She released the rest of the buttons on his shirt, grinning all the while. "I meant a suitable place to have a wedding."

He dispensed with his shirt and kicked out of his jeans and briefs, then said, "You just happen to be in luck."

"Oh boy, am I," she said as she noticed the extent of his arousal.

He went to work on her clothes, leaving her naked and needy in record time. After he took her down onto the bed, he told her, "I was talking about the wedding."

Kerry frankly wasn't sure she could talk at all when Ford sent his hands over her body. "What about the wedding?"

"I just happen to know this special place."

"You most certainly do," she murmured as he caressed her with his gifted hands, loved her with his tender mouth. All talk of the wedding ceased, but Kerry wasn't that concerned about the location or the time. Her only concern was Ford filling her completely, both heart and soul as he told her again and again that he loved her, while he made sweet love to her. She didn't care where they married, or when, as long as they spent the rest of their days together suspended in this lovely state of bliss.

Ford had taken Caroline up on her offer to hold the ceremony at The Vines, the one he'd scoffed at less than a month ago. They'd settled on a spot by the small lake, keeping the event simple, with only a select few family members in attendance. Abby had gladly agreed to serve as Kerry's attendant, and Grant had proudly filled in as best man. The ceremony had been brief but to the point, that point being that he and Kerry had vowed to be together for life. A life he'd once believed he would spend alone. Not anymore.

An all-around perfect day for a wedding, according to the guests. But Ford decided absolute perfection now stood only a few feet away, wearing the satin dress she'd borrowed from his sister, her blond hair burnished by the setting sun, the lake serving as a great backdrop for her beauty. She was chatting with Abby and Millie, Eddie standing nearby, looking and acting completely different from the sad, circumspect girl who'd almost sent his uncle to jail. According to Kerry, Millie was a master at working wonders with lost souls. From the looks of this version of one of those lost souls, he'd have to agree.

Ford was only mildly aware of Grant's and Russ's conversation involving cattle and commodities coming from beside him. The only thing that held his interest at the moment was Kerry Roarke Ashton. He'd arrived back in California two days before and had barely had time alone with her, much less made love to her. They'd communicated for two weeks by phone and, granted, some of those conversations had turned sexy enough to sear a few cornstalks. But it hadn't been the same as the real thing, and the prospect of the real thing had him ready to get out of there and get on with the honeymoon. He intended to do just that real soon.

"I need to talk to you and Abby for a few minutes, Ford. It's important."

Ford turned his attention to Grant and immediately noted his serious expression. "What about?"

"I'll tell you as soon as you get your sister over here."

"Do you want me to give you some privacy?" Russ asked.

Grant shook his head. "No. You need to hear this, too. So does Kerry."

Ford couldn't begin to guess what this was all about, but he worried it could be something that might ruin the day and his good mood. "I'll call them over."

Turning back to Kerry, he noticed Millie and Eddie had left and in their place stood Caroline's daughter, Mercedes. But she was only there for a time before a look of alarm crossed her face and she rushed away toward the house.

Ford whistled and gestured at Kerry. Abby followed her over and while they walked, he heard Kerry ask, "What do you think's wrong with her?"

"I'm guessing nothing that won't be cured in a few months," Abby muttered.

Ford suspected they were talking about Mercedes, and although he was somewhat curious, he was more concerned with Grant's sullen mood. Still, he couldn't help teasing his sister a little, for old-time's sake.

"Hey, Abigail, stick out your arms so I can tell if you're walking or rolling."

"Shut up, Ford, or I'll tell your wife all your dirty little secrets." She said it with a smile while rubbing her distended belly, prompting Ford to imagine what it would be like to see Kerry pregnant with his child. He figured he'd look as proud as Russ, who wrapped his arm around Abby and pulled her close to his side.

Ford did the same with Kerry, finding comfort in her presence, knowing Grant was about to lay some serious stuff on them. What, he couldn't say. But he knew his uncle well enough to know that what Grant was about to tell them would qualify as anything but light conversation.

"Now that you're all here," Grant began, "I have something important I need to say. I wasn't sure now was the time or place, but since I'm not going to be home for a while, I decided now is as good a time as any."

Abby looked as concerned as Ford felt. "You're scaring me, Grant."

Grant toed the grass beneath his boot. "I don't mean to scare you. In fact, I'm hoping you'll think this is good news, because it is."

Ford wondered if maybe he was about to announce his own engagement to Anna Sheridan, who was sequestered away with the rest of the guests beneath the white tent set up for the reception. But that didn't make sense. If Anna was involved, most likely she would be there.

"This is about Buck," Grant continued. "And his relationship with you."

Buck? Ford couldn't imagine what the ranch foreman had to do with this. "Is he sick?"

"No, nothing like that. He wanted to tell you himself, but I convinced him it might be better coming from me."

"Just spill it, Grant," Ford said.

"I will, but you two have to promise to listen with an open mind."

Abby shot a meaningful glance at Ford. "We can do that."

Grant let go a rough sigh. "Back when your mother and I were teenagers, Buck came to work for your great-grandparents. During that time, Grace was wild as a March hare and your grandmother had a hard time keeping her under control. But she tried as best she could, making sure Grace didn't leave the farm, at least not without Buck. As it turned out, she and Buck became involved."

Ford feared he knew where this might be leading, but his mind rejected that notion until Grant said, "And that's when Grace became pregnant with you, Ford."

He spoke around his shock. "Then you're telling me—"

"That Buck is your dad. He's Abby's dad, too."

Abby looked at Ford with disbelief. "Ford and I aren't half siblings?"

"No. Buck fathered you both."

Ford glanced at Kerry, who stood by silently, taking it all in, before regarding Grant again. "Why in God's name didn't you tell us before now?"

"Because I didn't know until now," Grant said. "Buck and I had a long talk last night and that's when he admitted it to me, although I guess I always wondered in a way. And before you start passing judgment on him, you have to understand why he didn't come forward. He loved your mother, but she told him he wasn't good enough for her. He was illiterate until Abby taught him to read. But he always believed Grace was right and that you two were better off not knowing."

"How could we be better off not knowing?" Abby said, echoing Ford's thoughts. "And why did he decide we needed to know now?"

"Because of the babies. He figured you'd want to know any medical history that he could provide. And because he loves both of you a lot. That's why he stuck around all those years, watching you grow and making sure you were treated well."

Ford had to admit that Buck had always been there for him,

but did that excuse him from withholding such an important fact? "This is a lot to handle, Grant."

Grant forked a hand through his hair. "I know. But you'll both handle it in time. When you get back to the farm, I expect you to talk with him, let him explain his motivation for keeping this a secret. He also said that he'd be willing to take a paternity test to prove it."

"That won't be necessary." And it wasn't, as far as Ford was concerned. Abby had Buck's hair color, and he had his smile. He just couldn't believe he hadn't seen it before now, but he had no real reason to see it. "After all this time, I'm not sure it really matters, Grant."

Grant leveled a serious stare on him. "It does matter. Buck's always been family, and now it's official. I expect you to treat him as you always have because he's done a lot for you."

"And so have you, Grant," Abby said. "This doesn't change the way we feel about you. You've been a father to us, too. I just want you to know that."

"I do know that." Grant glanced at the tent. "Now if you'll excuse me, I want to visit with a few of the guests." With that he walked away, leaving Abby and Ford staring at each other in stunned silence.

"Why don't we take a walk?" The first words Kerry had uttered since the revelations had begun.

"We'll do the same," Russ said, taking Abby by the arm and guiding her away.

Now more than ever Ford was glad to have Kerry by his side, holding his hand tightly in hers as they walked along the lake's edge in the opposite direction of the festivities.

After they'd put a good distance between themselves and the tent, Abby stopped and faced him. She laid a gentle palm on his jaw. "Are you okay?"

"I'm not sure." And he wasn't. Right now he felt like he was on information overload.

"This is a good thing, Ford," she said. "I never knew my real father, and the one that I did know didn't have a clue how to be a good parent. You've been lucky enough to have two great dads."

"And I've spent years trying to fill in that blank space of my heritage, and the answers were right under my nose. I can't believe Buck's been lying all along. I thought I knew him better than that."

"You heard Grant. He had his reasons. Good ones."

"His reasons just might not be good enough."

Kerry took both his hands into hers and gave them a squeeze. "Ford, I want you to think about this. When we met, you had your reasons for lying to me, and they involved protecting Grant. Maybe Buck thought he was protecting you."

"From what?"

"From what he viewed as shame. I don't know him, but I wouldn't be surprised if that's what drove him. When you have someone tell you often you're not good enough, you start to believe it. My stepdad had me convinced of that very thing. Had it not been for Millie, I still might believe it."

Everything she said made perfect sense, but the knowledge was still a lot for Ford to swallow. "I understand that, but it feels like such a damn big betrayal."

She surveyed his eyes for a long moment. "Do you love him, Ford?"

"Yeah, I do."

"Will knowing what you know now really change that? After all, once I finally understood you and your motives for deceiving me, I think that's part of why I fell in love with you, as crazy as that sounds. You were willing do anything for someone you loved. That's why I forgave you. And I hope you'll find it in your heart to forgive Buck."

Right now Ford would move every mountain in the state for her. "And I still can't believe how damn lucky I am to have found you."

"We're both lucky."

She circled her arms around his waist, he framed her sweet face in his palms and, regardless they were out in the open, he kissed his wife with all the gratitude, all the love for her he was feeling at that moment.

Once they parted, Kerry gave him a special smile, then one he knew very well. "You know, I'm really, really ready to get out of this dress and these heels."

"And I'm really, really ready to help you do that. But I think we're going to have to find a better place to do that first." He checked his watch and noted the lateness in the hour. "We have a plane to catch in less than three hours, so I'm thinking that's a great excuse to leave."

"True. How long will it take to get back to Nebraska?"

"With the layover in Denver, about four and a half hours. Then we have another few hours' drive to Crawley. Which means we won't be there until dawn."

"That's quite a long trip. You don't happen to be a member of the Mile-High Club, do you?"

He grinned. "Nope, but I'm open to getting a membership. Or to be on the safe side, we could stay in Denver for a few days and have a real honeymoon. We don't have to be back to the farm that fast."

She pressed her lips against his cheek then pulled back. "As much as I want to make love with you, I have my reasons for wanting to get to the farm as fast as possible."

"Oh, yeah? What reasons?"

"In my life, I've only wanted two things. Someone to love

who loved me back, unconditionally. And a home of my own. I have that someone in you, and now I can't wait to see the home where I plan to spend the rest of my life loving you well and raising our children. Can you understand that?"

Ford understood that completely. She'd never had a place where she'd belonged, and what she probably didn't realize was how firmly embedded she was in his soul, even deeper in his heart. He vowed to give her all those things and more.

Following another kiss, he took her hand, prepared to take her to the place that was as much a part of him as she was now. "Okay, sweetheart. Let's go home."

\* \* \* \* \*

# CONDITION OF MARRIAGE

BY
EMILIE ROSE

**Emilie Rose** lives in North Carolina with her college-sweetheart husband and four sons. This bestselling author's love for romance novels developed when she was twelve years old and her mother hid them under sofa cushions each time Emilie entered the room. Emilie grew up riding and showing horses. She's a devoted baseball mum during the season and can usually be found in the stands watching one of her sons play. Her hobbies include quilting, cooking (especially cheesecake) and anything cowboy. Her favourite TV shows include Discovery Channel's medical programmes, *ER, CSI* and *Boston Public*. Emilie's a country music fan because there's an entire book in nearly every song.

Emilie loves to hear from her readers and can be reached at PO Box 20145, Raleigh, NC, 27619, USA or at www.EmilieRose.com.

To the ladies of eHarlequin and the Brainstorming Desirables loop. You are a riot and I don't know what I'd do without our Wednesday chats.

# Prologue

Spencer Ashton kept his back to the door of his private library long after the maid announced his visitor and departed.

He'd give the no-account farmer his ex-wife had been foolish enough to marry time to see what true class and wealth brought—not that he expected a cellar rat like Lucas Sheppard to have the intelligence or the education to comprehend the value of the original artwork on the walls or the leather-bound first editions on the floor-to-ceiling bookcases.

Let him wait.

"You can ignore me as long as you like, Ashton. I'm not going anywhere."

*Cocky bastard.* Spencer spun his chair around, but he didn't stand. "To what do I owe the displeasure of your visit, Sheppard? Are you finally willing to concede you can't make a living off that scrap of land Caroline's mother left her?

Perhaps you want to sell it to me after all. Of course, I've lost interest now. My offer will be lower."

The look he sent Sheppard had sent many a wiser man scurrying away. This idiot held his ground and his gaze. "Not at all. I've come to talk to you about the children."

Son of a bitch. He wanted more money to take care of Caroline's brats. "You have thirty seconds. I'm a busy man."

For the first time since his entrance, Sheppard seemed ill at ease, and Spencer enjoyed his discomfort. "I love Eli, Cole, Mercedes and Jillian as if they were my own. I want to adopt them."

Anger burned through Spencer's veins like a lit fuse on dynamite—a short fuse. He might not want the brats underfoot, but they were *his,* by God, and Spencer Ashton never gave up anything unless he had a damned good reason. Making his ex-wife and Sheppard happy wasn't a good reason. "No way in hell."

"Ashton, you haven't seen the children once since you walked out on them three years ago. They need a father."

Spencer laughed. "They're better off without a father than to be saddled with a no-account like you."

Sheppard's nostrils flared, and anger flashed in his eyes. "You self-righteous son of a—"

"You're wasting my time. Remind Caroline that those brats belong to me. She made the deal. I expect her to abide by it."

"Then perhaps you ought to visit your children or at least send birthday cards."

Spencer rose slowly, menacingly. He parked his fists on the desk and leaned forward. "Don't cross me, Sheppard. If you do I'll sue for custody and take the children."

A bluff, but then a wise man always knew when to bluff. Caroline's own father had taught him that much—right before Spencer had beaten him at his own game. Spencer now owned everything that had once been Lattimer's, and he no longer had to endure Caroline or her whiny children to have it.

"You wouldn't stand a chance of winning a custody suit. You took almost everything Caroline owned and abandoned those kids when you divorced her."

"Ah, but lawyers can be so time-consuming and expensive, and I can afford the best. I'm sure you'd hate for your precious Caroline to have to sell Louret Vineyards to pay her legal fees. Do you think my mousy ex-wife would still love you if you cost her what little she has left?"

His barb hit the target. Spencer savored the defeat creeping over Sheppard's features.

"You are one coldhearted son of a bitch, Ashton." He stormed out.

Spencer sat back in his leather desk chair, steepled his fingers and smiled. "You don't know the half of it, Sheppard. But you will."

# One

"**S**tomach flu?" Jared Maxwell offered Mercedes Ashton a clean, damp washcloth.

"I wish." Mercedes released her hold on the toilet bowl, accepted the cloth and let Jared pull her to her feet in the tiny bathroom of his cottage. She swayed.

Jared cupped her elbows, steadying her. Her pale skin, combined with her unusual silence during dinner and the tension pleating her brow and pulling her generous mouth, concerned him. "Then it must be my cooking."

She offered a weak smile at his attempted humor. "Your cooking was excellent as usual. Why else would I appear on your doorstep every Wednesday night for the past eleven years?"

Puzzled, he leaned against the doorjamb. "Then what's going on?"

Mercedes pulled free and turned to wash her face and

hands. When she finished she fussed with her hair, trying to smooth the curly caramel strands back into the twist pinned at the back of her head. Mercedes usually let her hair down as soon as she entered his cottage, both literally and figuratively, but she hadn't tonight. She straightened the blouse of the suit she'd worn to work at the family winery earlier today. She wouldn't meet his gaze in the mirror, and Jared suspected she was stalling. Why? They had no secrets.

The sight of her trembling hands sent a sense of foreboding through him. What could she be afraid to tell him?

Finally she sighed, straightened her shoulders and turned. She avoided his gaze and focused on a spot beyond his shoulder. "Would you mind if I left a little early tonight?"

"Yes, I'd mind. Mercedes, I can't help, if you won't tell me what's wrong."

"You can't fix this." The agony in her voice and in her sea-green eyes pierced him.

"Did you ever listen to me when I said that to you?" Mercedes had stood by him through the death of his wife and child and his subsequent bout with alcohol abuse. She'd been his wife's best friend. Now she was his.

She winced. "No."

He tucked a stray curl behind her ear. "It's my turn to be the hero. Give me a chance."

She pressed her lips together, but not before he noticed a telling quiver. "Can we go back into the den?"

"Whatever you want."

"I want to go home." The irritable tone was completely out of character for his calm, controlled friend, but then she'd been fidgety for most of the evening.

He forced a smile despite his growing concern. "Except that."

She led the way back to the den, settled in her usual spot

in the corner of the sofa, but she didn't kick off her shoes, tuck her feet beside her or pull the afghan over her legs the way she usually did. Her stiff posture, tightly closed eyes and clenched fists spoke of an inner struggle. "Craig's gone."

"Good riddance." Jared wished back the words when surprise and hurt flashed in her eyes. He held up a hand to stop her protest. "I don't mean to be unsympathetic, but you know I never liked the guy. He wasn't good enough for you. None of the losers you seem to favor ever are. Frankly, Mercedes, your taste in men sucks."

A derisive smile curved her lips. "Don't hold back."

He shrugged. Mercedes was the only person he trusted enough to be one hundred percent honest with. Make that ninety-nine percent. He had one secret he'd never share. "If you try to tell me you're broken-hearted over his departure I'm not going to believe you. You weren't in love with him."

She sighed and pressed her fingertips to her temple. "No. No I wasn't, and I won't miss him, but…"

The mantel clock ticked off thirty seconds. He waited for her to complete her sentence. When she didn't, he prompted, "Did you have an argument?"

She grimaced. "Yes and no."

That certainly didn't sound like Mercedes's usual decisiveness. "Care to elaborate?"

Was that fear in her eyes? Adrenaline raced through his veins. He slid to the edge of his leather club chair. "Did the bastard hurt you?"

"Not physically. He—" She broke off and clutched her hands until her knuckles turned white. Her troubled gaze locked with his and she worried her bottom lip with her teeth. "He asked me to get an abortion."

For one stunned moment Jared thought he'd misunderstood, *prayed* he'd misheard, and then he hurt, as if a million shards of glass had exploded inside him. His throat closed up. His heart pounded like a jackhammer. His stomach clenched and his skin turned cold—as cold as that of his dead son. He gulped on the bile rising in his throat. "You're pregnant."

Mercedes chewed her lip and eyed him uneasily. "Yes. I didn't want to tell you until…until I decided what I'm going to do."

He was dying inside. He wanted to storm out of the house and keep running until the pain subsided. But he couldn't. Mercedes had led him out of the hell his life had become six years ago. He owed her. If not for her, he'd be buried beside his wife and child—if they'd ever found his body.

"You didn't tell me because you thought it would remind me of Chloe and Dylan." His flat voice broke when he said his son's name. Pain filled his chest and crept up his throat, choking him.

A tear streaked over the dusting of freckles on Mercedes's pale cheek and into the corner of her wide mouth. "Yes. I'm sorry."

For the first time since he'd given up alcohol five years ago, he wanted—no, he *needed*—a drink and the numbness it would bring. He fought to shove down his emotions and conquer the demons inside. "Have you made a decision?"

Again she hesitated. "I'm keeping my baby."

He drew in a ragged breath, stood and crossed to the mantel. Bracing both hands on the wide wooden slab, he fought to inhale but his constricted chest made that almost impossible.

"I'm not my father, Jared. I can't pretend this child never existed. My baby may not have been planned, but it will *never* feel unwanted or unloved." The painful neglect she'd suffered at Spencer Ashton's hands laced her tone with need, but conviction strengthened her voice.

He couldn't do it. He couldn't stand by and watch Mercedes's belly swell as the child inside developed. He couldn't risk seeing the baby move beneath her skin or coming to anticipate its birth. Caring for someone and losing them wasn't something he wanted to risk again. If anything went wrong he'd never survive the devastation a second time. If not for Mercedes, he never would have survived losing Chloe and Dylan.

A swish of fabric preceded the warmth of her hand on his stiff spine. "I didn't want to hurt you."

"Is he going to marry you?" He struggled to squeeze words past the noose around his neck.

Her bitter laugh held no mirth. "No. He claims the baby isn't his, and he says there is no way he'll tie himself down to someone else's brat."

Stunned, he faced her. "You weren't seeing anyone else."

Her lips turned downward in a cynical grimace. "I see you at least once a week, Jared, sometimes more, and then there are the occasional weekends we go away to B&Bs together. Craig thinks the baby is yours."

His jaw dropped. His brain scrambled to make sense of the insane allegation. At the same time mental and physical barriers slammed into place. His muscles tensed and his skin drew tight as if trying to armor himself against the pain he knew would follow.

"Those are business trips. We've never slept together. For God's sake, we don't have that kind of relationship."

"I know that and you know that, but Craig doesn't believe it. Or maybe he's using our relationship as an excuse to escape responsibility. Anyway, he's willing to pay for an abortion, but otherwise he wants nothing to do with this pregnancy or the baby. He accepted a job with a firm in southern California to reinforce his point in case I missed it."

He shoved a hand through his hair and hoped her brothers, Eli and Cole, and sister, Jillian, could be there for her during and after the pregnancy because he couldn't. "What did your family say?"

She ducked her head and fussed with one pearl earring. "I haven't told them, and I'm not going to. Not yet."

He didn't try to hide his surprise and confusion. Mercedes worked with her siblings daily. This wasn't something she could hide. "Why not?"

The pain in her eyes hit him square in the gut. "What do you want me to tell them? Guess what? I'm stupid enough to get pregnant by a man just like my father? And just like my father Craig's going to abandon his child?"

Pain stabbed his left temple. "Mercedes—"

She wrung her hands and paced the floor. "My family is going through hell right now. The press is crucifying us over the recent revelation that my parents' marriage was never legal. Instead of focusing on the winery's new marketing campaign that Cole and I sweated over, the press watches our every move like vultures hovering over roadkill waiting for a whiff of scandal. They want to see the factions of the Ashton family battle—preferably until blood is drawn."

He couldn't argue with that. The press had grown increasingly bloodthirsty since Spencer's murder in May. Jared's throat closed up. "How far along are you?"

"Eight weeks. I've done a home pregnancy test, but I haven't seen a doctor yet for fear of the press finding out. I know I can't keep the secret indefinitely, but as soon as Spencer's murderer is found the press will leave us alone."

"You won't have long before you start to show. A couple of months at the most. And you need to see a doctor now—before it's too late." Chloe had lost babies at eight- and ten-weeks pregnant.

"I know. I remember, too." She laid a hand over his forearm. His muscles knotted beneath her touch. Why did her fingers feel so hot? Was it because he was so cold?

If Mercedes remembered how much he'd loved his wife, how excited he'd been over the fact that their third pregnancy had nearly reached term after two earlier, devastating miscarriages, how could she forget he'd almost killed himself in his grief over losing his wife and son less than a month before the baby was due? Because he'd never told her how close he'd come to taking that final step. Mercedes had no respect for weak men, and he'd been weak.

"A baby will mess up your well-ordered life." *And his.*

She lifted her chin. "I know, and I don't care. Jared, I value your friendship more than anything. Please don't let this pregnancy come between us."

"Your family will help you," he said through clenched teeth.

She flinched, paled and pressed a hand to her chest. "And you won't?"

"I can't."

Seconds ticked past. "Do we have to give up our dinners?"

The tremor in her voice squeezed the breath from his lungs. Pushing her away was killing him, but his sanity—*his survival*—depended on putting some distance between them. "Not yet."

*But soon.* He didn't voice the words, but they hovered in the air between them.

He'd hurt her. Her pain was plain to see in the darkening of her eyes, in the strain in her features and in her quivering lips, but she nodded and stepped away. "I understand. All I ask is that you keep my secret until I'm ready to tell my family."

"You're making a mistake."

"No, my mistake was accidentally getting pregnant by a

man I knew I could never love." She gathered her bag and her blazer and paused by the door. "But, Jared, life goes on and you have to play the cards you're dealt. You can still win the game with a bad hand, you know."

How many times had she said those words to him back in the dark days when his life had been a black gaping void?

He cared more about Mercedes than anyone else. How could he let her down?

How could he not?

If anyone asked her—and they hadn't—Mercedes would swear that her family was coming apart at the seams, unraveling because of the threads Spencer Ashton pulled from the grave. Damn her father for his lying, conniving, narcissistic ways.

She swallowed her anger, her ever-present nausea and a rising panic over the loss of control in her own well-organized life and entered the bistro. She spotted her youngest—*as far as she knew*—half sister, Paige, across the dining room and waved away the hostess. Weaving her way through the tables, Mercedes scanned the patrons, on the alert for tabloid reporters the way a small animal would be for signs of a predator ready to leap from the brush and attack.

She probably should have refused the luncheon invitation rather than risk becoming ill in public and feeding the rampant speculation about the Ashton family saga. The last thing her family needed right now was more grief, and that's all a premature leak about her pregnancy would cause at this point. But she hadn't wanted to hurt Paige's feelings.

She'd get her life back together by herself—*thank you very much*—and then she'd tell them. She didn't doubt they'd rally around and support her…. Well, Mercedes conceded with an inward wince, she didn't doubt it much. Given the recent eye-opener that her father had illegitimate offspring all over the place—including her and her siblings—she couldn't be sure her family wouldn't frown on her decision to continue this pregnancy. But continue it she would, because everything happened for a reason, and this baby had a purpose, as yet untold, for being here. And then there was the fact that she was thirty-three, didn't believe love existed except for a rare few instances and didn't plan to marry. This could be her only shot at motherhood. Even though she liked children, she'd never planned to have any of her own, but from the moment she'd discovered she was pregnant she'd wanted this baby.

Paige smiled, rose and took Mercedes's hand. "Thank you for coming."

"Your request sounded urgent."

"Yes. I wanted to ask…" Paige's gaze skidded away and then returned. "How are you? I heard you'd broken up with your boyfriend."

Mercedes sighed, sat and reached for a bread stick. Craig had been gone for weeks, and she really didn't want to talk about him, but she could handle chitchat as long as her stomach cooperated. Paige would eventually get to the real reason for the impromptu Thursday luncheon invitation. Besides, if Mercedes hadn't accepted Paige's invitation she would have sat in her office and worried about how she was going to cope with the pregnancy without Jared in her corner. She counted on his strength and his friendship, probably more than she should. He'd been a fixture in her life ever since he'd met and married her best friend. As it was, she'd barely slept last night because worry had kept her up and pacing the floor.

"Yes, Craig is history, but I'm okay with that. Dare I ask how you heard? I didn't think his departure had made the tabloids yet." The bread stick tasted like sand. Great, even her taste buds had gone on strike.

"Kerry, my father's—*our* father's—assistant, mentioned it. I met Craig when you brought him to the fund-raiser back in February. He's quite attractive."

"And charming, funny and a great date, but he was also shallow, disloyal and not a guy you'd want to grow old with." A lot like her father actually. Definitely not a man she could love. That, of course, was one of her criteria for dating.

Paige blinked at Mercedes's bluntness, but the waitress arrived before she could reply. Mercedes ordered a ginger ale and the blandest pasta on the menu and prayed her stomach would behave.

She liked Paige. Her half sister reminded her of how young, naive and excited she'd been about life eleven years ago. It seemed like an eon since she'd been a twenty-two-year-old college student savoring the last days of freedom before joining the family business. A smile tugged at her lips. She had a permanent reminder of those fun, uninhibited days before she'd buckled down, hidden beneath her slim, pin-striped skirt.

Of course, Paige already worked for Ashton Estate Wineries, so maybe her half sister's carefree college days were already over.

"No wine?" Paige asked.

"No. I left a mountain of work waiting on my desk. I need to keep a clear head." How long would it take for people to pick up on the fact that the marketing and PR director of Louret Winery and Vineyard had given up drinking the company product?

Excitement sparkled in Paige's hazel eyes. She leaned forward. "Have you heard about the bachelorette auction fund-raiser we're hosting at Ashton Estates next month? Perhaps you could place yourself up for bid and find Mr. Right?"

Mercedes grimaced. Somehow she didn't think a pregnant woman whose stomach revolted unpredictably would be a great prize. "I think I'll pass."

Besides, she never dated a man who didn't have at least six characteristics from the "Twenty-five Ways To Tell Your Man's a Loser" list she and her friend Dixie had developed during their last year of college after both of them had their hearts severely dented. Screening the potential bidders for loser-list qualities was impossible; therefore, putting herself up for bid was not an option.

Everywhere Mercedes looked, the marriages around her ended in heartache. After years of infidelity, her father had abandoned her mother to marry his secretary. He hadn't been faithful to that wife, Paige's mother, either. Her sister, Jillian's, first marriage had been disastrous. Jared and Chloe's marriage had been magical, but when Chloe and the baby she carried had died in a car crash Jared had lost himself in grief. She knew his heart still belonged to Chloe and he'd never love another.

Mercedes doubted she was strong enough to endure the kind of pain loving and losing inevitably brought. Why risk it? To keep from falling into the love trap, she only dated men she could never fall in love with—men who didn't have the power to hurt her.

The waitress arrived with their meals, breaking into her dark thoughts. Mercedes sipped her ginger ale, nibbled her penne and hoped her meal would stay down. "How is your mother holding up?"

Paige's eyes darkened. "Dad was… He was such a dynamic person. It will be hard to go on without him. We're all struggling with our grief."

Finding out Spencer had fathered another illegitimate child while married to Paige's mother probably hadn't helped the grieving process. And the recent disclosure that Spencer had abandoned a wife and two children before marrying Mercedes's mother hadn't exactly been a eulogizing moment, either. Had Spencer Ashton loved anyone but himself? Poor Paige seemed to have no clue what a selfish bastard their father had been.

Mercedes's stomach started to churn. She reached for her ginger ale. How many half siblings did she have anyway? She could name six, but were there others? Would the publicity over the unsettled estate bring more relatives out of the woodwork? She'd certainly been taken aback by the value of Spencer's estate, and she wouldn't be surprised if others wanted a slice of the Ashton pie.

At the close of the meal Paige set down her fork and bent to withdraw several folded tabloids from the leather bag at her feet. She laid them on the table. "Actually, this is why I asked you to join me for lunch. Have you seen the latest?"

"No, and I'm not sure I want to." But Mercedes scanned the headlines, finding more of the same speculation and allegations that had hovered over Napa Valley like a fog for the past few months.

Will the Ashtons Become the Next Hatfield-McCoy Family Feud?

Will They or Won't They Contest the Will?

Will the Bastard Branch Harvest Their Father's Estate?

Mercedes pushed the papers away. None of these were as creative as her all-time favorite. Ashtons Aim Their Corks at Each Other. The reporter had gone on to dub the Ashton debacle as the Battle of the Vineyards. He'd compared the Ashton Estate Winery to Goliath and Louret's smaller boutique winery to David. It saddened Mercedes to think what the personal costs might be before the situation could be resolved.

Her father's death had turned his children into adversaries whose every move had become fodder for the tabloids Mercedes felt like a movie star with all the paparazzi bu none of the perks. Each intrusive headline reinforced he decision to keep her pregnancy under wraps for as long a possible. Maybe she could run off to work in France for year with her half brother Mason and return after her baby's birth. She sighed and nixed the idea. Her family needed her here in Napa. And Jared…she'd yet to figure ou what she was going to do about Jared, but she had no intention of losing his friendship. Besides, running neve solved anything.

Paige tucked the tabloids back into her bag. "We have to do something. Our families and our businesses are suffering."

Mercedes nodded. "I agree, but I don't know what we can do to turn off the publicity machine."

Paige hesitated a moment. "Could you speak to Eli and ask him not to contest the will?"

Ah…the true reason for the lunch invitation emerged. "My brother is doing what he feels is right. The land on which the Ashton Estate Winery sits, as well as the Ashton-Lattimer Corporation should rightfully belong to my mother since they were *her* father's properties. Since Spencer never bothered to divorce his first wife, my parents' marriage wasn't legal, either. Any divorce settlement he received from the dissolution of their marriage shouldn't be legal. As much as I wish it were different, there just isn't a simple way to heal this breach."

Paige gestured toward the papers. "I'm sure we can quietly come to an understanding instead of having our laundry aired in a public forum."

If only it was that easy to erase pain, outrage and betrayal. "Paige, I'm all for making peace between our families. I'm not sure it's possible, but I'll do what I can."

* * *

"You weren't leaving without me, were you?" Mercedes called through her open car window as she parked in the shade beside Jared's SUV.

The muscles in Jared's strong jaw bunched, and his thick, straight brows lowered. A cool breeze blowing off the lake ruffled his dark hair, and the midafternoon sun glinted off a scattering of silver strands at his temples. He wore khaki pants and her favorite polo shirt—the one that made his eyes seem impossibly blue.

He shoved his bag in the back of his vehicle. "I didn't think you'd want to go."

Mercedes swung her legs from the car and closed the door. "I've gone with you on every scouting trip for potential bed and breakfast purchases. Why wouldn't I go this time?"

He hesitated. "Are you feeling up to it?"

At the moment, yes. Five minutes from now was another story, but she kept that tidbit to herself. In the wee hours of her second sleepless night since telling Jared about her predicament, she'd decided that once the shock of her pregnancy wore off, their relationship would return to normal. She didn't want to lose her best friend, and she was convinced the way to attain that goal was to maintain the status quo. If that meant ignoring her pregnancy for the time being, then she would.

Mercedes slung the strap of her purse over her shoulder. "I'm up to it. If you don't want my opinion, then you're going to have to have the guts to say so."

He swiped a hand over the five-o'clock shadow covering the lower half of his face. "I value your input."

"Then let me get my bag and we'll go. To be honest, I'm looking forward to getting out of Napa Valley for the weekend. I feel like a bug under a microscope."

She hustled to the trunk of her sports car as quickly as she could in her heels. She'd rushed straight from the winery without stopping by her apartment to change out of her work clothes because she'd been afraid Jared would take off without her. He had a tendency to go off and brood when he was upset. And her news had upset him.

Jared beat her to the rear of the car and reached past her to retrieve her overnight bag. Their hands met on the handle of the case. A tingle traveled up Mercedes's arm. Jared's chest brushed her back. His heat penetrated through her thin rayon suit, and his larger frame seemed to enfold hers as he reached around her for her bag. The hair on her nape moved beneath the whisper of his breath, and an unwelcome sensation stirred in her abdomen.

Surprised, she turned her head toward his. Scant inches separated their mouths. His minty breath caressed her lips and his dark-blue gaze fastened on hers. He blinked and blanked his emotions. He'd done that with other people before, but she couldn't remember Jared ever blocking her out. That answered one question. *If* he felt the strange connection between them he planned to ignore it.

Good plan. One she heartily endorsed.

He frowned. "You shouldn't be lifting heavy items."

Surprised by the sudden dryness of her mouth, she wet her lips. "I packed light. We're only going to be gone overnight."

A tight smile slanted his mouth. "I've seen the way you pack. Light has nothing to do with it. I have your bag. Let go."

She released the handle and surreptitiously wiped her tingling palm on her hip while he carried her overnight case to the back of his SUV. Mercedes took her time securing her vehicle although her little car would be perfectly safe here beside the guest cottage on the grounds of the bed and breakfast inn Jared and Chloe had bought during the first year of their

narriage. She tried to regulate her choppy breathing and calm
her jangled nerves.

What was going on here? Jared was her *friend*. She'd never had a sexual reaction to him before. His heart belonged to
Chloe—always had, always would. He was off-limits.

So how could she explain her damp palms and racing pulse?

Damned pregnancy hormones. Her breasts were so tender
even the brush of her bra and blouse aroused her.

"Ready?" he asked.

"Yes. You know I wouldn't have to pack so much if you'd
tell me where we're going once in a while instead of always
trying to surprise me." She climbed into the passenger seat
and buckled up as she'd done dozens of times before, but today was different. She could feel Jared trying to put distance
between them, and she didn't intend to let him.

"You like my surprises. We're headed for the Sierra Neva-
das."

Surprised, she lifted her brows. "That's more than an
hour away."

She waved to Mr. and Mrs. White, the managers of Jared's
B&B, as Jared drove past the Victorian main house. Mercedes
had hired the couple six years ago when Jared, lost in his grief
over Chloe and Dylan, had been unable to keep up with his
duties as host. She'd expected the position to be temporary,
but Jared hadn't wanted to run the inn without Chloe. He'd
become a silent owner. In recent years he'd turned his hotel
management background into collecting financially struggling inns across the wine country and turning them into
profitable enterprises. She helped him hire the couples to
manage the inns.

She shifted in her seat and found his gaze on her. He nodded toward the innkeepers. "You did well in choosing the
Whites. I never would have hired them."

"No, you would have sold the place along with Chloe's an your dream. She loved this house with all its gables, fanc trim and deep porches."

A sad smile touched his lips. "So did you. I'm not sur which of you loved it more."

He was right. At the time, Mercedes had been a tad envi ous that Chloe had not only snagged the perfect man, one wh adored her and didn't register on the jerk-o-meter, but als because her friend would get to live in this dreamy, roman tic home with its delicate gingerbread trim and octagona turrets.

Mercedes shook off the uncomfortable memories. Okay so she didn't actually believe in romance, but she loved thi house, and Jared…Jared was a true gem. She couldn't los his friendship.

"Tell me what makes the B&B we're visiting today spe cial enough to add it to your collection."

He shrugged. "It's a family place."

She raised her brows. Until recently Jared had avoide B&Bs that catered to families with young children. Did thi mean he was healing? "Instead of a romantic couples' retrea or spa theme? That is a departure for you."

"The property is 160 acres in the California Gold countr north of Yosemite. There are twenty rooms inside the inn it self and thirty cabins on the grounds. The current owners of fer hiking, fishing, cross-country skiing and white-wate rafting along with the usual tourist attractions."

She nodded. "I can see the appeal. They offer all of th popular hobbies, but it's larger than your other properties an quite a bit farther away—out of the wine country, in fact. Wi we go rafting this weekend?"

"I might. You won't."

She sat back in surprise. "I beg your pardon?"

"It's too risky." He cut her a look as he turned onto the highway. "You need to think about the baby."

She understood his concerns. Chloe had lost two pregnancies early on, but she wasn't her petite, delicate friend. "Jared, I'm not fragile."

His fingers tightened on the wheel until his knuckles whitened. "You have no way of knowing that."

"I hike, raft and kayak with you on a regular basis. I'm in good shape."

His gaze raked over her. Every fine hair on her body rose at his thorough perusal—as did her nipples. Horrified by her body's reaction, she folded her arms and prayed he hadn't noticed, but with the snugger fit of her suit jacket over her pregnancy-swollen breasts, her distended flesh would be hard to miss.

Maybe she could blame her absurd reaction on the amount of time that had passed since she'd been intimate with a man. Her last encounter had been the time she'd conceived. Before that…well, she and Craig had been on the verge of ending their relationship, so there hadn't been much contact. As Jared had pointed out, she didn't love Craig. He was a convenient and charming escort who knew how to work a room at the numerous functions her job required her to attend, but he had an annoying tendency to flirt with her female friends, which made them all uncomfortable. It was amazing what a woman would tolerate when she didn't believe in love.

*Sayonara* sex and a birth-control failure had resulted in the baby she carried.

Jared's lips tightened. "Yes, but now that you're pregnant your balance will be affected."

"I haven't gained an ounce and my equilibrium is just fine, thank you."

"You've lost weight, Mercedes. Conserve your energy."

"You're not going to leave me in my room. For heaven's

sake, Jared, it's not like I'm insisting on going hot-air balloon-ing or bungee jumping with you this time."

"Good thing. I wouldn't allow it."

*He wouldn't allow it!* Anger stirred. "I have two older, overprotective brothers—thank you very much. I don't need another one."

His jaw muscles bunched. "I'm not your brother."

"No kidding." That had never been more apparent than now when her rebellious body seemed determined to misbe-have.

"All I'm asking is that you keep your feet on terra firma until after your baby is born."

As if she'd do anything to put her baby in jeopardy, Mer-cedes silently fumed.

They lapsed into a long, tense, uncomfortable silence—something that had never happened on their road trips before. Saddened, Mercedes closed her eyes and leaned back against the headrest. In addition to the rampant hormones, her preg-nancy left her exhausted much of the time. Her limbs felt weighted.

Jared's cologne filled her senses and she smiled, remem-bering the day ten years ago when she and Chloe had picked it out. The moment Mercedes had smelled the subtle blend of citrus, cedar and wood smoke she'd known this brand was perfect for an outdoorsman like Jared. He'd worn it ever since.

"Watch out." Jared's sharp warning jolted Mercedes back to consciousness. The heavy application of the vehicle's brakes threw her against the protective arm Jared had extend-ed in front of her. Adrenaline surged through her system.

"What happened?" She blinked groggily.

"A deer ran in front of the car." He slowly lowered his arm, but the imprint of his touch remained on her breasts. He ex-

...mined her with a concerned gaze. "Are you okay? I didn't hurt you?"

"I'm fine. Sorry, I must have dozed off. Are we there yet?"

"The inn should be around the next bend."

"Good, because I need the ladies' room in the worst kind of way." And she needed to get her pregnancy hormones under control, because she'd enjoyed Jared's touch in a most *un*-friendly way.

# Two

**R**esponding to a knock, Jared opened the connecting doc between his room and Mercedes's. His jaw dropped.

He'd seen Mercedes in her plain black one-piece swimsu dozens of times before, but she'd never filled it out quite th way she did today. Or if she had, he hadn't noticed. H shouldn't be noticing now, but her substantially expande cleavage was hard to overlook.

He swiped one hand over his face and struggled to mak sense of the words Mercedes had spoken. "You're goin where?"

She looked at him as if he'd lost his mind, and maybe h had, and then she folded her arms, which did not help the sit uation. The move lifted her creamy skin even higher out c the suit.

"I'm going swimming. The brochure says the pool is heat ed. I need to work out the kinks from the drive. Are you gc ng to join me after your usual walk around the grounds or corner the owners to go over the inn's financial statement?"

She knew him too well, but he hoped like hell that she didn't realize that the sight of her standing there with her curly hair falling over her pale, *exposed* chest had reminded him that he was very much a man. Disgusted by his base response, he shoved his fists in his pockets to hide his condition and studied the ornate washstand beside the door. "I'll walk the grounds and then take a look at the books."

His libido had been dormant since Chloe's death, and he didn't know what to make of the sudden awakening of his hormones. He didn't dare join Mercedes in the pool. "Stay out of the hot tub and sauna. Elevated temperatures are dangerous for the baby."

She took a sharp angry breath and nearly spilled from her suit. Sensing her impending explosion, he stepped away from the door, but the heat settling low in his groin and pulsing in unison with the throb in his temple wasn't as easy to evade.

Bad move. Increasing the distance between them brought her sleekly muscled, bare legs into the picture. Her weight loss combined with her increased bust measurement made her look like a centerfold model, and his body reacted predictably.

"I won't keep you from your swim." And then he wisely shut the door and strategically retreated into the hall.

He descended the stairs and let himself out onto the front veranda. With any luck the cool evening breeze would clear the inappropriate thoughts from his head. In the past two days his relationship with Mercedes had gone from easy and relaxed to decidedly uncomfortable.

Every mental corner he turned reminded him of Chloe, the excitement of each pregnancy, the crushing pain of the miscarriages and the devastating blow of her death. He couldn't go through that wringer again with Mercedes. He cared too

much, and the thought of losing her put a knot in his gut tha
no amount of antacid could dissolve as the half-eaten roll i
his pocket attested. No, he didn't love Mercedes in the sam
way he'd loved his wife, but Mercedes had become an im
portant part of his life. Too important.

He never should have let himself care about her. Carin;
brought pain. What kind of fool was he that he hadn't learne
that lesson by now? He'd lost his family—not to death but t
a gaping chasm of hostility—and then his wife and son, an
soon he'd have to let Mercedes go.

But how could he turn her away? She was as much a par
of his life as the sunrise. He counted on her friendship an
her business acumen. Thanks to Mercedes he'd made a suc
cess of the inns.

Thirty minutes later he came around the back corner of th
inn and found Mercedes swimming laps in the pool. Sh
spotted him, stopped at the edge of the pool and waved hin
over.

"Come in. The water's great, and before you ask, the poo
is in good condition. I checked."

They had a well-established routine when investigating po
tential properties. Examining the pool always fell into Mer
cedes's jurisdiction. He crossed the deck, stopping a yar
away. The weight of the water had straightened her cork
screw curls into a sheet of café-au-lait colored satin tha
reached just beyond her shoulders. Water droplets glistene
on her skin and eyelashes. The buoyancy of the water lifte
her breasts with each wave.

His mouth turned as dry as the desert. He'd seen her thi
way more times than he could count, but his new awarenes
of her as a woman disturbed him. "I should go over the book
tonight."

"Your loss." She lifted an arm, drew back and splashed

cascade of water over him. Typical Mercedes maneuver—at least it was typical when she was away from the pressure of her job with the family winery. There she seemed to be more driven than anyone he knew except himself—as tightly wound as the hair she kept pinned back on her head. If he hadn't been so distracted, he would have anticipated her horseplay.

He chuckled. "Witch."

"You know where to find me if you change your mind." With that parting salvo she ducked under the water and headed for the opposite end of the pool.

He watched her lithe form for a few seconds and then wiped the water from his face and turned away from the inn to continue his tour of the grounds. Desiring a few minutes to get his thoughts back on track before confronting the owners and their ledgers, he headed deeper into the aspen trees surrounding the cabins instead of returning to the primary structure.

The shadows and solitude of the woodland suited his mood. After Chloe's death he'd wasted a year camping, staring at the bottom of a whiskey bottle and avoiding people and life in general. Mercedes had been relentless in her quest to drag him back to the land of the living. She'd tried coddling and then bullying him out of his misery. He'd resisted her every step of the way.

One night while camping on the northern California coast he'd decided he couldn't go on without his wife and child. He'd stumbled drunkenly to the edge of the cliff and looked down at the waves breaking on the jagged rocks below. He'd been on the verge of taking that final step when Mercedes had called him back.

No, she hadn't physically been with him on the cliffs that night, but he'd heard her just the same and known that if he ended his agony, hers would begin. She'd miss him, mourn him in a way his own family wouldn't. His father had disowned him when he'd left the family hotel chain to marry Chloe and open the bed and breakfast. His two older brothers, caught in the middle of the feud with his father, rarely called.

Mercedes was the only one he had left, and he'd promised Chloe he'd look out for her. In the years since Chloe's death Mercedes had become his family, and she'd dragged him into hers. But soon Mercedes would have a baby, a family of her own, and he didn't know if he could bear to be around her and be reminded of what he'd lost and what he would never have.

It was a classic case of he couldn't live with her, but he seriously feared he couldn't live without her.

What in the hell was he going to do?

"What's your vote?" Jared asked as he joined Mercedes at the table in the sunny breakfast room of the inn.

Mercedes took in the gleam of Jared's freshly shaven face, his broad shoulders beneath a powder-blue polo shirt, and the jeans riding low on his hips. His cologne filled her senses and her stomach flip-flopped. She broke eye contact and glanced out at the amazing view of the meadow. He was too handsome for his own good. Her resistance was abnormally low, and her hormones were out of control.

"I vote yes, and if you buy the inn, I'm going to beg you to let me manage it for the next year or so." She could love it here away from the stress, the press and her complicated family situation. She hadn't been queasy once since they'd arrived last night. Her appetite had returned this morning with a vengeance, and she'd consumed an embarrassing amount of food. Despite that, the contents of Jared's plate made her mouth water. She reached out and swiped a grape.

He nudged the dish in her direction. "Hibernating is my thing, not yours. You love your job and family."

She shrugged. "You're right, but it's a tempting thought."

His expression turned serious. "I want you to see a doctor."

Her appetite vanished. "I will."

The determined set of his mouth suggested arguing might be a waste of time. "I mean today. I have a repeat customer who's an obstetrician. I've called Dr. Evans, and she's agreed to work you into her Saturday clinic. She'll be discreet."

Speechless, Mercedes stared at him. "We haven't finished inspecting the inn."

"I've seen enough to know I'm interested in sending up a building inspector and making an offer. The owners will fax me the rest of the information. If we leave after breakfast we can make it to Sacramento in time for your appointment. I want to make sure you're in good hands."

Before he dumped her. He didn't say it, but she received his message loud and clear. Anger percolated in her bloodstream. He wasn't going to shake her off that easily.

"Jared, I know you mean well, but making my doctor's appointment isn't your decision."

He covered her hand with his and his somber gaze locked with hers. "Do this for me. Please."

His concern defused her anger. The warmth of his skin permeated hers and her mouth moistened. That shimmery feeling she'd experienced when their hands had met on her suitcase handle multiplied ten-fold, traveled up her arm and descended through her torso to settle in the pit of her stomach and below.

She knew she should argue, assert her independence, but she couldn't seem to find the words to debate. "Fine, but if I'm going, you have to come with me."

He rocked back in his chair. "I'll drop you off."

"No deal."

"Mercedes—"

"Jared…I'm scared, okay? I need you there." She hated to admit it, but she remembered what Chloe had gone through, too. She'd shared the joy and the pain, and she'd accompanied her friend to doctor's appointments on the few times Jared couldn't get away. She'd been the one holding Chloe's hand the day the doctor couldn't find the second baby's heartbeat, and Mercedes didn't want to be alone if the news wasn't good. No, this pregnancy hadn't been planned, but she already loved her baby, and she was excited about the future they could have together.

*Her baby.* She pressed a hand over her belly.

Jared observed the gesture with a jaw set and blanked eyes. What she was asking wouldn't be easy for him. "I'll wait in the reception area."

Jared jerked to a stop inside the doctor's private office. His throat constricted and his pulse pounded in his ears. "What's wrong?"

Mercedes, already seated in one of the two chairs in front of the doctor's desk, looked surprised to see him. "Nothing…that I know of."

"Then why did you send for me?" How could he put distance between them if she kept dragging him into her pregnancy?

A frown pleated her brows. "I didn't."

A trickle of fear slithered down his spine. Why would the nurse bring him back here if there wasn't something wrong? His stomach clenched. Bile burned his throat. Memories of the past descended on him like a cold, lead blanket. He opened his mouth to insist that he shouldn't be here, but the worry clouding Mercedes's eyes made him hesitate.

She clenched the wooden arms of her chair with a white-knuckled grip. "Do you think there's a problem with my baby and they didn't want to tell me while I was alone?"

Before he could answer, Dr. Evans entered and waved him toward a chair. "Please have a seat, Jared."

Jared battled between his need to leave and his duty to Mercedes. Duty won. Could he be strong for her? Yes, dammit, he could. He owed her that much. He sat down beside Mercedes and took her cool hand in his.

The doctor, a middle-aged woman who'd been one of Jared and Chloe's first customers, settled behind her desk and smiled. "I'm happy to report that everything about this pregnancy looks good, excellent, in fact."

Air rushed from Jared's lungs in a relieved gush, but concern remained. "But…" he prompted.

She only hesitated a moment. "I've been a visitor to the Lakeside B&B for many years, so I know what a difficult past you've had, Jared. I also know the Ashtons are particularly newsworthy at the moment. As I told you on the phone, I can promise my staff will be discreet, but I can't speak for the patients in my waiting room. We whisked Mercedes through as quickly as possible, but…"

She shrugged and opened Mercedes's file. "You never know what the press will dig up. Now, the good news is Mercedes's health couldn't be better, and with the fetal heartbeat in its current range, the chance of miscarriage is less than ten percent." She paused and looked directly at Jared. "Your baby appears to be as healthy as can be. You should be proud parents in early to mid-April."

*His baby?* He recoiled. Where the hell did Dr. Evans get that idea? His gaze jerked to Mercedes.

She bit her lip, hesitancy and confusion plain on her face. If Mercedes hadn't misinformed the doctor, then who had?

Oh, hell, Jared realized the doctor must have misinterpreted what he'd said when he called her at home last night to request an appointment for Mercedes. Should he correct her? Or should he keep his mouth shut? If the people they'd encountered this morning thought he was the father, then they wouldn't look further. On the other hand, a mystery always drew interest, speculation and in the Ashtons' case, reporters.

He squeezed Mercedes's hand and silently urged her to follow his lead. "Good. What kinds of precautions should Mercedes be taking?"

Mercedes blinked. Questions filled her eyes, but she remained silent.

"Mercedes asked about exercise, and I've instructed her to use common sense and avoid risky sports, but I don't see a problem with hiking, biking, swimming activities in which she already participates on a regular basis. And you can resume sexual relations at any time. Mercedes said it had been a while."

His gaze ricocheted from Mercedes's stunned, red face to the doctor and back again. His mouth dried and his pulse missed a few beats before racing ahead at Daytona 500 speeds.

*Him.*

*Mercedes.*

*Sex.*

He'd never connected the three, and he didn't want to now, but fire raced through his bloodstream and need—shocking, unacceptable, and damned urgent—throbbed in his groin.

All he could think while the doctor rattled on about prenatal vitamins and diet was he had to get the hell out of here.

"Did I miss something back there?" Mercedes asked when the silence of the drive got to her. Tension filled the cab of the SUV like a dense, impenetrable San Francisco fog.

"I could have sworn I intentionally left the *father* part of the patient information form blank."

Jared's grip tightened on the steering wheel. "The doctor might have misinterpreted something I said."

Mercedes noticed the nerve ticking in Jared's jaw. "What *exactly* did you say, Jared?"

He didn't take his eyes off the road ahead. "I said, 'Someone very special to me is pregnant.'"

Her heart quickened, which was stupid, of course, because she knew her relationship with Jared was special—just not special in *that* way. She cringed. When the doctor had asked how long since she'd last had sex, Mercedes hadn't hesitated before answering. She hadn't known the doctor would leap to such an erroneous conclusion or mention Mercedes's celibate status to Jared.

Sexual relations with Jared. An image of hot, sweaty bodies sliding against each other flashed on her mind's movie screen, and surprisingly, her reaction was far from repulsed. In fact, her stomach fluttered and filled with heat—a totally taboo response.

Damned pregnancy hormones. "That's all you said?"

"That's it."

"I'll correct Dr. Evans on my next visit. I'm going to continue seeing her until closer to my due date, and then she'll refer me to a practice near home. I stand a better chance of avoiding the press that way."

He hesitated and his brows lowered. "What's the point of correcting her unless you want Craig's family history included in the paperwork?"

In a perfect world Mercedes would have the complete medical history of her baby's father, but this wasn't a perfect world. "I don't want to call Craig to get his history. I know enough. I made sure he was healthy before I slept with him. His parents are in their late seventies. He often complained that they were disgustingly hale and hearty and had no time for their only child. His father plays golf several times a week and his mother is on the seniors' tennis team."

Her baby would inherit good genes from his father's side. Apparently, that was all Craig intended to contribute.

Jared nodded. "Then let it ride. What harm can it do?"

"It's dishonest. I'd rather not start my baby's life with a lie. My father built a life based on lies, and look how that's come back to haunt us."

He sent her a glance so filled with understanding that warmth settled low in her belly and tears pricked Mercedes's eyes. "As you said, you're not your father."

"No, but I don't think lying is ever the best option, and unless you want to come to every appointment with me and play the devoted daddy-to-be, then I need to straighten this out."

Jared's shoulders tensed and his jaw knotted. He couldn't withdraw any further without getting out of the car. "I'll call her office first thing Monday morning."

Mercedes sighed and leaned her head against the headrest. Jared was determined to establish a barrier between them. How could she stop him?

Life as she knew it was about to change. Yawning, Mercedes pulled into her assigned parking space outside the apartment building and turned off the car's engine.

For starters, she'd have to move. There wasn't room in her studio apartment for a baby. And she'd have to get a new car. Her tiny two-seater wouldn't hold a car seat. She yawned and stretched. Maybe after a nap she wouldn't be too exhausted to plan for her future.

She unlocked the apartment door, stepped inside and froze. Craig Bradford reclined on her sofa. Her exhaustion vanished. "What are you doing here?" she said.

Craig rose, smiling his most practiced smile and assuming the posture that she'd learned meant he wanted something. She'd once found him attractive with his dark-blond hair and blue eyes and let's-have-fun attitude. Now she saw a man so much like her father that she couldn't believe she'd ever become involved with him. Stupid, stupid, stupid. And now she carried his baby.

"How did you get in?"

He produced a key from his pocket and held it up.

Mercedes silently cursed. She and Craig had never lived together, but she had loaned him a key once because she couldn't leave work to retrieve the cell phone he'd left in her apartment. He must have had a copy made. She crossed the room and reached for it.

He lifted it out of range. "I made a mistake. I love you and I want to marry you."

Shock stopped her midstride. "What?"

"I was scared. Mercedes, love, I've never thought twice about being a father. You surprised me, that's all. But now I'm ready."

She could see the lie in his eyes. "You don't love me, Craig. You love you. That makes one of us. What do you want?"

"I want us to spend the rest of our lives together."

"The rest of our lives." Skeptical, she folded her arms. "Just you and me, for richer and poorer, in sickness and in health, keeping only unto each other for as long as we both shall live?"

She glimpsed a touch of panic before his gaze danced away and then returned. His throat worked as he swallowed. "Yeah."

Mercedes laughed in disbelief. Not only did Craig avoid illness like the plague and rely heavily on his creature comforts, his blatant flirting with her female friends had almost cost her those friendships. He didn't know the first thing about fidelity—the kind of love that Jared had shared with Chloe. Mercedes wouldn't settle for less. Not that she believed she'd ever find it. And she certainly wasn't looking.

"Come on, Mercedes, let's run off to Vegas. When we get back we'll build a nice house using the money you're going to inherit from Ashton's estate and play mom and dad with style."

Did his voice break over the word dad? "Craig, I'm not inheriting any money, and I don't want to marry you."

"The papers are full of the news that your father was loaded, and your brother is contesting the will. All of your father's property will revert to your mother's children. That means one quarter of that estate belongs to you, sweetie."

Money. This was all about money? Why was she surprised? "Nothing has been decided about the estate, and I'm still not going to marry you."

Craig was an ambitious salesman dedicated to making acquaintances of the rich, famous and influential. For a while Mercedes had been happy to make those introductions because his smooth-talking and pleasant persona also helped her expand Louret's client base.

His expression turned petulant. "You will or I'll sue for joint custody of that little Ashton heir you're carrying."

Mercedes's knees collapsed as reality slapped her. She sank into her wicker rocking chair. Craig was more like her father than she'd thought. He didn't want her or her baby. He wanted to get his hands on the Ashton money, and he'd use this child as a pawn to do so. *Not as long as she was breathing.*

"What happened to your claim that this baby wasn't yours?"

He didn't try to varnish the truth with charm now. Bitterness flattened his lips. "I told you. I was upset."

"You ordered me to get an abortion, Craig."

Panic crossed his features. "You didn't, did you?"

It would be so easy to lie—but unfortunately, also so easy to disprove. "No. I told you I wouldn't."

His insincere, ingratiating smile returned. "Good. Let's get married."

"No."

"Mercedes," he sing-songed. "Come on. We're good together."

Correction. They were *okay* together. No stars, no fireworks, no weak knees. They'd been better at increasing each other's client base than as a romantic couple. "Give up, Craig. It isn't going to happen."

"Do you really want your child to be a bastard?"

He didn't have to add *like you*. Mercedes immediately relived the shock and shame she'd experienced eight months ago when she'd discovered her parents' marriage had never been legal. And now, she was repeating her father's mistakes. But she wouldn't let her child suffer. "Better a bastard than a pawn in a nasty divorce."

Anger flashed in his eyes. He stalked to the door, but paused with his hand on the knob and turned to glare at her. "Then you'll hear from my lawyer."

The door slammed behind him, jarring the picture of her family from the wall. The glass inside the frame shattered on impact with the floor. Mercedes feared her well-ordered life was about to do the same.

Her stomach revolted. She bolted to the bathroom and lost her lunch. When the retching subsided she sank to the floor, clutched her middle and sagged against the bathroom cabinet. What was she going to do? She couldn't let Craig get his hands on this baby. She'd experienced life with a father who, when he wasn't ignoring you, treated you like a necessary evil. My God, Spencer hadn't even recognized Jillian, *his own daughter,* at the reception the Ashton Estates Winery, her father's other company, had held earlier this year. Mercedes rubbed her tummy. Her child would never know the pain of being discarded and forgotten.

Panic clawed at her insides. She couldn't think for the pounding in her head. Jared would know what to do. He excelled at assessing a situation and formulating a logical plan of action.

She staggered to the phone and dialed his number. A sob skipped up her throat when his deep baritone answered. "Jared, I need you."

Mercedes opened the door before Jared could knock. She looked near shock. Her pupils were dilated and her skin waxy. "What am I going to do?"

He cupped her elbow and guided her back into her den. "First, you're going to sit down, and then I'm going to make you a cup of your favorite tea."

Mercedes wrapped herself in the quilt Chloe had sewn for her and curled in her rocking chair. Satisfied that she wasn't going to pass out at his feet, Jared crossed to her kitchen and prepared the tea. He visited often enough that he knew where Mercedes kept everything, including her favorite mug.

"Tell me exactly what Bradford said," he called over his shoulder.

"He read about Eli contesting the will in the papers. Craig said he wants us to run off to Vegas and then come back and build a house using the money I'll inherit. If I refuse he'll sue for custody."

Jared shoved the mug into her hands, pinched the bridge of his nose and tried to think of a better way to offset Bradford's claim—a way that didn't knot his intestines or make him

rave a shot of mind-numbing whiskey. He drew a blank. The
nsane idea that had forced itself into his mind on the drive
over refused to be supplanted by a saner one.

A sense of inevitability closed in, wedging him between
the proverbial rock and hard place. He exhaled slowly. "Tell
him the baby is mine."

Mercedes clutched her mug and gaped at him. Some col-
or returned to her cheeks, but the worry darkening her sea
green eyes to jade didn't fade. "We can't do that."

"We're only confirming what he already believes. Hell, it
was his idea."

"But it's a lie," she protested.

Yes, dammit, and he hated lying and liars which was one
of the reasons he'd never liked Bradford, the smooth-talking,
opportunistic bastard. But what other option did they have to
keep the parasite from following through with his threat? If
Mercedes felt like a bug under a microscope now, it would
be nothing compared to the media frenzy if Craig sold his story to the highest bidder. She and her baby would become the
next bone for the press dogs to fight over. The added stress
wouldn't be healthy for her or the pregnancy.

He crossed the room to stand before her. "Which is worse,
us lying about your baby's paternity or Bradford lying about
suddenly loving you and using the child you're carrying to
get his hands on the Ashton estate?"

"You're arguing semantics."

An urge to smooth her tangled curls blindsided Jared. He
shoved his fists in his pockets. "Do you have a better idea?"

"No, I don't, but I can't let him have this baby, Jared. He'd
be no better a father than Spencer, and no child deserves a father who makes her feel like an unwanted possession that he
can't wait to shed." She set the mug on the end table and
hugged the quilt tighter. "What if he demands a DNA test?"

"You can refuse to have the testing done until after the baby is born. Prenatal DNA testing is risky for the fetus. No court would require it. Do you think he'll hang around that long once he realizes that Spencer's estate isn't likely to be settled for years?"

"Honestly, no. I think Craig wants a fast buck and the publicity the Ashton name brings. He's a salesman. That kind of name recognition would help his career. But Jared, there's something else to consider." She hesitated and his nerves stretched taut. "My family didn't like Craig, and they'd never expect me to marry him... But they love you."

The quiet statement hit him with the force of a battering ram to the gut. He clenched his teeth and abruptly turned toward the window. His mind, his heart and soul screamed *no*, but he knew which path he had to take—the one he'd sworn never to travel again. Still, he couldn't force the words past his paralyzed vocal cords.

He heard Mercedes sigh. "I'll hire a lawyer and try to get Craig declared an unfit father. I have plenty of friends who can testify that he made passes at them while we were supposedly an exclusive couple, and the fact that he bolted as soon as I told him I was pregnant should carry some weight. God, I wish I'd kept the check he threw at me when he told me to get an abortion, but I was so angry I shredded it and flushed it. I'll just have to hope what I have is enough."

The doubt in her voice ripped him open. He set his jaw. Forcing one tight, aching muscle and then another to move, he turned until his gaze met hers. "We'll get married."

She gasped and her knuckles clutching the quilt whitened. "No. *No*," she repeated with more strength. "I won't let you do that."

"You'll have my name and my protection. We'll present a

nited front—not just the two of us, but your entire family
vill stand behind us."

Sad shadows filled her eyes. "I won't let you deface your
memories of Chloe that way."

*Chloe.* She'd loved Mercedes like a sister from the time
he two girls had met back in grade school. Chloe, his generous, loving wife, would want him to help—no matter what
he cost. "Mercedes, it's your only option if you want to avoid
a long, public legal battle."

Mercedes rose, and the quilt slid to the floor. Tension
strained her features as she crossed the room. The shadows
beneath her eyes looked darker than they had an hour ago.
"You are my best friend and I love you for what you're try-
ng to do, but I won't let you make this sacrifice."

He cupped her shoulders to prevent the hug he suspected
was coming, and her curls teased the backs of his hands. He
ouldn't handle close contact now when his nerves were on
edge and his body seemed to have its own agenda. "I wouldn't
lave made it through the last six years if not for the sacrifices
ou've made for me."

She lifted her hand to cradle his jaw. Mercedes could scale
a cliff and negotiate Class IV white water with ease. She'd
lone both with him countless times. He'd known she was in
great shape, but he'd never experienced the strength and
varmth of her muscles shifting beneath his fingers. A surge
of testosterone pumped into his blood, heading toward an unacceptable target zone. He lowered his hands and shoved
hem into his pockets, but the heat of her satiny skin lingered
n his palms.

Clearing his throat, he put the width of the room between
hem. "Once Bradford slinks back under his rock we'll qui-
tly separate and divorce. We're looking at a couple of years.
Three at the most."

Doubt clouded her eyes. "What would we tell my family?"

"If you want to keep the truth out of the press then w tell everyone the same story. We've been friends for years They'll buy that we've become...lovers." Saying the wor sent another shot of heat through his system. Fast on the heels of heat came pain. He'd never love another woma like he'd loved Chloe. He wouldn't—*couldn't*—risk it "When we end it we'll tell them we were better friends tha lovers."

"Would we be...lovers?"

Her quiet, hesitant question shook him like an earthquake "No. It'll be a marriage in name only."

Hugging herself, she paced to the window. "I'm not com fortable with lying to my family."

"Do you want to risk the truth getting out? We can't guar antee that family conversations won't be overheard. Servant talk and they've been known to sell secrets. Any hint tha we're not a happy couple will strengthen Bradford's claim b making it appear that we've concocted this story to deliber ately deceive him and exclude him from his child's life."

"We *have* concocted this story to keep him away from hi baby." Her shoulders slumped and she gave a resigned sigh "If we do this, then where would we live? This place is to small, and so is your cottage."

"We'll have to buy a house."

Worry pleated her brow. "What about us?"

"What about us?"

Her eyes beseeched his. "Jared, can you promise me marriage won't ruin our friendship?"

His chest constricted and it hurt to breathe. Everything ha changed the moment she told him she was pregnant. Lif came with no guarantees, but right now, Mercedes needed as surance more than she needed additional uncertainties.

"You have my word that I'll stand by you, Mercedes, for as long as I'm able."

And God help him, he'd do whatever it took to keep that vow.

# Three

Mercedes faced her mother and sister across her kitchen table on Sunday afternoon. She touched her queasy stomach and prayed this decision wouldn't come back to haunt her.

Setting down her teacup, she folded both hands in her lap to hide their trembling. "Thanks for coming over. I need your help."

"What kind of help?" her sister Jillian asked.

"Planning a wedding."

Her mother's cup rattled on the saucer. "To Craig?"

The dismay her mother couldn't quite conceal brought a sad smile to Mercedes's lips and reaffirmed her decision. Craig was a jerk, and erasing him from her life was the right thing to do for everyone concerned—especially her baby. "No. To Jared."

After a stunned moment of silence, Jillian squealed, jumped to her feet and pulled Mercedes into a bouncing hug. "It's about time you saw the prize right in front of your nose."

Her mother added her own hug and beamed. "Congratu-ations. You know Lucas and I love Jared as if he were one of our own. What did you have in mind? A spring wedding, or perhaps summer?"

"Actually, we'd like to get married right away." Mercedes licked her dry lips and took a deep breath. Her stomach churned. "I'm pregnant, but I'd like to keep that among the three of us for the time being."

Slack-jawed, Jillian sank back into her chair. Mercedes could see the questions in her sister's eyes, but she hoped Jil-lian wouldn't ask them, because Mercedes didn't know if she could look her in the face and tell a bold-faced lie. None of them needed to check their Day Planners to know that Craig had been gone little more than a month, and here Mercedes was pregnant and planning to marry another man.

Mercedes resettled in her seat and forged ahead. "We'd prefer a small, intimate wedding with only the immediate family present, and since Jared's in the middle of negotiating the purchase of the inn we visited yesterday, we're going to have to postpone the honeymoon."

Her mother eased gracefully back into her chair. "Perhaps we could hold the ceremony in my garden?"

Perfect. The eight-foot-high stone wall surrounding her mother's garden should keep out the press. "If you don't mind?"

"Of course not. The garden was always your favorite spot. You could say your vows in front of the fountain. Did you have a date in mind?"

Mercedes's heart raced. She couldn't believe she was ac-ually going to go through with this. "As soon as we can make the arrangements. Tomorrow is Labor Day. The court-house will be closed for the holiday. Jared and I will apply for the marriage license on Tuesday morning as soon as they

open. Do you think we could arrange it by Saturday afternoon?"

"I could call the minister who married Seth and me to see
if he's available, if you like," Jillian offered hesitantly.

"That would be great." Mercedes tried to smile, but her
numb lips wouldn't cooperate.

"We could shop for a dress tomorrow," her sister added
with a little more enthusiasm. "Everything will be on sale."

Mercedes swallowed. She hadn't thought about a wedding dress. If she didn't buy something, her family would ask
questions she didn't want to answer. "I don't want anything
fancy to remind Jared of his wedding to Chloe."

Her mother patted her hand. "His marriage to Chloe was
a long time ago, and she's been gone six years. He'd want you
to have your dream wedding, but if you'd prefer a simple ceremony, then you shall have one."

"Thank you. I'll prepare a press release, but I'd rather
nothing leak out until after the ceremony. I'm worried that
Craig might make trouble. We didn't part on the best of terms
and he's come sniffing around now that he believes I'll inherit some of Spencer's money."

Her mother nodded with a tightening of her lips. "We'll
hire extra security. Will Jared's father and brothers be attending?"

Yet another component Mercedes hadn't considered. "I
don't know. There's still a lot of tension between them, but
I'll ask Jared if he wants to invite them."

Her mother nodded again. "His family will be our family
now. They're welcome to stay here at The Vines. I'll call and
make the offer myself, if you'd like."

The lie grew more convoluted by the minute. Her family
loved Jared and would willingly embrace his family. They'd
all be hurt when the truth eventually came out.

So Mercedes lifted her chin. She'd have to do whatever she could to keep the truth from surfacing. Once Craig was no longer a threat, she and Jared would part as he suggested, claiming they were better friends than lovers.

*Lovers.* Her skin flushed hot and she couldn't seem to catch her breath. For the first time in her pregnancy, Mercedes thought she might faint. She and her husband could not, *would not* become intimate. She wouldn't betray Chloe's memory that way. Nor did she want to risk falling for the one man who had the power to breach the walls she'd built around her heart.

"Absolutely stunning," Caroline Ashton whispered in a tear-laden voice as she tucked the last of Mercedes's curls in place with a pearl-tipped hairpin. She stepped back so Mercedes could view her handiwork in her mother's bedroom mirror.

Mercedes swallowed to ease the tightness in her throat and met her mother's watery gaze in the mirror. This wasn't the wedding day Mercedes had pictured for herself, but then she'd never pictured herself ever trusting a man enough to marry him. "Jillian has incredible taste. The dress is lovely."

Given the circumstances of her hasty marriage, Mercedes had refused to wear bridal white. Nor had she wanted to look young or innocent since at thirty-three she was neither, and ruffles and flounces had never been her style. She'd suggested a simple, elegant suit, but her sister had refused to let her be so practical or staid.

Jillian had dragged her from shop to shop until they'd discovered this lingerie-style slip dress. The delicate beading edging the bodice, hem and the thin shoulder straps sparkled subtly on the antiqued ivory silk when Mercedes moved. The fabric skimmed her figure before flaring slightly around her ankles. The elegant and romantic wedding dress made Mercedes feel beautiful despite a huge case of nerves and tremendous reservations about the ceremony ahead.

She smoothed her hands over her hips and took a quick peek in the mirror to assure herself that the reason behind the rushed ceremony didn't show.

Jared didn't deserve this. Every step of the way had been painful for him—not that he'd uttered one word of complaint. He'd said nothing at the county clerk's office when he'd had to produce Chloe's death certificate as part of the application for a marriage license, but Mercedes's heart had ached for him. His fingers had lingered for a split second longer than necessary on the page, sweeping over Chloe's name as if he were saying goodbye again. His silence, the muscle ticking in his jaw and the rigid set of his shoulders had revealed far more about his pain than mere words could say.

If Jillian, their witness, had noticed Jared's reluctance, she hadn't mentioned it.

"Ready?" Jillian asked, draping a sheer shimmering silk stole over Mercedes's shoulders.

"As ready as I'll ever be." Mercedes quivered inside.

"I'll get our bouquets from the kitchen." Jillian slipped out the door.

As elegant and stylish as ever, Caroline Lattimer Ashton Sheppard dabbed a tear with a lace handkerchief. Mercedes would never understand how her mother could take a second chance on love after the way Spencer Ashton had hurt and betrayed her, but in her mother's case it had paid off. Lucas Sheppard, Mercedes's stepfather, treated Caroline like a queen. Their deep, abiding love was evident in every glance and touch.

Men like Lucas and Jared were few and far between. Seth, Jillian's new husband, looked as if he might be one of that rare breed as well. He'd certainly made her sister very happy in the past four months. Mercedes sighed and adjusted a curl. Why was it that the men worth a second glance were already taken?

Caroline's reflection joined Mercedes's in the mirror. "It's almost time to start. I'll get Lucas."

Mercedes turned, caught her mother's hand and squeezed her fingers. "Mom, thank you for putting this together so quickly. The garden looks like something from a fairy tale."

If her mother had guessed Mercedes wasn't in love with her groom-to-be she hadn't said so. Caroline had gone out of her way to turn the garden into the ideal location for a romantic fantasy wedding. Even the climbing roses lining the high white stone wall of her mother's private garden had cooperated by producing a fresh set of fragrant blossoms. Additional potted plants had been placed in every available niche and along the brick walk from the back door of The Vines to the fountain in front of which she and Jared would exchange their vows.

"Just be happy." Her mother kissed her cheek and left Mercedes alone in the room with her suffocating doubts.

Panic clawed at her stomach. What if this marriage was a horrible mistake? Others would be hurt. She pressed a hand below her navel and thought of her painful relationship with Spencer. Could she inflict that on an innocent child? No, she wouldn't make her child beg for crumbs of attention. She'd give her child enough love to make up for denying her a father. And maybe, just maybe, Jared would be a father figure for her baby once the shock of the situation wore off.

The bedroom door opened and Lucas Sheppard stepped inside. He'd married her mother when Mercedes was six and had brought a sense of normalcy back to their lives after her father's abrupt departure. Still handsome, tall and fit at sixty, Lucas walked with a slight limp—a remnant from the years of hard work in the vineyard. He'd combed every gray hair in place.

She smiled. "You look dashing in your tuxedo."

"And you're going to knock Jared right out of his shoes."

If only that were true. Mercedes blinked away the rogue thought. She wasn't out to seduce her husband-to-be.

Lucas took her hand and met her gaze. A solemn expression replaced the usual twinkle in his blue eyes. "This is the part where I'm supposed to remind you that it's not too late to change your mind. This baby is nothing we can't handle."

Her mother had asked if she could share the pregnancy news with Lucas, and Mercedes had agreed. Emotion welled in Mercedes's throat. She smiled and brushed a piece of lint from his shoulder. "And that's just one of the reasons I love you. No matter what kind of situation I found myself in, you were always there to guide me. You know I couldn't have dreamed up a more perfect father if I'd tried. I'm lucky to have you in my life, Lucas Sheppard, and my baby will be even luckier to have you as a grandfather."

Tears dampened his eyes, and Mercedes's own eyes burned. He yanked her into a big bear hug, and then drew back abruptly. "Don't want to muss the dress."

"*You* can muss me anytime." She straightened his bow tie and kissed his cheek.

"Ready to get this show on the road? Some of that stuff the caterers brought in looks mighty tasty."

Mercedes's stomach pitched at the thought of food. She took a deep breath and pasted a smile on her face. A simple ceremony and two gold bands could put her friendship with Jared on the line. He deserved the same opportunity to escape that Lucas had offered her.

"Could you give me a minute?"

\* \* \*

A cold calm settled over Jared as the clock inched toward noon. Moving forward meant leaving the past behind. He hadn't expected it to be so difficult.

Marrying a woman who wasn't Chloe seemed like a betrayal. But abandoning Mercedes to her opportunistic ex was no less disloyal. The past, his life with Chloe, was over. Handing over her death certificate had made that clear. Mercedes and her baby deserved a future without Bradford mucking it up.

Through the French door leading from the library to the garden patio Jared watched his sisters-in-law, niece and nephews and his older brother, Ethan, take their seats inside the walled garden with Mercedes's siblings. Behind him, his oldest brother and best man, Nate, lounged on the sofa, talking quietly with the minister.

Jared was surprised his brothers had come. His father hadn't. But then his father had never forgiven him for putting Chloe's dream of running a bed and breakfast inn ahead of family obligations. When Jared had refused to return to the fold after Chloe's death, the gap had widened even more. Both of his brothers were dutifully employed by Maxwell Hotels, Incorporated. They seemed happy enough under their father's controlling thumb. Jared hadn't been.

As the third son he was supposed to toe the line and do what he was told without question, but he'd needed to forge his own path, to succeed on his own merit and not just be the old man's puppet. And he had succeeded—albeit on a different path and a larger scale than he'd originally planned. He offered couples who had the desire but lacked the capital the opportunity to live their dreams of running cozy B&Bs. In a way he was keeping Chloe's dream alive, but from a safe distance.

A tap on the door sent Jared's stomach plunging toward

his polished shoes. *Time's up*. He flexed his tense shoulder as the minister rose to answer the summons.

Nate joined Jared by the French door. "I wish you'd le Ethan and me throw a bachelor party for you or at least let u take you out, booze you up and raise a little hell."

His brothers didn't know about Jared's bout with alcoho abuse. Only Mercedes knew.

"Mercedes and I wanted to avoid the publicity." And i wasn't as if he was saying goodbye to his freedom for the res of his life. He'd done that when he'd married Chloe.

Looking decidedly uncomfortable, the minister cleared his throat. "Mercedes would like a moment alone with Jar ed."

Jared's heart slammed against his chest. Did she have col feet? Didn't she realize this was the only way to protect he name and her baby? Surely she hadn't decided to acquiesce to Bradford's demands. Jared fisted his hands. God help Brad ford if he dared to show up today because—

The door opened farther, framing Mercedes in the dark wooden portal like a portrait and choking Jared off mid thought. His jaw and his fingers went lax. She looked…amaz ing. Beautiful. *Sexy as hell*. Jared sucked a sharp breath and took a mental giant step back. Every speck of moisture in his mouth vanished.

She'd pinned her curls haphazardly on top of her head. Stray ringlets caressed her neck and tumbled to her bare shoulders. Was that her wedding dress or the slip she'd wear underneath the dress? My God, she looked half-naked even though only her shoulders in the floor-length gown were bare. She shifted on her feet and the light reflected off pearls and sequins. Her dress, then, not her slip. Somehow the knowl edge didn't lessen the impact.

"Give us a minute," he croaked.

His brother punched his shoulder. Jared peeled his gaze off Mercedes long enough to see Nate's wink, smirk and thumbs-up. Nate didn't know the truth behind the wedding.

Mercedes entered the library, and his brother and the minister exited, closing the door quietly behind them.

Her alluring and exotic scent, so different from Chloe's sweet floral perfume, wrapped around Jared and made him dizzy with an adrenaline rush. "You look incredible, Mercedes."

A smile trembled on her lips. "Thank you. So do you."

She lifted a hand to straighten his tie, something she'd done countless times before, but dropped it before making contact. Her fabric stole fell off her shoulders to drape behind her back. Jared considered yanking it back in place, but he didn't want to risk contact with her velvety skin. Besides, the almost sheer fabric wouldn't hide anything.

Closing her eyes, she took a deep unsteady breath, drawing his eyes to her tantalizing cleavage. Her skin couldn't possibly be as soft as it looked. He tried and failed to stifle the thought. The response rioting through his system was completely inappropriate for a man to feel toward his best friend. He clenched his jaw and fought the unexpected and unwanted need snaking through his veins.

"Mercedes, is everything all right?"

"Yes. I…" She lifted her lids. Worry darkened her eyes to jade and a line formed between her brows. "Jared, I know how hard this must be for you. We don't have to get married. I can find another way to fight Craig."

The knot in his throat thickened. "Is that what you want?"

She hesitated. "I don't want to make your life miserable, and if you want to call this off—"

He laid a finger over her lips. She wasn't having second thoughts, but she thought he was. Mercedes worried about him way too much. She'd pulled him out of despair and along the road to recovery. She'd been the giver in this relationship and he'd been the taker. It was time he carried his weight. Payback time.

His finger burned. He removed it from her soft mouth and shoved his fist in his pants pocket. His knuckles bumped the coolness of the rings he'd bought for her and reminded him that he was here to protect Mercedes and her baby.

"How could having my best friend as a roommate make me miserable?"

"I don't know. I just thought…" She shrugged, and one pearly strap slipped off her shoulder. The front part of her dress—the bodice or whatever you called it—gaped slightly, but enough to shock him with the knowledge that she wasn't wearing a bra.

He gritted his teeth against a flash fire of desire, abruptly raked the strap back in place with one finger and then he knotted his hands behind his back. He shifted his gaze and battled his renegade thoughts. For crissakes, he didn't need to know the size and shape of Mercedes's breasts or the color of her nipples, but he'd had a glimpse, dammit. A tantalizing, torturing glimpse.

Why had he never noticed the delicacy of her shoulders? Sure, she was lightly muscled from their outdoor adventures, but she was also softly curved and feminine. At five feet six inches, she was just over a half foot shorter than he, and slender and petite. Chloe had been even smaller—so tiny and delicate he'd been afraid she'd break if he ever unleashed his passion.

*Mercedes wouldn't break.*

The mantel clock struck noon, jarring him from his forbidden thoughts with a swift stab of guilt. "Mercedes, stick with the plan."

She frowned at his abrupt tone. "Are you sure?"

"I'm sure."

"If you change your mind—"

"I won't." He considered pulling her into his arms to reassure her. Hell, they'd hugged before. But with the heat percolating beneath his skin and with the new knowledge that her breasts would fit perfectly in his palms, he didn't dare risk it. Taking her by the elbow, he turned her. In that brief second as he reached past her to open the library door, he battled an almost overwhelming urge to touch his lips to her exposed nape. My God, she smelled good. Too good.

He said a prayer of thanks when he found Nate and the minister waiting anxiously on the other side of the threshold. Their presence prevented him from making a mistake and crossing the line of friendship—a line he had no intention of crossing.

"Meet me at the fountain, Mercedes."

With a hesitant glance over her shoulder, she nodded and headed down the hall. The fabric of her dress molded her curves with a lover's detail to accuracy. There weren't any panty lines under her dress, and she wasn't wearing a bra. For heaven's sake, was she naked beneath that wisp of silk? His pulse drummed louder in his ears. He swallowed hard.

Struggling to breathe, he turned on his heel and marched back to the window. What in the hell was wrong with him? His relationship with Mercedes would not change. They'd share a home, companionship, not a bed or hot, sweaty nights. So why did his mind persist in catapulting him in the wrong direction when his hormones had been happily dormant for six years? Longer, if you counted the months he and Chloe had abstained because of her discomfort during the last half of her pregnancy.

"Are we going to proceed?" the minister asked tentatively.

"Yes." Jared reached for the brass lever handle on the French door and yanked it open. He strode to his assigned place beside the fountain, eager to get the formalities over with and to get Mercedes back into some real clothes. Any of her buttoned-up suits would be preferable to the dress that looked more like an undergarment than a wedding dress.

Nate and the minister caught up with him and flanked him. Jared ignored the wiseass smirk on his brother's face, clasped his hands in front and fixed his gaze on the opposite end of the aisle flanked by guests.

From the corner of the garden a harpist plucked out a tune. The double French doors leading from the main part of the house opened, and Mercedes's oldest brother, Eli, escorted his mother down the flower-lined brick walk. Caroline gave Jared a sweet, welcoming smile, and his belly knotted at the deception. She trusted him with her daughter. He wouldn't let her down.

Rachel, Mercedes's three-year-old niece, came next, scattering rose petals randomly over the bricks. When she reached the end of the aisle she rushed to her daddy, seated in the second row, and climbed in Seth's lap. Jared's heart ached. He'd never have a child wind her arms around his neck and his heart with such devotion.

Unless Mercedes's baby— He slammed the protective barrier back in place. He couldn't afford to love Mercedes's baby. Losing Chloe had been hard, but losing his son had nearly destroyed him. His marriage to Mercedes would end, and she'd move out and take her child with her.

By the time he found his composure and looked up, Jillian had made it halfway down the walk. Her mint-green dress resembled Mercedes's, but it wasn't anywhere near as sexy.

Mercedes stepped into the opening, and the knot in Jared's throat threatened to choke him. My God, she was beautiful.

Sunlight danced on her curls and sparkled on the beads and pearls of her dress. But Mercedes was marrying the wrong man. She deserved one who had a heart instead of a cold hunk of ice in his chest. She deserved a man who could be strong for her no matter what.

He would be strong, dammit. He squared his shoulders and awaited his bride.

On the verge of hyperventilating, Mercedes struggled to regulate her breathing, and then she met Jared's gaze across the garden and forgot about breathing altogether.

The strength in Jared's broad shoulders and in his eyes led her forward as surely as Lucas's firm grip on her elbow as he guided her down the steps and along the brick path. Mercedes's hyperalert senses identified the scents of flowers and her mother's herb garden mingled with the aroma of the candles burning in their glass globes beside the fountain, which gurgled in rhythm with the harpist. A gentle breeze ruffled her hair and caressed her shoulders. The silk of her dress slid over her skin like a lover's touch with every step. Her nipples beaded beneath the cool fabric, and there was nothing she could do to hide the telling reaction.

Not once did her gaze leave Jared's. When she reached the end of the short aisle he extended his hand. This is the right thing to do, his steady dark-blue eyes seemed to tell her. Lucas released her, kissed her cheek and stepped away. Jared took his place. His warm fingers curled around Mercedes's, and a sense of calmness settled over her. Her best friend would become her temporary husband. Their friendship had survived worse things than marriage.

Mercedes had made every effort to ensure this wedding was as different from Jared's first as possible. Chloe had written the vows she and Jared had spoken. Her friend had also insisted on a soprano soloist, twelve attendants to waltz down the cathedral aisle, hundreds of guests and custom-made wedding bands. Mercedes had requested simple elegance, and her mother and Jillian had provided exactly that.

The minister began the traditional service Mercedes had heard dozens of times before. The familiar words soothed her tangled nerves. She'd asked for a plain wedding band, but when she looked down at the engagement ring and wedding band set Jared eased onto her finger, she gasped. An emerald-cut diamond winked in the sunlight. The gold bands of the two rings fit together so perfectly that either would look incomplete without the other.

Jared repeated his vows in a firm and sure voice.

Mercedes's voice trembled and so did her fingers when she slid a wide gold band over Jared's knuckle. And then his hands, as warm and solid as a sun-baked rock, cradled hers and calmed her. Right or wrong, the deed was done. She'd married her best friend.

The minister closed his Bible and beamed. "Jared, you may kiss your bride."

Mercedes's heart stumbled then raced. Her shocked gaze jerked to Jared's. How had she forgotten this part? Duty and resolve filled his blue eyes, firmed his square chin. His hands curved over her bare shoulders, and each of his fingers spread a lavalike trail of heat over her body. She dampened her lips. His eyes tracked the movement. She thought she saw a flare of something besides surprise in the split second before he bent his head, but he lowered his lids before she could identify the emotion.

They'd shared numerous hugs and friendly kisses on the cheek, but she couldn't remember their lips ever touching. She barely had a split second to register that Jared had a really great mouth—a chiseled vee on top and lushly curved on he bottom—before his warm, firm mouth settled over hers. And then Mercedes's world went topsy-turvy, as if she'd been swept overboard by the swing of a sailboat boom.

Her eyes slammed shut, and she inhaled sharply through her nose. Jared's woodsy cologne filled her senses, and her head spun as if she'd been tumbled into the water and didn't know which direction led to the surface. Her muscles weakened and her knees buckled. She clutched the lapels of his jacket to keep from sinking to the ground at his feet. Jared's arm banded around her waist, pulling her flush against his lean, hard body. Hot. So hot. She gasped, and his mouth opened over hers. The flick of his tongue on her bottom lip struck her with the charge of a lightning bolt, and then he tasted her. A sip. A silken swipe.

She couldn't help but taste him back. Delicious. Jared. Familiar and yet so spicy and scrumptious she couldn't get enough.

Her hands slid up his neck to tangle in the springy, short hair on his nape. His palms eased down over the slick fabric of her dress to cover her bottom with a blanket of heat. A thick, insistent ridge pressed her belly and melted her bones.

A spattering of applause and laughter penetrated the sensual fog. Jared abruptly broke the kiss and stepped back. Mercedes stared at him in shock. He looked as stunned as she.

"Ladies and gentlemen, may I present Mr. and Mrs. Jared Maxwell." The minister's pronouncement reminded Mercedes of their audience.

She blinked and pasted on what she hoped looked like a blissful bride's smile, but her mind tumbled in chaos.

What was she going to do? She had the hots for her husband.

# Four

**T**he urge to run, to put some distance between him and Mercedes hit Jared hard. The wedding kiss had blindsided him. Shaken him. Scared the hell out of him because it made him feel too much.

And that hadn't been the end of it. The reception afterward had been sheer torture.

This marriage was temporary, a favor for a friend. End of story. If he let it become more… He ground his teeth. He wouldn't.

He unlocked the cottage door and shoved it open. A rustle of movement in the shrubbery followed by the reflection of light off a camera lens caught his attention. Damn. Reporters. Though everything in him shouted *distance*, Jared swept Mercedes up in his arms.

She gasped, stiffened and squirmed and kicked her feet. He tightened his arms and struggled to hold on to the slippery, silk-clad bundle in a wedding dress.

"Hold still before I drop you," he whispered against her ear. "What are you doing?"

"Paparazzi at nine o'clock. I'm carrying you over the threshold." He tried his best to block out her warmth and the exotic scent of her.

She stopped wiggling and wound her arms around his neck. "Already? But Cole isn't sending out the press release until tomorrow."

Jared stepped inside and kicked the door closed. He lowered her feet to the floor and stepped away as soon as she found her balance. Her body heat clung to him even after he put several yards between them. Making his way around the interior of the cottage, he closed the blinds and curtains, sealing out intrusive eyes and turning the room into an intimate, shadow-filled cave. When the last window in the main room had been covered, he ran out of excuses to avoid looking at her.

He snapped on a lamp. "I've cleaned out the second bedroom for you."

Her brows dipped. "Where did you move your office?"

"Loft."

Mercedes frowned at the darkened balcony area overlooking the sitting area of the cottage. The jackhammering of her heart almost drowned out the rustle of her gown and the tap of her heels on the hardwood floor as she moved farther into the room.

"Jared, that space was never intended to be used for anything other than a child's sleeping area. You'll be cramped, and the head clearance is low. There's definitely not room for the two of us to plot out a marketing campaign for the Meadowview Inn if you buy it."

Mercedes had volunteered her advertising expertise when he and Chloe bought the first inn. She'd continued to help him with each subsequent purchase. Because of her contributions his business had gone from one struggling inn to a string of eight flourishing inns, but proximity would be a problem unless he got his head straightened out.

He shoved a hand through his hair. Where would he go? Climbing? Hiking? Rafting? The cabin. Yeah, Mercedes didn't know about his cabin. "Would you prefer to sleep up there? There's not much privacy, and it will be hard to keep up the appearance of happy newlyweds if everyone knows we have separate bedrooms."

She frowned, removed and folded the filmy stole and draped it over the back of the sofa. "I guess you're right. I'm sorry to displace you. As soon as we find a house you'll have your own office again. In the meantime, we'll have to plot our strategies down here."

They'd agreed to buy a home since neither the cottage nor her apartment was large enough for two, let alone three who needed separate bedrooms. He hadn't wanted to be around while her pregnancy advanced, but with the tight housing market in Napa Valley he could be looking at months of being trapped in the guest cottage with Mercedes and her developing baby before they found a house. A duplex would be better. She could live on one side and he could be on the other. He made a mental note to contact a real estate agent Monday morning.

He ran a finger under his collar and loosened the tie that had tried to choke him for the better part of the afternoon. And then he turned on another lamp, but it did nothing to alleviate the intimate atmosphere. "I also cleared out most of the bathroom cabinet for you."

Having only one bathroom sandwiched between the two bedrooms hadn't been an issue before since he lived alone and didn't entertain, but then the cottage had never seemed this small and cramped, either.

He'd survive the shared quarters, but he didn't expect it to be easy. His office location wasn't going to be the main problem. The resurgence of his libido was. His resurrected hormones reminded him that Mercedes would be naked in his shower.

Wet with his water.

Slick with his soap.

He swiped a hand over his jaw and vowed to get out of here as soon as the reporter outside left. The knotted muscles in his shoulders protested when he glanced at his watch and mentally calculated how long it would take him to pack and load his hiking gear into his SUV. He could be at the cabin by midnight.

"Thank you, Jared. I appreciate everything you're doing. This is above and beyond the call of friendship." So formal and stilted, nothing like best friends. Or husband and wife. Mercedes looked as uncomfortable as he felt. And then he noticed the pallor of her skin and the pleat between her brows— a sure sign she had one of her tension headaches brewing.

She worked too hard. The only time he saw evidence of the carefree college girl Chloe had described was when he and Mercedes went on prospective-inn-buying trips. When they checked out the inns, they also checked out the available tourist activities. If he put Mercedes in a raft on the river, she forgot all about the pressures of the family winery. She probably wanted to get out of Napa as much as he did, but he needed time away from Mercedes to regain his equilibrium, not time alone with her. There would be no honeymoon during this temporary marriage.

He headed for the door. "I'll get your luggage and bring in the picnic basket your mother sent with us. You didn't eat much at the reception. You need to eat to keep up your strength. Take a hot shower, if you want. By the time you get out, I'll have something pulled together for dinner."

And maybe the reporter would be gone, and the reluctant bridegroom could take off for Yosemite.

"Jared…" Mercedes hesitated, biting her lip, and then she took an unsteady breath. "I need help getting out of this gown."

His insides clenched like an angry fist. Mercedes slowly turned to reveal dozens of tiny, satin-covered buttons running from her shoulder blades to the middle of her behind. He eyed the door and wished he were on the other side of it, but he couldn't refuse to help without explaining that his thoughts were far from friendly. He didn't want to embarrass her that way. This was his problem, and he would deal with it. His blood roared in his ears, and his legs felt numb as he moved forward on feet as heavy as concrete blocks.

She looked at him over her shoulder, and a lone curl glided over the pale skin between her shoulder blades. "I'm sorry. I should have changed before we left The Vines, but I had to get out of there. If anyone had asked us to kiss or mug for the camera one more time I think I would have screamed. I had no idea my family were such voyeurs."

"Mine, too." There had been an endless succession of guests—even in their small group—tapping on champagne glasses, demanding the required kiss and making the usual toasts. He'd been careful to plant those kisses on Mercedes's cheek. Her soft, fragrant cheek.

"It was nice of Lucas to provide us with sparkling cider. I doubt any of the guests noticed we weren't drinking real champagne."

"Yeah." His hands trembled as he reached for the top button. His fingers fumbled the first slippery devil free and then the next and the next, revealing inch after inch of bare skin. No bra, just as he suspected. His mouth dried. His throat closed. He tried to avoid touching Mercedes as he worked his way toward the buttons at her waist, but the snug fit of her

ress destroyed his plan. Her warm and supple skin teased his
knuckles. His pulse pounded in his groin, and his lungs
burned from trying not to inhale her intoxicating perfume.

The dress gaped and the straps slipped off her shoulders.
Mercedes caught the gown against her front before the fabric could fall to the floor, but not before a flash of deep red
beneath the thin band of an ivory thong plunged Jared over
the cliff of sanity.

*The tattoo.*

He swallowed a groan. He'd forgotten. Chloe had told him
about the tattoo on Mercedes's right buttock, about the heartache and the pitcher of margaritas that had led Mercedes into getting a permanent reminder that love hurt. The tattoo was
a red rose with thorns, Chloe said, and then Chloe had confessed she'd chickened out before getting her own tattoo.
She'd asked if he thought she'd be sexier with a tattoo, and
he'd assured his sweet, delicate wife that he'd never considered body art attractive.

The fierce desire to peel away the fabric of Mercedes's
dress, to see and touch the rose on her skin belied those
words.

"Thank you." Her husky voice made him grit his teeth.

Sucking in one painful breath and then another, he fisted
his hands, then stepped away. *Chloe.* Think about your wife—
*your first wife*—and how losing her almost destroyed you.
You are weak, Maxwell. You might not survive loving and losing again. And Mercedes's relationships ended real fast when
she found out her dates had feet of clay.

"I'll get your luggage," he ground out through clenched
teeth and then spun on his heel and headed out into the night.

*Don't do this to me,* Mercedes railed at her misbehaving hormones. Something she would just as soon not name stirred low

in her belly, a remnant of Jared's featherlight touch on her spine.

She'd never been the type to get hot and bothered by a look or a passing touch. Why now? And why Jared?

She'd never stayed friends with her past lovers. Her relationships ended bitterly—usually because the men let her down or her inability to commit became an issue. One thing was certain. Giving in to these outlandish new feelings for Jared guaranteed she'd lose her best friend.

And she couldn't lose Jared. He kept her sane. He was the only one she could let down her hair with except for her college friend, Dixie, but her brother Cole had married Dixie back in January, and Cole represented the family and the constant pressure Mercedes experienced to take Louret to the top.

Clutching the dress to her breasts, she retreated to her new bedroom and caught her breath. Jared had found the furnishings Chloe had originally bought for this room. Mercedes remembered her friend's enthusiasm in choosing each fabric, each knickknack. The cheerful colors and romantic ruffles were so reminiscent of Chloe that Mercedes's eyes stung.

Would Chloe see this marriage as a betrayal of their friendship? No. Chloe had valued family and children over almost everything else. She'd understand Mercedes's need to protect her unborn child.

Mercedes looked outside, but didn't spot the reporter Jared had mentioned, and then she closed the window blinds. A tap on the door made her jump. She clutched the bodice of her dress with both hands and turned. "Yes?"

Jared entered the room and laid her suitcases on the bed without making eye contact. "I'll start dinner before I change clothes."

The thought of putting food in her agitated stomach warred with the knowledge that if she didn't eat soon she'd be ill. If

he had her druthers, she'd close the door, climb under the
covers and hide from her tumultuous feelings. "Thank you.
I'll be out in a minute."

Jared left, closing the door behind him.

Mercedes stepped out of her gown and hung it up. She mechanically dug through her cases until she found slacks, a
blouse and a bra that still fit her swollen breasts. She didn't
dress to impress. That wasn't her goal here. One by one, she
pulled the pearl-tipped pins from her hair and dropped them
on the vanity. She ran her fingers through her curls, trying in
vain to make order out of chaos. Her hair was a rat's nest, as
usual, but she couldn't remember if she'd packed her bar-
rettes, and the noisy growls from her stomach warned her not
to waste time searching. Not for the first time she wished she
had Jillian's tame waves or Chloe's satin-slick hair. Instead
she'd been cursed with hair that she couldn't run a brush
through without turning it into a hedge. Natural curls were
the pits.

The beeping timer on the microwave penetrated the bedroom door. She yanked the panel open, took one step forward
and collided with Jared in the tiny dark hall between the bedrooms and the bathroom.

He grabbed her upper arms to steady her, but quickly released her and stepped back. "You okay?"

"Yes." Mercedes took in the way his snug white T-shirt de-
lineated his muscular chest and shoulders and how his jeans
snuggled his strong thighs and long legs. His feet were bare
as were hers.

He'd been undressing while she'd been undressing. *Stop.*
Irritated by her irrational thoughts, she shoved her unruly
hair off her face.

He averted his gaze and jerked his head toward the
kitchen. "Dinner's ready."

She resisted the urge to rub her hands over the warm spot where he'd touched her.

With a sweep of his arm, he indicated she precede him. Mercedes marched toward the compact kitchen. The simple addition of the rings on her finger made forbidden things no longer forbidden. Even though she had no intention of acting on her wayward thoughts, her rampant hormones seemed determined to run amok as much as possible.

"The ring set is beautiful. Thank you."

"You're welcome. Glad you like it," he replied stiffly.

The setting sun cast a dim glow across the colorful kitchen until Jared closed the curtains, filling the room with shadows and sealing them in an intimate cocoon. Although Chloe had never lived in the guest house, her presence permeated this room as much as it did the bedroom. The red and white plaid curtains matched the chintz chair cushions and the cheerful cherry wallpaper. Jared hadn't made many changes since he'd moved in after Chloe's death.

"Sit," he ordered.

Mercedes lifted a brow and sat at the table. "Are you always going to be in charge of the kitchen?"

He grimaced. "Sorry. Habit. Make yourself at home."

Forget you're married. Forget the man kissed better than any fantasy lover in your imagination. Pretend this is just another Wednesday-night dinner even though it's Saturday. Mercedes, trying to lighten the heavy mood, forced a smile to her lips. "I don't cook half as well as you."

Jared rewarded her efforts with a tight smile. He slid a loaded platter of the finger-foods her mother had served at the reception into the center of the small table, passed her a plate with fat cherries painted in the center and a chilled bottle of water. "I seem to remember you're a pretty good cook."

She'd brought him countless meals back in the dark days

immediately after the funeral when he wouldn't have eaten if she hadn't fed him. "You're better, but I'm willing to share kitchen duty."

Despite the fact that Jared fed her every Wednesday night, Mercedes didn't actually dislike cooking, but this cramped space wasn't big enough for the two of them to work simultaneously without a lot of body contact. With the weird way she'd been reacting to him lately, that wasn't a good idea—not if she wanted to get out of this marriage with her friendship intact.

"Would you like me to make up a schedule of who cooks when and post it on the refrigerator?"

"Mercedes," he practically growled, "rule number one. When you're here you relax. No uptight marketing and PR directors allowed. Stress isn't good for you or your baby."

She wrinkled her nose. "Does that work both ways? No overworked CEOs allowed? For someone who's his own boss, you put in a lot of hours."

"I'll shed my power suit at 5:00 p.m. if you will." The twitch of his lips as he settled in the chair across from her should have erased her anxiety, but her mind stayed stuck on the thought of shedding clothing.

*What was wrong with her?*

Their bare feet tangled beneath the table, and tension exploded with the suddenness of a popping champagne cork. She yanked her feet beneath her chair and crossed her ankles against the sudden surge of energy skipping up her shins. Ducking her head, she busied herself with her silverware, and then she stopped herself. Finger foods didn't require utensils.

Jared rose and picked up his plate and glass. "I'm going to read over the inn's prospectus while I eat."

He climbed the stairs to the loft, leaving Mercedes alone in the kitchen.

Her heart sank. This marriage had already taken a toll on their friendship. They couldn't even share a meal together. Was avoiding the publicity and a legal battle worth the price they'd pay?

Jared awoke with a burning need to escape. The house. Mercedes. The erotic dreams which had kept him up all night, in more ways than one.

He rolled out of bed cursing the hovering reporters who'd trapped him inside the cottage last night, tugged on his running clothes and headed out the door. He'd barely begun his prerun warmup when a reporter climbed from a sedan parked in the driveway.

"Leaving your bride so soon, Maxwell?"

Jared set his jaw, ignored the jerk and stretched his hamstrings.

"Mercedes awake yet? I'd like her statement on your hasty marriage."

Jared straightened. "Louret Winery will issue a press release."

"What do you think her boyfriend is going to say about your nuptials?"

Damn it. He didn't want to get dragged into this before he cleared his head. "Mercedes's relationship with Bradford is over."

"Does Bradford know that?"

Another car turned into the drive. A lanky, bearded guy climbed from the driver's seat. The camera hanging from his neck labeled him a reporter. The need to shelter Mercedes from an early-morning inquisition vied with Jared's urge to run.

"Do you want to explain the rushed-and-hushed ceremony?"

Jared clamped down on the *go to hell* that sprang to his lips and abandoned his warmup. Straightening, he forced his mouth into what he hoped looked more like a charming smile than a teeth-grinding scowl. "Gentlemen, we're on our honeymoon. Cut us some slack, would you? We will make no additional comments at this time. And you're on private property. Get lost."

Turning on his heel, Jared snatched up the Sunday paper and reentered the pressure cooker, which, until last night, had been his home, his sanctuary. He closed the door, locked it and leaned back against the wooden panel. He had to warn Mercedes about a potential ambush before he took his run. As soon as he did he was out of here.

A whisper of sound made him open his eyes.

Mercedes shuffled from the bathroom to the den. Her satiny red robe intensified the waxen pallor of her face and her colorless pinched lips. She pushed a trembling hand through her tumbled hair and continued toward the kitchen with single-minded determination.

The combination of her attire and her fragility hit him like a one-two punch to the gut. During their weekend trips they avoided intimate situations and kept the boundaries of their friendship firmly in place. Discussions were never held in nightclothes.

"Mercedes, are you okay?"

She turned her head and blinked as if surprised to see him. "Fine…or I will be as soon as I find the Cheerios."

"Cereal?"

"Yes."

Chloe had been delicate, but she'd rarely been sick during her pregnancies. Jared's protective instincts kicked up a notch. "I don't have any. Can I fix you some eggs?"

She grimaced, swallowed hard and pressed a hand to her stomach. "No…thanks."

"Toast?"

She hesitated. "That might work. Are the reporters still out there?"

"Yes."

"Ugh. I need to go to my apartment. I have to clean out the fridge and the kitchen cabinets and bring the food here, and then I need to finish packing my clothing and personal belongings. The movers are coming tomorrow morning to carry my furniture to The Vines for storage."

He shoved bread in the toaster and turned to find her gaze on him. The fabric of the satiny robe clung to the curves of her breasts with too much detail for his peace of mind, and her hair looked sexily rumpled. He savagely cut off the thought and attacked breakfast preparations.

She settled on a barstool at the counter and cautiously sipped from the glass of orange juice he poured for her. The overhead light reflected off the diamond engagement ring and matching gold wedding band he'd given her. She hadn't wanted anything fancy, and he'd intended to purchase a plain band, but the interlocking set reminded him of the face Mercedes showed the world. Buttoned up. Everything in its place. Understated, not flashy. But given the right setting and the freedom from her duties at the family winery, Mercedes sparkled with the same inner fire as the emerald-cut diamond.

She smothered a yawn. "Did you get to take your run?"

He jerked his thoughts back in line. She knew him well enough to know he ran five miles each morning. "No. There are two reporters waiting in the yard."

Sadness filled her eyes. "Jared, please don't let this marriage alter your routine any more than you have to."

He swallowed a laugh at the absurdity of her comment. She'd shot his routine to hell the day she'd informed him of her pregnancy. The wedding kiss had blown his mind, and he could only imagine what Mercedes had thought when he'd shoved his tongue in her mouth. My God, he'd lost control and crossed the line. Shame burned his ears. He couldn't explain why he'd betrayed her friendship and Chloe's memory, and no matter how hard he tried he could not subdue his resurrected libido. He raked a hand through his hair and fought the flicker of arousal licking through his blood that even shame couldn't quench.

But Mercedes had kissed him back, hadn't she? Or had her participation been purely to further this marriage charade in front of her family? She could hardly haul back and deck him without making them ask questions.

The toast popped up. He slid it onto a plate and shoved it across the breakfast bar. She mumbled her thanks and dipped her head to take a bite. A stray curl fell over her cheek.

He had to get out of the house before the need to smooth her tangled hair overwhelmed his good intentions. Five miles at a punishing pace ought to do the trick. "If the reporters don't leave, call the police and have them escorted off the property. After my run I'll drive you to your apartment."

"You don't have to do that."

"Your car won't carry your boxes. Should I rent a truck?"

"No, if we fold down the seats, your SUV should have enough room for the stuff I need to bring here…although I don't know where I'm going to put everything."

No kidding. The cottage was already cramped. They were practically on top of each other. Seeing her toothbrush in the holder next to his this morning had jolted any remnants of sleep fog from Jared's brain.

Mercedes licked a crumb from her plump bottom lip. The sight of her pink tongue hit him with breath-stealing force. He'd seen her do the same thing countless times before, but back then he hadn't known the taste and texture of Mercedes's mouth.

Someone knocked on the front door. Jared set down his glass of juice. "I'll get it. Finish your breakfast and have your shower. I'll take my run, shower and be ready to leave for your apartment in an hour."

He crossed the room and opened the door. A reporter shoved a tape recorder in his face. "Maxwell, did you marry Mercedes for her stake in Spencer Ashton's fortune?"

Anger roared in his ears. "No comment. Get off my property."

He slammed the door and turned in time to see Mercedes bolt for the bathroom. The sound of retching carried through the closed door and tied his stomach into knots. He hated feeling helpless. He didn't know what he could do except to get rid of the reporters and shield Mercedes from their intrusive presence and obnoxious questions.

After a quick call to local law enforcement, he rapped on the bathroom door. Mercedes eased it open. Her pale face put a lump in his throat. "Are you okay?"

She grimaced. "Sorry. My morning sickness—which you've noticed doesn't limit itself to mornings—seems to get worse when I'm stressed."

"Then I guess it's my job to keep your life as stress free as possible."

So much for his run and escape. He'd stick to Mercedes like a shadow today and keep the reporters at bay.

# Five

*M en!* She was sick of the lot of them.

Mercedes slid into her desk chair on Monday afternoon with a relieved sigh. She'd never been so happy to return to work. Yesterday Jared had hovered during the packing of her things, getting too close and reminding her of his electrified touch on her skin and the heat of his mouth on hers.

He hadn't let her lift anything heavier than a wine bottle. And when the movers had arrived this morning, he'd informed them that she was allowed to point, but not to lift. Lucas had been equally overprotective when the truck pulled into The Vines to unload her belongings.

"They mean well," she grumbled, and tossed her purse and a bag of disgustingly healthy snacks into the bottom desk drawer. But Mercedes felt smothered, antsy and out of sorts. She was used to doing what she wanted and coming and going as she pleased with only her brothers' eagle eyes to dodge.

Having Jared, Lucas and the nosy reporters monitoring her every move set her on edge.

She smoothed a hand over her hair and tucked an escaped curl back into her French twist. Turning in her apartment key—and the freedom it represented—had been more difficult than she'd anticipated, but the loss of the home she'd loved only seemed to symbolize how out of control her life had become. Now she had nowhere to go to escape the strange awareness of her new husband except here in her office where she was *supposed* to be concentrating on work and not on the series of bumps and brushes against her husband that had kept her hormones simmering all morning. She flexed her fingers, causing her wedding rings to sparkle in the September sunlight, took a calming breath in an effort to ease her nausea and pulled a file forward.

The day couldn't possibly get worse.

Jillian breezed in. "Everything settled?"

I wish, Mercedes said silently but forced a smile for her sister. "As settled as it's going to get until Jared and I find a house."

Like their mother, her sister had taken a second chance on love and it had paid off. The bounce in Jillian's step and the flush on her cheeks attested to a happiness Mercedes and Jared would never have. They'd be lucky to get out of this with their friendship intact.

Jillian dropped a paper on Mercedes's desk. "Ashtons on page one again. Our half sis Megan is pregnant, too. I swear the papers would report our shoe sizes if they thought it would sell copies."

Mercedes's stomach pitched. She dug in her drawer for a pack of whole wheat—*blech*—crackers and a bottle of juice and then skimmed the article. How long could she keep her own pregnancy a secret before finding her condition splashed across the page in bold-face font? It was bad enough that her marriage to Jared had made the Sunday paper. Reporters had swarmed the two of them like fruit flies while they tried to empty her apartment, but the press had apparently accepted the friends-to-lovers story Jared had concocted.

She sipped, grimaced and cursed her finicky taste buds. None of her favorite foods appealed anymore. Even her orange juice tasted of burned plastic. "The movers had to wade through reporters to get into my apartment this morning. I've also seen a few loitering in the winery parking lot."

Jillian grimaced. "They're lurking around every corner. We've upped security, but with the increased activity due to the harvest, they can't be everywhere at once. Are you okay? You're pale."

Mercedes grimaced. "It's nothing a few months won't cure. Morning sickness is the pits, especially in the afternoon, but please, keep that to yourself. I'd rather not have Cole and Eli pulling the heavy big-brother act."

Jillian flashed a sympathetic smile. "Agreed. Let me know if I can help in any way."

"Thanks, Jillian. I promise to return the favor and keep Cole and Eli off your back when your turn comes." Her sister left with a dreamy smile on her face—no doubt dreaming of the day she and Seth had a baby to keep Rachel, Seth's daughter, company.

Mercedes propped her elbows on her desk and rested her head in her hands. She hadn't lied when she told Megan's sister, Paige, that she wanted to heal the breach in this family. That meant Mercedes needed to call Megan and congratulate her on her good news. But what could she say to a woman she'd known about for most of her life but hadn't met until earlier this year? Should she confess to being pregnant, as well? It would be wonderful to have someone to compare notes with. Did her half sister suffer the same exhaustion, finicky taste buds and raging hormones?

She liked her younger half sister, Megan, and the two of them seemed to have quite a bit in common besides a lousy father, but she hadn't told her own brothers about the pregnancy, so it would probably be best to keep quiet a bit longer. She had enough on her plate dealing with Jared and her new reactions to him without stirring family and more reporters into the mix.

She dragged her Rolodex across her desk and flipped the cards until she found Megan's work number. Pulling the phone forward, Mercedes dialed.

"Megan Ash—um, Pearce," the voice on the other end answered.

Mercedes smiled. Her half sister hadn't gotten used to her married name yet. "Megan, it's Mercedes. I wanted to call and offer my congratulations on your pregnancy."

A half groan, half chuckle traveled down the phone line. "Those meddlesome reporters. They won't give Simon or me a moment's peace. But thank you. We're thrilled."

Happiness filled Megan's voice, and a twinge of envy nibbled at Mercedes. Her baby would only have one parent eagerly awaiting its arrival. But Craig wasn't good father material, and this was the right choice. She squared her shoulders and laid a hand over her own stomach.

"Congratulations on your wedding," Megan added.

Warmth crept up Mercedes's cheeks. "Thank you."

"The picture of Jared carrying you over the threshold was quite romantic."

Mercedes's skin prickled at the reminder of the picture that had greeted her yesterday morning. From the photographer's vantage point she and Jared had looked like a couple in love, and for a moment as she'd stared at the picture she'd wished—Mercedes cut off the thought.

She wished the spying reporters didn't make her nauseous. "Yes, it did look like something from a fairy tale."

She considered asking when Megan's baby was due, but bit back the question. If they managed to settle the family quarrel, then her child and Megan's could possibly be playmates, but she had plenty of time to worry about that later.

Mercedes twined the phone cord around her finger. "I'm hoping that once they find Spencer's murderer the press will leave us alone."

"We're hoping the same. It's difficult to live in a glass house, so to speak. And not knowing who killed our father or why is unsettling."

"Yes, it is. Megan, if you need anything…or if you just want to talk, please call me."

"Thank you, Mercedes. The offer goes both ways."

They said their goodbyes and Mercedes cradled the phone.

Three families had been torn to shreds by the selfish actions of one man. How could she have been so foolish as to let a man just like her father into her life? Not just one, but a series of them. As Jared said, her taste in men sucked.

Thank God for Jared. She didn't know what she'd do without him. And she didn't intend to find out.

Two cars occupied the winery parking lot—hers and another Mercedes recognized. Unfortunately.

Craig climbed from his expensive import. Mercedes silently groaned and cursed herself for working late as he crossed the lot. Tired, cranky and hungry, she stood her ground. "What do you want, Craig?"

He stopped a yard away. "Your marriage may have fooled the newshounds, but it didn't fool me."

Her stomach churned. "What is that supposed to mean?"

"That's my kid." He pointed to her midsection. "And you're

not keeping me from it. I'll get a DNA test. And then you'll have to pay palimony so I can keep the little Ashton heir in the manner to which he's accustomed during my visitation periods."

Her child was not an *it*. Anger stiffened Mercedes's spine, and bile rose in her throat. A part of her silently goaded, If you throw up on his expensive shoes he'll go away. But she didn't want to give him the power of knowing how much he upset her.

"Really? That's not what you said when you offered to pay for my abortion. As far as I'm concerned, Craig, the minute you uttered those words and shoved that check in my face you ceased to have anything to do with me or *my* baby."

"Tell it to the courts, sweetie."

"I will." The lie Jared had suggested resisted crossing her lips, but she forced herself to say the words. "Jared is going to be my child's father."

"We'll see about that, Mercedes. I devoted nine months of my life to you. That has to be worth something. And remember this, if you can't share, I'll sue for full custody. You'll hear from my lawyers."

Her blood ran cold. "And you'll hear from mine if you keep harassing me."

He turned on his heel, climbed into his car and peeled out of the parking lot.

Mercedes emptied her stomach behind a shrub. When the sickness relented she stumbled to her car and stabbed the key in the ignition with a trembling hand. She had to get home. And then it hit her. She didn't have a home anymore.

Damned hormones. She never cried, but she couldn't seem to stem the waterfall of tears.

*Sissies cry.* The childhood taunt from her brothers rang in her ears. Mercedes struggled to pull herself together. Self-pity solved nothing. She dug around her glove compartment until she found a paper napkin left over from some long-forgotten fast food lunch and mopped her face. She needed a plan—a foolproof plan—to keep Craig Bradford from using her baby as a pawn to get his hands on the Ashton money.

Jared's muscles clenched the minute he heard Mercedes's key in the front door. Dreading the quiet evening ahead, he rose from his desk, descended the stairs from the loft and jerked to a halt.

Red rimmed her eyes and the tip of her nose was pink. She'd been crying. His senses went on full alert. Chloe had cried over anything from birthday cards to chick flicks, but Mercedes didn't cry. His first thought was of the baby. His gaze briefly dropped to her belly and fear crept up his spine. "What happened?"

"Craig ambushed me when I left work."

Fear turned to anger. He swore and she flinched. "What did the bastard say? Did he lay a hand on you?"

"He didn't touch me and all he said was more of the same."

"Did you tell him the baby is mine?"

She glanced away, set her purse on the table behind the sofa and fidgeted with the clasp. "Not exactly."

He shoved a hand through his hair. "Mercedes."

Fisting her hands, she faced him. "I hate lying."

"For your baby's sake, could you get past that this time?"

"I'll try, but he—" Her voice broke. Tears filled her eyes and spilled onto her pale cheeks. "Jared, he says he's going to sue for full custody if I don't grant him access. But all he wants is the money. He admitted as much when he said I'd have to pay him palimony to keep the Ashton heir in the manner to which he'd be accustomed."

His protective instincts kicked in, full force. Jared pulled her into his arms, cupped his palm over her cheek and pressed her face to his shoulder. He rested his cheek on her hair and searched his mind for a way out of this mess. He cared more about Mercedes than anyone else, and he'd be damned if he'd let that selfish bastard hurt her.

"He won't win, Mercedes. I'll call my attorney first thing tomorrow. We'll do whatever we have to do to stop Bradford." Fresh tears scalded his knuckles. He drew back, tipped up her chin and swiped the tears from her cheeks with his fingers. He caught her gaze.

"I won't let him take your baby," he promised, and hoped like hell he could keep that pledge.

Her bottom lip trembled and her breath came in shuddery gasps. Jared pressed a thumb to her quivering lip as if stilling its motion could calm her. The warmth of her breath swept the back of his hand, and the mood in the room shifted in an instant. Desire slammed him. He became aware of the damp, soft flesh beneath the pad of his thumb and of the length and heat of Mercedes against him, of her breasts against his chest and her thighs interlocking with his.

He sucked in a sharp breath. Her redolence surrounded him. His heart stumbled and then his blood raced to pool where their hips touched. Gritting his teeth, he lowered his hands to her shoulders and searched for willpower.

Mercedes's eyes rounded and darkened from moss to jade. Surprise faded into awareness. The pink tip of her tongue swiped across her bottom lip and her nostrils flared. Her fingers tightened on his waist, curling into his skin instead of pushing him away.

God help him, he couldn't find the strength to release her. His muscles seemed locked in place and his brain shut down. His mouth watered and he swallowed hard.

"Mercedes." His intended warning sounded more like a hungry growl.

She tipped back her head and inhaled deeply. Her breasts nudged his chest, and he gritted his teeth against the rocket of fire screaming through his blood. Pulse-pounding seconds passed.

*Move away, Maxwell.* But the need to taste her overpowered his common sense. He lowered his head one agonizing inch at a time, giving her plenty of time to object, praying she'd have the good sense to stop him.

"Jared." Her whisper wasn't one of protest. And then she lifted her hand and cradled his jaw, scorching his skin with her touch.

He turned his head, pressed his lips to her palm and swirled his tongue over her skin. Her taste filled his mouth and his hunger expanded until he could barely draw air into his lungs. Her fingers threaded through the hair at his nape. A shudder racked him.

His mouth touched hers, lifted and settled again. Mercedes's lips parted in welcome, and he sank into her softness. Slick and hot, her tongue danced with his, tangling, retreating. He groaned.

*Back off, Maxwell.* Instead he angled his head and deepened the kiss. Common sense battled need. He dragged his hands down her spine, intent on pushing her away and ending this insanity, but the curve of her bottom fit his palms so perfectly that he hesitated. Mercedes moved against him and rational thought evaporated. He kneaded her buttocks and pulled her closer.

His groin throbbed. Desire ravaged his insides. Mercedes shifted, and the stiff peaks of her breasts raked his chest, forcing a hungry sound from his throat. Jared grazed his fingers upward over the curve of her waist and ribs until he reached the warm underside of Mercedes's breasts. He cupped her and stroked his thumbs over the beaded tips. She moaned into his mouth and the sexy sound filled him with an insatiable appetite.

Mercedes's nails scraped the sensitive skin of his nape, shooting a charge of electricity down his spine. Her legs shifted again. Her thigh brushed his groin, and her taut belly rubbed his erection. Fire coursed through his veins, consuming everything except the need to be skin to skin. She nipped his bottom lip. The love bite shocked and *inflamed* him. Chloe had never been an aggressive lover.

*Chloe.* He reared back and set Mercedes away. Fighting for control, he struggled to breathe. He'd not only betrayed Chloe, he'd betrayed Mercedes's friendship. He thrust his hands through his hair and put the sofa between them. His palms burned from the imprint of her flesh.

"I'm sorry. That won't happen again." He averted his gaze from her pointed nipples.

Looking as stunned and confused as he felt, Mercedes spread one hand over her chest and touched the other to her lips. "I—it's okay."

He'd expected her to curse him not forgive him. "Dammit, it's not okay. I can't love you, Mercedes. *I can't.*"

She lowered her hands and chewed her lip. "I know. But the kiss is my fault, too. My pregnancy has bent my hormones all out of whack. I'm more sensitive to just about everything. I'll ask the doctor about it at my next visit. There must be something I can do."

A muscle in his jaw jumped wildly. Mercedes wanted to take the blame for his loss of control, but the fault lay squarely on his shoulders. He'd crossed the line.

"For crying out loud, Mercedes, there's nothing wrong with you. It's me." He turned on his heel, snatched up his keys and headed for the door. "Dinner is waiting in the oven. I'm going out."

"Jared, you don't have to leave."

He hesitated with his hand on the knob, but didn't turn around. Guilt hadn't completely extinguished his hunger, and he couldn't guarantee what would happen if he stayed. "I need some space."

Without waiting for her answer, he yanked open the door. A flashbulb went off in his face, nearly blinding him. He slammed the door and swore.

"Reporters?" Mercedes groaned. "I didn't see any when I drove up."

He clenched his fists and wrestled his demons. "When the sun goes down the vampires come out to feed. Make sure the curtains are closed. I'll be in my office."

"Come and eat first. Please."

How could he refuse without sounding childish? He gritted his teeth and prayed for sanity. On leaden feet he headed for the kitchen, vowing to keep his libido under control and his hands to himself.

Mercedes's insides quivered, but she set her chin. She wouldn't let Jared know how difficult sharing a meal with him was for her right now.

Never had a man's kisses or caresses affected her so strongly. Could she blame her heightened response on pregnancy hormones or was it caused by something more? She chanced a peek at the tense line of Jared's jaw. Did her intense reaction to his touch have anything to do with the fact that she trusted him implicitly?

Jared would never intentionally hurt her. She couldn't say that about any man she'd ever dated—not that she and Jared had ever dated or even discussed taking their friendship to the next level. He was her safety net and she hoped she was his. Sex would only screw up their relationship—the way it had every intimate liaison in her past. She'd been badly burned by love twice during college, and she wasn't willing to buy into the third-time's-a-charm theory.

She followed him into the kitchen. Food held no appeal, but her baby needed nourishment. While he pulled plates from the cabinet and set the table, she opened the oven. Mouthwatering aromas filled the kitchen. Ever conscious of him moving around in the tiny space behind her, she set the casserole dishes on the stovetop and peeled back the foil.

Jared had cooked her favorite stuffed pork chops as well as a broccoli-and-cheese casserole. Her stomach rumbled in anticipation. Maybe her taste buds hadn't died after all. She opened the refrigerator, reached for a bottle of water and paused in surprise. Lime Jell-O. A smile tugged her lips. This morning she'd mentioned a weird craving for the jiggly green stuff. She lifted her gaze to his. "Thanks."

He shrugged. "As cravings go, yours seemed pretty tame. Chloe used to—"

He bit off the words and turned back to the silverware drawer. Love for Chloe had originally brought them together. Their shared grief and a promise Mercedes had made to her friend had bound them even after her death.

Mercedes didn't want him to feel uncomfortable talking about Chloe. "She used to have some pretty strange cravings. Remember when all she wanted to eat was crunchy peanut butter on strawberries?"

A smile lifted his lips, but sadness filled his eyes. "That wasn't as bad as sardines on chocolate ice cream."

They shared a grimace and some of the tension dissipated. Jared looked out for her as she did for him. She knew and accepted that he couldn't fall in love with her, and she didn't

vant him to, but he cared, the same way that she cared about
him. He kept her from overstressing about work. She kept him
from brooding too much about the family he'd lost. They kept
each other on an even keel.

She dusted her hands. So no more of those unbalancing
kisses. With a little nurturing, their friendship would carry
them through this uncomfortable period the way it had
through every other rough spot in their shared past.

But as Mercedes sat down across the kitchen table from
Jared, she couldn't help wondering what it would be like to
make love with a man who knew all her faults and liked her
anyway. And once the pesky thought planted itself in her
mind, it flourished like a weed and she couldn't seem to kill
it.

She studied Jared's long-fingered hands in a way she never had before. How would they feel on her skin? What kind
of lover would he be?

*Don't go there, Mercedes. Jared's too important to mess
this up.*

She jerked her gaze away and it landed on the tiny swollen spot on his lip where she'd bitten him. Her cheeks warmed
and her belly filled with shimmery warmth. Had he even had
a lover since Chloe? From the way he'd eaten her up—her
skin flushed anew just thinking about it—she didn't think so,
and that being the case, she had no right to inflict her misbehaving, overly estrogenized self on him.

They were both running a little low on resistance right now,
so she'd have to be strong enough for two.

Pretend the kisses never happened and forge on as before.
Friends. Just friends.

Yeah, right.

Avoidance. A simple plan.
Jared slowed to a walk and continued up the driveway.

Wiping the sweat from his face with the hem of his tank top, he congratulated himself on successfully dodging Mercedes again today. For the last three days he'd avoided her in the mornings by donning his running gear and taking off the minute he heard her stirring. For safety's sake he'd added an extra half hour to his run each day to allow her time to dress and get out of the house before he returned.

In the evenings he carried his dinner up to his loft office and tried to work, but he couldn't concentrate when he was vitally aware of her frustrated sighs, her restless energy and her every move in the den below. And he couldn't sleep worth a damn when he heard her pacing the floors at night.

He let himself into the cottage, grabbed a bottle of water from the fridge and headed toward the bathroom, stripping as he went. Peeling his tank over his head, he stepped into the bathroom, tossed the sweaty top into the hamper and turned to reach for the shower curtain. He jolted to a halt with his hand midair.

Mercedes's lingerie hung from the shower curtain rod. Peach, pink, cream and lavender bits of satin and lace caused a spike in his blood pressure. Chloe had worn white cotton underwear. Plain, white cotton. Nothing as lacy or sheer as the filmy sherbet-colored stuff in front of him. And Chloe definitely hadn't worn thongs like the one Mercedes had concealed beneath her wedding dress. The ivory bit of nothing now hung on the rod, drawing his eye like a flashing neon light.

Heat pumped through his veins and he swore. How was he supposed to take a shower with a week's worth of Mercedes's underwear guarding the cubicle like sentinels?

Worse, how was he supposed to look at her in the future and not wonder what tantalizing secrets she concealed beneath her clothing?

Cursing, Jared ripped the towels from a nearby towel bar

nd tossed them onto the counter. One by one he transferred he silky pieces from the shower rod to the towel bar. He lidn't linger over the task or allow himself to test the weight nd feel of the garments between his fingers although the emptation to do so whipped through him hurricane strong. t wasn't until he'd relocated the last item that he realized his nuscles had knotted from his jaw to his ankles.

He eased his jockstrap and shorts over his painful and traiorous erection, pitched them in the hamper and stepped into he shower. The frigid water made him gasp, but he welcomed he distracting sting and briskly lathered his chill-bumped skin.

How in the hell was he going to survive this marriage without crossing the line and making Mercedes hate him? He ell back on his tried-and-true method of overcoming difficulty.

Analyze the situation.

Divide it into manageable parts.

Set a course of action.

Problem one. Craig Bradford. Jared wanted to eliminate Bradford in the fastest manner possible. How, short of murler, could he accomplish the task? Research required.

Problem two. His marriage. The sooner he eradicated Bradford's threat the sooner he and Mercedes could separate, livorce and return to life as usual. Scrap that. The baby would rrevocably change Mercedes's life, and that meant Jared's had been permanently altered, as well. How could he mininize the damage?

Which led to problem three. The cottage. He'd call a real estate agent as soon as he dried off, and he cursed the fact that he hadn't done so already. Shortening their stay in this tiny, cramped cottage became more urgent and mandatory by the second.

Problem four. The press. With the media hounding them

at every turn, escape hatches had been sealed. How could they slip under the radar or shift the focus elsewhere?

His teeth chattered. He rinsed the shampoo from his hair. Now that his erection had subsided, Jared adjusted the water temperature and let the hot water thaw his chilled skin.

Step one. Call his attorney and see what legal steps they could take to block Bradford's claim on the baby. His attorney didn't handle custody issues, but someone in the firm would.

Step two. Call the real estate agent and find a house within a reasonable commuting distance for Mercedes to the winery. And room. Lots of room. Hell, he could afford it.

He turned off the spigot, scrubbed at the sting of soap in his eyes and reached for a towel. Out of habit he stretched toward the towel bar. Slick fabric in his hand had him jerking his eyes open despite the soap burn. A pink satin bra.

Swearing again, he shoved the garment back over the rack and snatched a towel from the counter. After drying off, he wrapped the towel around his hips and yanked open the bathroom door with almost enough force to rip it from its hinges. He stomped into the hall, accompanied by a cloud of steam.

Mercedes squealed and he jerked to a halt in the narrow hallway. Openmouthed, she gaped at him. "I…I forgot the notes I made last night."

Her gaze eased from his face to his shoulders over his belly, hips and legs. His body twitched to life. He gritted his teeth at his instantaneous reaction and thanked God he'd kept the towel around his hips. When he'd lived alone he rarely bothered, but with the threat of reporters shoving cameras against the windows, he didn't risk traipsing around in his birthday suit even though they'd kept all the blinds closed since their wedding day.

What color lingerie did she wear under her butter-yellow

suit? The thought flashed in his mind like a bolt of lightning—
hot, searing and destructive. Dammit. He forced his gaze
from the lacy cream-colored camisole covering her breasts to
focus on her face.

A flush pinked her cheeks. She licked her bottom lip.
When she looked at him like that—with a spark of curiosity
in her eyes—he didn't feel like a bitter forty-year-old who'd
lost interest in love and desire. He felt like a lusty college kid
with his own healthy share of curiosity about the sparks between them. And if he continued to stand here, his towel
wasn't going to be able to conceal his renewed interest.

"Excuse me." He tried to step around her.

She dodged in the same direction, grimaced and then,
holding her hands up, backed out of the hall. The overhead
light from the sitting room revealed dark shadows beneath her
eyes and delayed his retreat.

"Mercedes, when did you have time to work last night?"
They'd stayed up late to watch the news—a safe neutral activity.

She stared past his shoulder—no doubt noticing that he'd
moved her underwear. A frown puckered her brow. "When I
have trouble sleeping I work on the Louret marketing campaign. There has to be something I can do to divert the public's attention from our personal lives back to our products."

"You're not sleeping or eating enough, and you're still losing weight." His voice sounded harder than he intended,
more accusatory than concerned, and the light of battle flared
in her eyes.

Her lips flattened. "I can't help it. Nothing tastes good, and
the morning sickness hits whenever it damn well pleases."

His stomach muscles tensed, and a bitter taste filled his
mouth. "Are you having second thoughts about the pregnancy?"

Her eyes widened and she laid a protective hand over her

belly. "No. Oh, no. I want this baby, and I'm trying to do all the right things. I'm even drinking *milk*."

Her shudder startled a laugh out of him. "There are worse things than milk, Mercedes."

Her face was comical. "I'm sure, but you know I hate milk."

"Yeah, I know." He bunched the towel in his fingers and fought the urge to sweep a loose curl from her cheek. He had to keep a firm rein on the tender feelings she stirred in him.

If he touched her again...

He wouldn't. "I need to get dressed, and then I have a couple of calls to make. Afterward, I'll go to the grocery store and see if I can find something to tempt your taste buds."

"You don't have to do that, Jared."

"Yes, I do. For your sake. For your baby's sake." He'd do right by them, because there was a very good chance that one day soon—promise or no promise—he'd have to say goodbye to the best friend he'd ever had.

# Six

Mercedes pulled her car into a space at the far end of the winery parking lot and said a prayer of thanks for the other vehicles occupying the remaining spaces. Business must be up today. Or had Jillian scheduled a group event this morning and Mercedes had forgotten it?

Lack of sleep and caffeine deprivation had killed her short-term memory. She smiled wryly in the rearview mirror as she checked her hair and makeup. Maybe she could blame her forgetfulness on pregnancy hormones, too, but she had a feeling the real cause was stress.

She gathered her purse and briefcase from the seat beside her. Work brought unrelenting pressure to try to find a way to divert the press from their private lives to their product. Life at the cottage wasn't much better. She spent every waking moment and many when she should have been sleeping working on a potential marketing campaign for the Meadowview

Inn just in case Jared bought it. It was a surprise. She hadn't told him yet.

The minute she relaxed, worries over Craig's threats forced themselves forward like a nagging toothache. Keeping her mind constantly occupied kept her from fretting over her father's murder, her impending motherhood and everything that could go wrong with her pregnancy and her life in general. She especially worried about her relationship with Jared. He was avoiding her. They'd missed their first Wednesday-night dinner in years this week. Oh, Jared had been home and in plain view, but he'd isolated himself in the loft claiming he had work to do, and she'd eaten alone. She missed their easy friendship.

The upshot was that her life had gone to hell. She barely allowed herself time to scratch or pee—which she seemed to need to do every thirty seconds these days—right now, in fact. She shoved open the car door and hurried toward the winery entrance.

With her mind on the long list of problems needing rectifying, she barely noticed a nearby car door opening as she passed. "Mercedes, are you pregnant?"

Her muscles locked at the stranger's question. She stood frozen on the sidewalk and stared at the young woman climbing from the vehicle.

"Whose baby is it? Bradford claims it's his," shouted another voice she didn't recognize from behind her. She turned. Alarm skipped up her spine. Cornered. Why hadn't she been paying attention? And where was the security officer? She searched what she could see of the vineyard grounds looking for the car with the flashing green light on top. No car.

"When is your baby due? Bradford says April. Can you confirm that?" A third reporter asked as he joined the others.

Craig had gone to the press. The bastard.

"No comment."

She hustled toward the safety of the building. The group of reporters surrounded her, hindering her escape. Mercedes did the only thing she could think of. She hit the panic button on her key ring and set off her deafening car alarm. Sirens screeched. The horn blew repeatedly. With the reporters momentarily distracted, Mercedes darted through them and ran for the winery entrance. Jillian, evidently drawn by the racket, opened the door. Mercedes shoved her keys in her sister's hands as she passed.

"Lock the door and call that security man." And then she bolted to the private bathroom upstairs and lost her lunch.

After she'd washed up, she dragged herself to her office and shut the door. She never shut her door, because she preferred knowing what was going on with Louret Vineyards at all times. She liked the hum of voices from down the hall and the occasional sounds drifting up from the tasting room downstairs.

So much for keeping her secret. She hadn't wanted her brothers to know she was pregnant yet. They were incredibly protective. If they suspected the baby was Craig's and that he'd abandoned her there was no telling what they'd do. Whatever their response, it promised to be newsworthy, which was the last thing the family needed right now.

She ignored the blinking message light on her phone, since it was probably reporters, and tried to gather her scattered thoughts. Twenty minutes later someone rapped on the wood.

"In my office," Cole's voice called out.

Mercedes winced and freshened her makeup, blatantly delaying the confrontation as long as possible. She arrived just in time to hear the rumble of Jared's deep voice through Cole's partially open door. *Jared was here?* He never came to the vineyard.

"The obstetrician tells me that high levels of stress could be dangerous for Mercedes and her baby."

Mercedes's mouth dropped open in horror.

"So Mercedes *is* pregnant?" Cole asked.

Mercedes shoved Cole's door open the rest of the way, glared at Jared and then faced her brothers, Cole, seated behind his desk, and Eli, seated beside Jared in front of the desk. The men rose as she entered. Jillian gave her a sympathetic smile.

"Yes, I am, and I would have told you when the time was right."

"Should I offer congratulations?" Cole asked.

Mercedes lifted her chin and looked him in the eye. "Of course."

"You realize the commotion in the parking lot means you need to hold a press conference?"

She grimaced. "I was hoping to avoid that."

Cole shook his head. "Too late."

Jared continued, "Mercedes isn't eating or sleeping well, and every time we get ambushed by reporters or Bradford she gets sick to her stomach—and Jillian says she did it again this afternoon. She's losing weight she doesn't have to spare, and if the situation continues, then according to her doctor she could have problems sustaining the pregnancy or, at the very least, it could cause the baby to be more sensitive to stress."

"What do you propose?" Eli asked.

They were discussing her as if she weren't here. Mercedes sputtered with anger.

Jared glanced at Eli and then his gaze tangled with Mercedes's. "I'd like to get her away from here for a few days so she can regain some strength and catch up on her sleep. The press is only going to get worse now that Bradford's telling tales."

Mercedes held on to her temper by a fraying thread, but she did note that Jared had chosen to stick to their story.

She focused on Eli. Usually she could get her oldest brother to side with her. Cole was a harder nut to crack. "Jared is wrong. I don't need time off work. I'm fine. It's only morning sickness, and it will pass."

"Now that he mentions it, I caught you dozing at your desk yesterday, and you have been looking pretty ragged lately," Eli added.

A frustrated sound gurgled from her throat. "Thanks, Eli. I love you, too."

He shrugged off her sarcasm. "I think it's a good idea for you and Jared to take a belated honeymoon. I don't think any of the rest of us would be stupid enough to refuse an excuse to get out of the spotlight."

Mercedes stiffened at the implied insult and fought the urge to stamp her foot. "I'm needed here."

"Not right now," Eli countered. "We're in the middle of the harvest. Take some time off."

"I have a job to do."

Cole shook his head. "The marketing campaign is moving along. Unless you can figure out who killed our father, then there's nothing you can do here to change the fishbowl in which we're currently living. Get out of town and take care of yourself and your baby."

"I have customers to visit, and I need to check in with our distributors."

"Eli or I can cover the customers and distributors. I hate to pull rank, sis, but if you insist, I'm going to ask for your keys."

"*You can't do that.*" She shot a hard glance toward Jared. Did he have any idea what kind of trouble he'd stirred up?

Eli added, "Want me to call in the big guns—Mom and Lucas?"

This time Mercedes did stamp her foot and glare at Jared. He silently stared back. The concern in his eyes was the only thing that kept her from screaming in frustration. She'd lost her apartment, and now, thanks to Jared, she could lose her office, too. How could she hide from her crazy emotions if she had nowhere to go and no work to distract her?

But what was the point in arguing? Her brothers had sided against her, and if Eli called her mother and Lucas then she'd be out of a job indefinitely. Besides, catching up on sleep sounded like a good idea—even if being alone with Jared and her unwelcome fascination with him didn't appeal. Well, frankly, she corrected, it appealed too much and that was part of the problem.

"One week. That's it. I can't afford to be out of the office any longer."

Cole ignored her and looked at Jared. "Okay with you?"

Jared shrugged. "It's a start. I'll get back to you next weekend to let you know if she's made any progress."

Cole pinned her with his stern-big-brother look. "Then, Mercedes, starting now you are officially on vacation. But on your way out take a minute to make a statement to the press."

Mercedes trembled with a combination of fury at Jared for forcing her hand and fear over confronting the press. Normally facing the press wouldn't bother her, but normally it wasn't her private life under discussion. She either had to lie or risk saying something that would give Craig leverage over this child, and she didn't want to make that mistake.

"Could I speak to you in my office, please, Jared?" she said through her teeth, and then stormed from Cole's office and down the hall into her own. She quietly shut the door behind Jared when slamming it would have been *so* much more satisfying.

Bristling with anger, she confronted him. "What are you doing?"

He faced her stoically. "Trying to take care of you."

"Getting me kicked out of my office is not the way to go bout it."

Irritation sparked in his eyes. "Then tell me what is, because you're putting yourself and your baby in jeopardy."

"I am managing just fine."

"If you call hugging the toilet several times a day fine."

"It's morning sickness, Jared. It's normal."

His jaw hardened. He didn't bother to point out that more often than not she was sick when it wasn't morning. "How much weight have you lost?"

Direct hit. Her clothes hung on her, except for across her swollen breasts, and, yes, she was concerned. She'd planned to call the doctor herself this afternoon. Mercedes shifted in her pumps. "I don't know."

Jared's gaze narrowed on her. "When I spoke to Dr. Evans this morning she said she'd hospitalize you if you continue losing weight."

He'd called her doctor. "Why do you care? You're trying to cut me out of your life, anyway. You won't even eat dinner with me anymore."

She detested the telling wobble in her voice.

Jared paced to her window, presenting her with the rigid line of his spine. He rubbed the nape of his neck. "I don't want to care, but I can't help myself."

Her heart contracted upon hearing him confirm her fears.

Slowly he turned. Mercedes caught her breath at the agony on his face. "You can't keep food down. You walk the floors at night. You jump at the slightest noise, as if you expect Bradford or the press to spring from behind the bushes. I haven't seen you eat a decent meal since breakfast at the Meadowview Inn two weeks ago." He moved closer and stopped just inches away. "I lost Chloe and Dylan, Mercedes.

Don't expect me to stand by and let something happen to yo
when I have the power to prevent it."

The fight drained out of her in a rush, leaving her tired an
light-headed. Her eyes stung. Darn this new weepiness. Sh
hated it.

When had hers and Jared's roles shifted? After Chloe'
death Mercedes had become the caretaker in this relationshir
At the moment her shift toward being dependent on Jare
seemed like one more element of her life of which she'd los
control. She blinked back her tears and lifted her chin. "I'n
trying to take care of myself."

Tension accentuated the lines bracketing his mouth. "Le
me help. I have a lakeside cabin. Spend a few days there with
me. We'll swim, kayak, hike…" He shrugged. "Whateve
you want."

"I want to stay here and do my job."

His lips thinned. "Except that."

"What about your businesses? You can't turn your back or
an entire string of bed and breakfast inns."

"I trust my innkeepers. You hired the best. If any emergen-
cies crop up I can handle them by cell phone or laptop. You
can do the same with your work. I'm not asking you to drop
off the face of the planet, Mercedes, just temporarily step out
of the line of fire and out of Bradford's sight."

She pressed her fingers to the dull throb in her temple.
"What about the Meadowview purchase?"

"It's in my attorney's hands. I met with him this morning
before coming here. I've also asked his partner to look into
your legal right to keep Bradford out of the picture."

"Thank you for that."

"Get your things and let's go. We'll make a brief statement
on the way out. Your suitcase is in the car."

She did a double take. "My what?"

"Jillian called me and explained the situation. I packed for both of us and came over. If we take the time to go back to the cottage the press will follow us. This way, they don't know we're leaving town. With luck we'll get out of the valley undetected."

She grimaced and conceded his point with a nod. How could she be angry with him when he had her best interests at heart? "I should really hate you for this, you know."

Jared's smile reached his eyes for the first time since she'd informed him of her pregnancy. God, was it only three weeks ago that her life had fallen apart? "But you don't."

"No. I don't think that's possible." Mercedes gathered her purse and shrugged on her jacket. With a sense of dread she followed Jared downstairs. How was she going to keep her insane hormones under control for the next seven days?

The number of reporters had grown in the past hour. More than a dozen converged around them the moment she and Jared stepped outside the door. Jillian, Cole and Eli stood behind Jared and Mercedes, silently offering family support and, unfortunately, blocking Mercedes's ability to retreat.

Mercedes caught herself sidling closer to Jared and cursed herself for her weakness. Before she could move away, Jared's strong arm banded around her waist. The heat of his fingers penetrated her clothing as he pressed her against the length of his body.

He brushed a kiss on her cheek and whispered in her ear, "Keep it simple and smile. You're supposed to be a blushing bride."

"Mercedes, are you pregnant?" the first reporter asked before Mercedes could make a statement.

She wet her lips and forced a smile. "Yes."

"Whose baby is it? Your husband's or your ex-lover's?"

Her stomach pitched.

"Mine," Jared said before she could formulate a reply. His free hand settled low over her belly, heating her skin and drawing her blood to the spot surrounding her navel. "Mercedes is my wife and this is our child."

"Bradford claims it's his."

"My name will be on the birth certificate."

"But genetically whose baby is it?"

Jared's muscles stiffened against her. "Mercedes and I have known each other for eleven years. We've traveled together and been—" he looked into her eyes and lifted a hand to twine a stray lock of her hair around his finger "—special friends for the past five years."

Mercedes's knees weakened at the tenderness in his eyes. *Oh, my.* Why had she never noticed Jared had bedroom eyes? And then she caught herself. The loverlike intensity was pure pretense. Good thing. How could a woman resist such a bone-melting look?

Jared smoothed his knuckle across her cheek and lowered his hand. His gaze returned to the press. "She's known Bradford for ten months and she dumped him. My guess is he regrets blowing it with the best woman he's ever known and now he's crying wolf."

With that parting salvo, Jared hustled her into his SUV and peeled out of the parking lot.

Jared's trepidation increased with each mile his SUV covered. He'd never shared the secret hideaway his grandfather had left him. Letting Mercedes into this private compartment of his life seemed like an omen.

Mercedes sat in the seat beside him. She hadn't spoken a word in almost two hours, but he could sense her tension easing as if the wind whipped it out through the open window as they headed northeast and left Napa Valley and the vine-ard behind. The tight set of her jaw had relaxed, and her fingers had loosened on the edge of her purse. A breeze teased tendrils of hair from the tight twist on the back of her head. She'd quit trying to smooth it back in place about twenty miles ago.

She turned her head in his direction, and the dashboard lights illuminated her features. "Have you ever considered calling your father?"

Her question surprised him. He took his eyes off the road for a split second to shoot her a hard glance. "No."

"Not everyone is as coldhearted as Spencer. Or Craig. Your father might miss you."

His teeth clicked together. "If he does then he can pick up the phone."

"He won't if he's as stubborn as you."

He shifted in his seat, suddenly feeling his muscles cramp from the two-hour drive. "Mercedes, where is this coming from?"

"Something your brother Nate said at the wedding has been bothering me. He claims your father's lonely and that he misses you."

"He has Nate and Ethan and their families. My father cut me off, not the other way around."

"Jared, the only thing my father ever gave me was my name, and then he named me after his stupid car." Her sarcasm couldn't hide her pain. "Your father kept the three of you together after your mother died. When he traveled he took you with him. He didn't ship you off to boarding school or relegate your care to a nanny. For goodness' sake, he had your bus drop you off at his office everyday after school. He wanted you around. That has to mean something."

Mercedes's father hadn't wanted her around, and now Bradford only wanted their child for the money, connections

and, evidently, the publicity he could get out of the relation
ship. Compassion for Mercedes welled up in Jared's chest
but he shoved it aside and focused on her incorrect assump
tion.

"It means my father wanted peons to carry out his com
mands, and he wanted his secretary to double as a babysitter
From the time my mother died when I was seven, my fathe.
ruled with an iron fist. Having us close by meant keeping u:
under his thumb."

She twisted in her seat until she faced him. "I'm guessin;
that as the unruly youngest son you felt your father's firn
hand more often than your brothers. They seem like rule-fol·
lowers to me. You've always liked the challenge of trying
something new. But, Jared, I saw how much you enjoyed
talking to Nate and Ethan after the wedding. I think you
should try to mend fences with your father so they won't fee)
guilty for keeping in touch."

"I'll consider it." When hell freezes over.

"He's probably proud of you." Wistfulness tinged her
voice, and Jared wished he'd had the foresight to tell Spencer Ashton what a jackass he was before he'd been murdered.
"You've taken one struggling inn and turned it into a chain of
bed and breakfasts. You're mirroring his success with the hotels."

"I built the chain with your help, Mercedes, and my father
doesn't see my success. He sees my failure to toe the line."

"Maybe you're wrong about that."

He let the topic drop and checked his rearview mirror for
headlights one last time, making certain the reporters hadn't
followed. Mercedes was wrong, but Jared didn't want to
waste time or energy arguing.

No matter how angry Mercedes might be with him for
forcing this vacation on her, Jared was convinced he'd done

he right thing in colluding with her brothers. After talking to Dr. Evans this morning, he'd known he didn't have a choice. Protecting Mercedes and her unborn child was worth whatever costs he had to pay. He wouldn't fail her the way he'd failed Chloe and Dylan.

He turned into the almost-hidden path through the towering pines. Darkness swallowed the vehicle. The moonlight barely penetrated the canopy of trees.

The headlights illuminated the small, rustic log cabin as he pulled to a stop at the end of the long driveway. Mercedes straightened and faced forward. "I didn't know you owned a cabin, and I thought I knew everything about you."

"Not everything. Let me unlock the doors and turn on the cabin lights, then I'll unload our supplies." He killed the engine, climbed from the vehicle and took a deep breath of the pine-scented forest air. It failed to have its usual calming effect, but that could have something to do with the woman standing beside him in the headlight beam.

Mercedes teetered on the path as her heels sank into the pine straw, forcing Jared to cup her elbow and guide her over the uneven ground. As had happened too frequently of late, she got too close, and her exotic scent filled his lungs and muddled his thinking.

She glanced around at the dense woods surrounding the cabin. "You're pretty isolated here, aren't you? I barely saw any lights once we left that little grocery store behind."

"Very isolated." They'd stopped at a small grocer's thirty miles back for supplies. Jared knew he could rely on the couple who owned the place to keep his whereabouts quiet. They'd known his grandfather for decades, and folks up here respected each other's privacy.

She squinted. "Is that the lake behind the cabin?"

"Yes." The cabin sat a hundred yards from the shore. The

rising moon painted a white, undulating stripe across the wa
ter. "It takes about two hours to kayak around the perimete
or three hours to hike it. I hike the trail every morning wher
I'm here."

He unlocked the cabin and reached inside to turn on the
interior and exterior lights. Mercedes followed him into the
single boxy room containing the kitchen and the den. Two
smaller boxes, each containing a bedroom and bathroom
flanked the central space on the left and right.

"My bedroom's that way." He jerked his thumb to indicate
the wing on the left. "This one's yours."

He stepped into her assigned space, hit the light switch and
moved aside for her to enter. He scanned the area, trying to
see what Mercedes saw. The small room had rough-hewn log
walls. A double bed draped in a Native American blanket took
up most of the floor space, and a tall dresser had been shoved
in the corner. The wide window on the wall in front of him
would offer a breathtaking view of the lake during the daylight hours, but now the curtains were drawn.

These Spartan accommodations bore no resemblance to
his meticulously decorated cottage or Mercedes's monochro-
matic apartment. "Bath's through there. It's pretty basic."

He found her gaze on him instead of her new accommodations, and the intimacy of being in a ten-by-twelve room
with Mercedes and a bed hit him like a two-by-four to the gut.
No matter how wrong it was, he wanted her. There was no
use denying it, but he didn't intend to feed that hunger.

"Chloe's never been here."

It was a statement, not a question, since it was clear from
the sparse furnishings that Chloe hadn't contributed her decorating skills, but Jared responded anyway. "I inherited the
place from my grandfather during the last half of Chloe's
pregnancy. She didn't want to leave the inn."

And they both knew what came next. She'd died.

He came here when the memories weighed too much or when living in Chloe's perfectly decorated cottage grated on his raw nerves. The cabin held happy memories of childhood vacations with his brothers and his paternal grandfather, but no memories of the love and the life Jared had lost. He was careful to limit his trips to the days when Mercedes was on the road for Louret Vineyards. She was as protective of him as a momma bear was of her cubs. If she'd known he still had dark days—though far fewer than before—she'd have stuck to him like paint on wood. For the most part the cabin remained unused. He paid caretakers to keep an eye on the place.

He turned toward the door. "I'll unload the car."

"I'll help," she offered.

"No. Relax. Have a look around."

She looked ready to argue, but shrugged instead. He headed outside. Transferring the bags of groceries and their luggage to the cabin only took a couple of trips. When he finished he went looking for Mercedes. She'd draped her suit jacket over a chair in the den. The back door stood open, allowing a cool breeze to sweep through the screen door. Jared spotted the beam of a flashlight bobbing down by the lake and stepped outside. He paused on the rear deck long enough to light the gas grill and then joined her at the water's edge.

"It's beautiful," Mercedes said without looking at him. She'd let her hair down to drape over her bare shoulders and untucked her camisole from the waistband of her slim-fitting pants. A light evening breeze fluttered the hem of her top and made her disheveled curls dance in the moonlight.

"Yeah." He fisted his hands against the urge to twine one of those caramel-colored spirals around his finger. Why did sharing this quiet night with Mercedes feel so right?

Chloe had adored people. This place would have bored her

to tears, which is why he'd never brought her here when his grandfather was alive, but Mercedes had always appreciated the silence of out-of-the-way places. Guilt stabbed him. He shouldn't compare Chloe with Mercedes. The two women were opposites in too many ways to list. Chloe had needed to be needed. She'd relished pampering him and giving him the nurturing he'd lacked after his mother had died.

Mercedes treated him as an equal. She carried her own backpack—no matter how heavy—and expected him to do the same except for those times when he'd been too weak to shoulder his burdens. Then she'd stepped forward, dragged him back to his feet and gently administered a kick to the seat of his pants to get him going again. Mercedes didn't tolerate weakness in herself or those around her.

He picked up a pebble and skipped it over the water, sending ripples over the lake's mirrorlike surface. "Hungry? I've fired up the grill."

She looked at him, hesitated and then smiled. "Yes, I am, actually."

The surprise in her voice confirmed his decision to get her out of Napa. "I'll put on the steaks."

"I'll be right behind you."

"Take your time. We have all night." His mind spun the words into an entirely different meaning. Jared clamped his jaws shut and marched toward the cabin.

What would it be like to have the love of a man like Jared?

The errant thought exploded out of nowhere. Mercedes snuffed it and reached for her iced tea. She wasn't interested in falling in love with Jared. She loved and trusted him more than anyone, which meant having that trust broken—as inevitably would happen—would be all that much more devastating. She'd learned the hard way that, with few exceptions, men let her down. She couldn't bear to be disappointed by Jared too.

There was no denying that he cared for her. That much was obvious by the way he faced his fears over this pregnancy for her and her baby's sake. But he wasn't *in love*. And neither was she. Love was for tenderhearted souls like Jillian and Chloe, not for a realist like her.

She sat back and put a hand to her full stomach. The grilled steak had pleased her finicky taste buds, and she marveled at the amount of food she'd put away. "You're spoiling me."

His level gaze met hers. "You don't let anyone spoil you."

"You make that sound like a bad thing."

"A man likes to feel needed, Mercedes. You don't let anyone close—not even your lovers."

"And you do?" she quipped, but his reply hit too close to home. She didn't let anyone get close for a darned good reason. If she didn't love them, then saying goodbye wouldn't hurt. And saying goodbye was unavoidable.

"I don't let anyone close anymore," Jared said after a hesitation. "I need to turn off the grill. I'll be right back." He rose and stepped out the back door.

Mercedes dropped her head in her hands. She wasn't totally heartless, was she? She loved her family and Jared. But she'd never been *in love* in the unreserved, no-holds-barred way Jared had loved Chloe. She'd thought she was, in college, but she'd turned out to be wrong. Since then she dumped a guy whenever her feelings for him started to grow, because she was afraid to risk caring too much.

She wasn't a coward. She faced facts. Look at Jared. He still hurt from losing Chloe, and there had been times immediately after Chloe's and Dylan's deaths that the depth of his depression had worried Mercedes, times when she'd been afraid she'd never break through his pain.

Jared returned and dropped a deck of playing cards on the table. "Mercedes?"

Jared had come a long way since those dark days when he'd isolated himself from everyone—including her. He now kept himself in peak condition. Shallow crow's feet radiated from his thickly lashed blue eyes—eyes that still held shadows of sadness. A lock of dark hair tumbled over his forehead, and silver strands glistened at his temples. Lines bracketed his mouth, cutting into his lean, tanned face. Why had she never noticed what an incredibly attractive, mature man he'd become?

She shook herself out of a stupor. "Does a day ever go by that you don't think of her?"

He sucked in a sharp breath and then turned to the sink, busying himself with their dishes. He didn't ask to whom she referred. Finally he braced himself on the edge of the counter, clutching the countertop with a white-knuckled grip. "Yes, and it shouldn't."

"What do you mean?"

His head turned and his pain-filled gaze met hers. "It's my fault she and Dylan are gone. It doesn't seem right for me to keep living and to forget. Sometimes I'll think of her and realize that a week or even two has passed since I thought of her."

Mercedes blinked in confusion and crossed the room to stand beside him. "Why is Chloe's death your fault?"

"Because she asked me to go get a damned quilt and I refused."

Mercedes turned cold. Goose bumps raced across her skin. Her chest constricted and she thought she might pass out. She clutched the back of a kitchen chair for support. "She was going after a quilt when she had the car accident?"

"Yes. And before she left we fought about her buying more baby stuff, because money was tight back then. She wanted borrow from my father and I didn't. Borrowing meant strings, and I…" He shoved a hand through his hair and shook his head. "She stormed out of the house to go to the store, anyway.

"I never got to apologize. By the time I reached the hospital she'd been declared brain dead. The doctors did an emergency cesarean to try to save Dylan, but he'd sustained too severe a head trauma to survive. He never got to take his first breath."

He threw back his head and tightly closed his eyes. Pain and tension stretched every muscle in his body taut. "My wife and son died over a damned quilt."

Guilt settled over Mercedes like a smothering blanket. The delicious dinner weighed like a boulder in her belly. Tears stung her eyes, and the lump in her throat burned as if she'd swallowed a hot charcoal.

As horrible as the truth was, Jared needed to hear it—even if it made him despise her. "You shouldn't hate yourself, Jared. You should hate me. I called Chloe from my cell phone that morning to tell her about the quilt in the consignment store window. I passed the shop on one of my vendor visits, but I was running late, and I didn't want to take the time to stop at the shop and buy the quilt. So, it's not your fault, Jared. It's mine."

The grief in his eyes deepened and then turned to empathy. He cupped her shoulder and squeezed. "It's not your fault, Mercedes."

"Then whose is it? Not yours." She shrugged off his touch and, hugging herself, walked to the screen door to stare out at the darkness. An owl hooted in a nearby tree. She'd never heard such a sad, lonely sound as the owl calling to his mate and receiving no reply. Because of her, Jared's calls for Chloe would go unanswered.

She pressed icy hands to her cheeks. "I can't believe never knew."

"I never told anyone. It was my cross to bear." His voic drew nearer as he joined her by the door.

She blinked hard and ducked her head to hide her tear when what she really wanted to do was bury herself in Ja ed's strong arms and bawl like a baby. "And now it's mine

# Seven

Chloe, her dearest friend since third grade, was gone and it as Mercedes's fault.

Chloe's parents had lost their only daughter. Jared had lost is wife and son. Loss welled up inside Mercedes as if it were nly yesterday that Jared had called her to tell her that Chloe nd their baby boy had died.

Jared's long-fingered hands cupped Mercedes's shoulders. umbly she allowed him to turn her and pull her into his rms. He caught her cheek in his palm and pressed her face gainst his chest. A sob worked its way up her throat.

"Shhh." His breath stirred her hair and his heart beat steadi- beneath her ear.

"I'm so sorry," she choked out against the front of his irt. "I took away the two most important people in your fe."

His big hand stroked up and down her spine, but Mercedes

felt cold deep in her soul—too chilled to be warmed by hi brisk caress. "Mercedes, I'm not letting you take the blam for this. Chloe wasn't your responsibility. She was mine."

"I told her the design was perfect…the exact colors sh wanted for Dylan's nursery." Chloe had always done every thing she could to make those she loved happy. In return fo that generosity, Mercedes had selfishly put her needs and he driving desire to prove herself to her brothers *and her fathe* in front of anything or anyone else—even her dearest frien from childhood.

If she could relive those moments today, she would glad ly give back the ten minutes it would have taken her to sto and buy the baby quilt, if it meant having Chloe and Dyla here. But it was too late.

She swallowed the sob climbing her throat and lifted he chin to look into Jared's sad blue eyes.

His touch gentled, slowed. The grief in his eyes faded, an desire took its place. His nostrils flared as he inhaled deepl The fine hairs on Mercedes's skin rose, and her breath hitche The warmth and scent of him surrounded her. She suddenl became aware of the press of his muscular body against he and the strength of the arms enfolding her. Her body awoke clamoring with forbidden hunger. A flush radiated from he core.

Damned pregnancy hormones.

She couldn't seem to control the need blossoming insid her, but the length of Jared's hardening flesh against her na vel indicated he fought the same battle. She'd caused him un told heartache, which she couldn't cure, but she could off him comfort in the only way she knew how.

*Friends who became lovers,* he'd said, and suddenly th idea didn't sound as crazy as it had before.

Doubt nipped at the edges of her consciousness, and he

eart beat with hummingbird swiftness as she slowly rose on ptoe, cupped his jaw in her palms and pressed her lips to his. "I'm sorry," she chanted between kisses, "so sorry."

"Mercedes," Jared tried to protest, but his voice was little nore than a croak. Another kiss from Mercedes's soft lips and nother whispered apology smothered his words. Her tears ampened his lips and tasted salty on Jared's tongue.

Determined to end this insanity before he lost his tenuous rip on control, he caught her upper arms, but he couldn't nuster the strength to push her away. Her breasts brushed his hest and her thighs tangled with his. Silky, tumbled curls ased the backs of his hands and his wrists, sending a fris-on of need over him.

He cursed his base response to Mercedes's offer of solace. he'd despise him if she knew how badly he wanted to tan-le his fingers in her soft hair and lose himself in her mouth nd inside her body. It was a betrayal, dammit, a betrayal of is wife and of Mercedes.

"Mercedes," he said, firmly holding her an inch away. Their gazes met and held. The desire flickering in the depths f her deep-green eyes caused his pulse to pound like auto-natic gunfire. "We have to stop."

"I'm not Chloe. I can never be Chloe, but let me ease our pain."

He couldn't draw a breath and his knees nearly folded. He'd ead about the need to reaffirm life by making love, but he'd nev-r experienced it. He'd bet his newest B&B that was what Mer-cedes wrestled with now. "You don't know what you're saying."

She traced his ear, his jaw and then the curve of his bot-om lip with her finger. "I do."

His heart beat faster and an explosive pressure built in his ut. *Just say no.*

"Make love with me, Jared."

Damnation. He grasped for reason. "The baby…"

"You heard what Dr. Evans said. We won't hurt the baby"

He needed to be strong now more than ever before, b
when Mercedes leaned against him and sipped from his lip
again, his resistance wavered. The hard tips of her breas
gouged twin paths of fire across his skin, and he could bar
ly breathe. He struggled to analyze the situation, divide it in
to manageable parts or set a course of action.

*Analyze*… He and Mercedes were about to make an irrev
ocable mistake.

Blood pooled in his groin, and his pulse roared in his ear
His conscience urged him to run, but the need percolating ur
der his skin kept him right where he stood. He shook his head
trying to break the crazy magnetic pull between them, but h
failed. Miserably.

*Divide*…

Mercedes. Vibrant. Alive. Sexy as sin. She didn't love him
but then she never loved any of her lovers. Could their friend
ship survive intimacy? A moot point. Jared feared their relation
ship, like their marriage, was already running on borrowe
time.

She licked a hot, damp trail across his bottom lip, and he
tongue tangled with his. One kiss wouldn't hurt. His hand
slipped from her shoulders and into her hair. Her curls twine
around his fingers, holding him captive. He opened his mouth
over hers and deepened the kiss, drinking in the taste of he
like a starving man.

Instead of recoiling from his unleashed passion, Mercede
molded herself against him, fusing her body to his and wind
ing her arms around his neck. She matched him kiss for hun
gry kiss. Her nails teased his nape, and a shudder racked him
His heart pumped harder, and his skin felt electrified, but his

muscles weakened. No woman had ever affected him this way. Not Chloe or any of the lovers he'd had before he'd met her.

*Set a course...*

They were moving too fast and bound to have regrets if they didn't stop *now*. He gasped for air, clasped Mercedes's hips and struggled to clear his head by putting a little distance between them. His thumbs landed on the bare skin between her pants and top. Against his better judgment he stroked satiny warm flesh beneath her rib cage until she shivered. He wanted to caress her skin and inhale the exotic, spicy essence of Mercedes. He shouldn't, but she had him so rattled that the reasons why he should deny his desire and hers ebbed out of his grasp.

Mercedes reached for the hem of her camisole, pulled the fabric over her head and dropped the lacy top to the floor. Her sheer, butter-yellow bra hid nothing. He could clearly see the dusky pink areolas surrounding her tightly contracted nipples. Her breasts rose and fell rapidly as she panted for breath. He gritted his teeth on a groan and wrestled his rabid craving. Sweat dampened his brow and upper lip.

She grabbed fistfuls of his shirt and yanked the hem free of his pants. The light scrape of her nails on his flesh hit him like live electric wires. She whisked the fabric over his head and then tossed it on the floor beside her discarded top. Her fingers spread across his chest, tunneling through his chest hair with brain-melting amperage. She reached between them, unhooked the front closure of her bra and shrugged it off.

His hands ached to hold her round, firm breasts, but there was a reason why he shouldn't. He just couldn't remember what it was. She leaned forward to press a kiss over his nipple. The contact with her lips and body seared his skin. His breath whistled through clenched teeth. She danced her fingers over his waist, stroking him with a featherlight touch and stoking the urgency of his hunger. He folded like a house of cards, and his remaining reservations evaporated.

Jared backed toward the sofa, dragging Mercedes with him. He skimmed his fingers from her hair down her spine to the indentation of her narrow waist. Her supple skin rippled beneath his touch. He caught her moan with his mouth and devoured her. Slow, sensual kisses evolved into rough, impatient bites. He delved a finger beneath the waistband of her slacks, sliding it back and forth beneath the fabric. She drew back to tackle the button and fly of his pants. His stomach muscles contracted involuntarily as did hers when he returned the favor.

A blasphemy slipped past his lips as he fumbled like a clumsy adolescent, and then her pants and his lay discarded on the floor beside their shoes. The minuscule yellow panties barely containing her light brown curls nearly undid him. He yanked her close, sucked a sharp breath at the hot fusion of their torsos and took her mouth in another greedy kiss. He cupped her buttocks—*her bare buttocks*—and a groan erupted from his chest. Another thong.

He traced the strip of fabric dividing her cheeks and she whimpered. The tattoo. He wanted to see her tattoo. He'd dreamed about the damned thing every night since the wedding. But Mercedes's fingers tunneled beneath the waistband of his boxers and curled around him. The glide of her fingers down his rigid shaft cut off rational thought. Every muscle in his body tensed rock hard, and raging need consumed him. He grasped her wrist.

"Too much," he ground out.

She released him, but only to shove his shorts to the floor. He kicked them aside, hooked his fingers beneath the thin strips of her thong and whisked the fabric down her legs. She tepped free. Jared sat on the sofa, cupped her bottom and ulled her between his splayed legs. Beautiful. Pale, creamy kin. Her curves were slight but sexy as hell, and her tummy vas still too flat to reveal the secret within.

He hesitated again, thinking of the baby, but Mercedes angled her fingers in his hair and offered him her breast— n irresistible invitation. He teased her, laving and nipping efore finally sucking her deep into his mouth. A sexy sound urgled from her throat. More arousing noises slipped from er lips when he transferred his attention to the other breast.

Ravenous hunger chewed at his insides. Impatience urged im to hurry. He deliberately did the opposite, forcing him- elf to bank the fires, to savor the taste and texture of Mer- edes skin and the slick moisture he found between her legs. She arched into his searching fingers, threw back her head and vhispered, "Yes, right there. Just like that."

She rained down encouraging words, inciting his hunger o fever pitch. Sexy whispers were a new experience for him, and if he didn't get the show on the road he was going to go off early and solo—like a first-timer.

He trailed a string of kisses past her navel, buried his nose in her curls and inhaled her essence. Spicy. Exotic. Uniquely Mercedes. He lifted one of her legs and propped her foot on the cushion beside him. The position left her open for him to explore with his mouth and his hands. Her knees buckled at the first swipe of his tongue and only his firm grip on her buttocks kept her upright. She dug her fin- gers into his shoulders and let her head fall back. Her mus- cles quivered with each caress, and moments later, release rippled through her, flooding him with the taste of her pleasure.

"Jared, please." Her luminous, passion-filled gaze locked with his. She cupped his shoulders, urging him back against the cushions, and then she straddled his lap and lowered her self over his throbbing shaft.

A slick inferno engulfed him inch by excruciating inch. Her slow descent nearly drove him out of his mind. The ne cessity to pound mercilessly into her consumed him. Mer cedes must have read his mind and perversely decided t torture him instead. She rose and lowered, taking him infin itesimally deeper each time until she possessed him complete ly. He was ready to plead for mercy by the time she slowl picked up speed.

He captured her hips in his hands and her nipple in hi mouth. The sexy sounds she made and the aroma of their pas sion pushed him to the edge. He was close, so damned clos to blowing a circuit, but he wasn't doing this alone.

He combed his fingers through her damp curls, found th center of her passion and urged her to join him in his mad ness. She stiffened and then her orgasm rippled through he sparking the explosion of his climax. Lightning flashed be hind his eyelids and filled his veins with incinerating heat. H arched off the sofa, gripped her hips and pulled down on he narrow waist, burying himself to the hilt.

Mercedes collapsed against his chest with her head on hi shoulder. Their panting chests rose and fell in unison an their damp skin melded. He buried his nose in her hair, hop ing her distinctive perfume would tease him back to con sciousness, but the mission was doomed. His lids grew heavy His muscles turned to lead. He closed his eyes and allowe himself a few minutes to take pleasure in holding a woma close again.

Mercedes…his friend and now his lover. A mistake… O a miracle? Probably the former. His brain fogged and tim passed, but whether it was six minutes or sixty, he couldn' say. When he roused, Mercedes slept in a boneless heap i

is lap. Warm, soft, sated. He hated to disturb her, but neither
f them had been sleeping much lately. They needed their
eds. He slid to the edge of the sofa and stood, lifting her and
itching her legs over his hips. She stirred, tightening her arms
round his neck and her legs around his waist. "Where are we
oing?"

"Bed. Shhh," he said against her cheek and carried her to
er room. Jared yanked back the covers and lowered her on-
) the sheets. His body separated from hers, and instantly he
iissed the intimate embrace.

She caught his hand when he tried to rise. "Stay with me.
lease."

He hesitated. Without a doubt he'd just made the second
iggest mistake of his life. The first had been letting Chloe
torm out of the house after their argument over the quilt. But
Mercedes now believed herself responsible for Chloe's death.
No one knew better than he what a torturously destructive
urden that guilt could be. Hell, he'd walked to the edge of
cliff over it, and he didn't want Mercedes doing the same.
Ie had to convince her that he was the one responsible for
ie accident that had taken her childhood friend.

Against his better judgment, Jared slid into bed beside her.
he wiggled closer until her warm, lithe body filled his arms
nd a silky leg hooked over his. The rake of her fingers over
is hip revived his sluggish brain, and suddenly sleep was the
ist thing on his mind. He glanced at Mercedes's face. The
ultry tilt to her lips told him that sleep wasn't high on her
genda, either. His heart and a particularly demanding part
f his anatomy jerked.

Tomorrow. He'd convince Mercedes that Chloe's death
/as his fault tomorrow.

Tonight he wanted to feel alive one more time.

* * *

Mercedes awoke to silence and cold sheets. Where wa
Jared?

She sat up in bed and winced as her muscles protested the
passionate night. Making love with a man she trusted had bee
so…freeing, so…comfortable. *So incredibly different.* Neve
in her entire life had she been so uninhibited in bed. Her onl
concern had been bringing Jared pleasure. In return, he'd mul
tiplied her fulfillment tenfold. She shoved back her tangled hair

She and Chloe had never shared the intimate details of thei
love lives, so Mercedes hadn't known Jared would be a gen
erous and adventurous lover. He'd found erogenous zones sh
hadn't known she possessed, and she knew her body prett
well. And when he'd traced her tattoo with his tongue… /
delicious shiver skipped down her spine at the erotically
charged memory. She'd never had a lover do that before and
had no clue how potent the caress could be. A blush warmed
her from head to toe.

*Good grief, she never blushed.*

Together she and Jared had been white-hot. Stupendous
Orgasmic. She ducked her chin and smiled. Another wave o
warmth swept her skin and settled in the pit of her stomach
but then the sexual hum morphed into an anxious knot.

They'd shared nothing more than comfort and great sex las
night, right? But if it was nothing more, then why had making
love with Jared far exceeded anything in her experience? Sh
chalked up her outrageous response to pregnancy hormones.

Last night's intimacy would not change their friendship
She wouldn't let it. Jared was her escape valve. His B&B buy
ing trips and their Wednesday-night dinners took her off the
tense, competitive playing field where she butted heads with
her brothers. Jared was an integral part of her life.

She swung her legs to the floor, stretched out the kinks and hen crossed the room to dig in her suitcase for something to wear. She found her red robe and shrugged it on. Her hand paused over a collection of lingerie. Jared had packed these. How did she feel about him going through her underwear drawer? She considered it, but then shrugged it off. He'd packed her suitcase. No big deal. She'd do the same for him if the need arose. Friends did that kind of thing for each other.

Would Jared regret last night? Probably. He'd tried to talk to her as their pulses slowed and their bodies cooled, but she'd been afraid of what he might say, so she'd interrupted him each time with more hot kisses until they'd finally collapsed in exhaustion sometime in the middle of the night.

Massaging the crampiness below her navel, Mercedes went looking for him. She had to make sure he understood she didn't expect more than he was willing to give. They shared so many common interests. Biking, hiking, rafting, climbing—all physical activities. Sex could be just one more hobby they pursued together. Couldn't it? Although she'd never considered sex like climbing a mountain—something you did just because you could.

She hesitated in her bedroom doorway, chewing her lip. Maybe they should forget last night ever happened. No, last night had been too amazing to forget. As long as she remembered Jared would always love Chloe, and he remembered she wasn't going to risk loving anyone, they should be okay. No one would fall in love and no one would get hurt.

The kitchen and den were empty, as were Jared's bed and bathroom. His bed hadn't been slept in, so he must have stayed with her after she fell asleep. Comforted by the knowledge, she stepped out onto the back deck and scanned the yard and what she could see of the waterfront. No Jared. Where could he have gone?

Backtracking, she located his car in the driveway. Without

transportation he couldn't have gone far. If he hadn't returned by the time she showered and ate breakfast she'd go looking for him. She worried about him when he brooded, and she'd worry even more now that she knew he blamed himself for Chloe's death. That certainly explained why he'd closed himself off after the funeral. And of course their lovemaking could have heaped on more guilt. He probably thought he'd betrayed Chloe.

An itchy feeling settled over Mercedes's shoulders. Had she betrayed Chloe's friendship? She tugged her robe tighter against a sudden chill, and then opened the box of Cheerios and munched on a handful to settle her stomach. Not once during Chloe's life had Mercedes ever made an inappropriate move or had an inappropriate thought toward Jared—unlike the way Craig had hit on Mercedes's friends. And more than once Chloe had asked Mercedes to look after Jared if something happened to her. So, no, Mercedes decided she hadn't betrayed her friend. She was fulfilling a promise. Wasn't she?

She headed for a hot shower to ease her achy muscles. Ten minutes later she'd washed and dressed in shorts, a long-sleeved T-shirt and hiking boots. She slathered on sunscreen and still Jared hadn't returned. Mercedes swung through the kitchen for a bottle of water and saw his note on the refrigerator. How had she missed that before?

*Hiking.*

He'd said he hiked the perimeter of the lake each time he came up here. Jared was left-handed. When they hiked together he invariably chose the left fork in a trail unless they had a specific destination in mind—just like he'd chosen the left bedroom in the cabin. Smiling because she knew his habits so well, Mercedes let herself out of the cabin and set off to the right, hoping to intersect him.

The tightness in her abdominal muscles didn't loosen as

she hiked the clear but meandering path through the tall trees. In fact, it worsened. Even though she'd never had anything like that happen before, she blamed the discomfort on last night and brushed her concerns aside. She was in excellent health and great physical condition. A hike with no incline to speak of certainly wasn't beyond her abilities. The doctor had said so.

She hugged her arms around her chest as the pine-scented air grew cooler in the shade and trudged on. How much of a head start did Jared have?

The ache below her navel increased. They had overdone it last night. She needed to pee, but that was no surprise since the urge hit her ever thirty minutes or so. But she didn't relish the thought of ducking deeper into the woods. Thus far, she hadn't encountered any other hikers, but it'd be her luck to startle a pack of Boy Scouts by dropping her pants.

Her watch indicated that she'd been on the trail for less than an hour. Unless Jared had taken the right fork, she should meet up with him soon. The cramping in her belly increased, making her more than a little nervous and sending a trickle of fear down her spine.

*It's nothing. Keep walking.* But she didn't. Her steps slowed and Mercedes sank down on a sunlit boulder. She'd take a five-minute rest and then resume her hike. If the break alleviated her pain, then she didn't have to worry about her baby. If it didn't… She was very likely going to panic. In a worst-case scenario, she could use the cell phone in her pocket to call for help. Never mind she didn't know where she was or that she might have trouble with reception here in the valley. She'd worry about that if it became necessary.

Her discomfort lessened as she sat and contemplated the steep tree-covered slopes surrounding the lake. What was she going to say to Jared when she found him? Should they try to make this marriage work? It would involve carefully drawing boundaries and respecting them. Her child would certainly benefit by having a stable father. And she didn't doubt for a minute that Jared would be a great father. He was even tempered and logical, but he knew how to let loose and have fun.

"What makes you think Jared would be interested in parenting your child, Mercedes Ashton, uh, Maxwell?" she muttered.

He'd had the best wife on the planet. How could she measure up to a domestic goddess like Chloe? Her friend had been petite and motherly, kindhearted and generous. She'd had an amazing knack for decorating, incredible talent in the kitchen and a green thumb.

Mercedes stayed out of the vineyard for fear of killing the vines the way she'd killed every houseplant she'd ever been given. Puttering in the kitchen would never be her favorite activity, and she'd decorated her apartment all in the same shade of mocha so nothing would clash. Chloe had laughed and given her the quilt and other colorful items to brighten up the place.

Mercedes tended to speak her mind, whereas Chloe was more likely to be ladylike and polite. And Mercedes had already established that she was more selfish, driven and competitive than Chloe. They were so different it was a miracle the two of them had become friends.

No, Jared wouldn't be getting a bargain in her, but he would be getting a woman who would respect him for who he was and wouldn't try to change him.

She sipped from her water bottle and rechecked her watch. What was wrong with her? This wasn't her usual pregnancy icky feeling. Not that she'd been pregnant long enough to have a "usual," but she did feel more lethargic than she had over the past couple of weeks.

Branches snapped in the distance. She straightened. Please let that be Jared. And then his long-legged stride carried him into the open. Her heart hitched at the sight of his handsome mug. Morning stubble covered his strong jaw, and his eyes were as blue as the sky above. His snug black T-shirt revealed the depth of his pectorals and the breadth of his shoulders, and his snug, faded jeans accentuated long, muscular legs, a flat belly and the substantial male package in between. Her insides warmed at the memory of just how substantial.

Why had it taken her eleven years to notice Jared Maxwell had a killer body? In fact, her best friend was a certifiable hunk. Mercedes exhaled and shook her head. Thoughts like that were unnecessary and unwise.

Her relief in finding him didn't last long. His expression blanked as if he wasn't glad she'd tracked him down. She swallowed hard. If he apologized for last night she didn't know what she'd do.

Jared slowed when he spotted Mercedes sunning on a rock at the lake's edge. His pulse rate doubled. "What are you doing out here?"

"Looking for you." She rose slowly and dusted off the seat of the multipocketed hiking shorts he'd packed for her. He couldn't help wondering which bra and panty set her unisex outfit concealed. His heart hammered faster in memory of the sinful confections he'd found in her drawer.

The sun danced off her untamed curls and highlighted the spattering of freckles on her nose that she hadn't bothered to hide under makeup today—probably because he'd forgotten to pack her makeup. He'd also forgotten her hair toys, and for that he was glad. He liked her hair loose instead of scraped back into that twist thing she usually did.

"We usually hike together." Her cautious tone gave n[o] clue to what she was thinking.

He gazed out over the mirror-smooth water. The gentl[e] breeze barely disturbed the surface. All morning long he'd ha[d] a nagging suspicion that more than guilt had driven their love making. Had last night been a pity lay because she felt sorr[y] for him or a consolation lay because she'd needed reassuranc[e] that she was desirable after that jerk Bradford dumped her?

Did she feel he'd used her and betrayed her? Jared stud[ied] her neutral expression. "I needed some time to get m[y] head together."

Or had last night been a result of the overactive hormone[s] Mercedes had mentioned? Chloe's pregnancies had never af[-] fected her that way. As a matter of fact, once Chloe con[-] ceived she'd often pushed him away as if he'd done his jo[b] by making her pregnant, and she no longer needed him.

And Chloe had been shy in bed. She'd needed coaxin[g] and TLC.

Mercedes, on the other hand— Heat blasted through hi[s] veins. He'd never made love as wildly as he and Mercede[s] had last night. He shoved a hand through his hair and cleare[d] his throat. He only hoped she would forgive him for crossin[g] the line. "Last night—"

"Was pretty amazing," she interrupted.

Her answer threw him off balance. He searched her face and though his heart pounded like a jackhammer, his ches[t] muscles constricted at the doubt clouding her eyes. Did sh[e] have regrets? "Yes."

"Who'd have thought you and I would be so…" Sh[e] shrugged and looked away, clearly ill at ease.

*Explosive.* "Yeah."

Mercedes had been an aggressive lover. His need had bee[n] so great he'd been afraid he'd hurt her, and he'd tried to hol[d] back, but each time she'd pushed him beyond the limits of his control.

Had he only been one more man in the line of revolving men in her life? Not that Mercedes was promiscuous. She was extremely selective in choosing the jerks with whom she became intimate. Jared could tick off the fools' names on one hand since she usually confided in him, once the guys had been shown the door.

And why did the thought of being just another one of Mercedes's lovers make him want to crawl out of his too-tight skin? He shoved the unpalatable thought aside.

Chloe had once claimed that Mercedes always chose men like her father, men who couldn't or wouldn't love her. He certainly fit that description. Sure, he loved Mercedes *as a friend,* but a strong, passionate woman like Mercedes deserved more than a man who'd proven he had feet of clay. She deserved a man who'd be devoted to her heart and soul. And his heart was no longer his to give.

He'd left her bed this morning because from the moment he'd awoken beside her he'd wanted to make love to her again. The hunger she'd unleashed in him exceeded anything in his experience, but last night shouldn't have happened and if she'd turned away in regret or cursed him...

He ground his teeth, snatched up a pebble and skipped it over the lake's surface. Anger and regrets were only what he expected.

"Jared, last night doesn't have to change anything between us."

His jaw dropped open. He snapped it shut and examined her earnest expression. How could last night not change everything? He'd betrayed Mercedes's friendship. A man didn't screw his best friend.

And then there was Chloe. He'd betrayed his wife. His first

wife. He'd always love Chloe, and he could never risk that kind of love for another woman. Not even Mercedes.

He'd made a mistake, but he didn't have any clue how to rectify the damage. During his hike he'd tried to analyze the situation and divide it into manageable parts, but setting an action plan defeated him. For only the second time in his existence—the first being after he'd lost Chloe and Dylan—he couldn't see a viable path ahead. He wasn't ready to cut Mercedes from his life, but he couldn't foresee their friendship returning to the previous comfortable footing.

He shook his head. "How can last night not change our relationship?"

She shifted on her feet and turned toward the water. "As long as neither one of us expects this to turn into hearts and flowers and romance, then we should be okay. Sex can be just one more physical activity we enjoy together like kayaking or rock climbing."

He rubbed the back of his neck. Should he be insulted? Was she trying to say what happened held no more significance to her than a weekend hobby? That didn't sound like Mercedes. "You're saying you'd settle for sex without love?"

She looked at him over her shoulder. Sadness and resignation filled her eyes. "I always do. Love complicates a relationship. Feelings get hurt. Hearts get broken."

Understanding clicked in his mind. Mercedes had been hurt by a jerk or two in college and by Spencer Ashton. She'd watched her sister's first marriage go from blissful to verbally and mentally abusive. "Love doesn't have to be that way, Mercedes."

Her brows leveled. "I'm not willing to risk it. Are you telling me you're ready to jump back into the dating pool?"

"No."

She tilted her head at what he'd come to recognize as Mer

cedes's I'm-ready-to-debate-this-all-week angle. "And are you willing to live without sex for the rest of your life?"

Last month that question would have been easy for Jared to answer. Yes, he could live without sex. He had for more than six years. But today, simply being near Mercedes aroused him. He vividly recalled her scent, her taste, the satiny texture of her skin and the hunger she'd imbued in him. His jeans tightened over his expanding flesh.

A knowing smile curved her wide mouth. "Weighing the pros and cons again, Jared?"

"I always do." He'd never been able to have casual sex with a woman for whom he felt nothing, and what Mercedes offered sounded too good to be true. He'd discovered that in most too-good-to-be-true cases there were hidden faults running beneath the surface.

She tipped back her head, revealing the tender underside of her neck and tempting him to agree just so he could kiss her again. "You're the one who suggested we tell the press that we were friends who became lovers."

"Mercedes, I don't know if sex between us is a good idea. Our friendship is too important."

"We trust each other, and we both know not to expect more than the other is able to give. Sex between us would be safe sex."

"I'll think about it." Hell, he probably wouldn't be able to think about anything else. "Ready to head back?"

"Sure." She turned quickly and he caught her wince.

"Is something wrong?"

She shrugged one shoulder. "I might have set too quick a pace on the way up here."

"That's not like you. You know your limits."

"You're right. I do. Let's go." She took off down the trail

and Jared followed. They'd made it about a quarter mile when he noticed the unevenness of her stride.

He picked up speed to draw alongside her. The narrowness of the trail meant their arms and shoulders bumped with each stride. "Mercedes, what's going on?"

She glanced at him but didn't slow her pace. He noticed the rigid set of her jaw and the pallor of her skin. "I think we might have overdone it last night. Either that or you're larger than I'm used to." She blew a stray curl off her forehead. "Well, that was definitely the case, but—"

His blood chilled. He ignored her flattery and grasped her bicep. "Did I hurt you?"

She stopped and faced him. "No. Never. I think we just had a little too much of a good thing. Sort of like eating an entire pint of ice cream after being on a strict diet."

He didn't buy her excuse. "If you won't tell me what the problem is, then I can't help to solve it."

She rubbed her lower abdomen. Worry clouded her eyes. "I'm having cramps."

His muscles locked. And his eyes tracked the movement of her hand on her belly as if hypnotized. Was she losing the baby? Dear God, had his loss of control last night caused her to miscarry? He scanned the steep hills around them. There wasn't anywhere to fly in a rescue team. He'd left his cell phone at the cabin because he knew from experience that he couldn't get a signal here. "I need to get you to a doctor."

She shook off his hand and trudged down the trail. "We're almost a mile away from the cabin. Let's see how I feel when we get there."

"You're going either way."

Her step hitched, but she didn't stop. "We're hours from my doctor in Sacramento."

"Then you'll have to go to the nearest emergency room."

"Great. Press." And then she sighed. "Okay, I can deal with the press."

Her acquiescence worried him more than an argument would have. "Can you make it to the cabin?"

"Sure." But her breezy answer lacked confidence.

"But?"

"But it hurts more when I walk, and the faster I go the worse it gets." Her reluctance in making the admission was clear.

He stopped her again and held out his backpack. "Put this on."

She looked at him like he'd lost his mind. "You want me to carry your pack?"

"Yeah, and then I'll carry you."

"I don't think—"

"Don't think. For once, Mercedes, could you do what I say without arguing?"

She stiffened. "Don't think sleeping together gives you the right to boss me around."

"I may have caused this, so would you shut up and get on my back."

"Isn't the phrase supposed to be shut up and get *off* my back?"

Her forced levity didn't make him laugh. "Aren't you worried about your baby?"

The shadows in her eyes darkened and her shoulders drooped. "Yes. I am."

"Then let's go." He turned his back and squatted.

After a hesitation, Mercedes climbed on and looped her arms around his neck. "This is crazy. I'm too heavy."

"It's not crazy if it keeps you and your baby safe, and you're a featherweight. I've carried packs heavier than you."

A slight exaggeration, but she didn't argue. Straightening, Jar
ed hooked his arms under her legs and set off down the path
Adrenaline pumped through his veins lightening his load.

He couldn't live with himself if he hurt Mercedes or he
baby. Hell, yes, he could, but he wouldn't like it. Whateve
happened he'd be there for Mercedes. He owed her.

# Eight

"Newlyweds, huh?" the young male E.R. technician asked Mercedes. A smile twitched on his lips. "How long have you been married?"

Was this freckle-faced boy old enough to be out of school?

Mercedes tried to smile back, but it was difficult to be friendly when fear had turned her face into a frozen mask. The ache in her belly hadn't relented, and when she'd gone to the bathroom before leaving the cabin she'd cried out at the knife-stabbing pain. The tech had made her repeat that torturous procedure here.

Was she losing her baby?

"We've been married a week. I haven't had time to get my license or insurance card switched to my new name, but the health insurance is valid."

"Hey, I believe you. The doctor will be in as soon as we get your lab results. Call me if you need anything." He left with a casual wave. If his smiles and relaxed attitude were designed to make her feel less afraid, they failed.

Mercedes searched Jared's grave face, and guilt swamped her for dragging him through this. Losing his own babies had been hard for him, and his obvious tension told her that he was reliving those memories today. Even though he hadn't said one negative word during the hike back to the cabin or the drive to the hospital, she knew he thought she was losing her baby. The worst part was she did, too.

A sob stalled in her throat. "You won't leave until we talk to the doctor?"

He clasped her hand. His jaw went rigid. "I'm not going anywhere."

"Thanks." She took comfort in his support and wished she wasn't such a coward.

"Would you like me to call your mother?"

"Not yet." What could she tell her except that she was scared out of her mind? Her mother didn't need that worry. Besides, if she spoke to her mother, Mercedes suspected she'd probably break down and cry. "Let's see what the doctor says first."

Jared massaged the back of his neck with his free hand. "Did that guy examine you while I was filling out the admissions forms?"

"No. He's only a technician. He took my vitals and had me pee in a cup. That's it. But you'd think he'd be a little more concerned." She tugged at the hospital gown, trying to cover her bare back.

"We should have driven to Sacramento." Jared rose and reeled back the curtain as the young man passed by their area. "Why haven't you examined her? She could be—" Jared glanced at her and then back to the tech "—her baby could be in trouble."

The guy grinned. *He actually grinned.* "Look, sir, relax. The octor will examine your wife when he arrives, but you're new-weds. Your wife has the classic symptoms of honeymoonitis."

"What?" she and Jared said simultaneously.

The tech tried and failed to control his amusement. Tilt-ng his head, he whispered conspiratorially, "It's a bacterial nfection of the bladder caused by frequent sex. Honeymoon-rs are notorious for it."

Mercedes closed her gaping mouth. Her skin burned. That's it? But what about my baby?"

"The doc will be here in a second. He'll cover all the ases." He left again.

Jared paced the small curtained cubicle like a caged ani-al. The minutes dragged by at a snail's pace. He pivoted at e end of her bed and pinned her with his gaze. "I don't like is attitude. He's too damned flippant. Honeymoonitis, my utt."

She clasped her hands over her belly. What would happen she lost her baby? Would her marriage to Jared end? Would eir friendship do the same? Neither course bore thinking bout.

What seemed like an eon later, the curtain slid back and n older gentleman stepped in with a female nurse on his eels. "Mr. and Mrs. Maxwell, I'm Dr. Hicks, and this is Jan eed, your nurse."

The doctor shook hands with both of them and then flipped rough the chart before pulling the curtain closed. He did a orough exam and peppered Mercedes with questions. She ied to pretend Jared wasn't standing right by her shoulder hen she put her feet in the stirrups and the doctor got up lose and personal. If she hadn't been terrified of the diagno-is she would be embarrassed.

When the doctor finished the exam he tossed his gloves in

the bin, washed his hands and wrote on the chart. He had
quiet discussion with the nurse, which Mercedes couldn
hear no matter how hard she strained, and then Jan departe
The doctor helped Mercedes to sit up. Each passing secon
seemed like a lifetime's delay, and Mercedes's nerve
stretched until she wanted to scream.

Dr. Hicks observed her over the top of his half glasses. Th
older man's serious expression turned every one of Me
cedes's muscles into stone. "Mrs. Maxwell, I suspect yo
have a urinary tract infection, a UTI. Normally, we'd write
prescription for antibiotics and send you home, but your preg
nancy complicates the situation. The good news is your lac
of fever leads me to believe you haven't progressed into a kic
ney infection yet."

A kidney infection? That sounded scary. Mercedes's stom
ach clenched. "Why is that good news?"

He regarded her solemnly. "I'm not going to sugarcoat thi
A kidney infection could cause you to go into preterm labo
and ultimately, if we can't get the infection under contro
there's a risk of kidney failure, septic shock, respiratory fai
ure and death."

*Death!* A chill of terror raced over her. She wasn't read
to die, and she didn't want to lose her baby, either. She cra
dled her stomach. Labor at eleven weeks. Her baby woul
never survive.

It wasn't until the nurse dropped a heated blanket ove
Mercedes's shoulders that she realized she was shivering.

Mercedes searched Jared's set and pale face. He stood rig
idly beside the bed with his hands fisted by his side. "But
don't understand. I didn't have any symptoms until today. *I*
least, I don't think I did."

The doctor nodded. "You're probably right. In most case
a nonpregnant woman would notice the discomfort of

UTI relatively early on, but pregnancy suppresses your immune system to allow your body to tolerate foreign matter, like a fetus, a placenta or even bacteria. A pregnant woman usually has a sudden onset of symptoms, as you did today.

"Treatment of an acute UTI is serious business. Our goal is to stop the infection before it progresses into your kidneys, and chances are good that we will since you're not allergic to any of the preferred antibiotics."

*Chances are good.* Mercedes hugged herself. "You mean I could still lose my baby?"

"Yes, Mrs. Maxwell, the risk factors are there, but I'm going to do my best to minimize them."

"How?" Jared asked in a strangled voice.

"I'll admit your wife to the hospital. We'll run a course of intravenous antibiotics and retest her tomorrow. If she responds to the treatment, then we'll probably let you take her home in a day or two with an oral prescription and a promise to follow up with her doctor."

"And if I'm not responding?" Mercedes asked, but she was very afraid she wouldn't like the answer.

"Then you'll be our guest for as long as it takes. We'll tackle it one day at a time and face each obstacle as it arrives."

Tension deepened the lines bracketing Jared's mouth, and worry and guilt clouded his eyes. She knew what he was thinking. He blamed himself. He'd said as much on the trail.

She'd hate for her night with Jared to become fodder for the press, but she'd rather live with the public airing of her private business than have Jared hold himself responsible if something happened to her or her baby.

"Doctor, the technician called this honeymoonitis, but we didn't...last night was the first time we, um, consummated our marriage. We couldn't have caused this, could we?"

The doctor's brows lowered. "No, Mrs. Maxwell, this isn't

honeymoon cystitis. As I explained, changes in a pregnant woman's body make it the perfect breeding ground for this type of bacteria. Your bacterial counts have probably been high for days, possibly even a week."

So Jared couldn't take the blame. "Thank you."

Dr. Hicks looked surprised by her gratitude, and then he glanced at Jared and nodded as if he'd dealt with nervous husbands before. "Any more questions?"

Mercedes bit her lip. "Yes. How will this affect my baby?"

He patted her hand and then stepped aside for the nurse to insert an IV. "Studies show you're very likely to have a normal pregnancy and a healthy baby if we can get past this stumbling block. I won't kid you. This is serious business, Mr. and Mrs. Maxwell, but you and your baby are in good hands here at Mercy Hospital. Give us an hour and we'll have you snug in a private room upstairs."

Finally some good news. It was about time.

The scent of antiseptic, the hustle of people and the cries of pain from a nearby cubicle dragged Jared under the depths of his memories as if he'd gone over the side of the Golden Gate Bridge with concrete blocks tied to his ankles.

Chloe and Dylan had died in an emergency room, and though this was a different E.R., it felt the same, smelled the same, sounded the same. And the stakes were just as high.

He could lose Mercedes.

Fear grabbed his gut and squeezed with an iron-clad grip as history bore down on him. Another night. Another wife. Another innocent baby. Gone.

His heart pounded, and sweat broke out on his upper lip. He endeavored to remain stoic for Mercedes's sake, but a heavy sense of helplessness weighed him down.

He couldn't fix this.

"You can call my mother now." Mercedes's quiet voice jerked him from his painful rumination.

He forced his stiff neck muscles into motion and shook his head. "I can't use my cell phone in here. I'd have to go outside to call, and I'm not leaving you."

As much as he wanted to run, he couldn't leave her here alone with her fears, and as much as he wanted to pull her into his arms, hold her tight and smooth her unruly curls, he wouldn't do that, either. He wasn't convinced last night hadn't been a mistake.

Mercedes worried her bottom lip with her teeth. "The press is bound to get wind of this since my driver's license is still in my maiden name. I'd prefer that my family hear about my hospitalization from us rather than from a reporter calling to ask them for details on a situation of which they're unaware."

"The doctor promised he'd have you in a bed upstairs within the hour. As soon as you're settled you can call your mother from the phone in your room. Hearing your voice will reassure her more than hearing mine."

"I guess you're right. Dr. Hicks sounds like he knows what he's talking about." The fear darkening her eyes contradicted her words.

Why did he get the impression Mercedes was trying to soothe him when it should be the other way around? He pulled up a stool, sat beside the bed and covered her hand—the one not tethered by the IV slowly dripping the potentially lifesaving antibiotics into her veins. "He does, but I'll call Dr. Evans later to be sure. If she has any doubts about your care here, then we'll have you transferred to her hospital by ambulance."

Jared laced his fingers through Mercedes's and said a silent prayer, something he hadn't done since his pleas had gone

unanswered the night he'd lost Chloe and Dylan. He didn
want to lose Mercedes.

*He loved her.*

The knowledge hit him like a freight train at full speed. H
hadn't seen the locomotive coming and now it was too la
to step out of its path. The muscles in his chest constricte
and he couldn't draw a breath. Despite his vows to never lov
again after Chloe's and Dylan's deaths, somehow Mercede
had crept into his heart during the past five years.

He hoped Chloe could forgive him.

There was nowhere for Jared to hide in the confining cur
tained cubicle while he grappled with his discovery, his gui
and the realization that he and Mercedes didn't have a futur
together.

She'd married him solely to protect this child, and if sh
lost her baby she'd no longer need him. Even if she manage
to get past this crisis, Mercedes liked men who made he
laugh, men who could dance and schmooze at the cocktai
parties her job with Louret Vineyards required. He wasn't tha
man. Not anymore. He'd learned to avoid affairs that require
small talk with strangers, because folks invariably asked if h
had a wife and kids. He knew they didn't mean anything b
it. They were just trying to make conversation, but it was lik
a sneak attack every time and each time it left him reeling.

Could Mercedes be happy with a loner like him? Proba
bly not. Their occasional escapes were one thing, but Mer
cedes wouldn't find a steady diet of isolation palatable fo
long. Besides, she liked variety. None of her men had laste
long before she found a reason to cut them loose.

And if she ever found out how weak he'd been after los
ing his wife and son, she'd lose all respect for him.

The painful knowledge that their relationship was doome
settled over him and filled him with resolve. He wanted Mer

edes to be happy, and as soon as he got her out of here he
planned to set the wheels in motion to ensure her happiness.

Mercedes jerked awake as the car slowed. Blinking her
gritty eyes, she straightened in the seat and tried to banish the
lingering sense of longing brought on by her dream about
sharing a home with Jared and a houseful of dark-haired,
blue-eyed children. Thoughts like that would get her in trouble.

"Why are we coming here?" Mercedes asked Jared as he
drove up the long driveway of The Vines, her family's home
and the scene of their farce of a marriage. He passed the left-
hand turn that led to the winery and her office. Had she only
been gone three days? It seemed much longer since she'd
been strong-armed into a vacation. Some vacation.

"Your mother has agreed to take care of you while I'm out
of town." Jared pulled his SUV to a stop in the circular drive
in front of the entrance and cut the engine.

He was leaving and leaving her here? "You're going out
of town? On a B&B buying trip?"

"No. I have personal business to attend to." His short tone
warned her not to ask questions, and for once she didn't have
the energy to challenge him.

What was she? A piece of damaged merchandise being returned to her original owner? "You can take me to the cottage. The doctor said it would be okay to resume my normal
activities."

His expressionless gaze held hers. "Do you really want to
risk being alone on your first day out of the hospital?"

Was being alone really the issue? Did he not want her in
his cottage anymore? She didn't ask, because she was afraid
she wouldn't like his answer. "I guess not. How long will you
be gone?"

Jared's jaw remained tight. "Three or four days."

He exited the car and circled to her side. As soon as Mercedes's feet touched the ground, he startled her by sweeping her into his arms. She wound her arms around his neck and held on.

"I'm perfectly capable of walking," she protested, but surprisingly, she actually liked the warmth and security of being in his arms. His cologne teased her nose, reminding her of how he'd smelled when they'd been wrapped in the bed sheets and each other. Heat coiled in her abdomen.

"The doctor said for you to take it easy." He carried her toward the front door. His breath swept her lips with a hint of mint, tempting her to nibble that spot behind his ear that made him groan, but she didn't think the gesture would be welcomed.

During her stay in the hospital Jared hadn't touched her except to help her to the bathroom. Considering that she wouldn't have noticed the lack of contact a few weeks ago, she'd certainly missed it over the past two days. She yearned for the tangle and tug of his fingers in her hair, the moist heat of his mouth on her skin and the thick power of his body thrusting deep inside hers. She shivered.

Crazy hormones.

Her mother opened the front door as they approached and stepped onto the porch. "Nice drive?"

"She fell asleep the minute we hit the road and didn't awaken until we turned into the driveway," Jared answered before Mercedes could reply.

"I'm not surprised. Being in the hospital can be quite exhausting, but don't worry, Mercedes, you'll get plenty of rest here."

Jared followed her mother through the house and out into the walled garden where he set Mercedes down on a chaise and stepped away.

Her baby might be out of danger, but her relationship with Jared wasn't. Since leaving the cabin, Jared had built thick, impenetrable walls between them. The atmosphere remained strained and silent. And now she suspected he wanted her out of his house. The knowledge hurt.

He turned to her mother. "Caroline, thanks for agreeing to take care of Mercedes while I'm out of town."

"You know I'm always happy to have my children at home so that I can fuss over them."

"Will you call?" Mercedes hated that she sounded like a needy, whining wife.

Jared stayed silent for several moments. "If I can't make it home in time for your follow-up appointment on Wednesday afternoon I'll call to see what Dr. Evans has to say." He tucked a curl behind her ear and stroked a finger along her cheekbone. Mercedes's breath hitched and her pulse rate tripled. "Take care of yourself, Mercedes."

In her overly emotional state, the words sounded final, like a goodbye. Her eyes stung. "You, too."

And then he turned on his heel and left her. The quiet clang of the wrought-iron garden gate closing behind him drove a dagger through Mercedes's heart. His car engine started, and then the crunch of his tires on the drive faded in the distance. She lowered her head into her hands and clenched her teeth.

Would he come back? Or was this it? Was their marriage and friendship over? Pain crushed her chest.

A touch on her shoulder drew her gaze upward to her mother standing beside her chaise. "Are you ready for lunch?"

"No...not yet." Her baby was safe. Why wasn't she happy?

Because she wanted her old relationship with Jared back. She missed her best friend. Her bottom lip quivered. She bit

it and ducked her head to hide the telling sign from her ea
gle-eyed mother. When Caroline sank down on the cushion
beside Mercedes she knew she'd failed.

"What's wrong, Mercedes? Should I call Jared on his cell
phone and ask him to come back? Are you in pain?"

Yes, but this wasn't the kind of hurt a pill could fix. "I think
my illness reminded him too much of losing Chloe and Dylan."

Her mother brushed the hair off Mercedes's face. "I'm
sure it's been difficult for him, but you and the baby are fine.
In a few more months when you hold your son or daughter
in your arms, you'll both forget all about this little setback."

Mercedes inhaled a shaky breath. Her throat burned as if
she'd gulped scalding coffee. "I don't think Jared will be
around for the baby's birth."

Her mother's brows rose. "Why would you say that? The
man spent the last two nights in an uncomfortable hospital
recliner because he refused to leave your bedside."

Panic and fear welled inside Mercedes. What if he didn't
come back? She looked into her mother's understanding eyes
and confessed. "This baby isn't Jared's."

Caroline wrapped her arm around Mercedes's shoulders
and pulled her close. "I suspected as much, but I shouldn't
have to remind you that it doesn't take biology to make a man
a loving father. Lucas was a far better father to you than Spencer."

"I know, but Jared only married me because Craig's threatening to sue for custody. Jared's not in love with me."

Her mother waved a dismissive hand. "I've seen the way
your husband looks at you. And that kiss at the wedding…
You generated enough heat to wilt my roses. Don't try to tell
me Jared doesn't love and desire you. The question is do you
love him?"

Mercedes hesitated. She didn't want to tell her mother the

uth. Caroline already felt guilty about the horrible way
pencer Ashton had treated her children. The recent discov-
ry that they'd all been left out of Spencer's will had only
ade her mother feel worse. The last thing Mercedes needed
to tell her mother was that because of Spencer she didn't ev-
r plan to make the mistake of falling in love. "Of course I
ve Jared, but he'll always love Chloe."

"And you think one chance at love is all we get in our life-
mes? Surely my marriage to Lucas and Jillian's to Seth has
aught you differently."

"Yes, but…"

"Mercedes, I don't deny that I loved your father, and when
pencer left me I thought my life was over. But it wasn't. I
icked up the pieces and moved on because my children de-
ended on me. And then Lucas taught me to love again. It was
very different love than my first, and I was wary because
'd been hurt, but my feelings for Lucas were just as strong
s my feelings for Spencer." She paused and then shook her
ead. "No, my love for Lucas is stronger because I trust him
mplicitly—not because I'm young and naive and don't know
etter, but because I knew him as a friend first and then grew
o love him later."

Caroline covered Mercedes's knotted hands. "The biggest
art of love is trust, and you've had trouble trusting the men
n your life. But you've always trusted Jared, and he trusts
ou. Hold on to that now, Mercedes. Give him a chance to
rove you haven't misplaced your faith in him."

Caroline rose. "I'm going to get lunch, and I expect you
o eat it, young lady."

Hope unfurled in Mercedes's chest like a sail catching a
tiff breeze, but then the wind of optimism ebbed and hope
lackened. Doubts crowded in. Love wasn't in the cards for
er and Jared, but would he be willing to stay married and be

a father to Craig's baby? Not all men were as willing as he stepfather had been to take on another man's child.

How could she convince Jared that they belonged togeth er as friends and as lovers? They liked and respected each oth er and, good heavens, they were good in bed.

Would that be enough?

# Nine

Jared rapped once on the door to the upscale singles apartment Craig Bradford had moved into after leaving Mercedes and Napa. His briefcase seemed heavier than usual. It carried the weight of his future.

If he could convince Bradford to relinquish his parental rights, then Mercedes would be free of the threat to her baby and free to end their marriage. He wanted Mercedes to be happy, and that meant giving her the option of staying married because she wanted him in her life as her husband and her lover or going because she didn't.

If Bradford refused to sign the form, then Jared and Mercedes would stay married for the sake of her baby. He'd live with her and love her, but he'd never reveal his feelings because he couldn't bear to see pity in her eyes.

Jared rapped again with more force. Bradford's employer claimed Craig had left early for the day because he hadn't

been well. Jared heard movement inside and a male voic
cursing.

Seconds later Bradford yanked open the door. His clothe
and hair were askew, but he didn't look sick, although he di
look as if he might be pissed off and in pain. "What do yo
want, Maxwell?"

"To talk to you."

"I'm busy." Bradford tucked in his polo shirt and buckle
his belt.

Jared noticed a fresh hickey on the man's neck and a
smudge of red lipstick on his chin. Had he interrupted an af
ternoon nookie? Too bad. "This can't wait."

"Who is it?" a female voice called out from deep inside
the apartment.

Bradford glanced over his shoulder and then scowled a
Jared. "Come back later."

"Tell your girlfriend to get dressed. Is she your secretary?"

Red rose under Bradford's artificially tanned skin. "What's
it to you?"

"Nothing if you don't mind me calling your employer to
ask them if your secretary also took the afternoon off. And of
course, I'd probably point out that you were fired from your
job in Napa for sleeping with your secretary. Funny how you
forgot to mention that to Mercedes. She thought you changed
jobs to get away from her."

"Give me a minute." He shut the door in Jared's face.

Jared congratulated himself on doing his homework before
driving south. The additional ammunition could only work to
his advantage. Had Mercedes known Craig was being unfaithful during their relationship? No, Mercedes was into monog-
amy. She might not believe in long-term relationships, but she
was loyal to the jerks she dated for as long as the affair lasted.

The door opened again. A busty brunette scooted past him

with her head down. She scampered down the stairs and out of sight. Bradford opened the door wider for Jared to enter. "Make it fast."

The black leather sofas and chrome and glass tables screamed bachelor with bucks. What had Mercedes seen in the jerk? Scratch that. He was a great salesman. Mercedes said he'd been helpful in wining and dining prospective clients for Louret Vineyards.

"What do you want?"

Jared narrowed his gaze on Bradford. "I want you to relinquish your paternal rights to Mercedes's baby."

"Screw you." Craig folded his arms and rocked back on his wingtip shoes with a smartass expression on his face. "What's the deal? You figured out the kid's not yours? Tell me something I don't know."

"You don't know whether Mercedes's baby is mine or not, and you won't know until after the child is born and a DNA test can be run. That'll cost you and so will the attorney you'll have to hire if you choose to fight for custody. I'm warning you now, Bradford, that as Mercedes's husband I'll expect you to cover your share of all costs incurred until the child turns eighteen—if he's yours—and you'll be expected to chip in for college tuition." A lie, but a necessary one.

Jared set his briefcase on the coffee table and opened it. He extracted a spreadsheet and handed it to Bradford. "As you can see from this projection, the cost of raising the average child on the West Coast and putting him through college runs roughly one million dollars. Divide that by twenty-two years, and you'll be expected to ante up a minimum for forty-five grand per year in child support."

Bradford wadded the paper and pitched it back into Jared's briefcase. "This is a load of crap."

"Wrong. I've done my research. Those numbers come

from a reputable child advocacy agency. You might be expect
ing Spencer Ashton's estate to cover those costs, but it won'
If the courts overturn the will, then the money and propertie
will revert to Caroline Lattimer Ashton Sheppard. Her chil
dren won't see a penny of that money until after her death un
less she chooses otherwise. That's bad news for you for tw
reasons. One, Caroline hates you, and two, she's in excellen
health. She'll probably live another twenty to thirty years.
don't see any Ashton money in your future with or withou
custody of Mercedes's baby."

"I spent nine months with Mercedes. She owes me pali
mony."

"Wrong again. Palimony is for unmarried couples who liv
together in an exclusive relationship. You and Mercedes didn'
live together, and *you* sure as hell weren't exclusive.

"I've spoken to your previous secretary. She's pissed of
at you for getting her fired, and she's willing to testify tha
you were unfaithful to Mercedes throughout the duration o
your affair. And of course Mercedes's friends would also be
willing to testify that you hit on them and made inappropri
ate remarks during the relationship.

"If you make the mistake of taking this to court then I guar
antee Mercedes will countersue, and you'll end up owing her
money for misleading her about your intentions."

Bradford muttered a string of curses and stalked to the window. "You expect me to walk away from my kid?"

Jared set his jaw. "Is it yours? You seemed to think it was
mine three weeks ago."

"What do you expect me to think? Mercedes was fanati-
cal about birth control, and your damned name came up in
every conversation."

Surprise shot through Jared, warming him, giving him
false hopes. He nixed the feelings and forced a casual shrug.

What did *you* expect? Mercedes and I have known each other for eleven years. I've never been closer to anyone—not even my first wife."

He'd been bluffing, but as soon as Jared said the words he knew they were true. Mercedes knew him inside and out in a way that Chloe never had. Chloe had put him on a pedestal and ignored his weaknesses. Mercedes got in his face and made him confront the issues he'd rather avoid or kept him going until he found the strength to handle them. She'd taught him to be a survivor, to put one foot in front of the other and tackle one pain-filled day at a time. He couldn't have survived the past six years without her.

He'd never been a quitter. He hadn't given up when his father cut him off even though there had been plenty of days when it didn't look like his and Chloe's B&B would make it. It would have been easy to accept his father's loan offer, but instead Jared had sucked it up and worked ten times harder. He hadn't given up when his and Chloe's first and second pregnancies had ended in tragedy, and, thanks to Mercedes, he hadn't given up after losing wife and son.

Mercedes Ashton had made him a better man—*a stronger man*—than he'd been six years ago. Maybe he didn't have feet of clay after all.

"You're BS-ing me, Maxwell. You'd do anything for her."

"You're right. I would. Mercedes is my wife and I love her." Saying the words out loud for the first time filled Jared with a sense of rightness and renewed determination. He squared his shoulders and stared down at the shorter man. "Mess with her and you mess with me."

Bradford broke eye contact first. "Where can I get the damned form?"

Relief washed over Jared, but his job wasn't finished. He extracted the paperwork from his briefcase along with another copy of the estimated expense of raising a child. "Lucky fo you, I had my attorney draw up the papers. Take it to your and have him explain it word by word. I want you to know exactly what you're signing, because I don't want you cry ing foul later. I'll pick it up at your office Wednesday morn ing."

He shoved the batch of papers in Bradford's hand, snappe his briefcase closed and left the apartment with a combina tion of hope and dread in his chest.

Mercedes and his marriage were worth fighting for, an he'd just launched the first attack. But would this volley blov up in his face?

Would Mercedes stay? Or would she go?

Mercedes sipped her lemonade and fingered her cell phon as if touching it could make it ring. Jared had been gone fo two days. The fact that he hadn't called and probably wouldn be back in time for her doctor's appointment this afternoo or their Wednesday-night dinner bothered her far more tha it should have.

Before she could rationalize her discomfort, the back doc opened and Grant Ashton, Mercedes's oldest half brother an Spencer's firstborn son, stepped into the garden.

An interview Grant had happened to catch on TV ha brought him to California eight months ago to search for th father he'd believed dead. He'd discovered his father alive an well and married to wife number three. Grant's arrival i Napa Valley had sparked off a series of disastrous revelation for the Ashtons.

Mercedes, her mother and siblings had been shocked t learn that Spencer had left a wife and two children behind i Nebraska forty-two years ago. He'd married Caroline Latti mer without bothering to divorce Grant's mother, thereby mak ing Spencer's marriage to Caroline bigamy. Mercedes and her siblings had suddenly discovered they were illegitimate.

Grant's presence ought to make Mercedes uncomfortable, since one month ago Grant had been the chief suspect in her father's murder, but Grant's airtight alibi had cleared him, and his straightforward manner and genuine interest in uncovering the truth behind Spencer's lies made disliking Grant impossible.

"Hello, Grant."

"Feel like some company?"

"Pull up a chair." Mercedes looked into the same green eyes she saw in the mirror each morning—their father's eyes. She'd gotten to know Grant quite well. He'd been living at The Vines since January, but Mercedes hadn't seen him since Jared had dropped her off. She'd kept to her room and worried about where she'd go if Jared didn't come back for her.

Her apartment complex had a long waiting list, so returning to a larger one in the same complex was out of the question, and others in the area would be just as difficult to get into. She didn't make enough money to purchase a house on her own, and The Vines was overflowing with Ashtons from near and far due to her mother's gracious open-door policy. Mercedes wanted space for her and her baby to get to know each other without a lot of well-intentioned interference. She hoped Jared would be a part of those plans, but she was beginning to have her doubts. And that knowledge hurt more than it should.

A smile lit Grant's rugged face. "You look as if your stay in the hospital left you none the worse off. And congratulations on your pregnancy."

She grimaced. "Thanks. Word gets around, doesn't it?"

The papers had picked up the news of her hospitalization and broadcast it far and wide. Luckily, the intimate details of her night with Jared had been left out of the story. But she didn't want to discuss her precarious relationship with Jared or she'd lose her breakfast.

"Have you heard anything new about the investigation into Spencer's murder?"

Grant shook his head. "The detectives are still following the blackmail lead. Our father paid someone ten grand a month for at least a decade, and if they can figure out who was bold enough to bribe him, then we'll probably know who was bold enough to shoot him at point-blank range in his own office."

Mercedes couldn't help wondering if the hush money had been to cover up the secret of her father's marriage to Grant's mother or if another horrible secret would soon pounce on them unexpectedly. "So what's the news with your branch of the Ashton family tree? Have either Ford or Abigail heard from their mother?"

Grant's niece, Abigail, and his nephew, Ford, had also been her mother's guests at The Vines during the past nine months. It had been yet another surprise for Mercedes to suddenly find out she was an aunt to a twenty-four- and a twenty-six-year-old. Somehow she'd pictured herself bouncing her nieces and nephews on her knees and not having them arrive as fully grown adults.

Abigail had married Russ, Louret's foreman, in February, and the two of them had moved back to Nebraska for Abigail to open a veterinary practice. Last month Ford had married Kerry, her father's former executive assistant. What an insane year. There had been an Ashton marriage almost every month. How could Spencer's dishonesty bring happiness to so many?

Grant settled in a chair beside Mercedes. "We've had no word from Grace since she ran off with her salesman lover ten years ago. I'm trying to track her down. Before she disppeared, my sister liked being the center of attention, so if she's alive this media frenzy is bound to flush her out."

"I can't believe she'd abandon her children." Mercedes laid a protective hand over her baby. Dr. Evans had promised to do an ultrasound today. Mercedes couldn't wait to take a peek at her baby. She wished Jared were here to go with her.

Grant's lips twisted bitterly. "Like father, like daughter. My twin sister loved no one but herself."

Mercedes nodded. She couldn't believe there could be two people as heartless as Spencer Ashton in this world. He apparently hadn't loved any of the women he'd bedded.

Mercedes's heart skipped a beat and a chill raced down her spine. She hadn't loved any of her lovers, either. After getting her heart and ego severely dented in college, she'd deliberately chosen men she couldn't fall in love with, men who didn't have the power to devastate her the way her father had hurt her mother or the way Jillian's first husband had hurt her. Mercedes always warned her partners in advance that the connection would be temporary, and she entered relationships with an eye on the exit. She'd done the same with her marriage to Jared. They'd made plans to end the marriage even before they'd tied the knot.

*She was her father's daughter.*

Horrified, Mercedes clenched her fists until her nails dug into her palms. She'd hated Spencer because no matter how hard she'd tried to gain his approval, he couldn't love her, but was she any better than her father?

Was he too late? Jared hustled into the doctor's office and up to the counter.

The receptionist looked up. "Can I help you?"

"My wife, Mercedes Ash—Maxwell, had a three-o'clock appointment with Dr. Evans this afternoon. Is she still here?"

The woman checked the schedule on her desk. "She's with the doctor now. I'll take you back."

His heart pounded as he followed the woman through the rabbit warren of halls. Would Mercedes turn him away? And would today be the day she told him she wanted out of their marriage?

"Here we are." The blonde knocked on the door and poked her head inside. "Mr. Maxwell is here."

The door opened wider and Dr. Evans smiled in welcome. "Come in, Jared. We're about to take a look at your baby."

*Take a look?* His muscles locked. He forced them into motion and entered the room. Mercedes lay on her back on the examining table with a blue paper sheet covering her lower half. That drape meant she was bare under there.

He swallowed hard and dragged his gaze away from the blue paper and over the sage-green blouse she still wore to her face. He didn't see rejection in her expression, but he didn't see a welcome in her serious green eyes, either.

"You made it."

He jerked a nod. "Sorry I'm late."

A boxy machine with a viewing monitor stood on the floor beside the examining table. His stomach clenched. Dr. Evans pulled down the sheet to reveal the pale skin below Mercedes's navel. Not even Jared's tension could prevent the memory of pressing his face against the downy, soft area above a tangle of brown curls.

"This will be cold," Dr. Evans warned before she squirted clear gel on Mercedes's belly. She spread the gel with a device that looked like a shower head. "Jared, why don't you stand beside Mercedes's shoulder so you can see the screen? As I told Mercedes, the good news is the antibiotics have done their job. Her UTI has cleared up. We'll keep a close eye on her in the future to make sure it doesn't recur, but the important part is that it's unlikely to have affected the fetus."

His tension eased somewhat. Mercedes was out of danger.
ut Jared couldn't take his eyes off the ghostly black-and-
hite image on the screen. He'd been with Chloe during sev-
ral ultrasounds. He knew what it meant when the doctor
ouldn't detect the blip of a heartbeat. He reached for Mer-
edes's hand and laced his fingers through hers. When he saw
little flash of white, he said a silent prayer of thanks.

Dr. Evans examined him with a knowing expression on her
ace. "There's your baby's heartbeat. You'll be glad to know
at by the twelfth week the risk of miscarriage drops sub-
antially, and Mercedes's nausea should also ease. As you
an see, arms and legs have formed. Can you see the tiny fin-
ers? I'm going to take a few measurements to make sure
e're on target with your due date. Just sit back and enjoy
e show."

The little shadow on the screen wiggled and took a recog-
izable form. Mercedes's baby. A lump formed in Jared's
roat, and emotion welled in his chest.

He looked into Mercedes's happy, tear-filled eyes. He
ved her, and she was going to have a baby. A fierce desire
be around for this child's birth and to give the baby a broth-
r or sister filled Jared. Would Mercedes allow him to be a
ther to her child? Or would she take the document from
raig and run to the nearest attorney's office to file for a di-
orce?

"Do you want to peek and see if we can determine wheth-
r this is a girl or boy?" Dr. Evans asked. "It's early yet, but
e can try."

Mercedes blinked and broke eye contact. She shook her
ead. "No. I want to be surprised."

Dr. Evans looked at Jared and waggled her brows with a
asing smile. "Do you want to know? We don't have to tell
Iercedes."

He met Mercedes's gaze and squeezed her hand. "No. don't want there to be secrets between us."

"Then I'll print out a few pictures of the little Maxwell fo your scrapbook and let you two go. By the way, Jared, Mer cedes told me about the honeymoonitis business. It's ridicu lous, and you both need to know that sexual relations a perfectly safe. There are enough changes to adjust to durin pregnancy without having to throw celibacy into the mix."

*Him.*

*Mercedes.*

*Sex.*

Less than three weeks ago the idea had shocked him. To day, the thought of making love to Mercedes elevated h blood pressure, his temperature and an insistent part of h anatomy. And then he remembered the forms he'd left in h car. He wanted to hold Mercedes in his arms, look into he eyes and make love to her one last time before handing ov the document that made their marriage unnecessary.

He brushed a stray curl from her cheek and tucked it behin her ear before helping her to sit up. "That's good to know."

Mercedes's lips parted, and a flush climbed her cheek. Desire flickered in her eyes, and Jared's heart knocked hard er. Would she still desire him six hours from now? Si months? Six years?

Dr. Evans patted his shoulder. "I'll see you in three weeks She left, closing the door behind her.

Mercedes crumpled the edge of the paper drape in her fin gers and nibbled her bottom lip. "Should I move my thing out of the cottage?"

He frowned. "No. Why?"

She shrugged and looked away. "You left me at The Vine I thought maybe…"

*I love you* teetered on his tongue, but he held back. H

dn't want Mercedes to stay with him out of guilt or pity. She
uld make the decision to stay or go after he gave her the
rental relinquishment form, and if she chose to stay, then
'd have the rest of his life to show her how much he'd
me to love her over the past six years.

His gaze focused on her damp lips, but a doctor's office
asn't the place for the mind-numbing, doubt-blocking kiss
needed. Shoving his hands in his pockets, he stepped back.
wanted you to be safe. Do you feel up to driving home or
uld you prefer to get a hotel room?"

"I want to go back to the cottage."

He tried not to get his hopes up, but it was hard. "I need
make a stop on the way home, and then I'll meet you
ere."

Mercedes nodded. "I'll get dinner."

Jared turned on his heel and left her. He needed to put the
ast to rest before he could take the next step in his battle for
future with Mercedes.

# Ten

**M**ercedes sat in stunned silence after the exam room do[or]
closed behind Jared.

Evidently, she wasn't as heartless as her father after all, b[e-]
cause her heart had been breaking ever since Jared had left h[er]
at The Vines. All she'd been able to think about over the pa[st]
two days was what would she do without Jared? She'd bee[n]
afraid she'd lost him, and the rush of happiness that had swe[pt]
through her when he'd stepped into the examining room ha[d]
put it all into perspective. There had been something in Ja[r-]
ed's eyes that made her feel achy and tight, and this time sh[e]
knew better than to blame those feelings on her crazy ho[r-]
mones. In fact, she suspected her pregnancy had only made h[er]
more attuned to the secret she'd been unwilling to acknow[l-]
edge.

She'd fallen in love with her best friend. The knowledg[e]
both terrified and energized her.

How could it have happened when she'd tried so hard not fall in love with *anyone?* When had it happened, and how uld she not have recognized her feelings before now? When e looked back over the years since Chloe's death with hind-ght, there were so many clues.

Mercedes always returned to Jared when her relationships ded. He soothed her wounded spirit and bolstered her dam-ed ego.

Why else could no man measure up to her high standards? ecause she compared all her dates to Jared—the only man she ew who didn't register on her Twenty-Five Ways To Tell Your Ian's a Loser list. And Jared was the only man she'd ever met ho could make her forget the stress of her job and relax.

Her mother was right. Trust was a huge issue. Mercedes usted Jared more than anyone else. Had she driven him way by throwing herself at him at the cabin and then by forc-g him to face his worst nightmare—losing Chloe and Dy-n—in the emergency room? She hoped his presence here day mean she hadn't.

Mercedes mechanically donned her clothes. Doubts con-nued to plague her. Had that night in the cabin meant any-ing to him at all or had he been without a lover for so long at any woman—*or even a knothole in a tree*—would have ufficed? She'd been hurting and she *had* thrown herself at im without really giving him an opportunity to say no.

Had he wanted to say no? The thought bothered her too uch to contemplate. But his actions since that night gave lit-e clue to his emotions.

Where did they go from here? Did she set him free? Did he beg him to stay? No, no begging. She didn't want his pity.

But if he stayed… She pressed a hand over her pounding eart. Marrying Jared had been a bigger mistake than she'd riginally suspected, and destroying their friendship was the least of her worries. Without a doubt, Jared would break h[er] heart. He still loved Chloe, and even if by some chance Me[r-] cedes could convince him to take a chance on loving her, sta[y-] ing married meant always taking second place to Chloe in h[is] heart.

Not being good enough was a sore spot, since Merced[es] had always come in second to her father's new family. Or w[as] it third? Spencer had legally married the mothers of his fir[st] and third families.

Could she settle for being second best?

The lush green grass, towering shade trees, beautiful flow[-] ers hardly seemed like the right setting for heartache.

Jared stood in front of the small marble marker, and thoug[h] sadness filled his heart, it wasn't the crippling emotion he once experienced. He could actually see a glimmer of lig[ht] at the end of the dark tunnel in which he'd been living for th[e] past six years.

He had been happy with Chloe, just Chloe, but she' wanted a baby more than anything—more than him, he' sometimes thought. It seemed fitting that she'd share her ete[r-] nal resting place with their son.

Jared knelt to set the potted rosebush he'd brought wit[h] him at the base of the mother-and-child tombstone. The cem[-] etery caretaker had promised to plant the bush tomorrow. Jar[-] ed used to bring fresh flowers, but this plant would provid[e] a steady supply of blooms in the future.

For years he'd thought he'd let Chloe down by failing to pr[o-] vide the houseful of children she'd wanted and by letting he[r] get into the car and drive to her death. Jared had refused to ac[-] cept the investigator's ruling that the wreck had been a frea[k] accident despite the fact that the accident reports had reveale[d] that the blown tire, which caused Chloe's vehicle to roll an[d] crash into a tree, had been in good condition and properly inflated. Jared had wanted someone to pay for taking two innocent lives. For the past six years that someone had been him.

Hearing Mercedes try to take the blame had made one thing clear. Neither he nor Mercedes or even Chloe were at fault. Chloe and Dylan had been the victims of a tragic unforeseeable and unavoidable accident, and it was time he stopped beating himself up over it. It was time to move forward.

He sat back on his haunches. "I love her, Chloe. But you probably guessed that would happen. You said that I'd never have looked twice at you if I'd met Mercedes first, but you're wrong. You're both incredibly special women in very different ways. I'm lucky to have had each of you in my life."

He plucked a strand of grass and let it blow away in the breeze. "You asked me to look out for her if anything ever happened to you, and I'm here today to promise you that I'll be with her for as long as she'll let me. Mercedes needs me, even though she'd rather eat glass than admit it."

He rose and dusted off his hands. "I'll be back, but probably not as often. That doesn't mean I've forgotten you or Dylan. You'll always be here." He thumped his chest over his heart.

Jared withdrew a palm-size toy car that resembled his own SUV from his pocket and set it on the lip of the marker beneath Dylan's name. "You'll always be riding with me, son."

And then he turned his back on the past and took a step toward the future—a future he hoped to share with Mercedes and her child.

Mercedes lit the last candle and stepped back to view her handiwork. She hoped the table for two combined with dinner from Jared's favorite Mexican restaurant would set the scene for seduction. Anxious for his arrival, she walked to the window and peeked through the blinds. No Jared.

Craig and the men in her past had taught her a valuable lesson: sex without love didn't satisfy or fill the emptiness inside her. But making love with Jared had, even though she hadn't known she loved him at the time. She'd avoided falling in love because she hadn't wanted to be hurt, but she couldn't imagine anything hurting more than losing Jared.

No, she wasn't like her father. She'd rather love Jared and face the devastation of losing him than never experience love. Even if hers and Jared's relationship ended tonight, for once in her life she wanted to let down the walls she'd erected around her heart and make love knowing she loved her partner. But she'd keep her feelings to herself. She didn't want to make Jared uncomfortable. It wasn't his fault he couldn't love her back.

She glanced over her shoulder at the romantic table setting. She wanted it all; friendship and love, and she wanted it with Jared. Calculated risks like rock climbing and navigating white water didn't terrify her nearly as much as this simple dinner. But maybe one day Jared would be ready to love again, and Mercedes wanted to be the woman he chose.

The crunch of tires on gravel drew her attention to the driveway, and her heart leaped to her throat. Jared was home. She smoothed her hands over her pinned-up hair and met him at the front door, opening it before he could put his key in the lock.

He stopped on the welcome mat and his unblinking blue gaze locked with hers. Mercedes thought she might hyperventilate. She dampened her lips and studied his dear face. *She loved him.* "I picked up dinner at Casa Maria's."

"Smells good." He didn't make a move to come inside. Mercedes realized she was blocking the door. Heat climbed her cheeks and she moved out of the way.

He entered, set his briefcase on the sofa table, scanned the

losed shades, the candlelit table and then appraised her.
Special occasion?"

Her mind went blank. Where was her usual lay-your-cards-
n-the-table boldness? She knew what she wanted and how
o ask for it, but for the life of her she couldn't blurt out that
he wanted to make love with him because she was afraid he'd
efuse. And then what would she do? "Um, no, I'm just hap-
y to be home."

He shoved his hands in the pockets of his khaki slacks.
You were at home at The Vines."

She swallowed her rising panic. Was he going to ask her
o leave? "You know I feel more comfortable with you than
vith my family. Besides, it's Wednesday. We belong togeth-
r on Wednesday nights."

One corner of his lips twitched. "Only on Wednesdays?"

"I enjoy your company any day of the week." She silent-
y groaned. How tepid. "Thank you for staying at the hospi-
al with me. I know how difficult that must have been for you."

"I didn't like seeing you in pain."

She hated the awkwardness between them. "I meant—"

"I know what you meant, Mercedes, but your illness made
he realize Chloe's death was a horrible accident. It wasn't my
ault or yours."

"No, I guess you're right. I just wish…" What did she
vish? If Chloe were still alive, then Mercedes wouldn't
ave discovered love, but she didn't wish her friend dead,
ither.

"The past can't be undone. We have to move forward," he
aid in a neutral tone.

The perfect opening… She reached deep for courage. "I'm
lad to hear you say that, because I think we ought to try to
nake the most of our marriage."

His eyes narrowed. "In what way?"

"I want to be your friend…and your lover." She added th
last in a rush.

His nostrils flared on a sharp breath. "Are you sure?"

Her heart fluttered like a hummingbird's wings. "Yes."

He closed the distance between them in two long strides an
nudged up her chin with his knuckle. Mercedes held his gaz
and reveled in the expansion of his pupils. Jared may not b
in love with her, but he did desire her. "We're good together.

A smile trembled on her lips. "Oh, we're better than good.

Laughter sparked in his eyes. "You think?"

"I know. Let me show you." She lifted her arms an
splayed her hands across his pale-blue button-down shirt. Hi
heart beat steadily and rapidly beneath her right palm. Ris
ing on tiptoe, she kissed him.

Jared encircled her waist and pulled her close, fusing thei
bodies together from shoulder to knee. The thin silk of he
blouse and skirt were no barrier to the hard heat of his arous
al against her belly. Mercedes gasped and Jared took advan
tage. His tongue teased hers, dancing, dueling, advancin
and retreating until she wanted to groan.

She tangled her fingers in his short, springy hair. His mout
left hers to nip and suckle a trail of fire down her neck to th
top button of her blouse. His hands swept from her waist t
rest just below her breasts. Mercedes shifted on her feet a
anticipation built in her belly. *Touch me,* she urged silentl
He'd created magic with his fingertips that night in the cab
in, and she wanted to grab his hands and lift them to cove
her breasts for more of the same.

He lifted his head. "Are you hungry?"

She blinked? "What?"

"For dinner."

"Um, not really. I'd rather you kiss me again."

With a satisfied grunt, Jared swept her off her feet and ca

ed her into his bedroom. Looping her arms around his neck, Mercedes rested her head on his shoulder. She loved being carried, and she couldn't remember anyone—not even her father—carrying her before Jared. He set her down beside the bed. As soon as her feet touched the floor, Mercedes yanked his shirttails from his trousers.

He caught her hands and threaded his fingers through hers. He kissed her knuckles and then lifted her hands to his shoulders. "Don't move your hands."

She struggled to regulate her breathing. "Why?"

"Because I want to take it slow this time."

Their night in the cabin had been hot and devastatingly sexy, but each time they'd made love it had been rushed—as if they'd each feared one of them would come to their senses at any moment.

Jared's plan to take it slow tonight was evident in every lingering touch and the slow sweep of his mouth and fingers over her skin. He unfastened the buttons of her blouse one at a time, beginning at the top. His lips trailed his fingers in a slow, seductive descent toward the waistband of her skirt. Mercedes's blood raced. He inched her blouse from beneath her skirt and over her shoulders. Her blouse fell to the floor. Jared traced the lacy edge of her bra with his tongue, and then he caught her nipple, lace and all, with his teeth. She moaned. With a flick of his fingers, the front fastening gave way and her bra joined her blouse on the floor.

He lifted her hands back to his shoulders, and then the wet heat of his mouth engulfed her swollen and highly sensitive flesh. Mercedes dug her fingers into his supple skin and held him close.

His muscles bunched and shifted as his hands roamed, hot, ardent and thorough over her. He stroked her back, her waist, her hips and thighs, sending waves of goose bumps

over her skin. She trembled at the onslaught of sensation an
at the urgency building in her womb. Her knees weakened an
her impatience grew.

She wanted to look into his eyes as she held him deep in
side her, knowing that she loved him. Determined to reac
that goal as soon as possible, she reached for his shirt button:

"Not yet."

Jared released the button and zip on the back of her skir
and the fabric floated to her ankles. He rubbed his cheek ove
the area below her navel. The light abrasion of his afternoo
beard had to be the most erotic thing Mercedes had ever ex
perienced. A quiver shook her. She cradled his head an
threaded her fingers through his thick hair. His lips blazed
trail along the elastic waistband of her bikini panties.

He lifted his head and his passionate gaze meandered ove
her like a mountain trail traversing slopes and valleys. Her in
sides tightened with need.

"Turn around." His deep baritone voice sounded mor
gravelly than usual.

She frowned. "Why?"

"Just do it."

With any other man she would have refused. Because she
trusted Jared, she turned, stepping out of her skirt at the
same time.

"Put your hands on the bed."

She complied and her heart rate accelerated.

His rapid breaths steamed her skin as he kissed her nape
and then each vertebra in a slow descent of her spine. He
tugged her panties down her legs, and she stepped out of
them. His hands caught her ankles, positioning them at the
distance he desired and then his touch feathered upward light
as a butterfly.

She jerked at the electrifying touch of his lips on her tat-

oo and then smiled. Jared liked her body art. The rose tat-
oo, once a reminder of love and loss, had become a sexy invitation—one she hoped he'd accept frequently.

"Why a rose?" His tongue outlined the flower and Mercedes's brain and her muscles turned to mush.

"Love is like a rose. Beautiful, but sooner or later you'll
get jabbed by the thorns." Her voice faded when he kneaded
her bottom and stroked between her legs with his long, talented fingers. She was wet and so hot. She wanted him to
hurry.

Slowly he rose without putting an inch of space between
them. His cold belt buckle scraped lightly and erotically over
her buttocks until it rested against the small of her back. His
strong arms encircled her, enabling him to cup and caress her
breasts.

"You're beautiful." His rough whisper against the tendon
of her neck made the fine hairs on her body stand on end.

His torso pressed her spine, spooning her as they stood by
the bed. The contradiction of his hot body, the cool buttons
of his shirt and the cold metal of his belt buckle made reply-
ing impossible. He pulled the pins from her French twist and
dropped them on the table beside the bed, and then he buried
his face in her hair. She leaned against him.

"I like your hair down." His breath warmed her neck and
then his mouth opened over her fluttering pulse. He suckled
and laved her while one of his hands parted her curls and found
just the right spot to force a moan from her throat. "Like that?"

"Yes." Her breath came in shallow pants. The crest built
swiftly—too swiftly. She wanted to look into his eyes when
she climaxed, but he held her steady as release rippled over
her, causing her to buck against the hard evidence of his
arousal. He barely allowed her to rest before he brought her
to the peak again. The second climax rushed upon her.

Mercedes reached behind her, wanting to touch him, too, but Jared lowered his hands and stepped away. She turned and found him removing his shirt with abrupt, jerky moves. "Let me help."

"I don't think I could handle your touch right now," he said through clenched teeth.

If it weren't for the tension in his face and the fire in his eyes, she would have been offended. Mercedes yanked back the covers and climbed into his bed. She turned on the bedside lamp and reclined on her side to enjoy the show. Last time they'd made love with nothing but moonlight. This time she wanted more. She wanted to see and taste every inch of the man she loved.

Jared opened his shirt to reveal firm pectorals and ridged abdominal muscles. His tiny brown nipples stood at attention. She'd seen his bare chest before, but this time was different. This time she knew she loved him. This time she knew she'd soon have him in her hands and inside her body. He kicked off his loafers and reached for his belt. Anticipation hummed in her veins.

She'd had no idea how arousing it could be to be in love with the man about to become her lover, and the way he looked at her as if visually feasting on her made her want to confess her feelings. But she couldn't do that.

He reached for his waistband.

"Wait," she stopped him. "Turn around and go slower."

A naughty grin curved his lips. "You want a show?"

"Yes."

He pivoted and eased his pants and boxers over his hips. She thought he might have added an extra wiggle or two for her benefit, and it didn't go unappreciated. She loved the contrast of the tanned skin of his back and legs against the paleness of his tight rear. Jared had a great butt: firm and

ound atop long, muscular thighs and a runner's well-devel-
oped calves. A fine coating of dark hair dusted all the delicious skin below his waist.

She scooted to the edge of the bed and knelt on the mattress. Mimicking the way he'd held her moments ago, she flattened her front against his back and reached around him to
drag her nails across his hair-roughened torso. His muscles
undulated beneath her light touch and his breath hitched. She
sipped and nipped his neck, paying special attention to the
spot behind his ear and relishing this man in a way she never had another.

Touching him, smelling him, tasting him brought her tremendous pleasure. Now she knew the difference between
having sex and making love. This was so much more than
what she'd had in the past. She wrapped her fingers around
his thick erection and stroked him from the dense crop of curls
to the tip of his shaft. She spread the slick dew over his silk-
en flesh.

Groaning, he leaned back against her and allowed her
touch for perhaps ten seconds, and then he grabbed her hand
in one of his. He turned without releasing her, wrapped his
free hand around her nape and covered her mouth with his.
The force and passion of the kiss rocked her back on her heels.
She loved knowing that she could break his iron control.

He banded his arms under her bottom, lifted her and carried her back onto the bed. He sprawled above her, pinning
her to the mattress with the hard heat of his body. She wound
her legs around his hips. Excitement made her breathless.
Love and desire fueled her hunger.

She broke the kiss and met his gaze. "Love me, Jared."

With his ardent gaze locked on hers, Jared braced himself
above her and then entered her with one long, slow thrust. A
sound of sheer ecstasy bubbled from her throat as he filled

her. He withdrew and returned, his tempo increasing with every lunge. Mercedes arched to meet him. She looked into Jared's blue eyes and cupped his beard-stubbled chin. Love welled in her chest.

Pressure built inside her until she thought she'd erupt like a shaken bottle of champagne. And then she did exactly that, bowing up off the bed as wave after wave of pleasure washed over her in a tingling spray. Her internal muscles clenched him, and Jared groaned her name and plunged one last time.

He collapsed to his elbows above her. Mercedes held him in her arms and relished his weight, the dampness of their skins and the harsh sound of their rasping breaths. She loved this man, and she wanted to spend the rest of her life with him. Was it possible? Could friends really become lovers? According to her mother and Lucas they could.

He eased to her side and pulled her head onto his shoulder. Somehow they'd ended up catty-cornered across his mattress. Their feet hung off the edge, and the blankets were wadded beneath them, making for a lumpy bed. As far as Mercedes was concerned, this was as close to heaven as she'd ever been.

Slowly Jared disengaged. He brushed a tangle of hair from her face and rose to stand beside the bed. Sadness edged the passion from his eyes, and a nerve ticked in his jaw. "I have something for you."

A tingle of apprehension climbed her spine at the gravity of his tone. "What?"

He held up a finger to indicate she wait and then disappeared into the den. Mercedes sat up and dragged the sheet over her nakedness. Why did she get the feeling she wasn't going to like this surprise?

Jared returned and handed her a flat manila envelope. The name of a law firm had been imprinted in the top left corner.

Her stomach knotted and she grew queasy. Her fingers trembled as she unfastened the brass clasp and reached inside to withdraw the stack of a half-dozen pages.

Nervously wetting her lips, she glanced at Jared, standing naked beside the bed. He nodded once, indicating she needed to read the forms, and then he reached for his pants. That telling cover-up sent her hopes of a future together plummeting.

She read the first paragraph and then the next. Disbelief warred with happiness in her chest. She quickly skimmed over the remaining pages. "Where did this come from?"

Jared's face remained expressionless, his eyes blanked, shutting her out. "I had my attorney's office draw it up. Bradford signed it when I reminded him that if he insisted on claiming paternity he'd be expected to pay child support."

Mercedes pressed a hand over her heart. She didn't know whether to cheer because she wouldn't have to battle Craig for her baby or to cry because her child had been rejected by its father, too.

She looked at Jared through misty eyes and her heart expanded. Only a man who loved her would go to this much trouble. "That's where you were the past two days?"

"Yes." His jaw muscles bunched. "We don't have to stay married now."

His quiet words hit her with the force of a full wine cask falling off the racks. Devastated, Mercedes gaped at him.

He *didn't* love her.

He wanted to end their marriage.

Then why had he made love to her with such tenderness? More *sayonara* sex? That's what had started her problem in the first place.

She'd thought her heart broken back in college, but she hadn't had a clue how badly real loving and losing hurt. Her chest squeezed tight, and her throat closed up. She couldn't breathe, and she thought she might faint. Her stomach revolt ed. Mercedes tossed the sheet and the documents aside an staggered to her feet. Pushing past Jared, she raced for th bathroom and barely made it in time to empty her stomac in the toilet.

When she finished being ill, Jared cupped her elbow an helped her to her feet. He dampened a washcloth, pushed bac her hair and wiped her face. She snatched it from him, wipe her face and rinsed her mouth. Why did he pretend to car when he wanted her out of his house and out of his life? Sh snatched a towel off the rack and wound it over her nakednes

Her world had ended. She'd gambled and lost. Her frienc Her lover. Her apartment. She'd been thrilled to discover sh wasn't as coldhearted as her father. Now she wished she was so she wouldn't have to endure this pain.

She shoved past him and headed to the den. He followec Her nails bit into her palms as she turned to face him. "Ar you asking for a divorce?"

"I'm offering you your freedom if you want it." The pair in his eyes and the raspy edge to his voice confused her. Wa this as hard for him as it was for her? Was the legal legworl nothing more than a gesture of friendship? Or had he con fronted Craig because he loved her?

She lifted her chin. "And if I don't want my freedom?"

His Adam's apple bobbed as he swallowed. "Then you nee to know what you're getting." He looked away, took a dee breath and then met her gaze again. "I'm not as strong as yo think I am, and we both know you don't respect weak men. Af ter Chloe and Dylan died I wanted to die, too. I considered it.

Panic squeezed her chest. She could have lost him. "Jar ed, you're one of the strongest people I know to have bee through the trials you've faced and kept going." She laid hand on his arm. "I couldn't have stood losing you, too."

He covered her hand with his. "I know. And it was your voice that kept me from taking that last step—that and my promise to Chloe."

Mercedes frowned. "What promise?"

"To look out for you."

A surprised burst of laughter escaped. "Chloe made me make the same promise—to look after you if something happened to her." She clenched her fists and then asked because she had to know. "Is your promise to Chloe the only reason you allowed me to remain a part of your life?"

He hesitated. "No, Mercedes, you challenged me. You made me face each day. When I said I couldn't run the inn without Chloe, you're the one who suggested I find other couples that shared Chloe's dream but couldn't afford to live it. The idea of buying up failing B&Bs and hiring husband-and-wife teams to run them was yours. You even helped me find the financial backing to get the process started. You gave me a purpose for going on."

He lifted a hand and stroked her cheek. "And you let me remember, even though I know it hurt you to talk about Chloe, too. You'd known her a lot longer than I had."

She captured his hand and held it against her face. "Chloe brought us together and she kept us together. She was my best friend. Now you are. I don't want to lose that, Jared. You're too important to me."

She'd always thrived on challenges, but challenges came with risks. Should she play it safe or risk it all? All her life she'd avoided love to evade rejection, but if she didn't open her heart, then Jared could walk out of her life.

Releasing his hand, Mercedes braced herself. "If you want a divorce then I won't fight you, but there's something you need to know first. I love you, and not just as a friend. I'm *in love* with you, Jared."

Saying the words felt good, cathartic, but at the same time she teetered on a knife edge of tension. Her stomach knotted when he closed his eyes and exhaled a long, slow breath. She rushed on. "I don't know how it happened or when, and if you don't feel the same way, that's okay. I know I'm not Chloe. I'm not as loving or generous as she was. And I—"

His lids lifted and the emotion in his bright-blue eyes choked off her words.

"You don't need to be Chloe. You're perfect exactly as you are. And from where I'm standing you are the most generous woman I've ever met. You've devoted yourself to your family and to me. You've given unstintingly of your time and expertise in helping me find and promote the inns. You helped me rebuild not only my business but my life.

"I'm a number cruncher not a people person. I never could have done it without you. You have an uncanny eye for choosing exactly the right couples to run each inn. You help me make those peoples' dreams come true, and you gave me back my pride by keeping me from having to return to my father's company as a failure."

"I think you're underestimating your own strength and business savvy."

He threaded his fingers through her tangled hair and tipped her chin until only inches separated their mouths. Their gazes locked, and the passion in his eyes stole her breath. "I'm a stronger man and a better one for having known you. I love you too, Mercedes."

Hope and happiness filled her. Tears pricked her eyes, and a smile trembled on her lips. Her friend. Her lover. Her husband. Maybe they could have a future together after all.

Jared's brows dipped, and Mercedes tensed. "But I'm not like your other men. I'm not a charmer or a smooth talker."

Her muscles unknotted, and a wry smile twisted her lips.

'Thank goodness. As you said, I have a habit of picking out losers. I spent my entire life trying to earn my father's love. I think I must have subconsciously chosen men exactly like Spencer—men I knew I couldn't love and who were guaranteed to let me down. You, on the other hand, have always been my rock, and you keep me sane."

Mercedes worried her bottom lip with her teeth. "But I'm carrying Craig's baby, and I don't want my baby to feel unwanted or unloved. Not all men want to be a father to someone else's child, and I can understand if you don't."

Jared kissed her tenderly and stroked his hand over her belly. Heat settled beneath his palm. "I'll love your baby because it's a part of you, and the way I see it, he or she brought us together. I look forward to being a father to this child and any others that we might have together."

Mercedes had never wanted a houseful of children, so why did the thought of a crowded dinner table, sibling rivalry and the hectic mornings of her own childhood fill her with longing? "I'd like that, but if it doesn't happen…"

"If it doesn't happen we still have each other and this little tyke. Make a life with me, Mercedes."

A happy tear rolled down her cheek. "I can't think of anything I'd rather do than spend the rest of my days as your friend and your lover."

"Not just my lover…my love." And then Jared lowered his head and kissed her.

Mercedes rose on her tiptoes to meet him halfway.

# Epilogue

"**I**f you'd tell me where we're going once in a while I wouldn't have to pack so much," Mercedes said a week later as she squinted through the sunshine at the stately brick house ahead of them. "This doesn't look like a B&B."

"It's not." Jared glanced at her. She noted the apprehension darkening his eyes and tightening his jaw. Come to think of it, he had been unusually quiet during the drive. "It's my father's house."

Mercedes's breath hitched. "Is he expecting us?"

"I called and asked if he wanted to meet my wife. He said yes." He put the car in Park in front of the wide semicircular brick porch and turned in his seat. "You were right. My father may show his love in a different way, but he does love my brothers and me. I want to mend fences."

Mercedes cupped his jaw. "I'm glad you realized that before it was too late."

The front door opened and a man stepped outside. Mercedes stared, knowing Jared would look very much like this tall and handsome silver-haired gentleman in thirty or so years. She looked forward to being by Jared's side at that time. Perhaps they could retire to his cabin by the lake.

Mercedes pushed open her car door and met Jared in front of the vehicle. She laced her fingers through his and climbed the shallow steps beside him. His father's eyes—the same intense blue as Jared's—hungrily absorbed the details of the son he hadn't seen in years, and then his arms opened.

Jared hesitated. Mercedes was about to shove Jared forward when he moved into his father's arms of his own accord. The two men hugged. Tears rolled freely down Mercedes's cheeks. Damned pregnancy hormones. But she was smiling as she dug in her purse for a tissue to dry her face.

As Mercedes observed the reunion, she realized that if Craig ever asked to be a positive part of their baby's life, then she wouldn't keep them apart. Sadly, she didn't expect to have to make that decision.

Jared turned and extended his hand to Mercedes. "Dad, I'd like you to meet my wife, Mercedes."

Mr. Maxwell shook her hand and kissed her cheek. "I believe I have you to thank for today's visit, and for that I'm forever grateful. Thank you, Mercedes, for bringing my son home."

\* \* \* \* \*